THE BROKEN MAN

Josephine Cox was born in Blackburn, one of ten children. At the age of sixteen, Josephine met and married her husband Ken, and had two sons. When the boys started school, she decided to go to college and eventually gained a place at Cambridge University. She was unable to take this up as it would have meant living away from home, but she went into teaching – and started to write her first full-length novel. She won the 'Superwoman of Great Britain' Award, for which her family had secretly entered her, at the same time as her first novel was accepted for publication.

Her strong, gritty stories are taken from the tapestry of life. Josephine says, 'I could never imagine a single day without writing. It's been that way since as far back as I can remember.'

Visit www.josephinecox.com to find out more information about Josephine.

Also by Josephine Cox

QUEENIE'S STORY
Her Father's Sins
Let Loose the Tigers

THE EMMA GRADY TRILOGY
Outcast
Alley Urchin
Vagabonds

Angels Cry Sometimes
Take This Woman
Whistledown Woman
Don't Cry Alone
Jessica's Girl
Nobody's Darling
Born to Serve
More than Riches
A Little Badness
Living a Lie
The Devil You Know
A Time for Us
Cradle of Thorns
Miss You Forever
Love Me or Leave Me
Tomorrow the World
The Gilded Cage
Somewhere, Someday
Rainbow Days
Looking Back
Let It Shine

The Woman Who Left
Jinnie

Bad Boy Jack
The Beachcomber
Lovers and Liars
Live the Dream

The Journey
Journey's End
The Loner
Songbird
Born Bad
Divorced and Deadly
Blood Brothers
Midnight
Three Letters

Josephine
COX
The
Broken Man

HARPER

Harper
An imprint of HarperCollins*Publishers*
77–85 Fulham Palace Road,
Hammersmith, London W6 8JB

www.harpercollins.co.uk

This paperback edition 2013
1

First published in Great Britain by
HarperCollins 2013

Copyright © Josephine Cox 2013

Josephine Cox asserts the moral right to
be identified as the author of this work

A catalogue record for this book is
available from the British Library

ISBN: 9780007521104

Set in ITC New Baskerville by Palimpsest Book Production Limited
Falkirk, Stirlingshire

Printed and bound in Great Britain by
Clays Ltd, St Ives plc

MIX
Paper from
responsible sources
FSC C007454

To my darling Ken, as always.

To the musical Murphy family in Ireland. Hope all is well with you. Much love, Jo x

PART ONE

~

Bedfordshire, February

1952

CHAPTER ONE

THERE WAS SOMETHING disturbing about young Adam.

Deep inside, he carried a secret that he could never tell anyone.

Phil knew, though, because he recognised that certain look: the slump of the shoulders; the sad eyes that gave little away.

Having fought for king and country, Phil knew what it was like to carry a secret. Over the years he had learned to live with the vivid memory of terrible scenes he had witnessed.

He could banter with old companions, but the loneliness of guarding his secret was often unbearable.

Though his life was not empty, he ached for the company of a very special person, the one lovely woman he had loved with every fibre of his being. The only woman who was able to bring sunshine into his life, even on a rainy day.

He kept himself busy helping his neighbours and occasionally meeting up with locals down at the pub. He earned his living by driving the school bus, and when the working day was over, he would go home to an empty house, make his tea and, afterwards, sit in his chair and light up his faithful old pipe. Before it got dark, he would take a leisurely stroll through the countryside, his little mongrel dog, Rex, tripping along beside him.

Phil appreciated his few simple pleasures, though he would have given everything to turn the clock back to a time when he was younger and fitter, and fortunate enough to have a loving wife.

Now, though, he would make his way home as always, and except for the faithful little dog who was never far from his side, the house would be empty.

Now at night, he went up to his bed; alone. At first light he woke up; alone. He had no one special to laugh or cry with, no one to slide his arm around when he felt loving. And there was no one close with whom to share any titbits of gossip or maybe a smile at the occasional naughty tricks the schoolchildren got up to on the bus.

There was no one to chastise him when he left the tap running, or when he casually threw his worn shirt on the bedroom floor. It was a hard truth that after many happy years married to a wonderful woman, he was now a man on his own, with only memories and his dog for company.

The loneliness weighed heaviest on him in the evenings. He longed for things once familiar, like making a pot of tea for two, and sharing it over a cheery fire, or maybe cutting fresh flowers from his little garden, and seeing his wife's pretty smile as he handed them to her.

Those precious times had been dearly missed these past four years, since his beloved wife lost her fight against a long illness.

~

Phil's thoughts were suddenly interrupted by a flicker of movement reflected in the driver's mirror. Glancing up, he saw his last passenger, young Adam Carter, climbing out of his seat to make his way down the bus. He was far too quiet and serious for his age. There were times when Phil had caught the boy so deep in thought he was oblivious to the other children around him and he had no particular friend with whom he always sat. In Adam, Phil saw a troubled, frightened boy.

'We're nearly there, son!' he called encouragingly.

Phil manoeuvred the vehicle over to the verge, where he parked, applied the handbrake, and prepared to let the boy off.

'Right then, Adam, here you are, home safe and well.'

'Thank you, Mr Wallis, I'll be all right now.'

'The name's Phil . . .' he kindly corrected the child. 'Everyone calls me Phil.'

'But my father says it's rude to address your elders by their first name.'

'Mebbe, but not if they offer you the privilege . . . which I am very glad to be doing right now. Only if you feel comfortable with it, mind.'

Adam grew restless. 'I'd really like to call you Phil,' he admitted, 'but my father would be angry with me.'

Phil gave a cheeky wink. 'Well, that's easily settled. I won't tell him if you don't.'

Adam gave it a little thought, then with a wide smile said, 'OK. I won't tell him either.'

'Good! That's settled then.' Phil climbed out of the driving seat. 'Seeing as I need to stretch my legs and it's such a beautiful afternoon, I'll walk you down the lane to your front door. That's if you think your father wouldn't mind.'

Adam shook his head. 'He won't mind. Thank you, Phil.'

Phil laughed out loud. 'There you are. It wasn't too difficult to say my name, was it?'

He felt as though, at long last, this lonely boy was beginning to trust him. He hoped the day might come when the child would trust him enough to confide in him.

He now took a sideways glance at young Adam.

At seven years of age, Adam Carter was quietly spoken. With serious brown eyes, and thick dark hair that tumbled over his forehead, he cut a handsome young figure. Not naturally outgoing, he hardly ever laughed out loud, and smiled only on rare occasions. Yet when he did smile it was such a warm, genuine smile, it could light up a room.

Phil had noticed how Adam's nervousness increased

the nearer he got to home. Unlike the other children, who could never get off the bus fast enough, Adam hung back, waiting until the very last minute, almost as though he was reluctant to leave the safety of the bus.

'Right then, son, that's another week over. You go on; I need to secure the bus, especially after that young squirrel got inside and wreaked havoc.'

Adam went down the steps. On the last step he gave a short jump to the ground, his satchel catching on the handrail as he did so.

'All right, are you?' Phil released his satchel.

'Yes, thank you, Phil.'

After following Adam down the bus steps, Phil secured the door behind him.

'I expect you're glad to be home, eh?'

Except for a curt nod of the head, Adam gave no reply, but he wanted to tell this gentle, kind man that no, he was *not* all right; that he was *not* glad to be home. He wanted to confess that he was afraid and unhappy, and that he often dreamed of running away. But he would never do that, because it might be dangerous for someone he loved dearly. So he kept his silence and went on pretending. Even now, as they approached the house, his heart was thumping. Was his father home yet? Had his day been good? Because if not . . . oh . . . if not . . . Quickly, he thrust the bad thoughts from his mind.

Man and boy went down the lane side by side.

'By! This is a real treat.' Phil sniffed the air. 'This time o' day, the pine trees give off a wonderful scent.'

Adam agreed. 'Mum says it's even stronger in the summer. She says when the trees begin to sweat, they create a thick vapour over the woods, and you can almost taste it.'

Phil loved the lazy manner in which the worn path wound in and out of the ancient woodlands, skirting magnificent trees that had been there far longer than he had.

'You live in a really pretty part of the countryside,' he told Adam. 'And now you've got the whole weekend before you, so what might you be up to, eh?' He chuckled. 'By! I wish I were a lad again . . . climbing trees and apple-scrumping. The things we used to get up to, you would not believe.' He gave a great sigh. 'It's all a lifetime ago now. Mind you, I'd never be able to climb a tree these days, not with my gammy leg.' His pronounced limp was a painful trophy from the war.

'I'm not allowed to climb trees.' Adam's voice softened with regret. 'My father doesn't approve of it.'

'Well, I never!' Phil was dumbfounded. 'Climbing trees is what boys do. It's a natural part of growing up, like fishing, and football.' He gave a wistful smile. 'And who could ever forget the first time he kissed a girl?' He rolled his eyes and made the boy smile shyly; he still had that pleasure to come.

'I know it's not my place to ask,' Phil went on in a more serious tone, 'but, what's your dad got against you climbing trees?'

Adam shrugged. 'He says it's undignified.'

'I see.' In fact, he didn't see at all.

Deep in conversation, they were startled and delighted when a deer shot across their path. A few steps on, and Phil resumed their conversation.

'Do you know what I'd do, if ever I had loads of money?'

'No.'

'I don't expect I ever will have loads of money, but if I did, I'd build myself the prettiest little cottage right in the middle of these 'ere woods. And I'd be sure to make friends with every animal that lived here.'

Adam laughed. 'You'd be like the old man in the story.'

'Oh, and what story is that?'

'It's a mystery I once read, about a man who lived in an old shed in the woods. He cut his own logs for the fire, and everything he ate came out of the woods. Sometimes he would even sleep in the forest with the animals, and they never once hurt him.'

'Ah, well, there you go, then. He sounds like a man after my own heart. So, how long did he live like that?'

'A long time . . . years! Then one day he just disappeared, and was never seen again.'

'Hmmph!' Stooping to collect a fallen branch, Phil threw it into the verge. 'So nobody knows what happened to him, eh?'

'No. The story tells how one day he was seen collecting mushrooms; then he was never seen again. Some of the villagers were worried he might be ill, so they went to check the shed where he lived, but though the old man was gone, all his belongings were still there.'

'Sounds too spooky for me.' Phil was intrigued. 'But what do *you* think happened to him?'

'Well . . . I think maybe he got really sick and he knew he wouldn't get better, so he crept away where no one would ever find him. Just like the Indians of old used to do.'

Phil thought about that. 'Well, if that's the case, he's a very lucky man. Not many people get to choose how they live their lives, and then decide where to end them.'

There followed a short silence as they each dwelled on the fate of the mystery man.

'Phil?' The boy softly broke the silence.

'Yes, son?'

'I don't think I'll ever be able to choose what I want to do with my life.'

'Why do you say that?'

'Because my father has my future all planned out.'

'Has he now?' Phil prompted him. 'And you think that's a bad thing, do you?'

'He says I'm his only son and that he's decided there will be no more children,' Adam explained. 'So it's my duty to follow in his footsteps.'

'No more children, eh?'

'That's what he said.'

'And are you sure you don't want to follow in his footsteps?'

'Yes, I'm sure, but when I try and tell him, he gets really angry.'

He was careful not to reveal how his father often took a belt to him; that one time he split the skin on his back and forbade his mother to take him to hospital.

'Have you spoken to your mother about not wanting to follow in your dad's footsteps?'

'Yes, but Mum said it's best if I do what Father says.' He paused before confiding in a quieter voice, 'Sometimes if I disobey him, he takes it out on her. That's cowardly, isn't it, Phil?'

'I'm sorry, son, but without knowing all the circumstances, it would not be right for me to comment on that,' Phil apologised, although his mental picture of the boy's father was now deeply unsettling.

Thinking it might be wise to change the subject, he asked, 'So if you're not allowed to climb trees, what do you do when you're out with your mates?'

'I don't have any mates.'

'Oh? And why's that then?'

'Father says I must not waste my time. He says that if I've got any spare time after school, I must use it for doing extra studies, because I'll never make anything of myself if I don't study.'

He cast his gaze to the floor. 'Can I tell you something, Phil?'

'Course you can, son.'

'I don't like him very much. He makes me study all the time, and I'm never allowed to do anything else. I would like to have close mates that I could bring home and play with. But Father keeps me too busy for that.'

'I'm sure your father thinks it's all for your own good.'

'I know, but he asks too much of me, and he has

such a terrible temper, and if I get the questions wrong, he makes me do them all over again. Sometimes it's midnight and he still won't let me go. Mum argues with him and then . . . he . . . he . . .' his voice tailed off to a whisper. 'Sometimes, I really hate him.'

Saddened by what Adam had told him, Phil made him a promise. 'Always remember, son, if ever you feel the need to talk, I'll be here for you.' Not being witness to what happened in that house, Phil believed it was wrong of him to criticise. Instead, he quietly reassured the boy, 'I expect he has your interests at heart, but you obviously believe he's going about it the wrong way, so all you can do is to keep explaining how you feel.'

'I've made up my mind, I don't ever want to be like him!' A dark look crossed his face.

'Well, I'm sure that's your choice, Adam, but your father has made a success of his own life and, from what you tell me, it seems he wants the same for you.'

'I know that.' Looking ahead towards the house, the boy grew agitated. 'But he's not a good man. Sometimes he's really nasty. He doesn't laugh, and when he gets angry he shouts and screams. Mum tells me not to rile him, or he might . . .'

'Might what?' Phil could see the child was getting agitated. 'Apart from the shouting and wanting you to work harder, is there something else that's worrying you, son?'

'NO! No, there's nothing else.' Fearing he might have said too much already, Adam finished lamely, 'Me and Mum, we just do what he tells us, and then everything is fine.'

'Well, just remember what I said, Adam. If you ever need someone to talk to, I'm here.' Phil brought the subject to an end: 'I've an idea that you and your father will work it out, eventually.' Even so, he was genuinely concerned by what the boy had told him.

'Can I ask you something?' Adam said after a few moments' silence.

'Of course you can!' Chuckling, Phil lightened the mood. 'Unless you're after borrowing a shilling or two, because you know what they say: "Never a borrower nor a lender be", and that's the rule I live by.'

When he saw Adam's face fall, he laughed out loud. 'Take no notice of me,' he said, 'I'm just teasing. So, what is it you want to ask?'

Casting a wary glance along the lane, Adam quietly confided, 'Could you please not tell anybody what I've said, about my father?' Again, he nervously glanced down the lane towards his house.

'Don't worry, son. I've never been a gossip, and I can assure you that what's been said here today will not go any further. All right?'

'Thank you, Phil. Maybe you're right. My father doesn't mean to be like he is. It's only because he works such long hours and he has such a responsible job, he just gets on edge sometimes.'

'I understand that, son, but if you don't mind me saying, what suits one man doesn't always suit another. A man should be able to choose his own path. But you're not yet a man, and maybe your father is looking out for your future. D'you understand what I'm saying?'

'Yes, but I don't want to be bad-tempered and angry

like my father. I want to do something that makes me happy.' Growing increasingly nervous, Adam dropped his voice to a whisper. 'Already my father is training me into his kind of work.'

'How d'you mean?'

'Well, nearly every night he brings home a pile of paperwork and makes me go through it with him. It's all calculations of stocks and shares and money transactions. I don't understand any of it, not really, but sometimes he keeps me at his desk for ages, making me do tests and stuff. He says he's proud for me to follow in his footsteps. He wants me to learn all about high finance and dealing and stuff. And I hate it!'

Phil understood the boy's concern. 'Do you ever get any time to yourself?'

Adam's face lit up. 'Only when Father comes home really late, or stays in London overnight on business. That's when Mum and I have the best time of all, doing the things Father disapproves of. We play card games. Mum keeps the cards in a special hiding place. And sometimes we play loud music on the radio and Mum shows me how to tango and rumba and all that.'

His face broke into a proud smile. 'She was a champion ballroom dancer once. She won all sorts of trophies and she's got photographs of her in these beautiful gowns. She said Father asked her to give it all up when they got married, so she gave her dresses away and never danced again. She kept all her photographs and trophies, but Father locked them away. She knows where the key is, though, and when he's not here, she gets them all out.'

Growing afraid in case anyone was listening, he lowered his voice again. 'He doesn't know that Mum searched everywhere for the key. She found it under the carpet in their bedroom. When he's not here, she sets all her trophies out on the sideboard, and then she teaches me to dance. Oh, Phil, she looks so beautiful. It's not fair. Why would Father lock away all her precious things like that?'

Phil was shocked. 'I'm sure I have no idea, son.'

Feeling decidedly uncomfortable, Phil led the conversation in a slightly different direction: 'So, would your mum ever want to dance in public again, do you think?'

Adam nodded. 'Oh, yes! She says she's still young enough to take it up again. She even mentioned it to Father, but he said if she ever spoke of it again he would have to destroy everything, so she couldn't ever be tempted. I don't think she will ever dance again, though.' Glancing up at Phil, he smiled. 'Not in public, anyway.'

Phil was beginning to see a much wider picture of this family, and it was not good. 'Mmm, well, all I can say is, it's a pity your father has to work such long hours. But it's good that you and your mum get to spend that time together, isn't it?'

Adam nodded. 'It's really nice when Father isn't there. Sometimes, me and Mum go across the fields for miles and miles. We stay out for ages. Then on the way back, we get fish and chips, and sit on a park bench to eat them. That way we don't make the house smell, because then Father would know what we've been up to.' Breathless and excited, he went on, 'Oh, and sometimes we go to the pictures.' His face lit up. 'Last Saturday we went to see a cowboy film.'

Allowing the boy to chatter on excitedly, Phil instinctively eased him round a muddy puddle.

'Do you have a pet? A little dog, mebbe?'

'No. One time, Mum bought me a tabby cat, but it got run over. His name was Thomas and I really loved him. I taught him to do little tricks and he followed me everywhere, though Father would chase him out if he went into the house.'

Phil chuckled. 'I had a cat like that once. Up to everything, he was.'

'Thomas was the cleverest cat I ever knew,' Adam confided proudly. 'I cried a lot when he was run over. Father said I was a big baby and I should be ashamed of myself. And now I'm not allowed to have a pet ever again.'

'He got run over, you say?' That surprised Phil because, in his experience, most cats would head for the woods rather than risk going over a main road. 'That's a real shame. How did you find out?'

'Father told us that he found Thomas in the woods, and that he was hurt so bad that he died, so he buried him where he found him. I wanted to go and say goodbye, but Father wouldn't tell me where he was. He said that way I would get over him much quicker.'

'Oh dear, that's really sad. I'm so sorry.' Having learned a good deal about Adam's bullying father, Phil could not help but wonder about the cat's demise.

He had an idea. 'Look, Adam, being as it's such a lovely afternoon, I'll be taking my little dog for a walk through these lanes before it gets dark. You could ask your parents if you can tag along. What d'you say to that, eh?'

Adam shook his head. 'I'm not allowed.'

'Oh, but it doesn't hurt to ask, does it? You never know. My old dad used to say, "If you don't ask, you don't get."'

Adam shook his head. 'Father won't let me, but thank you anyway, Phil.'

'Ah, well, never mind, eh? Mebbe another time.'

'Yes, I would really like that.'

~

A few moments later they arrived at the house: a fine Victorian dwelling with tall chimneys, large windows and a sweeping drive. Set in beautifully landscaped grounds, it made an impressive sight. 'I'll be fine now, Phil, thank you.'

'All right, son. I'll just watch you go inside the gate, then I'll make my way home.' Reassured by the lit forecourt and drive, he waited for the boy to close the gate behind him.

'Oh, look! Father's home.' Adam pointed to the big Austin saloon parked in the garage entrance. His face fell visibly as he prepared to go in.

In that same moment a man who had to be Adam's father burst from the house. Lingering a moment in the shade of the porch, he appeared surprised to see the two of them at the gate.

'Afternoon, Mr Carter.' Phil raised his hand in

greeting, but the other man gave no response as he scurried to his car.

Leaning closer, Adam confided in a whisper, 'I'm glad he's going out, because now I'll be able to spend time with Mum, instead of being made to work in the office with Father.'

Phil understood, but thought it best not to stir up trouble. In his experience family problems usually sorted themselves out. 'Right, well, I reckon I'd best be on my way.'

''Bye, then, and thank you.' Adam went towards the house, while Phil turned and trudged back down the lane, deep in thought.

He had gone only a short distance when he heard angry yelling.

'You'll do as I say, or you'll feel the length of my belt! Get out of my way, damn you!'

A minute later, Phil heard the sound of a car door being slammed, then the revving of an engine.

Phil thought if that was the father shouting, it was no wonder the boy had little love or respect for him.

Deep in thought, he pushed on down the lane. Suddenly a car skidded past him at break-neck speed, the wheels sending a thick spray of mud all over Phil's trouser-leg. 'BLOODY LUNATIC! TRYING TO KILL ME, ARE YOU?' Shaking his fist as the car bounced out of the lane and onto the main road, he recognised the big Austin belonging to Adam's father. 'Bloody madman!' Phil yelled, brushing the mud from his trousers as he grumbled. 'You want locking up. You've not heard the last of this, I can tell you.'

18

About to continue on his way, he thought he heard a cry from somewhere behind him. Then he heard it again; this time closer. It was Adam. Running towards Phil, the boy was clearly distressed, 'Phil . . . help me!'

When he fell over, he made no attempt to scramble up. Instead, he remained where he fell, calling out, 'Come back! I need you, Phil . . . please.'

Slipping and stumbling on the uneven ground, Phil hurried back to him. By then, Adam was crumpled on the ground, frantically rocking back and forth, his two arms crossed over his head as though defending himself.

Shocked, Phil lifted him from the ground and held him close. 'What is it, son? What's happened?' It was clear that something terrible must have happened.

'We need you . . . please, Phil.' Trembling in the man's arms, the boy glanced about furtively, his eyes big with fear as he looked back towards the house. 'Phil, you have to come and see.' He lowered his voice to a confiding whisper. 'It was him, I know it was. It was him, Phil. I hate him, I hate him!'

'Ssh . . . take a deep breath, son. Tell me what's happened.'

'I don't know! You have to help me, Phil . . . please!'

'All right, son. Take it easy now. You and me, we'll go back together.' He knew it must be something bad to have affected the boy like this, but now was not the time for questions.

As they hurried back to the house, Adam kept asking over and over, 'He won't come back, will he? I don't want him to come back. Please, Phil, don't let him come back.'

Quickening his steps as best he could, Phil drew him close, constantly reassuring him, though he had no idea of what might have happened.

In the deepening hours of a February afternoon, he took quiet stock of the boy. At first he suspected his father had given him a beating, but the boy appeared to carry no visible cuts or bloodstains. He was thankful for that much, at least.

As they neared the house, Phil tightened his hold on Adam, while continuing to reassure him.

Clinging to Phil, young Adam seemed not to be listening. Instead, he shivered uncontrollably, while constantly glancing back to the main road.

At the gate, Adam drew back, his whole body resisting as Phil tried to move him gently forward.

Then in a sudden burst that took Phil by surprise, he broke away to run up the drive.

Phil quickly followed, then at the porch he hesitated. It went against his principles to enter another man's property without invitation, especially when that man was hostile. His concerns about the boy, however, urged him on.

A moment or so later, on entering the inner hallway, Phil was faced with a scene so shocking, he could never in a million years have prepared himself for it.

Adam was at the foot of the stairs screaming, 'She's dead, isn't she?' his school shirt covered in blood. He ran back to Phil. 'Look what he's done, oh, Phil . . . look what he's done.' The boy's cries were heart-wrenching.

Deeply shaken, Phil crossed to the foot of the stairs and kneeled to examine the woman. He recognised her as Peggy Carter, Adam's mother, and like the boy, he believed she was past all earthly help.

Lying in a pool of blood, she was covered in angry red bruises. Her eyes were closed and there seemed no immediate signs of life. Her body was grotesquely twisted, with both legs buckled. Her two arms looked as though they were wrenched out of their sockets. The right arm was loosely stretched out, while the other hung through the gap in the banister as though she had tried to use the banister railings to break her fall. Phil was of the opinion that she lost her footing as she tumbled down the stairs and had made a brave but unsuccessful attempt to save herself from serious injury.

'Adam! Phone for an ambulance.' There was no time to waste. 'Go on, son! Hurry!' He reminded him of the emergency number. 'Tell them there's been a terrible accident, and that your mother is unconscious. Tell them they must come at once!'

As the boy ran to do as he was bid, Phil called after him, 'Don't forget to give them the address. Hurry, Adam! Hurry!'

CHAPTER TWO

WHILE ADAM RAN down the lane to the public phone box on the main road, Phil attended to the injured woman. Taking off his coat, he carefully draped it over her. He then leaned closer to detect signs of breathing, but all he could hear was a deep, rattling sound that sent a shiver of fear through him. He knew he had to keep her warm and talk to her. Feeling more helpless than at any other time in his life, he mumbled, 'Oh, dear God, be merciful, for it's Your help she needs now.'

Not knowing whether she could hear him, he leaned closer, his tone reassuring. 'Mrs Carter, I want you to try and concentrate on my voice. I need you to keep listening to me.' He tenderly laid his hand over hers. 'My name is Phil. I'm the driver of the school bus. Adam's all right, but he's anxious about you. But don't worry, I'll look after him. He'll be safe enough with me. You just keep listening to my voice. Try and concentrate on what I'm saying, if you can.'

When he felt her hand twitch beneath his, he took it as a sign that he was getting through to her. 'Mrs Carter, listen to me . . . the ambulance has been called. They're on their way. It seems you fell down the stairs. You've been hurt bad, but they'll look after you. Don't try to move; it's best if you keep as still as possible.' Though, in her sorry condition, he doubted whether she could move even if she tried.

At that moment, Adam came running back. 'They'll be here quick as they can. They said we're to keep talking to her, and not to move her.'

Falling to his knees, he tenderly stroked his mother's hair. 'How did it happen, Mum? Can you hear me? Mum! Was it him who did this to you? Did he lose his temper again? Please, Mum, tell me what happened?'

Phil eased him away. 'No, son. That's not the way. For now, your mother needs gentle, encouraging words. I'm sure there'll be time for questions later.'

Adam understood. 'I'm sorry. She won't tell, but I will. If they ask me, I'll tell them how cruel he is.'

Crouching on the carpet, he kept his anxious gaze on his mother's distorted face.

'The ambulance should be here soon, Mum,' he reassured her. 'They said we had to keep talking to you. Me and Phil . . . we want you to listen, Mum. We want you to be all right, because if you aren't all right I won't know what to do. Please, Mum, try your very hardest. Just like you tell me to do, when I find my homework too difficult.'

Choking back his tears, he cast a forlorn look at Phil. 'She will be all right, won't she, Phil?'

'We have to hope so, son.' Realising that Peggy Carter's life hung in the balance, Phil softly measured his words. 'You can see for yourself. Your mother is badly hurt and there's no use pretending otherwise, but she's alive, and we need to be thankful for that. So, keep talking to her. If she can hear you, I'm sure she'll do her utmost to stay with you.'

For the next few precious minutes, Adam continued to talk to his mother, about school, and how his day had been, but all the while his heart was heavy with fear for his mother and loathing of his father. He recalled the many times when he himself had been thrashed; for no other reason than he had missed a question in his homework, or his father demanded more of him than he could give, which was more often than not.

Other times, when he was in the study, struggling over the homework his father had set, he would hear his parents loudly arguing in the parlour. Often the arguments were followed by the swish of his father's horse-whip, then his mother crying out in pain.

Minutes later his father, red-faced with anger, would storm out of the house. When Adam ran to his mother, she would quickly dry her eyes and reassure him that everything was all right, but it was not all right, and they both knew it.

In spite of her efforts to hide the bruises, Adam knew the truth. His father was a bully and a coward. This time, though, he had hurt her really badly, although she would not tell on him. She never did.

In that raw moment, Adam made himself a promise:

that when he was old enough, and however long it took him, he would make his father pay.

Seeing her like this was all too much. 'You won't admit it, but I know he did this to you.' His voice trembled. 'One day, when I'm bigger, I'll punish him, I will. You'll see . . . I'll make him pay for everything!' He tried not to cry, but the sobs took hold of him and he couldn't stop. 'I hate him! I hate him!'

Deep inside, Peggy heard Adam's angry words, and she feared for her child. Everything he said was true, but she could not let him be destroyed by the hatred he felt for his father.

With immense effort, and mustering every ounce of strength left in her, she whispered, 'No . . .' Her eyes flickered open to gaze on him lovingly. 'Don't . . . say that.' Having made this huge effort she was now struggling to breathe.

Seeing this, Adam reluctantly gave his promise. 'All right . . . ssh, Mum. Stay still. I won't say it any more. I'm sorry, Mum.' Ever so gently, he wrapped his arms round her neck and when she shivered, he backed away, sorry that he might have hurt her, and sorry he had worried her by the things he'd said.

Suddenly the high-pitched wailing of sirens filled the air.

'They're here!' Phil scrambled to his feet to go to meet the ambulance crew. 'Stay with her, son. Keep talking to her, but no questions. Just tell her the ambulance has arrived. Tell her she'll be in good hands now.'

Adam tried his hardest to be brave. He was grateful that his mother would get help, yet he was terrified she might be crippled or made to stay a long time in hospital. She would be unhappy about that, because her greatest joy was walking the countryside, just the two of them together.

'Move away, son,' Phil urged him, as the ambulance men hurried in.

Adam backed away as they brought the stretcher forward. 'I love you, Mum,' he whispered. The tears made a bright trail down his face. 'I'm sorry,' he said. 'I'm sorry, Mum. I'm truly sorry . . .'

But he was not sorry about the promise he had made, to make his father pay for what he had done. When he was big enough, he would go after him, and when he found him, he would make sure to punish him.

No, he was not sorry for any of that. The only thing he was sorry for just now was having made this vow out loud, and making his mother anxious.

From the back of the stairway, he watched as they treated his mother to ease her pain. He saw them cut into the rungs of the stairway and tenderly lift her clear, before securing her to the stretcher. Then they carried her to the ambulance where they raised the stretcher to slide her gently inside. In that moment, she made a feeble cry for her son.

He wanted to go to her, but he was too afraid. What if she was calling for him so she could tell him she would never see him again? What if she was in terrible pain and he couldn't stop it? What if . . .? What if . . .? Hopelessly mixed up inside, and more frightened than he had ever been in his young life, he took to his heels and ran.

Panic-stricken, he hid behind the shrubbery, where he sobbed as though his heart would break. 'Don't die, Mum,' he whispered brokenly. 'Please, Mum . . . don't leave me.'

Realising the boy's fears, Phil found him and lovingly drew him away. 'I know she called for you, son, but she's delirious. There is nothing you nor I can do for her. She's getting the best care. If you want to go in the ambulance with your mum, you'd best be quick.'

'Will you come too?'

'I'm surprised you feel the need to ask.' Phil was already hurrying him to the ambulance, where the attendants had executed the necessary safety procedures and were about to leave.

Phil and Adam climbed inside, and then they were swiftly away; the ambulance tearing along the lane with the sirens at full scream.

These fine, experienced men had seen it all before. They had learned to deal with desperate situations in a professional manner.

This particular call-out, however, was deeply disturbing. As they were both family men with young children, they found the boy's distress difficult to deal with. The disclosure that it was the child himself who had discovered his mother lying bloodied and broken on the stairway was shocking. Such a discovery could prove to be the stuff of nightmares for years to come.

Another concern was their shared suspicions with regard to the 'accident' itself. In their considered experience, the woman's extensive injuries did not appear to coincide with a tumble down the stairs.

For now though, getting her to hospital was their main priority.

~

Inside the ambulance, Adam sat quietly beside Phil, his attention riveted on his mum, and his eyes red and raw from crying. Every few minutes he would whisper to Phil, 'She will be all right, won't she?' And Phil would pacify him as best he could, though secretly, he had his own doubts as to whether Peggy Carter could survive.

He wondered about Adam's father, and the way he'd fled from the house like a guilty man. His instincts told him there was far more to Mrs Carter's so-called accident than met the eye.

Throughout the journey, the medic remained by Peggy's side, softly reassuring and constantly tending her while she drifted in and out of consciousness. Not once did he glance across to the two anxious figures seated on the small bench at the back of the ambulance. He had a job to do, and if there was the slightest hope that this patient might survive, then time was of the essence.

~

To Phil and Adam, the journey to the hospital seemed to have taken for ever, when in fact they were there in under an hour.

On arrival, the ambulance doors were thrown open and Phil and Adam scampered down onto the tarmac.

The driver ran from his cab and climbed into the back, where the two men set about securing Peggy to the stretcher again. Phil and the boy waited anxiously, but it was only the briefest of moments before the two medics manhandled Peggy out of the ambulance. With one of them at each end of the stretcher and Peggy now deeply unconscious, they went at a run towards the hospital emergency doors where, having been forewarned, the medical staff were there to collect the patient and rush her straight to theatre.

While Peggy was hurried away, Adam and Phil were taken aside; though Adam tearfully insisted that he wanted to go with his mum. 'Where is she?' he wanted to know. 'What have they done with my mum?' Traumatised by the fear that he might never see her again, he called for her over and over.

The nurse gently assured him, 'The doctors are helping your mother now. Don't worry, she's in safe hands, and they'll come and tell you when you're able to see her. Meantime, there is nothing you can do. She truly is being taken care of, so please . . . I know how hard it is, but you must try to be patient.'

She knew the boy might have a very long wait; especially since the message relayed from the ambulance crew to the hospital as they drove there had described the patient as having suffered life-threatening injuries.

'Look, I'll tell you what . . .' She pointed to the little tuck cabin down the corridor. 'If you go and see Mavis, she might let you have a bottle of pop. Tell her Nurse Riley sent you, then she won't charge you a single penny for it.'

Phil understood her kindly motive. 'That's a good idea, Adam,' he encouraged the boy. 'In fact, I wouldn't mind a bottle of pop myself.'

With sorry eyes, Adam glanced at the green baize door through which they had taken his mother. 'All right then.' Reluctantly, he gave a little nod. 'But you have to promise you'll wait here, Phil. You won't leave me, will you?'

Phil choked back a tear. 'Me? Leave you?' He cradled the boy's face in his hands. 'I would never leave you, never in a million years!' Digging into his trouser pocket he withdrew a shiny coin, which he handed to the boy. 'There! You run off and see Mavis . . . there's a good fellow.'

'Your grandfather is right,' Nurse Riley said. 'Mavis will be pleased to see you.'

Phil and the boy exchanged curious glances at her reference to Phil as 'your grandfather', but wisely, neither of them made mention of her remark.

A short time later, when they had drunk their pop and were seated in comfortable chairs in a small room off the main corridor, the silence between them was heavy.

All they could think of was Adam's mother, who lay just a short distance away, fighting for her life.

Every few minutes either Adam or Phil would go into the corridor and look to see if there was anyone they could speak to about how the boy's mother was doing, but there was no one about, except a man in a long white coat, in a great hurry, and a nurse rushing about with a trolley, piled high with newly laundered linen.

'They all have jobs to do,' Phil reassured Adam. 'I know you're worried, but we have to be thankful that the doctors are looking after her. No doubt someone will come out soon and tell us what's happening. Until then we'll have to be patient.'

Adam was desperately concerned for his mother. He was also concerned about what might happen to him. He reasoned that she would have to stay in hospital for at least a short while. His mother told him long ago that she had been adopted, and that when she met his father, her adoptive parents took an instant dislike to him, and forbade her to see him.

There was a huge row. Having just turned eighteen, she defied them and married his father without their blessing. Shortly after that, her parents emigrated to Australia, and she eventually lost all contact with them.

That was all Adam knew of his grandparents on his mother's side.

The only mention of his father's parents was during a heated argument between his own mother and father. He had learned that his father's older sister and both his parents were devoutly religious, while Adam's own father grew increasingly rebellious against their rigid and highly disciplined way of life. There were constant rows until, in his early twenties, he cut himself adrift from his family.

Now he had no idea where they were, nor did he want to know, because as far as he was concened, they did not exist.

During the many rows with his own wife, he claimed that she was much like his own mother; that she was domineering and saw no worth in him. He argued that instead of being grateful for the good life he provided for them both, she and Adam took him for granted. During his wild, unpredictable rants, he said they were like strangers to him; that they darkened his life and gave him nothing, yet they continued to feed off him like parasites.

He also threatened Adam's mother that if she ever mentioned his parents and sister again, she would be made to regret it. So, knowing from experience that he was more than capable of hurting her, Peggy wisely never again spoke of them.

Once, when Adam was caught eavesdropping outside the parlour, he was punished with the bunched knuckles of his father's fist across his head 'for hiding behind the door and listening in on a private conversation', he was told.

Now, with his father gone, hopefully for ever, he felt able to speak out.

'Phil?'

'Yes, son?'

'Can I tell you something?'

'Of course.'

'All right then.' In a whisper, and with a wary eye on the door in case his father should suddenly burst in, Adam told Phil everything.

He described the awful rows and the things he had learned about his father's family; that his father hated his sister and his parents, and had cut them out of his life. 'He said they were wicked, spiteful people, and that they made his life a misery, and now I'm frightened they might come and take me away, to look after me until Mum's better. But what if they never bring me back? I'm frightened, Phil. I don't want them to come and get me.'

Phil took it all in and when Adam fell silent, looking up at him with fear in his eyes, he assured him, 'If they're as bad as all that, they'll not be allowed to come for you.'

Adam then told Phil of his grandparents on his mother's side. 'Mum said her parents wanted her to go to Australia with them, but she didn't want to, and so they fell out and she left home. Then a while ago, some old neighbour told Mum that they'd gone to Australia, but she didn't know where, and Mum never heard from them again.'

'I see.' Phil nodded thoughtfully. 'By! That's a sorry situation and no mistake. So, it seems you've no close family other than your own parents, eh?'

Because Adam was already in pieces, Phil made no mention of his deep concern with regard to the boy's care. In the light of what he had just learned, he feared there could be all manner of trouble ahead.

'Phil?' Adam grew concerned when the older man lapsed into deep thought. 'Phil!'

Brought sharply out of his reverie, Phil put on a smile. 'Sorry, son . . . I was just dwelling on what you said: no aunts nor uncles, nor family of any kind, except for your parents. By! It doesn't bear thinking about.' Fearing that Peggy Carter might not survive, he was deeply anxious for the boy's welfare.

Adam voiced his own concerns. 'If Mum has to stay in hospital for a long time, I don't want to stay in the house all on my own, so will you please stay with me until Mum gets home?'

Taken aback by the request, Phil wisely avoided answering directly. 'Aw, look, son. It's not good to get ahead of yourself like that. Let's just wait and see how things go, and then we'll decide what's best to do.'

Adam had another question: 'If you don't like to live in my house, can I come and stay with you then?' Growing tearful, he finished lamely, 'Please say yes, Phil, 'cause there's nobody to look after me until Mum comes home.'

Phil glanced about nervously. 'Ssh!' He pressed his finger to his lips. 'It's best not to discuss these things just yet. Let's leave it for now, son. Let's wait and see what the doctor says, then you and me . . . we'll sort summat out. Try not to worry, and the less you say just now, the better.'

'All right, Phil, but if you stay with me at the house, I promise I'll be good. I'll do my homework, and if you want, you can fetch your little dog to stay with us.'

Phil's heart went out to the boy. He knew the situation could never work, and besides, it wasn't right – not for him and not for Adam. And yet he was made to ponder what alternative there might be.

'Listen to me, son . . .' Sidling closer to Adam, he spoke in a whisper. 'It seems they think I'm your granddad, but you and I know that is not the case.'

'We don't need to tell them, though, do we, Phil? You can still pretend to be my granddad . . . until Mum comes home.' His voice shook with emotion. 'Please, Phil . . . please!'

Phil felt torn. 'I'm sorry, son,' he said, being sensible, 'I don't know as I can move into your father's house. It would be wrong of me, and what if your father comes back? Like as not he'll have me arrested, and who could blame him?'

'All right! I'll come to your house and stay with you.'

'Aw, son . . . I don't know.' Phil was growing more unsettled by the minute. 'It's a bad situation. I don't want to think on it right now, not until we see how it goes with your mother.'

'This is all Father's fault, isn't it?'

'I don't know, son. I'm not altogether party to the facts.' Wisely, Phil was reluctant to commit himself to such far-reaching accusations.

'It's true, Phil!' Adam spelled it out: 'He's always hitting her, and she never tells anyone. And now he's hurt her so bad, he's got frightened and run away. He should be locked up for ever!'

Phil didn't really know what to believe, except what he had seen for himself today. And, talking about his father's brutal treatment of his mother, Adam seemed genuinely afraid.

Phil now voiced his own concerns. 'There's a possibility that you could be wrong about what happened. Maybe they had an argument and there really was a terrible accident, and if that's the case, your father will be worried sick when he gets home. I know one thing for sure, though, he will not be best pleased to see me and my dog taking up residence in his house. After all, I'm not even a relative. I'm just the driver of the school bus who's got himself caught up in a shocking accident—'

'It wasn't an accident! He did it, I know he did!'

'Sssh!' Phil instructed Adam, slightly unnerved. 'Like I say, just now, it's best not to talk about it too much. Let's just wait and see how things go. We'll have a better picture of the situation once the doctor tells us what's happening. Until then, however difficult it is, we have to be patient.' He looked the boy in the eye. 'Agreed?'

With a reluctant nod of the head, Adam had little choice but to agree. 'When Mum comes home, everything will be all right, though, won't it, Phil?'

'Let's hope so, eh?' Phil was well aware of the seriousness of this situation.

'Adam?' Phil asked.

'Yes, Phil?' Adam looked up.

'I have an idea to pass the time.' The child's small, anxious face made Phil immensely sad. 'Do you know what I was just thinking?'

'No.'

'Well, I was thinking how you and me could say a little prayer for your mum. What d'you think?'

'Oh, yes, please, Phil, I'd like that.' The tears brimmed over. 'Do you think it might help Mum to get better? I so much want her to come home. She will, won't she, Phil?' Throwing his arms round Phil's neck, he hugged him so hard that Phil found it difficult to breathe.

Phil held him at arm's length. 'Listen to me, Adam. Even if we say a prayer it doesn't mean that everything will come right. It doesn't always work like that. All I'm saying is, at certain bad times in my own life, I've always found a deal of comfort in saying a little prayer; hoping that somebody up there in the Heavens might be listening, and that somehow they would try and help. The thing is, sometimes, however much they might want to help, they just can't do it, and we will never know the reason for that. D'you understand what I'm saying?'

'If you said a prayer, why did they not help you?'

Phil took a deep breath. 'Well, it seems they weren't able to give what I really asked for, but they did help me . . . a little.'

'In what way?'

Phil was beginning to wish he had never started this, because the painful memories were flooding back. 'Well, you see, when my dear wife was very ill, I prayed for the Lord to make her better . . .' Composing himself, he went on in subdued tones: 'Sadly, my prayers were not answered, because that was not to be. Thankfully, though, they did stop her pain and I was grateful for that. Maybe she had to leave me, because she had important work to do in Heaven. Maybe someone up there needed her far more than I did.' Though he could not imagine how that might be, because for almost thirty years she was his world. His reason for living.

And now he had to stop tormenting himself, or the boy would see him cry and that would never do.

Adam's angry voice penetrated his thoughts: 'So, you said a prayer and asked for her to get better, then she died and you were sad. I think that was cruel.'

Phil nodded. 'It was cruel for me, yes, because I miss her every waking moment. But in a way, it was not too cruel for her, because you see, she was no longer in pain. Maybe she would never have got better, and that was why the Good Lord stopped her suffering. Yes, you're right in one way, because she was taken away from me, and I miss her. But I have so many wonderful memories to keep me warm.'

'You loved her very much, didn't you, Phil?'

Phil simply nodded.

'Did you love her as much as I love my mum?'

'Oh, yes. I'm sure I did. Y'see, we were together for a very long time.'

'So, did she say a prayer as well?'

'Well, I don't know for sure, because if she did send up a prayer, she never told me. Maybe her pain was so bad, she prayed for it to be gone, and in their wisdom, and because it was her that was in pain and not me, they decided to grant her wish instead of mine. That's fair enough . . . don't you think?'

'I don't know.'

'Me neither, son, but we have to believe it was the only way.'

His life was not the same since losing his one and only love, and as long as he lived, it would never be the same again. Like it or not, he had to accept the situation.

He returned to his question: 'So, knowing that you can't always have your wish granted, do you still want us to say a little prayer for your mum?'

The boy smiled through his tears. 'Yes, but I only

know the one that Mum used to say before I went to sleep.'

'Right, then!' Phil was glad to have diverted the boy's attention. 'Only you'll need to tell me what it is.'

Adam remembered it well. 'When I lay me down to sleep, I pray the Lord my soul to keep . . .'

'Ah, yes, that's a good prayer. I like that. We'll say it together . . . quietly.'

As they shared the prayer, they had no idea that someone else was listening. Someone who had also heard every word of their conversation.

An auxilary nurse had stopped to stack the linen cupboard next to the visitors' room where Phil and Adam were quietly talking. The dividing wall was thin and she had innocently overheard every word of their intimate conversation.

Some of what she had overheard was shocking, especially regarding the father. Then the fact that the boy had no relatives, except a brutal father who had left the mother battered . . . seemingly to within an inch of her life. Unbelievably, after the event, he had callously abandoned his son to whatever fate awaited him; knowing he had no one to turn to.

Having been made aware of this important information, which she suspected may not have been made available to the duty nurse, she was unsure of what to do. Eventually, torn between compassion and her sworn responsibility, she concluded that there was really no choice at all. She softly closed the wide cupboard doors and made her way down the corridor at a smart pace.

In view of Mrs Carter's life-threatening injuries, she realised there was not a moment to lose.

～

As the auxilary nurse arrived at the door of the main office, the matron entered the room where Phil and Adam were impatiently waiting for news.

'How is she?' Phil enquired.

'She's out of surgery,' the matron said. 'Mr Hendon is a very reputable surgeon. I can assure you no one could have done better. He will answer all your questions, I'm sure, but for the moment he's been called away to advise on another emergency. He needs to speak with you, and of course he's aware you will have questions, so I'm sure he won't be too long.'

'Where's my mum? Can I see her? Can she talk to me?' Anxious for information, Adam pushed between the matron and Phil, his questions coming thick and fast. 'Please, Nurse, can I just see her? Is she awake?'

In a reassuring manner, the matron informed him, 'Your mother is out of surgery and in the recovery room. She's tired and a bit groggy, which is understandable. A moment ago she opened her eyes and asked for you, so I do believe it would do her a world of good to see you. But you must not excite her, and you can only stay for a minute or two.'

Looking up at Phil, she explained, 'She desperately needs to rest, but as she's so very anxious to see her son, the surgeon has agreed for you both to visit, with myself in attendance.' She lowered her voice. 'You understand, she is not long out of major surgery. So when the nurse beckons you away, you will be expected to leave immediately.'

Nervously, Phil dared to ask, 'But she did come through the surgery well, didn't she?'

The matron glanced again at the boy, then she gave Phil an aside look that made his heart sink; for it seemed to warn him that things had not gone as well as they had hoped. 'Like I say, the surgeon will speak with you presently.'

As she turned to leave, the door opened and the surgeon walked in.

A man of impressive stature and authority, he greeted Phil and Adam with a warm, sincere smile. 'I'm sorry to have kept you both waiting, but I was called away.'

Phil's questions were direct: 'How is she . . . really? Are you concerned, or did it all go as well as you would have liked?'

Aware that Adam was also awaiting his answer, the surgeon chose his words carefully. 'As you must understand, there were major injuries to deal with, and yes, of course there were some very worrying moments, but she put up a good fight and we must pray that she makes a good recovery.'

He now directed his advice to the boy. 'Your mother is very weak. You must not expect to be with her for longer than a few minutes, and when the nurse indicates that it's time to leave, you must do as she asks. You do understand, don't you?'

Even though he ached to see his mother, Adam

wanted what was best for her. 'Yes, sir, I understand. I just need to see her.'

'And so you will.' He turned to the nurse. 'Matron, please will you take these gentlemen along to see Mrs Carter?'

'Of course.'

'Thank you. Oh, and I'm afraid I need to commandeer two of your nurses.'

Matron pursed her lips in disapproval, but her smile soon reassured him. 'As long as I get them back.'

'Don't worry.' After working together for many years, these two understood each other.

Before excusing himself from their presence, he turned to Adam. 'From the little your mother could tell us, she lost her footing and tumbled all the way down the stairs. Did you see her fall?'

Adam glanced nervously at Phil before answering, 'No, sir. I wasn't there. I came home from school and found her lying near the bottom of the steps.'

'I see.' He took a breath. 'Your mother will be pleased to see you, but she'll be a little groggy from the anaesthetic. She may not be able to say much, but she will hear you when you talk to her . . . Remember, a few minutes only.'

'Will my mum be strong enough to come home soon?' Adam asked.

The surgeon gave the only answer he could. 'We can't say at this time, because she still has a long way to go. Your mother was very badly injured, but I can assure you, we have done everything possible to help her. I'm sure your mum wants to get home to you as soon as possible. Oh, and you mustn't be too frightened when you see her. She's surrounded by machines; all there to assist her recovery. Both her arms are wrapped in plaster casts, and she carries a great number of nasty bruises.' He deliberately made no mention of the numerous internal injuries; some of which would take many months to repair.

He placed his hands on Adam's small shoulders. 'I'm telling you now so that you won't be alarmed when you see her. All right?'

'Yes, sir.' Adam was shaken, but determined. 'When she gets better, she'll be coming home, won't she . . .? When her bones mend and all that?'

The surgeon tried to put it tactfully. 'We can't really say how long it will take her to recover. Your mum has been through a shocking ordeal, and hours of major surgery, and now it's imperative that she gets rest and care.'

'Then she'll be all right, won't she?' Adam was relentless in his need for reassurance. 'We'll be able to take her home soon, won't we?'

The surgeon was equally determined not to raise the boy's hopes. 'In these early stages of recovery, we must not even think of her as being in a hurry to get home. I'm sorry, I know it's hard for you, but you have to try to understand.'

Tearful now, Adam appealed to Phil. 'Tell him, Phil. I want my mum to come home really soon. I'll look after her, you know I will.'

Phil nodded. 'I know you would, son, but like the doctor says, your mum needs time to recover where the doctors and nurses can keep an eye on her. And besides, I'll bring you to see her every day. Meantime, she'll want you to be attending school and trying to get on with your life as normal. You know that, don't you?'

Reassured by Phil's persuasive remarks, the boy looked up at the surgeon. 'Please, can I see my mum now?'

'Of course.' Being a family man, Mr Hendon was full of sympathy for the boy. 'Matron will take you along.'

The surgeon departed ahead of them, while directly behind him, Matron led Phil and Adam along the same corridor, to the recovery room.

Throughout the long, worrying walk, Adam kept his gaze to the floor, while Phil looked ahead, his mind troubled by the look in the surgeon's eyes when asked about Peggy Carter's condition.

He watched as Mr Hendon, still ahead of them, turned into what looked like the main office. His interest was heightened when he drew alongside the office and he saw the surgeon earnestly talking with two official-looking people.

As Phil glanced in, one of the officials caught sight of them passing by the window. He then beckoned his colleague, and she looked out of the window, directly at young Adam.

Phil's concern intensified. Discreetly, he put his hand on Adam's shoulder and hurried him along.

'Who were those people?' Adam asked. 'Why were they looking at me?'

'They probably heard our clattering feet hurrying along, and were curious,' he reassured Adam.

Phil, however, felt decidedly nervous. He was in no doubt that the officials were interested in the boy. Also, they had appeared to be engaged in deep conversation with the surgeon. Maybe it had nothing to do with Adam or his mother, but Phil had a bad feeling, which he could not shake off.

He glanced at the boy. Such an innocent; his young heart filled with loathing for his cowardly father who had left such a trail of devastation in his wake. And now, he was so afraid his mother would never get well again. Yet through all his crippling unhappiness, Adam gave no thought to himself. Nor did he realise the precarious position he had been put in by his father's abandonment of him.

~

At the door of the recovery room, Matron peered in through the glass panel. 'Don't forget, a few minutes, that's all,' she warned.

After Adam gave an appreciative nod, she turned the handle and pushed open the door to usher them inside.

Phil and the boy were shocked to see the small, vulnerable figure lying in the high bed, her face turned away and her two arms wrapped in thick, stiff plaster. There was a kind of pulley over the top of the bed, with support-joints stretching down; two ends attached to the root of the pulley, and the other ends attached to the plaster-encased limbs, which were very slightly elevated above the patient.

Phil's interest was immediately drawn to the heart-tracking machine.

'Carefully now.' Matron accompanied Adam to the bedside, where she sat him down on a chair right beside the bed and close to his mother, whose badly bruised face was turned towards him. She appeared restless, intermittently shifting her head back and forth, and making a low, whining sound, much like an animal in pain.

Unsettled by this sound, Phil fixed his troubled gaze on the heart monitor; he was greatly relieved to see the screen showed a steady beat.

Taking a seat beside the boy, Phil rested his arm on the back of Adam's chair, while his sorry gaze also travelled the visible dark bruises on Peggy Carter's body. Deeply unsettled, she appeared to be unaware of their presence.

'Mum?' With a shaky voice, Adam called out twice. 'Mum, it's Adam. I've come to see you.' Reaching up, the boy tenderly clasped the tip of his mother's fingers where they jutted from the plaster cast. 'Phil's here too, Mum. He's been looking after me.'

When the tears rolled down his face and his voice began to tremble, Phil slid a comforting arm around him. 'Easy, son. You remember what the doctor said: your mum might not be able to speak, but she might possibly be able to hear you. So, just try and tell her the things that are in your heart. Let her know that everything is all right, that she's not to worry about you. And tell her you'll be here to see her often, until she's well enough to come home.'

So that was what Adam did. He told his mother how very much he loved her. 'I'll be so glad if you can get better really quickly, and then you'll be able to come home and we'll be together, and I'll take care of you until you're strong again.'

Both Phil and Adam were astonished when her eyes flickered open and she looked straight at her son. Her lips were moving, but when she attempted to speak, the mumbled words were lost in a choking sound.

'What's wrong with her?' Appealing to Phil, Adam began to panic.

Quickly now, Matron crossed to the bed. Leaning to examine her patient, she told them, 'It's all right. She's trying to say something, but she's not yet fully awake.' She glanced up at Phil. 'Another moment, and you must take Adam back so she can get her rest.'

As Matron moved away to check the machine readings, Peggy attempted to speak again. This time, Adam drew closer, trying to decipher the incoherent whispers.

With great tenderness, he wrapped his hand about her fingers. For a moment he was silent, painfully reliving what had gone before. Presently, with his other hand he reached out to stroke her thick, wayward hair. 'I love you, Mum. I want you to come home, so please get better soon.'

Peggy heard his every word, and she so wanted to rest, but she had to know first. In a snatched breath, she asked him, 'Is he . . . here?'

Relieved to hear her voice, Adam leaned closer, his

voice small. 'If you mean Father, he ran away like a coward, and he never came back.' Anger consumed him. '*He* did this to you, didn't he?'

'Sssh!' Her voice shivered with fear.

Exhausted, she momentarily closed her eyes. She was not afraid for herself, but for her only child. She needed to take care of him, this precious boy, who had seen bad things that no child should ever see.

'Mum!' Adam leaned closer. 'Don't be afraid, because if he comes back, I won't let him in. Phil's taking care of me, and we'll be all right till you come home. We really will . . .'

When she made a slow, deliberate movement to touch his face, he realised she was anxious to say something else.

'Don't talk, Mum. It will be all right,' he assured her. 'I'll take care of everything until you get home. If he comes back . . . I'll tell them what he's like . . .'

Deeply distressed, Peggy's furtive whispers were for her son's ears only. 'No. Don't say . . . that.'

'But he hurt you, Mum. He did!'

'Please . . . promise me.' Exhausted, she fell back into her pillow.

'All right, Mum.' Adam stood up and, gently laying his face on hers, he reluctantly put her mind at rest. 'I won't tell,' he whispered, 'I promise . . .' He found it hard to believe it was what she wanted, but he would keep his promise.

All he needed was for his mum to get better.

'Love you . . . Son.' Relief shadowed her face and now she was silent again.

'Mum?' Cradling her face, he was shocked at how cold she was. 'Mum!'

There was no response.

'Mum! Wake up . . . Mum!'

Matron hurried across the room. One glance at Peggy and she pushed the panic button. 'Take the boy away now!' she said to Phil.

Glancing at Peggy's face, Phil was afraid. 'Come on, son. We'd best do as Matron says.' Deeply shaken, he led Adam away. As they hurried out the door, a number of medical staff were coming up the corridor at the run.

Keeping a strong hold on Adam, Phil quickened their steps. He did not want even to consider what might be going on in the recovery room.

Quickly now, he took Adam down the long corridor and into the waiting area where they had previously been.

Adam fought against him. 'I have to go back . . . my mum needs me.'

'They're taking care of her, son.' Phil kept a tight hold on Adam. 'They'll let us know how she is, soon enough.' After seeing her so pale and empty, Phil secretly feared the worst.

CHAPTER THREE

IN THE VISITOR'S room, Phil anxiously paced the floor. Occasionally, he paused to look through the window into the corridor, but there was no one in sight.

He turned his gaze to Adam, who was curled up on the couch, quietly sobbing.

With every minute that passed, Phil began to lose faith, though he kept his disturbing thoughts to himself.

Presently, he glanced across at the boy, who was quieter now, deep in thought. Phil's heart went out to him. Again, he made his way over to him. 'I know you want news of your mum,' he started, 'but we must try and be patient, however hard it might be.'

After what seemed an age, there was a tap on the door, and the surgeon entered, his face sombre.

'What happened? Is she all right?' Phil asked.

Simultaneously, Adam ran over, asking anxiously, 'Is my mum all right?'

The surgeon quietly suggested to Phil, 'It might be best if I have a quiet word with you first.'

Sensing the tense atmosphere, and made increasingly nervous by the knowing glances that passed between the two men, Adam backed away. 'What's happened? Why won't you let me go to my mum?'

Moved to tears, Phil took hold of him. 'I'm sorry, son, but you can't go to your mother,' he said gently. Though well aware that it was Adam's right to see her, Phil realized it would not be wise. After all, he was just a child and, at the moment, dangerously vulnerable.

'Why can't I see her?' All of Adam's instincts told him the awful truth. In his heart and soul, he knew she had left him. 'Get off me!' His screams reverberated through the room. He fought Phil off and would have run from the room, but Phil caught him and held him.

'Listen to me, son.' His kind voice was calming. 'D'you recall what I told you . . . about my darling wife and how the only thing I wanted in the whole wide world was for her to be all right?'

Tearfully, Adam nodded.

'And do you recall how, for reasons we may never understand, the Good Lord took her all the same?'

Another reluctant nod.

'Well, then, I've been thinking. Maybe your mum, like my dear wife, could never be made better on this earth. But up there, in God's Heaven, she doesn't feel pain any more; she's comfortable and at peace, and though you will always miss her, she'll be watching over you. She will never leave you.'

Deeply moved by Phil's gentle words, the surgeon cautiously approached Adam. 'I'm so very sorry. I know how hard it must be. I can promise you, we did everything humanly possible for your mother, but her injuries were many and her heart was not strong enough to carry her through.'

Adam looked up, his eyes marbled with grief. He began to sob, and soon it was an avalanche of grief. The devastating loss of his mother and the all-consuming hatred for the man who hurt her could no longer be contained.

In a trembling voice, he murmured, 'One day, when I'm bigger, he'll pay for what he did.'

'Who will, Adam?' Mr Hendon probed for the truth. 'Do you want to tell us about this person . . . the one who must "pay for what he did"? Adam, can you tell me who you mean?'

Adam looked away. The surgeon's words were a timely caution to him, for he knew he must never tell. Not because he didn't want to, but because his mother had made him promise not to.

Just then the door opened and a nurse entered. After she had imparted her message to the surgeon, he politely excused himself. 'I'm afraid I'll have to leave you for a while, but please wait here. Someone will be along in a moment to have a word with you.'

They watched him leave.

'Phil?' Adam's voice trembled.

'Yes, son?'

'When the person comes, will they let me see my mum?' He felt as though his world had fallen apart. It was a strange and frightening feeling. 'I have to tell her something.'

Phil knew that feeling, and he saw it in the boy's face now. 'Adam, listen to me.'

'No! I don't want to.' Tearful, Adam turned away.

Phil persevered. 'Think about what you're asking, son. I know how much you want to see her, but it isn't right for you just now. Later, when everything is in order, I'm sure you can see your mother . . . if you are still of the same mind.'

'Please, Phil, I need to see my mum!'

Phil tried gently to dissuade him. 'I do understand, but do you really think your mother would want you to see her now? Or do you think she'd rather you remembered your last conversation with her, when she was still able to tell you how much she loved you? Don't you think she would feel your sadness, if you were to see her now?'

Phil's wise words reached home. After what seemed an age, the boy took a long, deep breath and tried to be the man his mum would want him to be. 'Is my mum really safe now, Phil?' He needed reassurance.

Phil promised him that she was safe.

Adam accepted what Phil had told him, though he found it incredibly difficult to believe that he would never again see his mother, never again hear her voice. Never again hear her laugh, nor run with her across the fields. In his heart he could see her beautiful smile, and that funny way she had of wrinkling her nose when she laughed out loud.

Suddenly the awful truth began to sink in, and the enormity of it all was too much for him to bear.

In a voice that was almost inaudible, he whispered to Phil, 'I'm really sad.' Winding his arms round Phil's wide waist, he confessed brokenly, 'I don't know what to do.'

'Aw, son, we can none of us do anything, because when the Good Lord calls us home, we have to go.' Phil held the boy tight to him. 'But you're not on your own, son, because I'm here for you. If I'm able, I will always be here for you.'

Thankful that he had Phil, the boy confided in a whisper, 'Phil, I don't know if she heard me promise. I need her to know that I made the promise.'

Choking back his emotion, Phil told him, 'Don't you worry about that, because she heard it all right – I heard it too – but y'know, son, sometimes we make promises and then, later, we regret them. You might need to think about that particular promise, the one you made to your mother. Maybe you won't want to think about it just yet. But maybe later, when you're not so very sad.'

Adam was resolute. 'If Mum had not made me promise, I would have told them everything . . . about how he hurt her, time after time, hitting her and making her cry. I hate him for what he did, but she didn't want me to tell. Why did she not want me to tell?'

Phil measured his words carefully. 'Because she loved you so much, she did not want you to do something that might hurt you in the long run. I believe that was why she asked you to make that promise.' He lowered his voice. 'I think she wanted you not to tell, because if you told, then you would have so many awkward questions to answer. It would be a nasty business, with you caught up in it.'

Leaning forward, Phil placed his hands either side of Adam's face. 'All you need to know is that your mother loved you, and that no one will ever be able to hurt her again.'

Looking into Phil's kind, weathered face, Adam saw such honesty.

'Phil?'

'Yes, son?'

'She's died, hasn't she?'

'Yes, son.'

'Has she gone to the same place as your wife?'

'Yes, I'm sure she has.'

'Will they be friends?'

'I would like to think so.'

'But I'd rather my mum could be here with me, because then, when I get older, I could keep her safe always.'

'Ah, but that's not your job, son, because now she's in the safest place of all. Your mum was an angel on earth, but angels belong in Heaven. She'll be well looked after there.'

'I want her back, Phil. I miss her . . . I really miss her.' Suddenly the full truth had hit home. He could no longer be brave; and his grief was overwhelming. Hiding himself in Phil's musty old coat, he sobbed as though his heart would break.

Holding him close, Phil took him to the couch, where he sat beside him, holding him until he sobbed himself to sleep.

A short time later, Matron arrived. On seeing the boy asleep on the couch, she went out and returned with a fleecy blanket, which she handed to Phil.

She watched him wrap it around Adam before quietly informing him, 'I'm afraid we have to discuss official matters.' She beckoned Phil to the other side of the room, lowering her voice as she told him, 'I am led to understand that you are not the grandfather after all. Is that true?'

Knowing he must, Phil told her his name and the whole story: how he had dropped Adam from the school bus and walked home with him down the lane; how he was on his way back to his bus when he heard the boy shouting. 'In a shocking state, he was, finding his mother like that, and his father running off like a spineless coward. I don't know if it was the father who hurt her, but Adam seems convinced of it.'

'So, why did you not inform us of these circumstances right away?'

'I gave as much information as I could, but it was your staff who chose to believe I was his grandfather, and besides, there were more urgent matters to deal with at the time, as you well know.'

'Well, I'm sorry, but since we have become aware of the truth, I'm afraid it was our duty to call in the authorities.'

'What authorities?' Phil recalled the officials in the office, and all his fears returned. 'Look, Matron, I make no apologies for letting you believe that I was his grandfather, because as far as I'm aware, he's got no one else.'

'I see.' As a woman, Matron was deeply sympathetic, but duty was her priority, along with the boy's welfare.

She explained, 'In the light of what we now know,

this is a very serious situation. The boy's mother has died under suspicious circumstances, and the father has run away. Moreover, we are led to understand there are no close relatives at hand to take care of the boy.'

'I'll take care of him then. At least until the in-laws can be found.'

'I'm sorry, but I don't think that will be an option.'

'So, what will happen to him?'

'That's for the authorities to decide.'

Before he could answer, she left with the parting words, 'You do seem to have his interests at heart, and he obviously trusts you. If you could please continue to keep an eye on him, I'll be back presently.'

When she had gone, Phil paced the floor. *This is a sorry state of affairs and no mistake*, he thought, walking over to where Adam was sleeping. *I can't imagine what might happen to you now, son.* He gazed down on the boy and he shook his head in despair. *No family to speak of, and no one but me to stand by you.*

He understood the gravity of the situation. Unless Adam's father was found there was little hope of getting the child home. Possibly not even then.

Physically and emotionally exhausted, he sat down in a chair, laid himself back and closed his weary eyes.

Some few minutes later the nurse arrived with two other people.

Phil clambered out of the chair, one eye shut and the other on the boy. He still clung to the hope that, one way or another, he might yet be able to take the boy home.

'These people need to speak with you,' the nurse

advised him. Having waved the visitors forward, she went to sit by Adam. When in his sleep he occasionally whimpered in distress, she tenderly lulled him quiet again.

Phil had been greatly unnerved at the sight of the two very officious-looking people standing before him. The woman was middle-aged, dressed in a dark two-piece. The man was older, serious-looking, smart in light grey jacket and black trousers. He also carried a document case. They were the people Phil had seen in the office earlier.

The woman introduced herself and her colleague: 'My name is Miss Benson, and this is Mr Norman. We're here on behalf of Child Welfare and Social Services.' Her gaze shifted to Adam.

Phil had already guessed at their reason for being there, and he expected the worst. 'Child Welfare, eh? And may I ask, what it is you want from us?'

'I understand you are Phil Wallis?'

'That's right.'

'You accompanied Adam and his mother, yes?'

'I did.'

'Well, Mr Wallis, first, I apologise for all the questions.' She paused to glance at the sleeping boy. 'Please be assured, we're not here to cause distress at this unhappy time, but having been made aware of some rather unsettling issues, we're duty-bound to examine the facts.'

Phil was already on the defensive. 'Well then, I'll explain the "facts" to you, shall I?' He pointed to Adam. 'That poor child there has just lost his mother in the cruellest way imaginable. His father's run off and the boy thinks the world has come to an end. I would not describe that as being an "unhappy time". I would call that catastrophic, wouldn't you?'

'Well, yes, of course. As you say . . . but as I've explained, we have a job to do, and in view of the notification we received, we will first need to clarify the details of your relationship with the boy.' Without waiting for Phil to respond, Miss Benson plucked a black notepad from her document case.

After quickly scanning her own notes, she had a number of questions, which she put to Phil in a quiet manner, being acutely aware that Adam could wake at any moment. 'If you could again confirm that you are Phil Wallis, and that you are no relation to Adam Carter.'

'That's right.'

'I'm sorry,' she seemed genuinely so, 'but I need you, please, to go through what happened.'

Phil was irritated. 'Why can't you let me get him home and we can answer your questions there?' He lowered his voice to an angry whisper. 'What good will it do Adam, sitting here just yards from where his mother lies dead? For pity's sake, let me get him home. I can assure you, neither me nor the boy is about to leave the country!'

'I understand your anxiety, Mr Wallis. Believe me, we also have Adam's best interests at heart. So, if you could, please, quickly run through the events that brought you and Adam here . . .? Once we know exactly what the situation is, we can then decide which course of action to take.'

Phil had no doubt about what she meant. These were official people, and he appreciated that their specific task was to protect children from harm. If they decided Adam needed taking into care, temporarily or otherwise, there would be nothing that he or anyone else could do to stop them. Especially considering not only the seriousness of events, but the fact that he himself was neither a relative nor even a long-term friend. He was merely the driver of the school bus; in the wrong place at the wrong time.

Miss Benson now casually informed him, 'Oh, and incidentally, because of the information we received, the police have been notified. I understand, they are on their way as we speak.'

Her serious-faced companion, Mr Norman, now took a step forward. 'Of course, the father will obviously need to answer to the police. Adam, however, will initially come under our jurisdiction.' Gesturing to a nearby chair, he suggested, 'Maybe you would care to sit down, while we take you through the procedure?'

Phil flatly refused to sit down. 'Ask your questions.'

'Firstly, as we've already established that you are not Adam Carter's grandfather, can you please explain how you came to be here, with the boy?'

Phil explained, 'I drive the school bus and have done these many years. I had already dropped all the other children off, and as Adam was the last, I decided to walk him up the lane to his house. When we got to the gate, I saw the man I assumed to be his father; he came rushing out of the house, and stood on the porch. I greeted him cordially, but he made no reply.'

He paused before confiding, 'It didn't bother me that the boy's father chose to ignore me; he's got a reputation of being a miserable sod, to say the least. Anyway, thinking the boy would be safe enough with his father, I took my leave of them.' He relived the scene in his mind.

'Please, go on.'

'Well, I was on my way back down the lane, when I heard Mr Carter yelling at Adam. Then all of a sudden this car sped past me. Seeing as it was the very same car that was parked in the drive, I thought it must be Adam's father. Whoever it was, they must have taken leave of their senses, tearing down that narrow lane like a bat out of hell! Splashed mud all over my trousers, so he did, damned lunatic!'

'What did you do then?'

'Well, what else could I do but go back and find out why the boy was now calling. I found him in the lane – crying and shaking he was – and then I went back to the house with him and saw his mother, all broken and twisted at the bottom of the stairs. By, she was in a terrible way; she needed help, and quick. So, I did what needed doing: I sent Adam to call for an ambulance, while I sat and talked to his mother. I didn't even know if she could hear me, but I was hoping she could. That's what they say, isn't it – talk to them, just in case they can hear you?'

'So then what? Did the father come back?'

'No! We saw neither hide nor hair of him. It wasn't long before the ambulance arrived. They tended the mother and put her in the ambulance. Me and the boy jumped in alongside. And now we're here, and that poor boy has lost his mother. And there you have it.'

'Thank you. So now we'll need to discuss the implications of what you've told us.'

'What will happen to Adam?' Phil asked anxiously.

Miss Benson's reply was curt: 'We'll be back shortly, and inform you of any decisions made with regard to Adam.'

No sooner were they gone than the door opened to admit two police officers – a woman and her male colleague – who were interested to learn what exactly Phil might know about Adam's father. Concerned that they were not of the same quiet disposition as the Child Welfare officials, Phil inched them over to the furthest side of the room. 'I don't want Adam to hear us talking,' he explained, and they fully appreciated his concern.

Over the next ten minutes or so, Phil impatiently answered all their questions; most of which he had already gone through with Miss Benson and Mr Norman.

The officers were sympathetic, but they questioned Phil about various aspects of his account. 'First, the medical staff were led to believe that you were the boy's grandfather. How did that come about?'

As before, Phil answered truthfully. 'First of all, I can assure you that at no time did I give the impression that I was his grandfather. They just assumed that I was, and because of what was going on I didn't bother to put them right. Mind you, I wish to God I *was* his grandfather, because then I might have some say in what happens to him.' He told them that he was the driver of the school bus, and had fallen into a situation that no one with any compassion could have run away from.

The questions were thick and fast: 'How did you come to be here now, with Adam Carter? How much do you know about the manner in which Mrs Carter's injuries were caused?'

'I don't know any more than I've already explained,' Phil told them. 'I was on my way back to my bus, when the boy called for me to help him. I neither heard nor saw anything of what took place up to that point.'

'All right, so could you just go through it again, say what you do know, and explain how you got involved? Don't leave any detail out, however small and insignificant it might seem to you.'

Quickly, Phil went through it all again: about how he had dropped the boy off and walked him down the lane to his house. 'Like I told the others, his father was with him when I left, so I told the boy cheerio and went on my way.'

'And then what?'

'Well, I heard this man's voice. He sounded angry . . . screeching and yelling, he was. I assumed it must be the father as I'd seen no one else about, and the Carters' house was the only one down that lane. Then the same car I'd seen in the drive went skidding past me and onto the main road like a damned lunatic!'

Uneasy that the woman police constable was making entries in her notebook, he reluctantly continued, 'No sooner was the car out of sight than I heard Adam yelling my name, pleading for me to help him . . . in a right state he was, poor little devil. I ran back to him and when we got into the house I was shocked at what I saw there.'

He described finding Peggy Carter, as before. 'I've no idea what went on in that house, but if you ask me, nobody falls down the stairs and ends up as damaged as that poor woman.'

He was not surprised to see the two officers exchange glances, because he suspected they must be thinking the very same as himself.

Having explained the run of events, he glanced over at the boy. 'No child should ever see his mother like that, and now she's gone, and he's like a lost soul. I gave him my word that I would not let him down.'

'When you "gave him your word", what do you mean exactly?' the male police officer asked.

Phil hesitated. What use was his word anyway, now that Child Welfare had got involved? But then, he must have been crazy if he had ever believed it could be any other way.

'I meant that he was not to worry about anything, because I would look after him. So now I'd like to get the boy home as quickly as possible. It's not right for him to be here just now, especially after what's happened. He needs looking after. As far as I can tell, I'm the only one he's got.'

The male officer was sympathetic, but having dealt with deserted children for many years, he was also realistic. 'I'm afraid it isn't as simple as that.'

'What's that supposed to mean?' Phil's concern was heightened by his remark, even though he was sensible enough to know that what he proposed would never be allowed.

The officer spelled it out. 'As you're well aware, the boy's mother has just died, and as far as we can tell, his father has abandoned him. Then there's the question of how Mrs Carter actually received her injuries. There are still far too many questions left unanswered. As for the boy, he is not altogether your concern. You must understand, it's our duty to see that he is kept safe until every effort is made to locate any relatives there might be.'

'Yes, of course I understand that, but he's a very frightened child, without anyone close to turn to. The thing is, he knows and trusts me. I'm offering to keep him safe, at my home, or if it helps matters I'll stay with him at his house. Either way, he'll be taken care of, and, more importantly, by someone who's known him these past many years; since he was old enough to attend school.'

'I'm afraid this is not an option, Mr Wallis. When a child appears to be in danger, for whatever reason, we have a legal responsibility to examine those circumstances and take whatever steps we have to take in the best interests of that child. From information received, we consider Adam's situation to be highly sensitive; therefore needing an immediate response. As you have already explained, you are not a relative. That being the case, Adam's welfare is a matter for the Child Welfare Department.'

He concluded, 'Under the circumstances, there is no question of allowing the boy to return home. As I understand it, the case has now moved into the realms of a possible murder inquiry. So, until the investigation is concluded with regard to Mrs Carter's fatal injuries, the family home will be cordoned off and kept secure. As for relatives, you can be assured that the search is already underway. Meantime, as I've already explained, the boy's safekeeping remains the responsibility of the courts, and the Child Welfare Department.'

'Yes, and that's what I'm worried about.' Phil spoke his mind. 'I'm worried that they'll put him in the children's home, and if his father doesn't come back, what'll happen to him then, eh? Like as not he'll be fostered out, and how many foster parents would choose a deeply troubled seven-year-old in preference to a younger child? Not many, in my opinion!'

'Have you any idea where the father might have gone?' the woman police officer asked.

'I've no idea at all. How could I?'

'So, you wouldn't know if Mr Carter ever intended coming back?'

'I haven't a clue.'

When the official questions were over, Phil had a few questions of his own, such as what would happen with Mrs Carter now, and when might they be able to make plans to move her. 'When can we begin making arrangements for her to be laid to her rest?'

Again, the answers to all of his questions were negative and unsettling. And he was grateful that Adam had remained asleep; unaware of what was being said.

~

Following an agonising wait, Phil was informed by the Child Welfare officers that, after discussing the case, they had reached the only decision available to them in the circumstances.

Peggy Carter's son would be taken into care until it was established whether or not he had relatives who might want to apply for custody.

Heartbroken, Phil asked if he might be the one to relay the news to Adam. Being sympathetic to the boy's plight, and having already realised the bond between these two, the officials agreed. So, while the officers remained by the door, Phil woke Adam up.

Seated beside Adam, Phil choked back his own emotion as he explained how everyone was concerned that they should do the right thing by him, and therefore every effort was being taken to locate his father, and track down any other of his relatives.

'Meantime, son, you must go with the people whose responsibility it is to keep you safe and well.'

Nervously, Adam looked across at the two Child Welfare people. For what seemed an age he did not speak. Then he looked back at Phil and, in a small, quivering voice he asked, 'Are they waiting to take me away now?'

Trying hard not to show his sorrow, Phil took a moment to reply, and even then was able only to nod, for fear of letting his emotions run away with him.

Then they looked at each other a long while, and the boy fell into Phil's chubby arms. Holding onto him as though his own life depended on it, he confided tearfully, 'I don't want to go with them, Phil. I want to go with you.'

'I know, son, and I would take you home in a minute, but it isn't possible. But you're not to worry. You'll be safe enough with these people. They'll look after you, and who knows, they might even find your real granddad, and possibly a cousin or two. You'd like that, wouldn't you?'

Adam gave no answer. Instead, he asked, 'When can I see my mum?'

'Not yet, son, but when the time is right, I'll be sure to let you know.'

'Will you, Phil? Honestly?'

'Oh, yes! You can depend on it!' It was getting harder for him to hold back his emotions, but somehow he continued to remain calm and reassuring, for the boy's sake.

'And you'll come and see me, won't you, Phil?'

'You bet I will!'

'Are you coming with me now?'

'No, I'm afraid not, but you've got Miss Benson and Mr Norman with you.'

'But I want you there! Oh, please, Phil, don't leave me!' He started to cry again. 'Don't go, *please.*'

Phil addressed the Welfare officers. 'It wouldn't hurt if I went along too, would it?' he asked softly. 'It's been such a bad day for the little chap.'

Of course, they could not deny the sobbing child this request.

'Where are we going?' asked Adam.

'To the place where you'll be living, while they look for one of your relatives,' Phil explained. 'Oh, Adam, wouldn't that be wonderful . . . if they found someone who wanted to love and take care of you . . . someone of your very own?'

Adam looked away. 'I want my mum.'

'I know that, son. But like I said before – and I want you always to think of what I'm telling you now – your mother has gone to a better place. She's not suffering any more, and no one can hurt her ever again.'

'Is she still watching over us, Phil?'

'Oh, yes. More than ever, and she always will be.'

A small, sympathetic gesture from one of the watching pair told Phil it was time to go.

Phil gave a nod, then, as he held Adam by the hand, they were led down the corridor, outside and across the car park, and into a waiting vehicle.

At first Adam resisted, but Phil stayed beside him, coaxing him into the back of the car, before climbing in alongside.

Throughout the short journey, Adam was unusually quiet, head down, his thoughts back there in the hospital with his beloved mum. Occasionally he would choke back a sob, and lean into Phil for comfort.

Phil talked calmly to him. He reminded him that he would come and see him as often as he was allowed, and that he would never let him down.

'I mean to keep track of you,' he said. 'Tomorrow I'll bring you pen and paper, and my home address, so if you feel the need to write to me, you'll have the means. Oh, and I'll fetch you a notebook.'

'What for?'

'Well, if ever there's a time when I'm not able to visit and you might be worried, or sad, or maybe you've done something you feel proud of, you can put it all in your little book. Make sure to keep it safe, and we'll talk it through when next I see you. Mind you, it'll take a herd of horses or the end of the world to keep me from visiting. So, Adam, my boy, is that a deal?'

'Yes, please, Phil.'

Seated upfront, the Welfare officers were touched by the very special relationship between the man and the boy.

'The old fella was right,' Miss Benson confided to Mr Norman. 'If there was any justice in the world, he should have been the boy's real grandfather.'

Mr Norman glanced in his driving mirror to see the boy smiling up at Phil, and he had to agree.

~

Within the hour, they arrived at the children's home. An impressive, proud old building with long windows and a great oak door, it gave an impression of great strength.

'Here we are then, Adam.' Mr Norman climbed out of the car, and opened the door on Adam's side. 'We have many other children here, children much as your-self, who, through no fault of their own, have found themselves in unfortunate circumstances. I do hope you'll be content here, while the search is on to find a relative who might offer you a loving home. In the meantime, I'm sure you'll find a friend or two here. Oh, and I'm sure your good friend, Phil, will be calling in from time to time.'

'Come rain or shine, you can count on it!' Phil assured them all.

Walking across to the front door, Phil felt Adam's hand tremble in his, and his heart was like a lead weight inside him. As was his way, he gave up a silent prayer: *Don't desert him, Lord, for this boy will never need You more than he does right now.*

He glanced at Adam's forlorn face, then he looked up at the impressive building with its long, arched windows and grand oak door, and he hoped it would not be too long before Adam could be reunited with his own long-lost relatives. Or, if that was not to be, then maybe he would be offered a special place in the heart of a loving family.

At that moment, the door opened to reveal a portly woman of middle age. Her pink face, with merry blue eyes, was wreathed in a broad smile, and her mass of brown hair was haphazardly piled on top of her head. She introduced herself as Miss Martin, and brightly invited them to, 'Come in . . . please, do come in.' She had a singsong voice that made Phil and Adam share the tiniest of smiles.

As they were ushered inside, Adam clung to Phil; and Phil felt that Adam was resisting every step. 'It'll be all right, son,' he confided. 'She looks like a nice, jolly sort. Oh, and look!' He pointed to one of the long casement windows. 'The children are waving at you. Oh, Adam! I really think you'll make friends here, but I've a feeling it won't be too long before you're settled into a fine, loving family.'

Adam was not listening; nor was he looking at the

children. Instead, he was thinking of his mother, of her smile and her laughter, and the way she always cuddled him, too tight, and too often; almost as though she could not let him go.

Now, she would never cuddle him again, or laugh out loud, or wave him off when he climbed onto the school bus.

When the inevitable tears came, he quietly wiped them away with the cuff of his sleeve.

Phil had seen the tears, though, and wrapping his arm round the boy's shoulders, he drew him close.

Minutes later, as they walked through the door and into the huge, wood-panelled hallway, Phil had a feeling of dread.

He feared for the future, and with the boy still reeling from the loss of his mother, and his heart heavy with hatred for the man who he believed had caused her death, he was at his most vulnerable.

Phil could not help but wonder how this sad and lonely child would ever again find a sense of peace.

He felt as though somehow he had been appointed guardian. And so, come what may, and for as long as it took, he promised himself that he would watch over Adam as though he were his own flesh and blood.

Miss Martin seemed friendly enough, and as she waddled ahead, they were informed of occasional events that took place in the home.

'We keep an orderly house, but that is not to say we don't ever have fun. We also like to reward hard work and good behaviour. We're privileged to have at least one summer trip to the seaside, and we always celebrate Christmas.'

There were many rooms in the house, and it took the best part of an hour to visit each one. The great hall was very much designed in the manner of the hallway itself, with wall panels above the skirting, and tall, arched windows. At one end there was a raised pulpit.

'This is where we gather for morning prayers and address the various matters of the week,' Miss Martin said.

As they toured the downstairs, Adam remained silent, as did Phil, though the officials did ask questions now and then, in order to gain more information for the benefit of Phil and Adam.

At the front of the building there were classrooms and other, brighter, rooms for play. Adam and Phil had the opportunity to watch the younger children playing happily, with the staff being very caring and supportive.

Of the other rooms, some were dedicated to early learning, while another, with rows of seats and a huge screen, was set aside for additional education and the occasional film treat.

From one small room came the sound of music, and when they peeped inside, Phil and Adam were surprised to see a boy of about Adam's age playing the piano.

Miss Martin was very proud. 'I had to fight the authorities tooth and nail in order for piano lessons to be agreed,' she told them, 'but the piano is mine, so there was no cost to be made.'

She gestured to the old man overseeing the playing. White-haired, and with a slightly bent back, he had his eyes closed, and was obviously intent on the boy's playing.

'That's my uncle,' she explained. 'He's a retired music teacher, and lives quite close. He kindly gives his time freely in order to encourage the talented amongst us.' Softly, she closed the door. 'There is more for you to see,' and with a wide and pleasant smile, she urged them onward.

The back of the house was given over to the kitchens, toilet facilities, and accommodation for junior staff.

Upstairs was divided into two. The lesser area was dedicated to the senior staff. 'We have no need to tour this side,' Miss Martin informed them. 'It's merely private offices and accommodation.'

The larger and better secured half of the upper floors was the children's dormitories, with a small office close by for the duty night officer.

All too soon it was time for Phil to say goodbye to Adam. 'Remember what I said,' Phil reminded him. 'Anything that worries you . . . anything at all, we'll discuss it tomorrow, when I come and see you.' He turned to Miss Martin. 'Do you have specific visiting times?'

'Of course. We can't have people popping in and out at will. It's necessary for both staff and children to work with an orderly timetable, although, of course, in cases of emergency, we can be flexible.'

Bypassing Phil, she enquired of the officials, 'So, does Adam have any belongings with him?'

'I'm afraid not.' Miss Benson walked her away from the group. 'I assume you've been informed of the circumstances?'

'Of course, yes, I do understand. But Adam will feel more comfortable if he could possibly have a few of his own things with him . . . his regular clothes and personal things.'

'Yes, I understand. I can't promise anything, but I will try.'

'Oh, please do. It really will make all the difference to him settling in.'

There followed the inevitable tears, with Adam clinging to Phil.

'I don't want to stay here, Phil.'

Phil's heart ached as he confided, 'For the moment there's nothing we can do about it, son. Just remember. I won't be far away, and I'll be back every day. So you're not alone. Always remember that.'

'Phil?'

'Yes, son?'

'What about my mum?'

Phil took him by the shoulders. 'Listen to what I say now. Your mum is in a safer and happier place, and she's watching over you. If you ever need to confide in her, then do so any time, any place, and she will hear you clear as a bell. As for everything else, just you leave it to me. I'll talk to whoever's in charge, and I'll get all the answers you need, I promise . . .' he laid his hand across his chest, '. . . hand on heart, I truly will.'

'You mustn't worry too much about Adam,' Miss Martin informed Phil. 'We'll soon have him settled in, and he'll be fine. You wait and see.' She smiled at Adam. 'I'll do my best to get some of your personal possessions brought in. It would certainly help if you could make

me a list of the things you cherish most.' When Adam
gave no answer, she added, 'Just have a little think about
it.' She then plucked a leaflet from the hallway table,
and handed it to Phil. 'You'll need this, Mr . . .?' She
recalled that Phil had been introduced already, and she
was irritated that her memory was not what it used to
be, although she never lost sight of what was most important: the children and their welfare.

'Wallis . . . the name is Phil Wallis, and you can be
sure I'll be back here tomorrow, and every day I'm
allowed.'

'I see.' She made a smile, but behind the smile she
was wondering if this determined man was a pain in
the making. She could see, however, that Phil Wallis
was sincere in his concern for the boy.

A few minutes later they were outside in the porch.
'I'll be thinking of you, son,' Phil promised. 'Happen
when I come back tomorrow, you'll have made a friend
or two.'

Adam began to panic. Throwing his arms round
Phil's ample belly, he pleaded tearfully, 'I'm frightened.
Please, Phil, let me come home with you.'

It took every ounce of strength for Phil to speak
calmly and reassure the boy. Holding him at arm's
length, he stooped to his level, and, looking into his
eyes, he asked, 'Do you think I would ever lie to you?'

Adam shook his head.

'So, you must know that what I've told you is the
truth, that your mother is watching over you, and that
she won't let any harm come to you. And don't forget,
you'll always have me looking out for you.'

Fishing into his pocket, he took out a pen and a tatty old envelope. 'Look, I'm writing my address down for you, and if ever you need to tell me things that you can't tell anybody else, just write me a letter.' He glanced at Miss Martin. 'He is allowed to do that, isn't he?'

'Of course, but there are certain regulations, so we will need to see the letter before it goes out.'

'Huh! Well, I'm sure he won't be planning a bank robbery with me . . .' He gave an aside wink at Adam.

When Adam chuckled, Phil grabbed him in a hug. 'Aw, son, you'll be fine. Just be yourself. Try not to fret too much, and don't let yourself dwell on the bad things that have happened.'

Fishing into his pocket for a second time, he drew out a handful of coins, which he gave to Miss Martin. 'This is Adam's money . . . for stamps, or whatever other small thing he's able to buy.'

'Thank you, though we do have a small budget for certain incidentals.' All the same, she slipped the coins into her pocket. 'But I'll keep them safe for him.'

''Bye for now, son.' Phil kissed the top of Adam's head. 'Remember . . . the sun nearly always shines after the rain. I'll keep my fingers crossed that the authorities will find your relatives.' He made a point of not mentioning Adam's father.

When Phil climbed into the car alongside the Welfare officers, Miss Martin held onto Adam, who waved until his arms ached. Then, as the car went out of sight, his sobbing was pitiful to hear.

Her heart being slightly softer than her authoritative exterior, Miss Martin slid her arm round his shoulders.

'Your friend Phil has promised he'll be back tomorrow, and I'm sure he will.'

'He will! I know he will!'

'Well, there you are then.'

Adam confided brokenly, 'My mum . . . she . . .' he took a deep breath, '. . . she died. Did you know that?'

'Yes, they told me, and I'm so sorry, but we will care for you here, Adam. We will look after you. For as long as it takes.'

'I don't want to be here.'

'I know, and I do understand.'

'NO! You don't, because you didn't know my mum. You didn't know how kind she was, and how funny, and sometimes she would race me across the fields, and now . . . and . . .' he could no longer hold back the heartbreak, 'I want her back . . . I miss her.' Knowing he would never again see his beloved mother, never again hear her voice or feel her small, strong arms around him, he wept bitterly and his cries were terrible to hear.

Miss Martin understood. 'Listen to me, Adam. I do know what it's like to lose your mother, because I lost mine when I was not much older than you.' She had an idea. 'Do y'know what? I would love to know what your mum was like. She sounds wonderful. So, how about you and I go and have a chat? Then we can talk together, and ask each other all the questions that are in our minds. Afterwards, we can meet up with some of the staff and children. Would you like that, Adam?'

'I don't know.'

'Well, shall we just go and have a little chat on our own? Afterwards, you can decide whether you want to meet some of the children, and maybe one or two members of staff? Is that all right with you?'

Again, Adam nodded, but really he just wanted to run after that car, and his only friend, Phil.

'Right then! So that's what we'll do.' Taking hold of his hand, Miss Martin quickened her steps.

Adam was reluctant. Pulling back against her iron grip and dragging his feet, he glanced towards the windows, his forlorn gaze constantly drawn to where the car had taken Phil out of sight.

He could not understand why or how everything had happened so very quickly, and he was so afraid. This morning he had gone to school as usual, and afterwards, Phil had walked him home. And now Phil was gone, his mother was gone, and his father had run away.

'Come along, Adam,' Miss Martin interrupted his thoughts. 'There's no time for wasting. Lots to do . . . lots to talk about.'

She led him smartly along the corridor and through the house to the parlour, which doubled as her office. 'Here we are, Adam. Now then, how about a glass of fresh orange juice?'

Unceremoniously plonking him onto the sofa, she firmly closed the door and cut across the room to the sideboard. 'I think we deserve a little treat, don't you?' Without waiting for an answer, she took out a small tumbler and a fluted glass.

Humming a merry tune under her breath, she first poured the orange juice into the tumbler, and then she poured a sizeable helping of sherry into the glass. 'One for each of us,' she chirped.

While she bustled about, Adam felt more lost and frightened than at any other time in his life.

Everyone he knew had gone away. Everything familiar had changed, and now he was alone among strangers.

PART TWO

~

The Unwanted Visitor

1957

CHAPTER FOUR

ANNE WYMAN LOVED the little house, formerly her aunt's, on the outskirts of Bedford. It was her pride and joy, but most of all, it was her safe hideaway.

When she'd arrived in Bedford some thirteen years ago, she was a frightened young woman on the run.

Fearful that the man from her past would find her, she would wait until the street was empty before venturing out. When a kindly neighbour might attempt to make small talk, she would merely give a brief nod of the head, before hurrying away.

Back then, after she fled, she was at her most vulnerable. When night fell thick and heavy, she would climb up the stairs to her darkened bedroom and cautiously inch open the curtains just enough for her to peer through to the street below. Then she would kneel by the window and peek out until her eyeballs were sore and her bones ached from the kneeling.

Haunted by the memory of Edward Carter, a madman

who had twice beaten her to within an inch of her life, she had learned over the years to remain ever vigilant. Night after night, and even in the daylight hours, she made herself ready for when he might emerge from the shadows.

At first, having finally escaped from him, she would hardly dare close her eyes to sleep. Instead, aching with tiredness, she would listen to every sound, every slight movement, fearing the moment when he might snatch her away.

So she watched and waited, and eventually she would fall asleep, but it was not an easy sleep. Not then.

And not now.

Today was Saturday. Both herself and her friend Sally had completed their weekly quota of hours working at Woolworths, so this was their day off to do with as they liked.

The thought of spending quality time with Sally brought a smile to Anne's face.

The weather had been bright and sunny all week. Having already decided that, if the weather held, they would drive to Yarmouth, it now seemed that a day at the seaside would be a reality.

Anne hummed a little ditty as she went into the hallway to the telephone. Grabbing up the big black receiver, she dialled Sally's number. It was a while before her friend answered.

'Hello?' She sounded sleepy.

'Sally, being as it's a lovely day, I was wondering, are we still on for Yarmouth?' She kept her fingers crossed, because if Sally didn't go, then neither would she, and she was really looking forward to it now.

Sally, however, was of the same mind. 'Yeah, I'm up for it.'

'Great!' Anne did a little dance on the spot. 'So, d'you want *me* to drive?'

'Well, my car's leaking oil again, so if we go in yours we might actually get there. I meant to deliver mine to the garage but I haven't had time.' She groaned. 'To tell the truth, I keep putting it off, because the mechanic will probably tell me to dump it anyway. He reckons it's well and truly worn out but it's all I can afford, so I'll have to make do with it for now.'

'Look, I've got savings,' Anne said. 'I can lend you some, and you can pay me back whenever.'

Sally would not hear of it. 'I know how long you've scrimped and saved to put a few quid aside. That money is your security and peace of mind, and I would never dream of taking it.'

'It's OK, really. I don't mind. It would be a real pain if your car broke down altogether.'

'Oh, don't worry. It's like an old soldier. It's been patched up before and it'll be patched up again. Meantime, I'll have to stop gadding about and save a few shillings every week until I've got enough to get it put right.'

'OK, so I'll pick you up in what . . . an hour?'

'I'll be ready in half an hour.'

'Are you sure?' Anne knew from experience how

long it took Sally to get ready, and by the sounds of it, she had only just got out of bed.

'I'll be ready, don't worry.'

~

'Right!' Growing excited, Anne resumed her humming as she swiftly cleared away the last of the breakfast things. Glancing at the clock, she saw that it was already half-past eight. 'Crikey! I'd best get a move on.' It was a fifteen-minute drive to Kempston where Sally lived, and at this time on a Saturday the roads could be busy.

Having tidied the kitchen, she made sure the back door was locked and bolted before running upstairs and into the bathroom. She quickly cleaned her teeth, ruffled her fine blonde hair and ran back downstairs; grabbing her coat and bag as she went out the front door.

As always, whenever leaving the house, she made doubly sure that the front door was secured. She then glanced up at the bedroom windows to satisfy herself that they were closed. For good reason, she had learned over the years to keep her wits about her as far as her own security was concerned.

These days, though, she was slightly less paranoid than she had been on first arriving in this quiet back-street many years ago. Even so, the bad memories and a dark, nagging fear that Edward Carter might find her still lurked at the back of her mind.

Clambering into her beloved Morris Minor, she slammed shut the door and then checked through her handbag. She opened her purse: three pound and six shillings, more than enough.

Next, she drew out a stick of rouge and a powder compact. She looked at her reflection in the compact mirror while she dabbed a little make-up over her cheekbones. 'Anne Wyman, you're no oil painting, but you're all you've got, so you'll have to do!' she muttered to herself. Retrieving her lipstick from her handbag, she painted her full, plump mouth with the pale pink lipstick.

She then returned the items to her handbag, started the engine, checked for oncoming traffic, and drew away from the kerb.

At the top of Roff Avenue, she slowed and checked in the driver's mirror. Her eyes were instantly drawn to a tall, dark-haired figure heading away towards the far end of Roff Avenue. He was walking slowly, almost strolling. He seemed nervous, his head turning this way and that, as though searching for something or someone.

Anne's heart skipped a beat. She could hardly breathe. 'Stop that!' she chided herself. The past is long behind you.

The man was out of sight now and, with an irate driver honking his car horn behind her, Anne shifted into gear and drew away.

Some short distance down the road, she pulled over and switched the engine off. Wrapping her trembling fingers around the steering wheel, she gripped it so tight her knuckles turned white.

'Pull yourself together, girl!'

She reminded herself that this was not the first time she'd imagined he was actually in her street searching for her. And each time she'd been wrong.

After a few minutes, feeling calmer, she restarted the engine and set off again. By now, there was no sight of the man who had truly unnerved her.

~

Edward Carter was in a foul mood. Having been up and down the back alley, peeking into yards and hanging about, he had still not been able to catch sight of her. He knew the house was in this street. He'd seen the address in the past enough damned times to know he'd got the right place. Roff Avenue, Bedford.

Unkempt and agitated, he had been on the run far too long. He needed a place to hide to keep his head down for a while. He had a plan, and it involved Anne Wyman, the girl he had married all those years ago. The naïve, trusting little girl who eventually ran off and left him. She owed him, and she was still his wife . . . whether she liked it or not.

He chuckled to himself. If she really thought he might never come looking for her, she was in for a real surprise.

He continued to wander up and down the back alley, growing increasingly agitated, his sharp eyes constantly scanning the houses.

When a couple of people turned into the alley and wandered past him, he flattened himself against the wall, pretending to light a cigarette. As they went past, he nodded amiably to them. 'Morning.'

After a fleeting acknowledgement, the couple walked on, though they turned once to take another look at him. When he stared back, they made a hasty exit.

The policeman had not long turned the corner into Roff Avenue when he saw the man head into the alley, and now, as he noticed the couple hurrying out, he grew curious and crossed the street to investigate.

Edward Carter saw the policeman approaching, and, speaking in his finest voice, he cunningly made his way towards him.

'Good morning, officer. I wonder if you might be able to help me?'

Surprised by this untidy man's refined voice and manner, the policeman replied in a friendly but authoritative tone, 'If I can help you, I will, but it's not wise to be loitering about these back alleys. It tends to make people nervous, and that makes me nervous.'

'Of course. I do understand, but I'm looking for an old friend . . . a woman by the name of Anne Carter. When she moved away from her previous address, she gave me the street and town, but forgot to write down the number of her aunt's house . . . that's where she's staying.'

He began to rummage in his pocket. 'I can show you what she wrote . . . Roff Avenue, Bedford. I promised to visit when I was able. The thing is, her old aunt Ada doesn't have a telephone, doesn't like them, so I'm told.' He gave a warm smile.

The policeman nodded. 'I know a lot of people who

seem a bit timid of the idea. I expect they're used to going down to the red box outside. My mother's exactly the same . . . won't even hear of a telephone in the house.'

Still putting on a show, Carter pulled a crumpled piece of paper out of his pocket, feigning a groan when he read it. 'Oh, wrong one. Sorry, officer. It must be in my inside pocket . . .' He made a big fuss of digging about in his pockets.

The policeman accepted his story hook, line and sinker. 'Look, I understand. I'm afraid I can't help you, but I tell you what –' he pointed back down the alley – 'go back the same way you came in, and turn left. You'll see a pub on the corner. The landlord's always up and working, and there's an old fella keeps the place spick and span. Like as not he might know where your friend is living, especially if there's an old aunt, because the old 'uns do have a communal spirit round these parts.'

'Well, thank you very much, officer. I was about to go and knock on a couple of doors, but I'll have a word at the pub instead.'

'I'm sure that's the thing to do, because you won't find her wandering about in the back alleys, will you?'

'No, you're right. I don't suppose I will.'

'The pub isn't open yet but if you knock on the door, the landlord or his wife will be sure to hear you. Ted and Mary have lived round these parts for some time, so they know the locals better than anybody.' The policeman gave a knowing little smile. 'Oh, and you might even find a few old codgers playing darts in the corner, enjoying a crafty pint out of hours. They think we're not on to them yet, but sometimes we find it wiser to look the other way . . . but don't tell anyone I said that.'

Satisfied that there was nothing to worry about here, he continued on his beat, thinking what an odd sort the stranger was. He found it hard to reconcile the fact that the man was dressed little better than a tramp, while possessing the confident, refined voice of a gentleman. It looked like he'd come on hard times. No doubt he was hoping for a few days' lodgings and a cash handout from his old friend. The policeman did not approve of scrounging, and he thought the stranger should be ashamed, especially when it seemed there appeared to be no reason for him not to hold down a job of sorts.

~

Pausing outside the public house, Edward Carter took a moment to run his fingers through his thick dark hair and briefly brush a hand over his clothes. Best make a good impression, he thought, or they might not be so ready to reveal what they know.

The constable was right. The first thing he saw as he gingerly entered the public house was a group of aged men seated round a table in the corner. They were engrossed in a game of dominoes, and each man had a pint of brown ale before him.

As the door closed behind him, everyone looked up to see who it was. Nobody spoke. Instead, once they had taken stock of him, they resumed their game.

Carter slowly walked past their table. 'Morning. Nice day.' He nodded to each and every one, and they nodded back, curious to know who this weary-looking stranger might be.

'If it's beer you're after, you'll not get it here, at least not till opening time.' The bulbous, whiskered landlord cast a wary glance to the table where the men were now paying attention. 'Oh, and before you go making assumptions, these are friends of mine,' he added warily, 'a private party.'

Carter smiled. 'You've no need to worry about me. I haven't seen a thing,' he assured the landlord. 'To tell the truth, I'm not here for a pint, though I wouldn't say no, especially as I've travelled a long journey to get here.'

'I see. And what is it you want from me?'

'I'm looking for someone. I just thought you might be able to help. I expect you know most people round here?'

The landlord seemed reluctant to answer. 'Maybe I do know a few people, yes, but I'm not the sort to get caught up in gossip. From my experience, poking your nose in other folks' business can get you in a heap o' trouble.'

'That's all right by me, because I'm not the sort to gossip either.' Carter was careful to choose his words. 'The thing is, I'm searching for an old relative.'

'Oh?' The landlord remained cautious.

Carter gave a sad little smile. 'The thing is, when I was sixteen, things got really uncomfortable at home between my parents. Then, when they went their separate ways, Ada took me in.'

The landlord made no response.

Carter continued, 'Ada had a nice, roomy house in Hampshire. I lived with her until I was twenty-one, and then I needed to get out and see the big wide world.'

'Wanted to spread your wings, eh?' The landlord was growing curious.

'I suppose that was it, yes. But my relative didn't want me to leave, so we had a bit of an argument before I left. After I'd gone, I wrote often, but she never answered. Then I was told she'd moved here to Bedford. The sad thing is, she was like a mother to me, so when I heard she was ill, I was determined to find her. I've always regretted us falling out.'

He lowered his voice to a sorry murmur. 'She's quite old now, and I just need to put things right between us . . . before it's too late. If you know what I mean?'

Being a family man himself, the landlord approved of his motive. 'So, if you know where she is, what's stopping you from "putting things right" between you?'

'Because after she moved, I never got her full address. All I was told, was that she'd moved to Bedford . . . Roff Avenue, they thought. I just arrived here this morning and a policeman suggested that I should ask you. He said you might know.'

'What did you say her name was again?' the landlord asked.

'Ada . . . Ada Wyman.'

'Mmm.' He gave it some thought. 'And she's of an age, you say?'

'That's right. I never knew her actual age – you know what women are like about telling – but she must be in her late seventies by now.'

The landlord scratched his head and called for his wife, who was busy washing pots. 'Mary!' his voice rang out. 'Have you a minute?'

'No!'

He raised his voice: 'There's a fella here who's looking for his relative, a woman by the name of Ada Wyman, in her seventies!'

'I don't know any Ada!'

Blowing out his cheeks in exasperation, he apologized, 'I'm sorry. We mostly only know the folk who frequent my pub. Does she have a husband?'

'As far as I know, she never married.' Carter cunningly played his most precious card. 'She might have a niece staying with her, though. Her name is Anne Carter . . . she's in her early thirties. She and Aunt Ada were very close. I was told that Ada was really ill, so her niece might well be taking care of her.'

'I see. And what does she look like, this niece?'

Before he could reply, a voice from across the room called out, 'I know that young lady. Quiet little thing, she is; wild, fair hair and really pretty. Keeps herself to herself, she does. But if you happen to pass her in the street, she always lights up your day with her bright smile.'

Carter could not believe his luck. 'That sounds like her all right!'

The old fellow who'd spoken beckoned him to the table, where they sat together while the other men listened in, waiting to add their own small pieces of information.

'I'm sorry to tell you, but your relative Ada passed

away some years back,' one old, slightly deaf fellow butted in. 'Like you say, the girl did look after her aunt. Did everything for her, she did. She even took her out in the wheelchair most days. You're right, they were very close.'

'That's right!' the little man in the corner who'd first spoken said. 'The old dear was so thankful to have the girl with her, she left her the house, lock stock and barrel.'

'Really?' Carter was so flushed with this discovery, he could hardly sit still. 'Would she be at home now, d'you think?' Carter suppressed his excitement, while feigning the sad expression of a bereaved relation.

'Oh, but you may well have the wrong name for the niece, because this one goes by the same name as her aunt – Wyman. Not Carter . . . Anne Wyman. At least that's how she introduced herself to the postmistress,' said the little man.

Though burning with rage at that unfortunate snippet of information, Carter managed to keep his cool. 'Ah, yes, well, as I recall now, she was indeed a Wyman.'

'Oh, and it's no use you going along there just now because she'll not be back from work just yet.' This further disappointing comment came from a new source. 'Best to leave it till later, I reckon.'

Carter grudgingly thanked the men. Though quietly satisfied with the information he had gathered, he was in a murderous mood. The knowledge that Anne had callously discarded his name while still being married to him was hard to take.

'I wonder if the landlord would mind me having a pint of beer alongside you kind folk?' He needed to keep their confidence. 'You seem to know a lot about my family. It might be nice to sit and chat awhile.'

He was eager to know everything about his runaway wife. Where did she work? How long had her aunt been gone? Did she have a relationship? What was the house worth?

It was beginning to look like he'd fallen on his feet. His bad mood lifted and he had to stop himself from laughing out loud. This morning he was beginning to wonder if he might ever find the woman who was still his legal wife. And now not only had he found his wife, but he'd stumbled across a fine property. As her husband he surely had certain legal rights . . .

He was nobody's fool. He knew that if he played his cards right, he could have it all.

CHAPTER FIVE

'Hang on! i'm on my way!'
Hopping along the passageway with one high
heel on and one in her hand, Sally cursed under her
breath, 'Stop pipping that damned hooter. You'll have
the neighbours out!'

Slinging her shoulder bag round her neck, she flung
open the front door and locked it behind her. She then
slipped her foot into the shoe, dropped the key into
her pocket and ran down the path.

Seeing her friend make her way down the path, Anne
leaned over and threw the passenger door open. 'What
did you say?'

'Oh, now suddenly you've gone deaf, have you?'
Red-faced from hurrying, Sally clambered into the car.
'Well, I can't say I'm surprised, what with all the noise
you've been making. Old Mother Benton next door
threw a bucket of water over the ice-cream man, just

for ringing his bell. So I reckon she must be out just now, because with the racket you created, she'd have been charging at you with the hose-pipe!'

Anne laughed. 'In that case I'm glad she's out. I'm just excited, that's all. It's been ages since we went to the seaside, and now that we're actually on our way, I can't wait to get there.'

In truth, she had felt oddly uneasy these past few days, and the idea of getting away from Bedford, if only for a day, had eased her mind.

As they drove off, Sally took a sneaky look at her. 'Are you all right?' She had noticed how tired Anne looked, and how every now and then she would nervously glance in her driver's mirror. 'Anne?'

Anne was too deep in thought to hear her name being called.

'Anne!'

Anne gave a little gasp. 'Oh, sorry . . . what?'

'You seem to be miles away. Tell the truth . . . have you changed your mind? Would you rather not go to the seaside? It's a long drive, and I know you're not too keen on driving long distances.'

'No, I'm fine, honestly. I'm really looking forward to a day at Yarmouth. I was just thinking, that's all.'

'About what?'

'Nothing in particular.'

'I'll drive, if that's what worries you?'

'No, like I said, I'm absolutely fine. I just didn't sleep too well last night.'

'Why not?'

Anne gave a little shrug. 'Dunno . . . overtired, I suppose.' She had never told anyone the truth of her past, not even the lovely Sally. She still believed that keeping quiet was the right decision, because that way she had a better chance of putting the horror behind her.

So far, that particular plan was not working.

Sally's voice gentled into her thoughts. 'OK. Well, when we get to Yarmouth, you can park the car and we won't go anywhere near it again until it's time to come home. In fact, if you want to, we could lie on the beach all day, and do nothing.'

Anne laughed out loud at that suggestion. 'Huh! I can see *you* lying on the beach doing nothing. You'd be bored out of your mind.'

'I expect I would, but if it's what you want . . .?'

'It isn't.'

'There you are then! And besides, where's the fun in "doing nothing"? And what's the point in going to the seaside and not trying the rides, or eating candy floss? Or having a go at winning some money in the amusement arcade? And what if we meet up with a couple of good-looking fellas who might want us to be with them for the day?'

'And you a happily married woman! No, thanks all the same . . . about the fellas, I mean.'

'Hmm! So are you saying that if some gorgeous bloke made a pass at you, you would actually turn him down?' She gave a knowing little grin. 'I don't believe that for one minute.'

'Well, you'd better believe it,' her tone darkened, 'because I'm off fellas for good!'

Sally was saddened by Anne's remark, and surprised by the angry manner in which she had said it.

She had to ask. 'Anne?'

'Yes?'

'What's wrong?'

'What d'you mean?'

'I'm not really sure, but you seem to be in a strange mood. Going to Yarmouth was your suggestion, and now you don't seem so sure. Just now, you decided to wake the whole street by honking your car horn, and then you go all quiet on me, like something's playing on your mind. And just now, when you said you were off fellas for good, why is that?'

'Forget about it. I suppose I'm just not ready for settling down, that's all.' She hoped that would be the end to Sally's questions.

'But you sounded angry . . . as though you'd had a bad experience.' Unaware that she had touched a raw nerve, Sally went merrily on, 'Most women look forward to a happy marriage, and children.'

Anne regretted having made that controversial statement. 'I'm sorry if you thought I was angry, because I wasn't.' She gave a little shrug. 'It's like my head's all over the place at the minute. I don't really know what I want, that's the trouble.'

'I reckon you're tired. You said yourself that you're not sleeping. I'm worried about you, Anne. So, what's the problem? We're like sisters, you and me, and you should know by now you can talk to me about anything, and you can rest assured it won't go any further.'

'I know, and I'm sorry.' Anne felt vulnerable. 'There's nothing to talk about. I got out of the wrong side of bed this morning, that's all. And now I'm spoiling everything. Look, take no notice of me. I promise, we will enjoy ourselves. I'll make sure of it.'

Still not altogether convinced, Sally had to accept her explanation. 'Just remember, though, if there is ever anything on your mind and it's causing you a problem, I'm a good listener. And I do know how to keep my mouth shut.'

'I appreciate that, but there is nothing to tell. So now, can we please stop the chatter, and let me concentrate on my driving?'

'OK, and if I open my mouth again, feel free to kick me out.'

Sally's light-hearted remark lifted the mood, but she had known Anne long enough to realise that something was worrying her, and one way or another, she was determined to get to the bottom of it. Meantime, she had to play along.

'Right! So now let's turn our thoughts to enjoying ourselves. OK?'

When Anne seemed deep in thought, Sally asked her again, this time louder, 'I said . . . OK?'

'Yes . . . OK!' Anne gave her answer with a willing smile.

All these years she had kept her dark secret, but now she wondered if it was time to share her fears. After all, Sally was her best friend, and if you couldn't tell your best friend, who could you tell?

And yet the idea of confiding in anyone, even Sally, filled her with dread.

~

Through the final leg of the journey, Anne concentrated on the road, while Sally's thoughts were focused on Anne.

She had suspected for some time now that Anne had a past she did not want to reveal. In all the time she had known her, Anne had never spoken about her family, or the circumstances that had brought her to Bedford.

She had spoken often about her aunt Ada. It was clear she had adored the old woman, but not once had she mentioned her parents or other family. When one of their workmates asked her about her family, Anne always excused herself, claiming that she had something urgent to attend to or somewhere she should be.

Sally, though, remained curious. But her affection for Anne meant that she must respect her friend's right to privacy. Even though, as the years went by, Anne's obvious need to bury her past was of some concern to Sally.

She noticed things that worried her. First, Anne's obvious reluctance to talk about her family did seem unnatural. Also, whenever she had been invited to Anne's house, Sally soon realised that apart from one faded photograph of her old aunt as a young girl, Anne had no photographs on show of either herself or anyone else. And whenever the discussion turned to family, or girlish talk about when they were teenagers and experienced their first love, Anne would swiftly change the subject.

It was a strange and curious thing, but it was Anne's right not to discuss her private life. And it was Sally's intention never to pry.

Over the years, Sally had learned to tread carefully, and because of her discretion, her friendship with Anne had flourished.

She had no idea what had brought Anne here to Bedford, and she had no idea of what her life had been before, or what her future plans were. In the end, it didn't really matter.

Since she came to work at Woolworths, Anne had been a great friend to Sally. She had proven herself to be a kind and compassionate young woman, who cared very much for those close to her. Now Sally could not even imagine what it would be like without Anne. To Sally it seemed as though Anne had always been there, and always would be.

Sally herself had no brothers or sisters, so always having Anne around made her feel complete in a way; kind of warm and happy inside.

Lately, though, she had become concerned that whatever secrets Anne was hiding had begun slowly to destroy her peace of mind.

～

For a time, the two of them were lost in thought: Anne training her attention on the road ahead, which was getting busier by the minute, Sally looking ahead to a wonderful day out, and the fun that might await them.

While she was concentrating on driving, Anne was thinking that she was even more determined than ever to distance herself from the dark memories that had robbed her of a normal life. Sometimes, she could go for weeks, even months, without letting the past invade her peace of mind, then out of the blue something would happen to trigger it all off again – like this morning, when she caught a glimpse of that stranger through her driving mirror.

Try as she might, she could not get the dark-haired man out of her memory. She could see him now in her mind's eye, clear as a bell and larger than life.

It was the way he had walked along the street, in that same, confident manner as her tormentor.

It was the shifty manner in which he had glanced about . . . like a cat watching for a mouse.

It was the shock of dark hair, and the straight shoulders . . . like the posture of a military man.

She had tried so hard to put him out of her mind, and now, thanks to Sally and her innocent chatter, she was beginning to feel a little bit easier.

So, as they neared Yarmouth, Anne promised herself again that she would make a concentrated effort to put the past behind her once and for all. She knew it would not be an easy promise to keep, because Edward Carter had made her suffer badly, and that was not something she could shrug off. It went too deep. It had a life of its own.

That man, that monster, had taken a bright, young girl, and robbed her of all trust and innocence.

He taught her how to be subservient in order to survive. He taught her the very depths of hatred.

Until she met Edward Carter, she had never known the true meaning of fear. Now, try as she might to overcome it, that fear continued to haunt her in her nightmares and in her every waking hour.

All the promises in the world could not make her forget the pain and terror he had put her through. The memories were too strong.

The fear that he might one day track her down still haunted her every waking hour.

CHAPTER SIX

TWO HOURS AFTER leaving home, they were on the outskirts of Yarmouth.

'Look, there's the sign to the front.' Sally pointed the way, straight on.

Anne headed the car towards the sea. 'It's just what the doctor ordered.' She was really looking forward to their day out. 'Sun, sea, and time on our hands.'

'We-hey!' Sally could not contain her excitement. 'Yarmouth, here we come!'

'Behave yourself.' Anne laughed out loud. 'You're like a kid on her first outing to the seaside.'

'Oh, but I do love the seaside!' Sally would not be quietened. 'We'll go on every ride there is. And afterwards, if it's warm enough, we'll go for a swim in the sea. Let's hope there are no sharks or anything nasty like that. Then we'll lie in the sun and get a tan . . . and after that we'll get ourselves one of them pedal-things and whizz down the promenade—'

'Woah! For now, let's just concentrate on getting a parking place.' Anne laughed.

'No worries. We're early enough, so there'll be plenty of space on the front. Look!' She drew Anne's attention to a second sign. 'Parking, turn right.'

'Good. But it's Saturday, don't forget, and it's looking a bit busy already.'

Anne turned right, only to find that this particular car park was full. 'Let's drive along the front. You never know, we might just be lucky.'

She drove the entire length of the front, and there was not a parking place in sight.

'Dammit!' Sally groaned. 'I expect we'll have to park miles away.'

Then she had an idea. 'Why don't we park in that hotel car park?' She brought Anne's attention to the newly refurbished Victorian hotel opposite the beach. 'Perfect!'

'We can't park in there.' But Anne smiled at her friend's mischievous idea.

'Why can't we?' Sally was not easily put off.

'Because all the places are allocated for guests, look.' She pointed to the large white-painted numbers in each parking place.

'But half of them are empty.'

'That doesn't matter. They could turn up any time, and anyway, with our luck the manager's bound to turf us off.'

'Worth a chance, though.'

'Hey! Who's driving this car?'

'You are, more's the pity. If it were me, I'd have been in there like a flash!'

'Then it's a good job I'm the driver, isn't it?' Anne's gaze roved along the seafront. 'Hey! Look! There's a fella pulling out of a parking place . . . up there, d'you see?'

'Where?'

'There, right in front of that little café.'

Sally began to panic when she saw the driver backing out. 'Hurry up, Anne, before somebody else nicks it.'

Anne manoeuvred into position, but as they drew close, the driver of a black Austin Morris tried to edge in front of them from the other direction. 'Cheeky devil!' Sally wound down the window. 'Hey, you! That's our place, so back off!'

Seeing the whites of her eyes, the man backed off, and Anne shot in quick. As the irate driver pulled away he made a rude sign at them.

'And you!' Sally did the same back.

Anne started chuckling, then Sally was sniggering, and now the two of them erupted in laughter.

'You'll get us arrested,' Anne told her.

'Huh! If the arresting officer is tall and handsome, and extra kind with his truncheon, you won't see me putting up a fight.'

'You're a liability, and with a doting husband at home!' Anne was beginning to relax. It was so good to get away for a day.

~

The next few hours were filled with non-stop fun.

Their first ride was in the caterpillar.

'I hope they don't roll the roof over,' Sally whimpered as they climbed in. 'I don't like closed-in spaces. They make me nervous.'

'Let's get out then,' Anne suggested. 'There are plenty of other rides we can go on.'

'Not likely!' Sally was adamant. 'We've paid our money and we're staying on.' She yelled out to the fairground attendant, 'They won't roll the roof over, will they? I don't like it.'

'Naw!' Skillfully throwing his chewing gum from one side of his mouth to the other, he assured her, 'We don't roll the roof down unless it's raining.'

'There you are!' Anne said.

Sally settled into her seat and tried to relax. 'I hope they don't go too fast . . . I get giddy when they go too fast.'

Anne climbed into the seat beside her. 'Let's just enjoy the ride. Oh, look! We're off already.' The ride started slowly at first, then it gathered speed, and as the caterpillar flew round and round the tracks, they held onto the bar, laughing and giggling, and occasionally screaming with delight.

Sally noticed it first. 'Can you hear that?' she yelled above the screams and laughter of other joyriders.

'What?'

'Just listen!'

Anne listened but she couldn't hear anything untoward.

Suddenly it began to get dark, and the screams grew louder. Sally was panicking. 'The roof's coming over! Look at the roof. Bloody Nora, get me out of here!'

She screamed so loud, the ride was stopped and they both climbed off.

'You lied to me!' Sally vented her anger on the ride-owner. 'I asked about the roof and your man said it would not go over unless it rained, and it didn't rain, so I want my money back.'

'You'll not get no money out o' me!' The burly ride-owner sent them on their way. 'You knew what the ride was about and you still got on it, so don't come that old game about getting your money back. Go on, bugger off out of it!'

As they made their way back to the main walkway, he continued to swear and curse after them. 'You want locking up, trying to cheat a poor bloke who works hard for a living. Don't show yer faces round 'ere again, not unless you want a kick up the arse!'

Sally was all for going back to sort him out, but Anne took hold of her and marched her to the goldfish stall. 'Can we please have two fishing-lines?' She handed four small coins over to the homely-faced woman.

Just as Anne had planned, the two of them got engrossed in trying to catch a fish. In the end, though, they came away empty-handed.

Half an hour later, they made their way over to the rifle range.

Whether it was anger because she failed at the gold-fish pond, or maybe it was her determination to get the better of something after her row with the ride-owner, but Sally proved to be a hotshot with a rifle.

She quickly won two big adorable teddy bears; one for her and one for Anne. 'Am I a hotshot, or what?'

Punching the air with a clenched fist, she did a little dance on the spot. 'I'm ready for anything now.'

Anne was amazed at Sally's brilliant shooting. She herself hadn't even hit a single coconut, while Sally had sent them all flying. 'How did you do that?' Anne asked.

'Easy. I imagined I was aiming at the ride-owner,' Sally quipped. 'It worked a treat, didn't it?'

Anne smiled but wisely gave no comment. 'Come on then. Let's see what else is on offer.'

A few minutes later, they stopped to rest their aching feet. Sally dropped onto the sandy bench like a sack of potatoes. 'I'm worn out!'

'Stay here a minute,' Anne suggested. 'I'll go and put the bears in the boot of the car.' She took hold of the prizes. 'And no swearing at anybody while I'm gone.'

Just then a couple of middle-aged men sauntered by. They glanced at the two young women, then looked away. Then one of them glanced back to have another look as they wandered on. Unfortunately, Sally was still in fighting mood after the caterpillar ride.

'So what are you two staring at?' she snarled.

'Hey!' Anne calmed her down. 'Don't take it out on strangers, just because that ride-owner got the better of you.'

'It's not that! Did you see them, turning round to stare at us? Did he think we were on the lookout for a couple of paunchy, middle-aged men, or what? Bloody cheek of it! And anyway, that boy on the ride told us a lie, so the ride-owner should have given us our money back.'

'Forget about it.'

'Am I being a pain?'

'Yes.'

'Sorry,' Sally apologised. 'It's just that I always panic if the roof comes over.'

'Yes, I got that one.'

'I'll shut up about it, shall I?'

'Might be an idea.'

'Not another word, I promise.'

'Good.'

'We can still have a good time, though, can't we?'

'Course we can!'

'D'you want an ice cream?'

'OK, I'll take the bears back to the car, and you get the ice creams?'

'Good idea!' Sally's sour mood quickly disappeared. 'So, what kind of ice cream do you want?'

Anne didn't have to think too hard. 'A double dollop of vanilla ice cream with a chocolate flake on top.'

'Right! It'll be my treat.' Sally's mood brightened. 'You can get the fish and chips after we've been on the other rides, and no more mention of the caterpillar. Deal?'

'Yes, deal! And you can stop apologising. To tell you the truth, when I saw that cover coming over, I didn't like it either.'

'Ah! You didn't kick up a fuss, though, did you? In fact, you never seem to get het up about anything. I remember when you first started at Woollies and the manager piled more work on you than any of us. And you just got on with it, without a word of complaint. If he'd done that to me, I'd have been up in arms!'

Anne had her reasons for keeping quiet, but she kept them to herself. 'In my experience it pays not to make ripples.'

'Even when you're being taken advantage of?'

'Yes, even then.'

Anne's memories carried her back over the bad years, when she'd been unafraid to speak out. But then she'd been made to pay dearly for her boldness. 'Sometimes confrontation can lead to more trouble than you can handle.' Her answer came in a whisper, almost as though she'd forgotten Sally was there.

'Anne?' Sally had a feeling that something was wrong. '"More trouble than you can handle"? What's that supposed to mean?'

Lost in the horror of her past, Anne did not hear.

'ANNE!' Sally raised her voice.

'Oh . . .' Anne took a deep breath, 'I was just . . . oh, sorry.'

In her mind she could see the baby, small and vulnerable. Her baby. Her own flesh and blood. She shut it from her mind. But she could not shut it from her heart.

'You'd best queue up for the ice creams. I'll only be gone a few minutes.' Grabbing the two bears, she hurried away, while secretly wiping away the tears.

Seeing the stranger earlier had really shaken her and now she could not get Edward Carter out of her mind. She could see his face, angry. Hateful.

She could hear his voice, so refined, so wicked.

Shivering, she quickened her steps, silently praying, *Dear Lord, will I ever be free of him?*

~

At the car, Anne retrieved from the boot two brightly striped shoulder bags, each containing a towel, swimsuit and sunhat. She then climbed into the front seat of the car and sat for a time, her thoughts covering the years before she sought refuge with her beloved aunt Ada.

You're free of him, Anne, she felt the need to reassure herself. *He hasn't found you all these years, and he won't find you now. Besides, he's probably found some other poor woman to terrorize. With luck he's forgotten you ever existed.*

Feeling calmer, she hoisted one bag onto her shoulder, and carried the other over her arm. As she walked back, there was the tiniest of smiles on her face. When she caught sight of Sally, she waved and grinned, and for the moment all seemed well with the world.

'Where the devil have you been?' Sally had expected her back ages ago. 'It's a good job there was a long queue at the ice-cream van. What took you so long?'

'It only took a minute to leave the teddies and collect the bags, but I sat inside the car for a minute or two . . . had to think.'

'What about?'

Anne shrugged. 'Just something and nothing.'

'Is everything all right?'

'Yes, everything's fine.' She reached out to collect her ice-cream cornet. 'Thanks, that looks good.' She licked the trickling ice cream from the sides of the cornet. 'What next then?' She sat down next to Sally.

'What d'you mean?'

'Well, we haven't been on any other rides, and we said we'd spend some time in the amusement arcade trying to win a bit of spending money. Then there's the beach. We promised ourselves a swim and a lie on the beach to try and get a bit of a suntan. But I was thinking, it might be best if we leave that till last. What do you think?'

Sally was in agreement. 'But don't forget, we'll need to get something to eat along the way.'

Anne chuckled. 'You're always hungry.'

'I know.' Sally made a face. 'I reckon I've got worms.'

Anne laughed again. 'What do you want to do next?'

Sally had it all worked out. 'I know I said I was hungry, but I'd rather not eat till later. And anyway, it'll be quieter in the café later on. If that's all right with you?'

'I'm easy.'

'OK. So, how does this sound? We'll finish our ice creams, then we could go on a couple of other rides. After that we could spend an hour on the machines in the arcade, and maybe win a fortune. Then we can go for a swim, and spend an hour or so on the beach, to maybe get a tan before we clean up and finally make our way to the café on the promenade. We'll relax and enjoy a leisurely meal, before setting off home. How's that?'

'Perfect!' Anne clapped her hands in agreement. Whenever she was with Sally, she always felt lighter of heart.

They sat awhile on the beach wall, chatting and finishing off their ice-cream cornets.

'Right!' Having nibbled the small remains of her cornet, Sally wiped her face with a tissue and threw the tissue in a bin. 'Time for action.' She set off down the promenade.

Anne quickly finished her cornet and set off at a run to catch up with Sally. 'Wait for me!'

By 4 p.m., they had seen and done everything they had wanted to. They rode in the flying aeroplanes, and went mad in the crazy bumper cars. They went round and round on the waltzer, and had a wonderful time.

Afterwards, they spent a full hour in the amusement arcade, where between them they won the amazing amount of six pounds.

They had a leisurely swim, and after they had dried themselves off, they persuaded the donkey-man to let them ride on his two biggest donkeys.

'There you go.' He smacked the donkeys' rumps and set them off at a good pace. 'Enjoy yourselves.'

Sally and Anne laughed and squealed as they bounced up and down. Then the donkeys got spooked and took off down the beach with Sally and Anne hanging onto their manes for dear life.

'Help! Get me off!' Sally's cry caused other holiday-makers to laugh at their antics.

Eventually, the donkey-man came to their rescue. 'That's never happened before,' he said breathlessly. 'I never knew they had such spirit in 'em.'

Scrambling off the donkeys, the two women were stunned into silence as they made their way up the beach. Then Anne started giggling, and soon they were both helpless with laughter.

Sally's hair was up on end as though she'd been in a hurricane, and Anne's legs were raw on the inside where she'd gripped the donkey's belly.

'Well, that was fun!' Sally remarked wryly. 'It's the first and last time I ever get on a donkey.'

Anne agreed, but added that she had never laughed so much in all her life.

Afterwards, sore and exhausted, they lay on the towels on the sand, and lapped up the sun.

'This is the life! I could lie here all day, every day, and never do another day's work as long as I live.' Sally sighed.

Anne was also loving the feel of the sun on her bare skin, but time was ticking by, and they still hadn't eaten.

'Sally? I thought you were hungry?'

'I am.'

'So, do you still want to go to the café?'

'Course I do!'

'Do you realise what the time is?'

'No, and to be honest I'm so comfortable, I don't care.'

There followed a short span of silence before Sally asked, 'So what time is it then?'

'Half-past four.'

'Oh, crikey! We'd best get packed up and go, don't you think?'

'What, go home, you mean?'

'No, to the café. We've still got time.'

'I'm a bit peckish,' Anne admitted.

'Me too.' Sally groaned. 'I'm surprised you can't hear my stomach rumbling.'

Anne made the first move. She stood up, brushed the sand from her body and, wrapping the towel around her, she skilfully removed her swimsuit without displaying her attributes to all and sundry.

Sally, though, standing some distance away, was not so careful. Her towel kind of slipped, and when the two young men playing football along the beach wolf-whistled at her, she gave them a quick flash of her buttocks.

'Hey, I reckon he fancies me,' she told Anne, with a naughty twinkle in her eye.

'Behave yourself.' Anne knew only too well what her friend was up to. 'I'm beginning to think I daren't take you anywhere.' She had to laugh, though. 'What would Mick say if he saw you flirting like this?'

'Mick knows I adore him,' Sally said dreamily. 'No one could ever replace him in my heart. *And* he appreciates my sense of mischief.'

Some ten minutes later, as they were trudging along the beach, the football came bouncing their way and landed at Anne's feet.

'See, I was right!' Sally was delighted to see one of the men come running towards them. 'They did that on purpose, just to get our attention.'

As it was in her direct path, Anne stooped to collect the ball and had her arm raised to throw it back, when the fairer-haired fellow of the two bounded up and reached out as though to take it.

'Sorry, I hope it didn't hit you.' His smile was friendly.

'No, it didn't.' Anne thought he was about to take the ball and leave. Instead, he took the ball with one hand and suggestively slid his other hand down her bare arm. 'I don't suppose you and your friend would like to couple up with me and my brother. We could have a bit of fun . . . if you know what I mean?' His knowing wink left nothing to the imagination.

Anne shook her head. 'Sorry. We're on our way to get something to eat, and then we're starting home.'

'Ah, well, me and my brother could do with a bite to eat, so why don't we make it a foursome? It'll be our treat.' Gripping her wrist, he gently drew her towards him. 'Please, say yes.'

From a short distance away, Sally witnessed the exchange between Anne and the stranger.

Moving closer, she was surprised to hear Anne say, 'Thank you, but we haven't actually decided whether or not we will go to the café. We've got a two-hour drive before us, and we have to get back.'

Stepping away, she tried to release herself from his hold, but when he gripped her wrist all the tighter she began to feel threatened. 'Please . . . I have to go now.' Making a determined effort, she pulled free from him.

As she made her way to Sally, her heart was pounding. Then she was panicking. Was he behind her?

Turning to see him already heading back to his brother, she gave a sigh of relief and slowed her steps.

Sally was not best pleased. 'What were you thinking of? He was practically throwing himself at you, and then you frightened him off. Why? I mean, think about it. You haven't been out on a date in ages. All this time, and you still haven't found the right man. For all you know, he could have been the one. As for me, I'm already spoken for, as you well know.'

Anne smiled. 'So, stop looking in the shop window if you don't intend buying. Mick and you have been married for, what . . . eight years?'

'It's just a bit of fun, but having a bite to eat with two good-looking strangers doesn't really mean anything, does it? Besides, I was hoping you might strike lucky.'

Sally had witnessed Anne's nervousness with that man, and she had seen her react like that before when any man got too close. It troubled her.

'Seriously, I'm only thinking of you, Anne. If you don't start going out more, and meeting new people, you may never find the right man.' She tried to lighten the situation. 'Honestly, anybody would think you were afraid of making a commitment.'

When Anne fell silent, Sally realised that somehow, she had touched a nerve. 'All right then, forget I said that. Come on, let's get something to eat, before we head off home.'

Sally continued to chat as they walked down the beach towards the café.

Anne only pretended to listen. She could still feel the strength of the man's fingers gripping her wrist. It had awakened so many memories. Her tormentor had kept her trapped so often by those very same means except, unlike just now, his iron grip had left indentations on her bruised skin for days after.

Often, that was how the real violence began . . .

Anne quickened her steps to escape from the beach and the two men, so that Sally had difficulty in keeping up with her. 'Hey! Slow down.' Running up alongside, she linked her arm with Anne's. 'We're not in that much of a rush.'

As they hurried along, Sally noticed how pale and nervous Anne was, and how every so often she would glance over her shoulder as though worried someone might be following.

'Jeez! You're trembling! Anne, what's wrong? Did he say something to frighten you?'

'No, and there's nothing wrong,' Anne assured her. 'I'm just thinking about the drive home and the traffic getting busy.'

'If it's worrying you that much, we can leave right now. I don't mind one way or the other.'

She did not believe Anne's explanation, especially as Anne was an experienced driver, more than capable, even in the thickest of traffic.

Anne would not hear of abandoning their plans. 'No, we said we'd go to the café and head off home after that. So that's what we'll do. And stop worrying about me, I'm just cold, that's all.' She feigned a shiver. 'I'll be right as rain with a hot drink inside me.' Squeezing Sally to her, she forced a smile. 'I've had a really wonderful time today. I'm so glad I've got you as a friend.'

'Me too.' Sally gave her a little hug. 'We're good together, you and me . . . like sisters, eh?'

'Yeah.' As they climbed the steps to the little café, Anne felt guilty. 'Sally?'

'What?'

'I'm sorry for being a pain just now.'

Sally feigned surprise. 'What? You being a pain? Never!'

They were in brighter mood as they entered the café. 'Can you get the order?' Anne asked. 'I need the loo.'

'Course. What do you want?'

'Coffee. And chips, please, with peas and a slice of bread and butter.'

While Anne went off to the toilet, Sally glanced about, relieved to see there were only two other people in the café, because that meant they would be served quicker, and then they could get a start home that much sooner. That would be a good thing as Anne still appeared to be unnerved by that man's advances.

Sally found a table right in the corner.

'Can I take your order, please?' The woman looked to be in her forties, prim and tidy, with a frilly white cap perched jauntily on her dark hair. 'Is it just the one?'

'No, two; my friend's gone to the loo, but she's left her order with me.'

'That's fine.' The waitress had her pen and notepad at the ready. 'Drinks?'

'One coffee, and one lemonade, please, no ice.'

When the entire order was given, Sally settled back in her chair and gave a lazy yawn. 'Whew! It's been a long day.'

Five minutes passed, and the drinks were delivered.

Then another five minutes, and by now Sally was

growing impatient. *What the devil is she doing in there? The meals will be here soon.*

Picking up the menu, she began to browse through it absent-mindedly. After a minute or so, she replaced it on the table.

In the toilets, Anne washed her hands at the basin, and for a long moment she just stood there, deep in thought.

Leaning against the towel rack, she lowered her head and closed her eyes. She had so much on her mind, what with that stranger this morning, and then the man at the beach. She gave a whimsical smile: he must have thought she was a bit crazy, the way she backed away from him as though he were a mass-murderer.

Her smile slipped away. What was it about today? It was meant to be a fun time away from everyday life. But two incidents had deeply unnerved her. Two incidents in the space of one day.

Over the years she had done everything possible to put it all behind her, but now, because of two strangers, she was taken back, mind and heart, to the most unhappy and frightening time of her life.

~

For what seemed an age, Anne remained in front of the mirror, anxiously murmuring to herself. One minute, she would be staring at the floor; the next, she was nervously glancing about.

'You got Sally really worried,' she chided herself. 'You'd

better get your act together, my girl. Or one of these days, they'll be coming to take you away.'

Leaning forward, she placed her hands on the edge of the basin, her eyes closed and her heart palpitating.

'Edward Carter!' She whispered his name over and over. 'Edward Carter . . . Edward Carter, the monster who ruined my life. Never again will I be able to trust any man. I'll never get married, and I will never have children. Oh, I would have loved to have children, but now I can't. Thanks to him!'

Clenching her fist, she punched the wall. 'I hope you rot in Hell! I hope you suffer like you made me suffer. I pray that you will never have any peace in the whole of your miserable life!'

Unaware that Sally was standing in the half-open door, she began crying; softly at first, and then she was sobbing helplessly.

'Who's Edward Carter?' Sally's voice cut softly through Anne's pain.

'Oh . . . Sally!' Swinging round, Anne was shocked to see her friend standing there. 'He's no one . . . just someone I once knew . . .' Hurriedly wiping away the tears, she was devastated that Sally might have heard everything.

Without a word, Sally wrapped her arms around her friend, and for a long moment neither of them spoke.

Then: 'I'm sorry, I didn't mean to listen to what you were saying, and you don't have to tell me about it. But I want you to know, your happiness means a lot to me, and I don't like to see you hurting,' Sally gently assured her.

Anne felt ashamed. 'It was a long time ago . . . best forgotten.'

'Let me help you, Anne . . . please?'

Anne shook her head. 'I can't.'

'All right. If you'd rather not confide in me, then that's your choice. I'm sorry. I promise I won't ever ask again.'

Leaning into Sally's embrace, Anne tried to gather her senses.

Neither of them spoke for a while.

Presently, Anne drew away, washed her face and, putting on a smile, she said brightly, 'Take no notice of me. I just got upset at something and nothing.'

Sally did not believe a word of Anne's explanation. What she had seen and heard was a woman in turmoil. A woman who was deeply affected by something that had happened to her. 'Like I say, I won't ask you again about what happened, but if you feel the need to confide in me, I'm always here for you. Remember that, won't you?'

'I will.' Anne was greatly relieved. 'Thank you, Sally.'

Deliberately changing the subject, Sally asked her, 'So? Do you want cold chips?'

'No.' Anne was surprised at the question. 'Why?'

'Because I expect they're on the table, waiting for us. The waitress is probably thinking we've changed our mind and run off without paying.' All she wanted was for Anne to come back to the table.

Taking a deep breath, Anne composed herself. 'I'm all right now. Just give me a moment, I'll be right behind you.' Over the years, she had become skilled in the art of putting on a brave face, when inside she was falling apart.

Sally understood. 'OK . . . two minutes, though, or I'll be back.'

Anne watched her go, and gave herself a stern warning: *If you go on like this you'll be put away in some awful place, and they'll never let you out again.*

She tidied her hair and checked herself in the mirror, before going across to the door. Whatever did Sally think of her now? When they got back home, she'd probably avoid her like the plague, and who could blame her? She gave a sad little smile; another friend lost.

Because of her self-imposed secrecy and non-committal, over the years she had lost many friends. And now she convinced herself that she was about to lose Sally, the only real friend she had.

Sally was waiting for her at the table. 'I put a napkin over your chips,' she told Anne. 'Nobody likes cold chips.' She deliberately made no mention of what had taken place back there.

The two of them began their meals, although after Anne's upset neither had an appetite.

'Do you fancy another drink before we head off?' Because of Anne's bizarre behaviour, Sally was not ready to leave just yet.

'Thanks, yes. I'll have a ginger beer.' Right now, Anne was in need of something with a bit more zing than coffee.

'Ginger beer coming up.' Sally went off to order at the counter.

When a few minutes later she returned with the two

drinks, she was concerned to find Anne seemingly deep in thought.

Sally placed the drinks on the table. 'You seem to be lost in a daze. Preparing yourself for the journey back, are you?'

'Not really. I was just thinking, it's so peaceful and pretty here. To be honest, I don't think it would matter if I never went back.'

Sally had no answer to that, but she made an observation: 'You look done in. If you'd rather I drive home, I wouldn't mind one bit. After I see you home safe, I can easily get the bus back to my house.'

Anne dismissed the idea. 'No. Thanks all the same, but I enjoy the drive.'

'Really?'

'Yes, really!'

They sipped their drinks, and talked quietly of anything and everything – except the one thing that burned in both their minds.

'Anne?' Sally's voice was almost inaudible.

Thrusting the bad thoughts from her mind, Anne took a few gulps of her drink and replaced her glass on the table. She could feel Sally's attention on her. 'Oh, I'm sorry, Sally.' She quickly started gathering her belongings together. 'Are you waiting to go?'

'No, we're all right for a while yet. But I do need to ask you something. Don't worry. Like I said before, I won't pry. So if you don't want to answer, that's fine.'

Anne had half expected her to ask questions, and she was ready. 'You can ask, but I can't promise to answer.'

'Earlier, at the fairground . . .?'

'Yes?'

'When I reminded you about the man at Woollies?'

Anne was somewhat relieved. Initially, she feared the question might be linked to what Sally had overheard in the loo. 'Oh, him! Yes, what about him?'

'It's just that afterwards . . . you said something.' Sally had not forgotten. 'It just made me wonder, that's all?'

'What did I say?' Anne grew nervous. 'I can't remember. And anyway, it was probably something and nothing.'

'It might not be word for word, but,' Sally leaned closer, 'as I recall, you said . . . "confrontation sometimes brings you more trouble than you can handle", or words to that effect.'

Anne feigned ignorance. 'Did I really say that?'

'Yes, you did.' Sally was gentle. 'It was a really strange thing to say. So, what exactly did you mean by that?'

Anne measured her words carefully. 'There are times when you might really want someone to leave you alone, but they never do. So you tell them straight. You stand up to them. Somehow, you have to find the courage to speak your mind.' She took a moment to calm herself. 'Sometimes you try and protect yourself, but then you might find that you've made the situation worse. That you've let yourself in for more trouble than you could ever have imagined.'

For what seemed an age, there was silence between them.

Then Anne tried to explain further: 'All I meant was

128

that you should be careful how you say no. Some people don't like to take "No" for an answer.' Grabbing her drink she took a long swig, then put the empty glass down with a heavy thud. 'Think about it, Sally. I'm sure you've been in that same, uncomfortable situation, at one time or another.'

Sensing a chink in Anne's armour, Sally played along. 'You're absolutely right! Do you remember when the randy foreman asked me to climb the ladder at work. He said he had a bad back and wanted me to get the stock down from the top shelf. I was on to him straight away! Bad back be damned! He thought he'd stand at the bottom of the steps, peering up my skirt and getting an eyeful, dirty old sod! Oh, but he didn't like it when I said no. I pretended I was afraid of heights. He lost his rag. Just like you said, he flew into a spiteful mood. Slamming and banging about, he was, and yelling at everyone for no good reason.'

She gave a nervous little chuckle. 'Nobody ever knew the reason for his bad mood, and I thought it wise not to tell. But I had the feeling he would have loved to give me a battering. As it was, he made some feeble excuse to take me off my regular duties. That same day, he shifted me to the cramped back office, where they carry out stock checks and ordering.'

'But I thought you hated that kind of work?'

'I do. It was my first job on starting there, and he knew it had bored me to tears. But it's what you were saying before, he was just punishing me because I stood up to him. So I do know what you mean. And you're absolutely right.'

'It's true. Some men are like that.' Anne knew only too well. 'They're just naturally vicious. They like to hurt women. They like to see them in pain. They torment their minds, and break their spirit, and they think it's all right. But it's not all right, it's wicked!'

Realising she had already said too much, Anne picked up her glass, and pretended to drain the last few drops.

Sally deliberately ignored Anne's short burst of rage. 'D'you want another drink before we go?' she asked casually.

Anne had lapsed into her own little world again.

'Anne?'

'Yes?'

'Do you fancy another drink?'

'No, thanks. I've had enough.'

'Well then, I'm ready to leave whenever you are.' For one minute, Sally had hoped that Anne might be ready to confide her troubles. Now she collected her belongings. 'Let's hit the road, as they say.'

As always, Sally's bright humour put a smile on Anne's face, although she was fully aware that she had come way too close to revealing the shocking truth. For the first time in all these long years, she had very nearly let her feelings get the better of her.

Yet somehow, even though she had let her guard slip for only that one brief moment, she felt better for it. She felt calmer inside.

The dark memories remained, of course, along with the firm belief that she would never be like others. She would never hold her own child in her arms, or be at the centre of a loving family.

Because of the damage he had done, a normal life was denied her. And as long as she lived, she would never forgive him.

Edward Carter was more devil than man.

At least, she had found the courage to flee from him. In the safe haven that was her aunt Ada's house, she had tried so hard to make a life for herself. But in spite of everything, in spite of all her efforts to shut him out of her mind and her life, he had won.

A short time later, having piled their bags into the boot, Sally and Anne set off home.

'We've had such a lovely day, haven't we?' Sally gave an almighty yawn.

'Yes, and wasn't it great that the weather held out for us?'

'How are we for petrol?' Sally had a phobia about running out of fuel in the middle of nowhere.

Anne assured her that the tank was still half full.

Within minutes of starting out, Sally was fast asleep, her rhythmic snoring making Anne smile.

Glancing down at Sally's crumpled figure and pretty face, she thanked her lucky stars to have found such a loyal friend. *I hope she didn't hear too much of what I said in the café toilets,* she thought.

Even though she knew her friend was the soul of discretion, the idea of her having heard everything played on Anne's mind, especially because Sally had actually asked who Edward Carter was. Somewhere deep inside, Anne desperately wanted to confide in her.

All these years she had been carrying the truth, and

it was a heavy burden. Her fear that one day he might somehow find her was terrifying indeed.

~

As the miles flew by, Anne found herself wondering what Sally would say if she knew the truth. But dare she tell? Was it time? And could she really trust Sally that much?

As they neared Bedford, she constantly tried to push the idea of confessing to the back of her mind, but it persisted.

Eventually, she headed the car down a quiet side street on the outskirts.

Having now parked the car, she gently tapped Sally on the shoulder, 'Wake up, Sally.'

Sally leaped up, eyes wide awake and her voice slurred. 'Oh . . . sorry, Anne! I must have dozed off. You should have woken me. Oh, are we home already?'

'No. We've still got a little way to go yet.'

Feeling groggy, Sally glanced out the window, puzzled by the unfamiliar surroundings. 'Where are we?'

'We're just off the Goldington Road.'

Sally gave a tired groan. 'Oh, bugger it! I knew it: we've run out of petrol, haven't we?'

'No, we've still got more than enough petrol to get us home.'

'So what's going on?' Raising both hands, Sally ruffled her flattened hair.

When Anne hesitated, Sally's concern deepened. Now wide awake, she sensed that something was wrong.

'Anne, why are we parked in a quiet side street?' she asked worriedly. 'I don't understand.'

She knew instinctively that this was to do with the incident at the café and wanted to ask why Anne had been so upset, and who was the man she had cursed over and over. But for now, she thought it best to let things lie. It seemed enough damage had already been done. Besides, if Anne had wanted to confide in her, she would have done so by now.

'Sally . . . what you said back there . . .' Anne began.

'What? What did I say?'

'It was the question you asked me.'

'Well, whatever it was, let's just forget it. It's not my business, and I don't need to know the answer.'

But Anne could not let it go now. 'Sally, can I trust you . . . implicitly?'

'Absolutely! Whatever you tell me won't ever go any further, I promise.'

Anne fell silent for a moment. She needed to be sure she was doing the right thing. She had always intended that Sally should never know anything of her turbulent past, but now, having come to a new decision, there was no turning back. 'Sally, while you were sleeping, I was thinking,' Anne told her. 'And I feel I owe you an answer.'

'You don't owe me anything, Anne. Maybe we should just put it out of our minds and forget it ever happened.'

'No!' Anne stopped her. 'Please listen, Sally. I've never been able to make friends; not even when I was a little girl. You see, my mother had me when she was forty-five years old. When I was born, my parents were already set in their ways. I was not allowed to bring friends home from school, nor play out with them, nor walk to school with them. Mother took me to school and she picked me up, and once she got me home, I was very rarely allowed to go outside, though I could play in the back yard on my own. So, y'see, you're the first real friend I ever had.'

Sally reached out to take her hand. 'It doesn't matter to me what's in the past, because I'll always be your friend. And I hope you will always be mine.'

Anne was grateful for Sally's loyalty, but it was now time for the truth to be told. 'I need to be honest with you, Sally. There are things you don't know about me. Bad, terrible things that I need to share with you. I'm a weak person. What happened was partly my fault. After I've told you, if you want to walk away from me, I won't blame you.'

'It doesn't matter what you tell me, good or bad, I would never walk away from you.'

She was intrigued by what Anne had described earlier. 'You said your mother was in her mid-forties when she had you.'

'That's right, forty-five. My father was three years older.'

'Crikey! So, did you have older brothers or sisters?'

'No. I was an only child, more's the pity. Mother never mixed with anyone, and she raised me to be the same. When I was about ten years old, I was invited to a birthday party, but she refused to let me go. It seemed like a punishment to me, so I argued with her. I wanted to know why she would never let me play out with other children.'

'And what did your mother say?'

'She sat me down and told me I should never have been born. She said I was an accident of nature, that I was never planned, especially at their time of life, that I wore them out and that she had nothing in common with the other mothers. She said if I went to the party she'd be expected to have the other girls back when it was my birthday, but she had no intention of doing parties. She said that Father was coming up to sixty now, and if it weren't for me, they'd have been planning his retirement; looking for a smaller house on the coast. She said all they had to look forward to now was bringing me up, and by the time that was done, they would be too old to make any plans for themselves.'

Sally was shocked. 'That explains why you found it so hard to make friends when you started at Woolworths. It's why I had to tease you out of your shell. I noticed at first you found it so hard to mix with other people.'

'You helped me, Sally,' Anne admitted. 'I could never have done it without you . . . and lovely Aunt Ada. She was older than my parents, but she was so kind and unselfish. She took me in when I needed someone to help me. She made me laugh. She brought me out of my shell, and made me believe that I was special.' She gave a fond little smile. 'She said I deserved a chance to shine.'

Sally remembered the old woman. 'I met her only a couple of times, but I really liked her. She seemed a genuine soul.'

Anne's voice broke with emotion as she confessed, 'I owe her so much, and, oh, I do miss her terribly.'

'I'm sure you do.' Sally knew how close these two had been. 'I don't mean to pry,' she ventured, 'but I've always wondered how you came to be living with your aunt.' She was already learning more about Anne in these few minutes than she had learned these past years. 'Did you leave because of the things your mother said to you? Did you think your parents would be happier if you moved out of the family home as soon as you were able?'

Anne smiled wryly. 'I always knew they'd be happier without me in their lives,' she acknowledged sadly. 'In a way I felt sorry for them. I felt as though I'd ruined their lives. But the truth wasn't as simple as me just "moving out".'

Though she was determined that Sally should know the truth, she was finding it difficult to bare her soul. 'When I was seventeen, I did something really bad. There was a terrible row. Mother threw me out. She told me she and Father never wanted to see me again . . . that I was never to come back. She said, as far as they were concerned they did not have a daughter.'

Sally was beginning to realise what had made Anne so very shy and private. 'Whatever did you do that was so bad it made them throw you out?'

Anne fell silent for a while. In her tortured mind it was almost as though she was back there, caught up in a nightmare.

Having taken time to focus her thoughts, she explained, 'It was a couple of weeks before my seventeenth birthday. Mother had found me a job in the local dressmaker's. I was working long hours and earning decent money; half of which I gave to Mother for my board and keep. She even seemed proud that I was doing so well.'

'So what happened to make it all go wrong?' Sally was intrigued.

'I should have known better. It was the day of my birthday. Irene, the dressmaker's daughter, asked what I had planned. When I told her that my mother did not agree with parties or celebrations, she insisted that the two of us should mark my seventeeth birthday by going out somewhere.' Anne gave a knowing smile. 'Irene was a bit of a rebel on the quiet.'

'So, did you go?'

'Yes, and that's when I deceived my mother for the first time in my life. When Mother asked where I was going, I said I was meeting up with Irene, and that we were going to see one of Irene's friends. When I was ready to leave, Mother gave me the once-over, to make sure I was dressed accordingly. She did not approve of make-up and stockings, and girls who flaunted themselves. She also reminded me that the house would be locked and bolted at 10 p.m. as usual, and that if I wasn't back before then, it would be no use banging on the door, because neither she nor Father would get out of bed to let me in.'

'And were you back on time?'

Anne shook her head. 'Irene insisted on the two of us going out on the town. She said it wasn't every day a girl was seventeen, and that it was cause for a special celebration.' Anne laughed out loud at the memory.

'By the time we left Irene's house I was a different girl. Irene had plastered my face with make-up. My hair was curled, and as we were more or less the same size, she sorted me a strappy dress from her wardrobe. Honestly, Sally, when I walked out of there, I felt like a film star!'

'Wow! And I bet you had a good time, didn't you?' Sally couldn't help but smile at the idea of Anne being plastered in make-up, with her hair curled, and wearing a naughty dress. It was hard to imagine.

'This is where I did a bad thing,' Anne recalled. 'We really enjoyed ourselves. We met up with one of Irene's friends. She was a few years older than me and Irene, but she was so lively, and such fun. I had never met anyone like her. We talked about going to the pictures, but then Irene had an idea, and we ended up dancing to the band at the Palais. Irene's friend got us some drinks. I asked for a lemonade, but she told me to try one of their specialities, which I did.'

'Oh, what kind of "speciality"?' Sally had her suspicions.

'I never knew, but I went with the mood, and I drank it. Then I had another. I felt a bit woozy after that, but by that time I didn't care. For the first time ever, I was out on the town with these lively girls, and I was having fun.'

She explained how, after they left the Palais, they walked the streets looking for a taxi home. 'A big black taxi pulled up and we all climbed in.'

In her mind she could see the driver vividly: long-boned, handsome and dark-haired, he had a smile you believed you could trust. 'The driver was really friendly.

He said his name was Edward Carter, and that he meant to make his mark in the world. He told us he owned the taxi firm and that every now and then, especially on a weekend, he enjoyed coming out of the office to drive a taxi himself. Apparently, his uncle had built up the firm. He had promised Edward he could buy it when he was more experienced, and Edward eventually bought him out.'

'Quite the businessman, eh?' Sally thought he sounded very enterprising. 'Did he get you home safely, though?'

'He took the others home first, then he drove to my house. It was gone midnight. I banged on the door, and called up to the bedroom window, but got no answer. Either my parents were fast asleep and couldn't hear me, or Mother meant what she said and had locked me out.'

'So, what did you do?'

'Well, Edward Carter refused to leave me there in the dark on my own. He asked me if there was a relative he could take me to, and when I told him there was no one, he got me back to the car. He said he could not believe they would lock me out like that.'

'So, where did you go?'

'He took me to a really nice hotel. He even offered to pay my room for the night, but I wouldn't let him. Fortunately I had enough money in my purse to cover it.'

'I think I can guess what happened when you got to the hotel.' Sally was worldy-wise. 'I bet he insisted on escorting you safely to your room. Am I right?'

Anne blushed with shame. 'When we got there, he made a play for me, and like a drunken, gullible fool, I fell for his smooth talk.'

She fell silent, deeply regretting that shameful night, and the fact that it had cost her so dearly. 'I can't put all the blame on Edward Carter,' she confessed. 'I should have been strong enough to resist his advances.'

Sally was angry. 'That's all very well, but don't forget you were a young girl of seventeen. You'd been kicked out of house and home in the middle of the night, with little money and nowhere to go. You must have been really scared. That man took advantage of you. He was the one who should have known better, not you!'

Anne made no response to Sally's wise words.

'So, did you ever see him again?' Sally was curious.

'Yes, I did, more's the pity. My parents never knew, but over the next few weeks, we met up a lot. Things got serious. He began talking about getting married, but I didn't want that. I said it was too soon. I felt I was too young to be married. But then it became clear that I didn't have a choice.'

'What do you mean? Of course you had a choice.'

'No, I didn't, because I got pregnant. Edward didn't know and I was too afraid to tell anyone. I was two months gone, and one morning I was too sick to go to work. Mother guessed and forced the truth out of me. She went crazy!'

Anne choked back the tears. 'It was awful! When Father came home she told him, and there was a huge row, shouting and screaming like I've never heard. They called me a slut. They said I'd brought shame on them . . . that they did not want me under their roof. They threw me out that night, with nothing but the clothes on my back and a couple of personal items. I had a small amount of money, but it wasn't enough to carry me through.'

Sally was shocked. 'That was so cruel. You must have felt really frightened.' She could hardly believe anyone's parents would do such a thing.

'I remember it was pouring with rain,' Anne went on. 'I ran to the telephone kiosk and called Edward's number, but there was no reply. So, I called Irene. When she told me to get a taxi and come straight over, I was so thankful.'

'That was good of her, especially at that time of night.'

Curiously, Anne made no comment. 'When I got to Irene's house, she was watching out of the window for me. She said she knew someone who could get rid of the baby for me, but it would cost. I said no, that it wasn't the baby's fault, and I didn't like the idea of doing that. She got angry, saying I was a fool for having got myself into that situation, and that she couldn't help me, and that I'd best go before her parents found me there.'

Sally was disappointed. 'Hmm! So she wasn't such a friend after all?'

'She was, but I don't really blame her for turning me away. She urged me to go and see Edward that very night, and tell him the truth . . . that he was to be a father.'

'And did you?'

'Yes. I went to his house, but it was in darkness, so I took a room in a small boarding house nearby. I caught Edward at the office early the next morning, and I told him about the baby. He seemed delighted that he might have a son, who he could train up to take over from him one day. He started talking wedding plans and all that, and a short time later we were married at the registry office.'

'Well, at least he seemed to have done right by you.' Sally had been taken aback by what she'd learned. Her quiet, unassuming friend, who most times had little to say, had poured out her heart and soul. She had confided her extraordinary and shocking past, and now those awful times, and her suffering, were clearly evident in her face.

For a moment, Anne spoke not a word. Instead, she sat fidgeting, her head turned away to look out through the car window.

When Sally looked up, she was deeply moved to see tears flowing down Anne's face.

Instinctively, she wrapped her arms round Anne's small shoulders. 'What you've told me won't go any further,' she promised. 'But what happened between you and Edward? The fact that you're on your own now must mean it didn't work out. Am I right? Is that the way it was?'

When Anne merely nodded, Sally went on, 'As far as I can see, you've had a hard time of it. Up to Edward marrying you, there was never anyone there to help you . . . except later, when your aunt Ada took you in. But you've got *me* now, and I'll always be here for you, but I'm sorry things didn't work out with the marriage, Anne, I really am.'

Hugging Anne closer, she asked, 'You take it easy now. I'll drive from here, and when we get back, I want you to come and stay with me for a while. OK?' In the back of her mind, she suspected she had not yet heard the whole story.

Anne, however, was reluctant to leave just yet. 'Please, Sally, I need to tell you everything.' Drawing from Sally's embrace, Anne continued, 'Edward Carter was not the man I believed him to be. He was a spiteful bully. He beat me often, sometimes for no other reason than that he'd lost a good client, or a lucrative hotel-booking had been cancelled at the last minute. Sometimes he beat me so I could hardly walk. When I was eight months pregnant, he came home from a night out. He'd lost a great deal of money gambling. He was in a foul mood and so drunk he could hardly stand up. He was looking for a fight, and things turned nasty. It was awful, Sally . . . I really thought he would kill me.'

Realizing that Anne was badly shaken, Sally held onto her. 'Don't think about it, Anne. You shouldn't be on your own tonight. Please, come and stay with me and Mick, for as long as you like.'

Anne graciously declined the offer. 'I'll be fine, honest. At least I know I'm safe now. Edward Carter is long gone. He can't hurt me any more.'

'Is it helping you – to talk about it, I mean?'

'Oh, Sally! You can't know how long I've wanted to tell you, only I'm so ashamed, I thought you wouldn't want to know me any more.'

'Huh! If I couldn't share your troubles, what kind of a friend would that make me?' She gave Anne a friendly little push. 'You might as well go on, now that you know we understand each other.'

'He hurt me so much that night, Sally. I lost the baby.' Anne fell silent, and for a moment she could hardly breathe. Then, in an almost inaudible voice, she went on, 'Edward Carter killed our baby. At the hospital, they induced me into labour, and I had to give birth.'

The trauma of seeing the baby afterwards was too awful a memory. 'I'm sorry.' At first, she tried not to cry, but then the tears flowed and her heart broke. 'I will never forgive him, Sally. For as long as I live . . . I will never forgive him!'

For a seemingly long time, Sally held her while she cried. And, though silently, Sally cried with her.

After a time, Anne drew away. Her voice was breaking as she continued, 'Afterwards, they brought him to me . . . so tiny . . . a perfect little man.' She gave a muffled laugh. 'He had a look of my mother . . . his grumpy face and that tuft of hair on his head.'

Relieved that for the first time, Anne was able to pour out her heart and soul, Sally urged her to go on.

Anne told her, 'After they took him away, the chaplain came to see me. He said they were bringing in Social Services, because I'd been beaten up. They had pictures of my broken fingers and the bruises all over my body. They said the police had also been informed and would want to ask me some questions.' In her mind, she relived the moment. 'I was frightened they might blame me.'

'So, what did the police say?' Sally asked gently.

Anne shrugged. 'I didn't wait to find out. After the nurses had treated my injuries and settled me down, I waited until they were out of sight, then I scrambled my clothes on, and got as far away from the hospital as I could. I planned to make my way down to Aunt Ada. Edward knew of her existence, but he had never met her, or asked about her. As far as I know, he had no idea where she lived, except it was down south somewhere.'

'So, you made your way down here, knowing you should be safe?'

'Yes. It was my only chance. My parents had disowned me; I had no friends who could help, so the only person I could turn to was Aunt Ada. I thought I'd be safe with her . . . if she didn't mind taking me in. The trouble was, I hadn't seen her in such a long time, I had no idea if I'd be welcome.'

She gave a warm smile. 'I should never have doubted her, because she welcomed me with open arms.'

Sally listened quietly; at times shaking her head and other times shedding a tear.

The longer she talked, the more Anne relaxed. 'When I got there, I was exhausted and close to collapse. Aunt Ada took it all in her stride. She put me to bed, then she sat beside me, holding my hand. When I said I had some bad things to tell her, she said it could wait until I was rested. She reassured me that after I'd had a good long sleep, I could tell her, or not tell her, whichever I felt comfortable with. Either way, she would be there for me, and would nurse me back to health. And that's exactly what she did.'

Sally had met the old woman on only a couple of occasions. 'That was a wonderful thing for her to do, but that's what friends are for. Even so, as a young girl in need, you should have been able to turn to your parents.'

Anne nodded sadly. 'I know,' she murmured, 'but my parents were the last people I could turn to, and to tell the truth, I do understand now. They had me too late in life and it was all too much. Aunt Ada, though, was wonderful! I told her everything: how my parents had turned me out of the house; about Edward Carter, and the spiteful beatings.' Her voice broke. 'I told her about the baby, too, and we cried together. I felt so very sad.'

'What did your aunt say you should do?'

'She said I ought to report him to the police and tell them everything; that it wasn't too late. But she didn't know Edward like I did. If I had reported him, the police would have tracked me down, and then he would have got to me somehow. He would have killed me without a second thought. I know it, Sally. I know it!'

Sally reminded her, 'They would have questioned him anyway, what with the bruises on you, and the baby . . . and everything.'

'Aunt Ada said that, but I know Edward. He would have wormed his way out of it, somehow or another. He probably blamed me. I wouldn't put it past him.'

'Anyway, thankfully, he never did find you, did he? And thanks to Aunt Ada, you now have a whole new life.'

'That's true.' Anne smiled at Sally. 'And I have the best friend in you.' Talking to Sally was as though a great weight had fallen from her shoulders.

For a time, the two of them sat holding each other and thinking of the bad times.

After a while, Sally asked, 'Anne, you don't have to answer this, but something has just occurred to me. How did you divorce Edward Carter, without him somehow discovering where you were?'

'I never did divorce him.'

'Oh, my Lord, why not?'

'For the very reason you just mentioned: because I was afraid that if I applied for a divorce, I would have been found. He would know where I was, and I could not risk that.'

'But doesn't that mean you are technically still his wife?'

'I suppose I must be. I've never really thought about it and, thankfully, no one has ever served me with official papers, but I don't care. I don't want anyone – lawyers or police, or anyone else – to find out where I am.'

'Oh, Anne, you must find someone who can help you. Otherwise, you'll never be free of that monster. Neither of you will ever be able to move on with your lives.'

'I don't care about that!'

'But what if you find someone in the future? There might come a day when you want to get married. But you won't be able to.'

'I will never again want to get married.'

'All right then. But if you truly want to be rid of him, you need to find a discreet lawyer and tell him everything. He'll be able to free you from Edward Carter once and for all. I'll help you, Anne. I'll do all I can to help you, I promise.'

'No!'

'But maybe there's a way in which they can protect your address, so he can never find you.'

Growing fearful, Anne drew away. 'No! I won't do it. Please, Sally, don't ask me to. You can't know what he's like. He's unhinged.'

Sally urged her to think about it all the same.

'I won't ever let myself get drawn into another deep relationship. It's too frightening,' Anne said.

'Anne, listen to me for a minute, please—'

'You're wasting your time. Please, Sally, don't make me wish I'd never told you.'

Undaunted, Sally had one more try. 'If you don't go to the police and tell them what he did to you, who's to say he might not do the same to some other poor, unsuspecting woman? What if he was to hurt her, like he hurt you?'

'It would not happen.'

'But, how can you know that?'

'Because I know I was partly to blame. I was just a stupid, naïve young girl who could not handle a deep relationship like that. I didn't know how to deal with his moods. I was too easily bullied . . . too afraid. No other woman would ever be so gullible. No woman would ever let him hurt her like he hurt me. She would stand up to him, protect herself, or tell someone.' Her voice dipped. 'Only I had no one to tell.'

Glancing about nervously, she suddenly drew closer to Sally. 'I thought I saw him,' she whispered huskily.

'Who?' Sally was taken by surprise.

'Him! Edward Carter!'

'When?'

'This very morning, when I was leaving home. I saw this man, and for one awful minute, I could have sworn it was him!'

'It wasn't, though . . . was it?'

'At first I was sure it was him. He was walking close to the house. I'd never seen him before, but at first glance he looked uncannily like Edward . . . same build. Same dark hair. But then I realised that Edward is older now, so the stranger could not have been him. He couldn't, could he?'

Sally calmed her. 'No, of course not. Can't you see, he's haunting you, Anne. This is why you need to punish him for what he did to you and the baby. Trust me, Anne. You really must take legal steps. Divorce him. Close that episode of your life and stop being afraid.'

'No! You don't understand. If I stir things up now, he will never stop until he's found me. I know him. I know what he's capable of.'

Growing nervous even at the possibility that Edward might somehow find her, she started the car. 'We'd best make tracks.' She grabbed Sally's hand. 'I'm really grateful for you listening to me. You can't know how hard it's been, living with the truth, and not being able to tell anyone.'

Thrusting the engine into gear, she moved the car out of the side street and onto the main road.

~

As they headed further into Bedford, neither Sally nor Anne spoke a word.

And then out of the blue, Anne confessed, 'The odd thing is, even though he was cruel and he hurt me badly, I never hated him.' She took a long breath before finishing. 'Until he killed my baby.'

Sally made no comment, but when she noticed a solitary tear rolling down Anne's face, she reached out and squeezed her hand, to reassure her that she was not alone any more.

And the gesture was enough.

CHAPTER SEVEN

HAVING ARRIVED AT Sally's house, Anne drew up to the kerb. 'I'll see you on Monday then?' She waited for Sally to climb out of the car.

'Wait a minute!' Sally had noticed that her husband's car was not in its usual parking space. 'It looks like Mick's not home yet. He said he was popping in to see his mum on the way from work, so how about I come back with you? Afterwards, I'll get the bus to Mick's mum's, and drive home with him.' She gave Anne a way out: 'Or have you had enough of me for today?'

Still reeling from the shocking things Anne had confided in her, Sally was concerned about her being on her own just now.

Anne, though, was receptive to Sally's idea. 'OK, that'll be nice.'

'Good!' Sally slid back into her seat, a little smile of satisfaction curling the corners of her mouth.

~

Edward Carter was quietly congratulating himself. After learning as much as he could from the old geezers in the pub, he impatiently bided his time while hiding in a derelict builder's yard.

The day had seemed a lifetime long. Twice he'd returned to the house on Roff Avenue, but each time there were no signs of life. Then there was that officious-looking bobby, constantly patrolling the streets, and seeming to peek into every little hidey-hole, presumably looking for the man he saw lurking about earlier.

So, remaining wary of the bobby, Carter watched and waited. When she got back, he would be ready for her.

Yet again, he cautiously emerged from his hiding place. Snaking his way through the maze of back alleys and less inhabited places, he made his way back to the house. 'You've been a thorn in my side for too many years,' he muttered insanely. 'You moved far away, but you should have known I'd find you eventually, and now that I have, we need to finish it, once and for all.'

~

A short time later, unaware that he was lurking out the back, Anne slid the key into the front-door lock and stepped back for Sally to enter.

'You put the kettle on,' she said, 'I'll call the cat in. Little devil! She ran off again this morning, before I could feed her. I've no idea where she goes.'

Sally chuckled. 'Leave her alone. I expect she's got a boyfriend.'

While Anne rushed ahead, Sally followed her down the passageway and through to the kitchen, where she placed her handbag on the windowsill.

Making a small bowl of meaty titbits, Anne then threw open the back door. 'Pusscat! Come and get your feed . . . come on, I won't call you again!'

Meantime, Sally busied herself making the tea. 'Milk, and one sugar, isn't it?' she called out.

'Please.' Anne returned with the bowl of food. 'I expect she'll come back when she's ready. I would leave her food out, but stray cats will wolf it down.' She covered the bowl with a plate and put it inside the sink cupboard.

'Come on then, let's you and me have our tea in the front room, eh?' She placed a packet of gingerbreads and two cups of steaming tea onto the tray, and made her way to the front room.

Anne padded happily along behind her. 'Sounds good to me.'

As they left the kitchen, not for one moment did they realise that they were being watched.

~

A short time later, Sally threw her coat on, jingling the change in her pockets. 'I'll ring you when I get to Mick's mum's house.' She gave Anne a parting hug, 'Thanks for a smashing day out.'

'Thanks for listening to my troubles.'

'Ah, but don't you remember what I said: that's what friends are for?'

'I know.'

'Listen, Anne, about doing something to end the marriage . . . you will think about it, won't you? You never know, maybe you're already free, but you just don't know it. I have heard that they can declare a marriage null and void in certain circumstances, but I'm not sure.'

Anne gave a little smile. 'Don't forget to ring me when you get to Mick's mum's.'

~

Having seen them arrive, Edward Carter had kept his distance. Now he was placed in a vantage point at the end of the alley where he was able to see out while no one could see him.

He watched Sally hurry past the opening. He saw her turn and wave.

''Bye, Anne. See you!'

He smiled to himself. *Will you now?* His plan did not include a third party.

At the bus shelter, Sally checked the time of the next bus. Still twenty minutes to wait. *Oh, bugger, I could have stayed with Anne another ten minutes,* she thought impatiently.

Back at the house, while collecting the tray from the front room, Anne glanced through the window to see the tabby cat, strolling lazily across the busy road. Quickly replacing the tray on the table, she ran out of the front door and swept the cat into her arms.

'You silly little devil! You could get run over.'

Carrying the wriggling bundle inside, she placed the dish of food on the floor, and stood the grateful cat in front of it. 'There! Make sure you eat it all up.'

While the cat tucked into its food, she returned to the front room, and collected the tray. As she walked back into the kitchen, she had a sickening feeling that someone else was in the house.

Through the corner of her eye she saw the swish of a dark jacket. Panicking, she turned to run, but he was on her, gripping her so tight by the neck, she struggled to breathe.

The more she fought to escape, the more his grip tightened, and there was no way out.

'Missed me, have you?' His warm, thick breath fanned her face. 'Long time, no see, but you haven't changed much. Still the same, tight little figure . . . same mop of hair. Mmm!' Gripping a lock of her fair curls in his teeth, he buried his face in her hair. 'You smell real nice . . . all woman.' He gave a long, deep groan as he ran his free hand over her private parts.

Frantic, Anne tried to push him away, but he held her fast. He swung her round to face him, his narrow eyes boring into her. 'You ran away from me. No woman ever ran away from Edward Carter!' Pushing his face close to hers, he whispered in her ear, 'That was not a nice thing to do. You really are a prize bitch, aren't you?'

'Leave me alone!' However hard Anne struggled, she could not free herself from his vice-like grip. 'You mean nothing to me. I don't want anything to do with you.'

His laughter rang through the house. 'Is that so?' he growled. 'Little Miss High-and-Mighty doesn't want anything to do with me? Well, you listen to me, bitch! This is your husband you're talking to. The same husband you dumped back there. The same husband who helped you when even your own parents turned you out. You might be surprised to know that I've made a few friends since I got here, and by the way, I've done my homework. Oh, yes! I know you don't have a man-friend, and you should thank your lucky stars for that, because if I thought you had set up with another man, I would need to deal with him . . . and it would not be nice. If you know what I mean?'

He craftily slid one arm over her shoulders and across her breast. When he began roughly fondling her, she fought viciously. 'Get off me! Get out of my house! My friend has just gone to the shop. She'll be back in a minute—'

'Liar!' Screeching with laughter, he licked her neck from the hairline to the collarbone, making her cringe with disgust.

'I've been watching you,' he crowed, 'and your friend. I know she's gone, and I know she's not coming back. I heard her say cheerio. So, to my reckoning, that leaves just you and me. You may not believe it, but it's been a while since I had a woman. Oh, but that can wait for now; until we've discussed the legal stuff.'

Anne knew the depth of his badness, and she was desperate. 'What are you talking about? What legal stuff? There's nothing between us any more, and never will be. Like I told you, I want nothing to do with the man who killed my baby! I hate you. Every minute of every day, I've wished you dead. Do you hear what I'm saying?'

Her words were cruelly cut short when he grabbed her by the face. 'You want me dead, do you? Well, it won't happen. I'll tell you what will happen, though, shall I?' Lowering his voice, he growled in her ear, 'Like I said, I've made friends. They very kindly filled me in on a thing or two. For instance, I know the old biddy left you this house. Only it's not your house now. It's mine! I'm your husband. What's yours is mine. I'm entitled to whatever you have, and that includes this house.'

'NEVER!' Anne screamed at him. 'You'll get my aunt's house over my dead body.'

'Oh, don't you worry, that can always be arranged.' Thrusting his face close to hers, he took delight in boasting, 'After you ran off, it didn't take me long to find myself another woman. I never loved her, though; not like I love you. She meant nothing to me. She was weak. She had no spirit. I despised her for that.' Anne was shocked when he added casually, 'She died, you know.'

'What do you mean, "she died"?'

'She had an accident. She fell down the stairs . . . broke every bone in her body, I shouldn't wonder. I had a son too . . . Adam. I left them both behind, because of you. Y'see, it's you I want.' He smiled. 'It's always been you. So, what d'you say to that, eh?'

'I say, I've always known that you're completely mad.' Now she was more convinced of that than ever.

'Still feisty, eh?' Her spirit pleased him. 'If I'm "mad", it's prison that made me that way. I did time because of that weak, spineless woman. Even when she was dying, she was too afraid to accuse me.'

'Was it your fault she died?' Anne dared to ask.

'Hmm! Don't you think if it had been my fault she would have said so, and I would have been put away for a very long time?'

He abruptly changed the subject. 'The boy was made in her mould. I've no idea where he is now. Nor do I want to know. He meant nothing to me, and neither did his mother, although I'm grateful that she chose not to say it might have been me who caused her early demise.'

His manner darkened. 'There were others who tarnished my name, though. Apparently, the medical team found a number of bruises on her body, and made certain suggestions. One or two other things were said that marked my card and got me put away. My own son turned against me, and some old man gave an account of me supposedly running away on the day it all happened. I got a prison sentence. Oh, but it was rough in there, I can tell you. The place was filled with rogues, murderers and bad people you could never imagine. But the experience has made me stronger. It's taught me that I must do whatever it takes to survive.'

He smiled. 'It even gave me the will to find you . . . and lay my claim to this house. So now, I'm back in your life, and that pleases me.'

He sniggered. 'You should be delighted to see me. Instead, here you are, calling me all sorts of names, and even wanting to fight me.'

Suddenly, taking him by surprise, Anne pulled away and ran down the hallway, but he caught her and pinned her against the wall. 'Don't make me angry.' He dragged her into the front room. 'You'll only come off worse.' With one mighty shove he sent her sprawling onto the sofa. 'Now be quiet or I'll have to gag you!' Keeping a wary eye on her, he swiftly drew the curtains shut. 'We don't want anyone being nosy, do we?'

In the half-light, he watched her every move. 'No point in trying to escape, my dear. It will only rile me, and make matters worse for you.'

Knowing what he was capable of, Anne remained quiet. Hurt and bleeding, she let him rant on, while training her frantic thoughts on a plan of escape.

~

Sally ran all the way back from the bus stop. *What an idiot,* she muttered to herself, *leaving my handbag on the windowsill.*

She hurried up the front path to Anne's house, and was about to knock on the front door when she heard sounds much like soft laughter. Someone else was there . . . a neighbour, probably. She knocked on the door but there was no answer. She knocked again, louder this time, but still no answer. That was really odd.

Growing curious, she sidestepped onto the lawn, and stretched up to peer in the window, but she was too short to see, and the curtains were closed. Why would Anne close the curtains at this time of day? Sally smiled.

Maybe Anne had got a secret admirer, and didn't want to say.

Tapping on the window, she called, 'Anne, are you in there? I left my handbag on the windowsill . . . I'm sorry!'

When there was still no answer, she grew concerned.

She looked about the garden. Spotting a large plant pot, she dragged it to the base of the window where she turned it upside down, and climbed onto it.

Gripping the windowsill to steady herself, she leaned forward, towards the impossibly narrow slit between the two curtains. Peeping through, she found it difficult to make out anything. There were no sounds, but in the half-light from the hallway, she imagined she could just about see the two figures seated on the sofa. She called out, 'Anne, are you in there? I need to quickly collect my handbag . . . please?'

Suddenly, there was movement, but she couldn't make out what was happening. 'Anne, if you could please hand me my bag, I'll be off and catch the bus.'

Inside, Anne was desperately struggling. Hearing Sally, she tried to call out, but Carter punched her hard across the mouth. Dazed and bleeding, she fell back onto the sofa.

Realising that something was not right, Sally remembered Anne's words: *He hurt me . . . he killed my baby.*

Horrified at the possibility that Edward Carter was inside the house, Sally bunched her fist and banged hard on the window. 'Carter! I know who you are. I know what you did. You'd better not hurt her. I've seen you now . . . I can identify you.' She banged on the window again. 'I'm calling the police!' Scrambling off her makeshift platform, she ran down the path, all the while yelling at the top of her voice, 'Help! Call the police! There's a madman . . . He's got my friend . . . He's hurting her . . .'

She ran to the pub, thankful that the landlord was on the pavement putting out his boards advertising the evening darts match. He saw her running as though her life depended on it.

'Good Lord! What's wrong?' He caught her in his arms.

Breathless, Sally shouted, 'Call the police! Quickly. It's Anne! He means to kill her . . . he will. He'll do it . . . please hurry! Get the police!'

The landlord ran inside, with Sally following. As he dialled the number, Sally told him, 'Hurry! He's got her trapped inside the house, and he's hurting her . . . he means to kill her! Please hurry!'

It seemed like no time at all before the squad cars were racing down the street, sirens screaming.

They found Anne lying on the floor, bruised and bloodied.

Edward Carter, though, had already fled.

Some half a mile away, the foot-patrol officer was on his rounds when he heard the sirens. They alerted his memory of the shifty-looking man who had been lurking about in the back alleys earlier.

Being the kind of officer who took his work seriously, he decided to check the back alleys yet again.

As he came round the corner, Edward Carter ran straight into him. There was a vicious set-to as Carter tried to escape, but he was out of breath and weakened, while the officer was a big, capable fellow, and not one to be brought down easily.

This time, Edward Carter had met his match. Being well trained in the art of apprehending a violent suspect, the officer gave better than he got. There was a desperate struggle, but even though the officer was slightly injured, he soon had his prisoner safe against the wall, arms behind his back, and strong handcuffs securing him there.

While keeping Carter trapped, the officer used his walkie-talkie and within minutes help arrived.

A short time later, Carter was unceremoniously bundled into the car and taken away.

As he went, he glanced out the window. *Don't celebrate too soon, little wifey*, he mouthed in a whisper. *I'll be back.*

~

Pale and shaking from her ordeal, Anne told the constable, 'He's beaten me up before, but this time he really wanted to kill me. I saw it in his eyes.'

'Right! Well, he can't hurt you where he's going.' The kindly constable could see how Carter must have terrified this young woman.

After checking her bruises he made an entry in his notebook. 'I'm sorry, but I need you to tell me exactly what happened here.'

As Anne described the frightening series of events, he meticulously recorded them.

After the police had gone, Sally took charge. 'Come

on. Let's get you upstairs . . . A freshen-up and change of clothes might help you feel better.'

After escorting Anne upstairs and helping her choose a comfortable outfit, Sally told her, 'You finish here, and I'll go down and tidy up. When you're ready, we'll get into your car and I'll drive you over to my house. You're staying with me and Mick . . . and I am not taking no for an answer! Don't worry, Pusscat can come too.'

Anne did not need asking twice.

Half an hour later, the two of them set off. Sally was driving, but she kept a careful eye on Anne, who was very quiet, shaken by what Carter had done to her . . . again.

PART THREE

~

Dangerous Times

1957

CHAPTER EIGHT

WHEN THE KNOCK came on her office door, Miss Martin was head down, browsing through paperwork.

'Come in!' She was expecting a senior member of her staff to deliver Adam Carter to her door. In anticipation, she took off her spectacles, laid them on the desk and waited.

Nancy Montague flounced in, ushering Adam before her. 'I've brought Adam as instructed,' she advised Miss Martin. Placing the flat of her hand in the centre of Adam's back, she gently urged him forward.

Miss Martin offered him a smile. 'Good morning, Adam! And are you feeling good, this bright and beautiful morning?'

'Good morning, Miss Martin.' He stood before her, his two hands clenched before him. 'I'm all right, thank you.'

She nodded to Nancy. 'Thank you, Nancy. We'll be

fine just now.' With a flutter of her chubby hand she waved the nervous little woman away.

When the door was closed and she was alone with the boy, she instructed him with a warm smile: 'Please, Adam, do sit down.' She gestured to the deep-bottomed chair strategically placed at the side of her large, well-polished desk.

Adam stepped forward and did as he was asked.

Momentarily, Miss Martin took quiet stock of him, especially noting the subservient manner in which he had stood, hands clenched in front, eyes down. Staring at the floor.

With his thick brown hair and serious brown eyes, he was a handsome boy; quiet with a soulful disposition and a heavy heart.

Now aged thirteen, and having been at the children's home for a number of years, Adam had forged no real friendship here. He was a loner, plagued by events of the past, and ever anxious about whatever future awaited him.

'Please, Adam, look up!' When he raised his head and looked directly at her, Miss Martin asked him, 'Did you enjoy your birthday party last week, Adam?'

'Yes, Miss Martin, thank you.'

'Good! And did you enjoy your outing with Miss Nightingale and your friend Phil?'

Adam's face lit up. 'Oh, yes, I enjoyed it very much, thank you.'

'Excellent!' She always made a point of giving praise where it was due. 'You have a fine friend in Phil.'

Her manner and tone grew serious. 'So, Adam, what are we going to do with you, I wonder?'

'I don't understand, Miss Martin.'

'Very well then, I shall explain. Here you are, now thirteen years old, and still not settled with a foster family. Why is that, do you think?'

'I don't really know, Miss Martin.'

'So, Adam. Now that you've had time to think about your month with the last foster family, can you tell me what really happened there?'

'I'm not sure, Miss Martin. I just wasn't very happy.'

'And why was that? Did someone beat you?'

'No, miss.'

'Were they spiteful in any other way?'

'No, miss.'

'So, they were good to you, then?'

Adam hesitated before giving his answer. 'Yes . . . only . . .' Falling silent, he returned his gaze to the floor.

'Adam! Look at me.'

Reluctantly, Adam raised his gaze.

'Dearie me!' Exasperated, Miss Martin clambered out of her chair, to pace anxiously back and forth. 'This is not good, Adam! After three attempts to place you with fine, God-fearing families, you are still here, with us. Why is that?'

'I don't know, miss.'

'Well, I *do* know! Mr and Mrs Shaler have now officially reported to us. They claim that not once did you even try to fit in. They said you were sullen, disobedient, and that one time, you sat outside in the garden for hours, refusing to come in, even though you had no coat on and it was pouring with rain. Is that true, Adam? Did you do these things?'

'Yes, miss.'

The atmosphere grew heavy, while Miss Martin, loudly tutting, padded her way up and down the carpet.

Meanwhile, Adam closed his mind to that particular foster family and his bad behaviour while living there. He even closed his mind to Miss Martin as she paced back and forth.

Inevitably, his thoughts wandered back to the house where he had lived with his darling mother and the devil who took her from him.

Recently, both Phil and Miss Martin's staff had gone to great lengths to keep the newspapers from him, but he heard the gossip, and what he had learned was more than enough. They said his father had been arrested and locked up for a long time. That it was to do with another woman, that he had beaten her up . . . just as he had beaten his own mother.

So, Edward Carter was in prison. Adam was glad about that.

But it was not enough. It would never be enough!

'I so need to see you settled,' Miss Martin went on, 'but it has not gone well so far. Which is why I continue to ask myself, how on earth *are* we going to get you settled with a good family? Adam, do you hear what I say?'

Miss Martin's question jolted him back to the moment, 'Yes, Miss Martin.'

'Well?'

'I'm sorry, miss . . . I don't know.'

'Hmm.'

Flummoxed by his negative attitude, Miss Martin

stole a moment to study this troubled but capable boy, and reflect on the dreadful experiences he had encountered through his short life. Not for the first time, she was deeply saddened.

'Adam, you do realise you could have a great future, if only you would set your mind to it?'

When he chose not to comment, she persevered. 'I'm told by your teachers that you have a natural talent for painting. I understand they've told you as much. Isn't that so?'

'Yes, miss.'

'Do you enjoy painting?'

'Yes, Miss Martin.'

'Why is that, Adam? What do you see in painting that brings you pleasure? They tell me that most of the images are somewhat dark and brooding, and yet somehow they quicken the heart and fire the imagination.' She paused, before asking softly, 'What makes you want to paint these dark pictures, Adam?'

Adam had never been asked that before. In truth, he had never even thought about it, but now, the answer came to him so easily. 'Most of all, I like painting my mother.'

'Really? And why is that, do you think?'

Adam gave a whimsical smile. 'I paint her when she's walking along the hill rise behind our house, because then she was happy, and so very pretty. It's like springtime. But then *he* hurts her, and everything becomes dark and ugly. It's like . . .' he struggled for the right words, '. . . it's like she's running away, but she can't get through the trees . . . it's dark and shadowy. The trees are like giants. They stretch out their branches and trap her inside, and then it becomes a prison. I can hear her calling for me, but I can't get her out. I can't save her.'

His voice hardened to a harsh whisper. 'That's what I draw, because that's what *he* did to her.'

'And does it help you, Adam? When you draw these pictures, how does it make you feel?'

'Sometimes happy, sometimes sad. Especially when I draw a picture where I make *him* be the prisoner. He's the one in the dark, afraid and trapped. In my paintings, I punish him. And then I feel better inside.'

Miss Martin was shocked at the hatred in Adam's face, whenever he referred to his father. She shared Adam's abhorrence of his father's cruelty to his mother, but to hear the boy talk with such loathing she found deeply upsetting.

More than that, she feared for this sad and lonely boy. He had done no wrong, and yet it seemed his punishment was never-ending. His bad experiences appeared to have crippled him, both mentally and emotionally.

'Adam, I know life has not been kind to you, and I truly am sorry for that. But maybe now it's time to try and put the past behind you. Sometimes, through no fault of our own, terrible things happen to us, and we wonder why.'

Adam simply nodded.

'It's foolish, Adam, but often we blame ourselves when we are just the innocent bystander. You, in particular, have had to deal with things that most children of your age would never encounter. But you really must try very hard to face up to the sequence of events that brought you here, because if you don't face up to them, they will always haunt you. Do you understand what I'm trying to say, Adam?'

Choked with emotion and unable to speak, Adam nodded again.

'No, Adam!' Miss Martin raised her voice. 'A nod of the head will not do! You must say it out loud. Say it, Adam: "Bad things have happened to me, and I have to face up to them. It's the only way I can move forward and build a life of my own." Say it for me, Adam. Say it loud and clear!'

A moment passed and still he could not say it. Miss Martin waited hopefully.

When Adam continued to be silent, she took it to be a simple matter of wills between the two of them. In a way she had always known it would come to this. So, she rose to the challenge in her indomitable way.

Taking a sheaf of typed paper from her drawer, she laid it on the desktop, slowly and deliberately put on her spectacles, and, appearing to ignore him, she pretended to be reading, occasionally adding a little tick alongside the writing, merely for effect.

In the corner of the room, the grandfather clock ticked sombrely. The rhythmic sound of the swinging pendulum was the only sound in the room.

Moments passed, and still Miss Martin kept her head down, seeming not to care if Adam was there or not.

After a while, Adam's hesitant voice began: 'Bad things happened to me . . .' He paused, thinking of his mother, before going on. 'I have to . . . face up to them. It's the only way I can build . . . a life . . . of my own.' There was a moment when his voice seemed to resonate with the ticking of the clock before his muffled sobbing filled the room.

'There!' Miss Martin got out of her chair in a flurry. 'Ssh, child. Well done for being strong enough to say that out loud. I know it can't have been easy. Yes! Well done, my dear.' On an impulse, she wrapped him in her chubby warm arms and held him to her ample bosom for a moment, before dipping into her pocket and flourishing a pretty white handkerchief. 'Here . . . wipe your eyes.'

With a tear in her own eye, she sat beside him, and for a while neither of them spoke.

Presently, she addressed him kindly. 'I do realise how very hard it's been for you losing the mother you loved, and then learning how your father is now imprisoned.' With some embarrassment at showing the softness of her character, she admitted, 'Believe me, Adam, when I say that if I could take away your pain, you know I would.'

'I'm glad he's in prison.' Adam wished that man all the harm he'd caused his mother. 'I hate him! I hope they never let him out.'

Having momentarily dropped her guard, Miss Martin chose not to remark on what Adam had said. Instead, she abruptly returned to her formal self.

'Now then, Adam! I have good news for you.' Having got his attention, she informed him, 'We have another foster family who, I hope, might give you the home you deserve . . . and before you get worried, you won't be the only child, as in the previous home. This family already has two children: an eighteen-month-old baby girl and her nine-year-old sister. Oh, and a dog called Buster.'

Having seen his face light up at the mention of a dog, she asked him, 'Have you ever had a dog, Adam?'

'No, Miss Martin. Phil has a dog, though. He takes it for walks every morning before he drives the school bus.'

Adam's whole manner had lightened, and for the moment he was not consciously thinking of his parents. 'What kind of dog is it, Miss Martin?'

'As I recall, Buster is a little brown terrier. That's all I know. And that's only because they asked if having a dog might stop them from fostering. But in actual fact, we sometimes welcome a pet of sorts. It helps the foster child to fit in. Mind you, if the child is nervous of pets, then that's a different story. We would never send a child where he or she might feel threatened.'

Delighted by Adam's response, she went on, 'So now, Adam, do you have any more questions?'

After giving it some thought, Adam was concerned enough to ask, 'Miss, if they've got two children of their own, why do they want to foster someone else's child?'

Miss Martin began, 'Of course you must understand, that this subject is not for discussion outside of this room?'

'Yes, miss.'

'Very well then, and because I have secured their permission, I may partly share their confidence with you. Suffice for you to know that for medical reasons it is not possible for them to have another child. Apparently, they had planned a large family, and they had hoped their next baby might be a boy. Unfortunately, that cannot happen now, and so they decided to apply for fostering . . . with a view to adopt, if you fit in all right with the family.'

Adam was curious. 'Miss Martin, why would they want me? Why not a baby?'

Miss Martin had gone as far as she was allowed. 'I am not privy to that information, although if I were to make a guess, I would say that as they already have a baby they maybe wanted an older child. Also, they might think a sensible brother could befriend and guide their nine-year-old daughter. But, as I say, that is only my opinion, and you must not quote me on that. Do you understand?'

'Yes, miss.'

'Good!'

Whenever Miss Martin put on her spectacles, she meant business; and she meant business now.

'Now then, Adam. I can tell you that I gave them information on several children, including you. And because I believe in you, Adam, I did not hesitate to sing your praises.'

'Thank you, miss.'

'Fortunately, they seemed to warm to the idea of having you. But of course, I needed to arrange a meeting with them, so they can take stock of you, and you can also take stock of them, so you can see how you feel when you meet them in person. You will spend some time together, approximately half an hour initially, right here in this office. Afterwards, you must say whether or not you feel happy to go with them – if they indeed choose you . . . because, of course, it's a two-way thing. So, Adam, is that all right with you?'

'Yes, miss.' In truth, mainly because of the dog, he found himself growing a little excited. 'I would like to meet them. Oh, and will they bring the dog?'

Miss Martin laughed. 'Bless you, child. You have to look at the family first. As for whether they might bring the dog, I have no idea.' She gave a merry little smile. 'Although I will admit I did not forbid the little dog's presence.'

After Miss Martin dismissed him, Adam danced all the way down the corridor, a wide smile on his face.

Maybe, at long last, things were about to change for the better.

~

Since Adam had first been placed in the children's home, Phil had been a regular visitor. As promised, he continued to remain a constant friend and advisor throughout Adam's feelings of insecurity.

In his own wise manner, he guided Adam through his anger and his sadness, and in doing so, he had not only brought a measure of companionship and love to the boy, but he had unexpectedly found a friend in Polly, one of the staff members at the home.

Whenever Phil had been allowed to take Adam into town to watch a football match, or merely walk along the canal towpath, Polly was officially recruited to accompany them, as part of the security measures.

Neither Phil nor Adam had any problem with that. In fact, through the early months when Adam found it difficult to settle, and through the bad, painful period when he was rejected from his first foster family, Polly had worked with Phil in building Adam's badly bruised confidence.

In the process, both Adam, and Phil in particular, had come to respect and admire Polly; so much so, that whenever he arranged an outing with Phil, he also looked forward to seeing the homely little care assistant.

Today, they had planned to sit by the canal and feed the ducks. It was one of Adam's favourite pastimes.

'Make sure Adam is back here by two-thirty.' Being a stickler for the rules, Miss Martin went on to list the regulated dos and don'ts that accompanied any child on a trip from the children's home. 'Remember, Adam . . . do as you're asked, and always follow Polly's instructions. No changing the plans, or wandering off on your own. And you must stay in sight the whole time. Do you understand?'

'Yes, Miss Martin.'

'Good!' She issued similar instructions to Polly, then she waved the three of them on their way. 'Off you go, then.'

As Phil was about to go out of the door, she called him back. 'A moment, please, Phil.'

Phil hurried back to her, while Polly and Adam waited in the porch.

Pre-empting her reason for calling him back, he assured her earnestly, 'Don't you worry, Miss Martin. We'll have Adam back by two-thirty, as requested.'

Bold enough to speak out of turn, he told her what was on his mind. 'If I may say so, Miss Martin, it really doesn't give us much time together.' He valued his time with Adam; and Polly too, if he was truthful.

Unmoved by his remark, Miss Martin glanced at the grandfather clock. 'It's now twelve-thirty. To my reckoning, that allows you two hours.'

Unable and unwilling to reveal delicate official information, and because Phil was not the boy's official guardian, she gave a certain little smile, which offered Phil the smallest clue to her reason for cutting short the outing.

'The reason I need him back here is because I care about his future . . . as I know you do.' She paused while the remark sank in, then went on in a softer tone, 'Adam might have important visitors arriving to see him. He needs to prepare himself, and I need a short time with him before the important event.' She put on her most official tone of voice, 'If you consider it a problem to have him back by two-thirty, then I must withdraw permission for the outing.'

Again, she gave that certain little confiding smile. 'I'm sure you understand what I'm saying.'

Phil believed he understood exactly what she might be saying, and it brought a smile to his face. 'You can trust me, Miss Martin. I will have Adam back here, in good time for the "important visitors".' He had an impulse to give a little wink. 'Thank you.'

'Ah! So we do understand each other?'

'I believe so.'

'Good man!'

Phil went away with a bounce in his step.

A few moments later, Adam surprised him by saying cautiously, 'I think I might know why they want me back.'

'Oh, do you now? And why might that be then?'

'Because there might be a new foster family coming to see me.'

'Really?' Phil gave a sideways wink at Polly. 'Well now, and if they *were* coming to see you, how would you feel about that?'

Adam gave a little shrug of the shoulders. 'I don't know.' Beyond that, he would not be drawn. After enduring the previous fostering experience, he had grown very wary.

Polly had said very little up to that point, but now she said, 'Try and keep an open mind, Adam. One bad experience does not mean you won't be placed with a good, loving family. In my experience, there are more decent, deserving people out there than there are bad ones.'

While Phil readily endorsed her comment, Adam kept his silence, and brooded on his dark memories.

Though, everything else aside, he was greatly excited about seeing the little dog.

The new family would be bound to ask him questions, and he must answer truthfully, even if it put them off choosing him to be part of their family.

Miss Martin had advised him to ask questions of his own, but Adam decided that he would know anyway if they were kind people and truly wanted him. And, because he had yearned to be part of a real family, he desperately hoped that at long last it might really happen.

More importantly, today was a special day because it was the day when Phil took him to the churchyard to see his darling mother.

Just as Adam was thinking about her, Phil drew him back from the kerb. 'Mind out, son. The bus is here.'

When the bus arrived, Phil saw Polly on, then Adam, then himself.

'Now then, Adam,' he said, 'being as we haven't got much time, we'd best make it hot-foot to the florist and get your mum's posy. Then we'll walk up to the churchyard and spend a few minutes there. After that, we should still have time enough to treat ourselves to an ice cream and a sandwich.'

He consulted Adam and Polly. 'How does that sound to you folks?'

Adam agreed that it was a fine plan and, by way of approving, Polly insisted on paying the bus fares.

~

At the florist's shop, Adam chose a small posy of pink flowers.

'Mum always liked pink best of all,' he told Phil and Polly, who had already learned that from previous visits to the florist.

The florist was a round, smiling woman who always wore green. On more than one occasion, Polly had innocently remarked on how much the florist resembled the flowers, 'all pink and green and wearing a smile'.

Her description brought a little chuckle from the other two.

The florist wrapped the posy in a cornet of stripy paper and tied it with a big floppy bow. 'There!' She was well pleased with herself. 'That's a very pretty posy, even if I do say so myself!'

The churchyard was just a short walk up the hill. When they got to the top, Phil was puffing and panting, with Polly, sprightly as ever, springing ahead. 'You need to do a bit of exercise,' she told Phil, 'get some of that fat off your belly.'

Adam burst out laughing, while Phil replied haughtily, 'I'll have you know, I do a lot of walking and lifting, and I drive a bus full of sprightly children. If you ask me, that's more than enough to keep a fella's weight down!'

Smiling secretly to Adam, Polly took the hint to drop the subject, while Phil took her comment on board and vowed not to beg any more of the children's sweets.

As always, whenever Phil had taken him to the churchyard, Adam ran ahead. Before the other two had even reached the top of the hill, Adam was running down the path to the church entrance, and then through the shrubbery to the pretty green area where his mother lay.

Dropping to his knees, he told her in a whisper, 'I'm here to see you, Mum. Look, I've brought you flowers. Phil's with me . . . and Polly from the home.' He placed a kiss on his fingers and pressed it to her name etched in the stone.

A few minutes later, seeing Adam kneeling there, Phil stopped in his tracks. 'Happen we should stay here for a while. Let the boy have some time with his mum.'

For the slightest moment, Polly was torn between compassion for the boy and her duty to Miss Martin.

Compassion won the day. 'Yes, we'll wait here.' She smiled up at Phil. 'Besides, it's so pretty here . . . don't you think, Phil?'

Phil nodded. 'Pretty it might be, but only for visiting.' He gave a little shiver. 'I'm not ready to overstay my welcome, at least not for some long time yet.'

Polly wagged a finger. 'If you feel like that, then it's more reason for you to lose some of that belly.'

Phil patted his stomach. 'You might be right, but it won't be easy. I've had this belly for a while.'

'There you go then! Cakes and sweets and sticky buns won't help, will they?'

'How do you know I've got a soft spot for sticky buns?'

'Because it's what you order every time we take Adam into a café.'

'That's only once a fortnight or so.'

'Hmm!' Polly gave him a knowing look before seating herself on the nearby stone wall.

Having placed the flowers, Adam told his mother in a whisper, 'He can't hurt you any more, Mum. And now he's been put away.' Leaning forward to wrap his two arms around the memorial stone, he whispered, 'I

183

kept my promise, Mum, but it's hard. I peeped in the newspaper and it said he had hurt this other woman. But they caught him, and he was put in jail, and I hope they never let him out.'

The tears were never far away and now he could not hold them back. 'I hate him! He took you away from me and now everything's changed.'

Wiping his eyes, he told her sternly, 'Sometimes when I'm in bed and I think of what he did to you, I want to hurt him . . . to kill him . . . I really do!'

When the memories became too hard to bear, he cried, because he was sorry, and because he was frustrated that he could talk to his mum but he didn't know if she could hear him. He wanted to see her pretty smile. He wanted to feel her hand over his, and he so wanted to hear her laughter . . . and see her as she suddenly raced him to the top of the hill when they had been walking out together.

'Oh, Mum, I miss you so much. I will love you . . . for ever and ever, Mum . . .' His voice broke beneath the weight of his sorrow, and he could say no more.

Just then, he felt Phil's loving arms about him, lifting him up to his feet and holding him close. 'It's all right, son. It's all right to feel angry, but wanting to kill someone is not the answer. And besides, I have no doubt he'll get his just deserts in prison.'

'Do you know what, Phil?'

'What, son?'

'I hate him! I want to hurt him, like he hurt my mum.' Adam clung to this man who had brought such comfort into his lonely life.

'I understand that.' Phil searched for the right words. 'But . . . like I said, it's not good to harbour thoughts of killing . . . Your mum would never want that, and you know it, don't you?'

When Adam was slow in responding, he asked again, 'Adam, you do know it's very wrong to think of killing, don't you?'

'Yes.' There was a span of silence, before Adam angrily announced, 'I hope they treat him badly in prison. I hope he's really unhappy, just like he made my mum unhappy.'

'Ssh, now.'

Phil held him for a time, while Polly could only look on helplessly.

Over her years at the home, she had seen many friends and do-gooders who might occasionally give a much-needed treat to one of the children at the home. But she had never before witnessed such devotion as she had seen between Phil and the boy. He was more than a friend to Adam. He was more like a father figure. And the love that had grown between these two was humbling to see.

Polly understood how Adam had flourished under Phil's protection. She had long realised that Phil was one of those selfless men – warm and giving – who asked for nothing in return.

She realised it was not too hard to love a man like Phil because, in truth, whenever Miss Martin asked her to accompany Adam and Phil on a trip to town, her heart would turn over. And that had not happened these many years.

185

A short time later, the three of them made their way down the hill, with Polly walking beside Phil, and Phil keeping a protective eye on Adam.

'All right, son?' Phil playfully ruffled Adam's hair. 'Ready for your ice cream, are you?' After years of coping with the children on the school bus, Phil had a natural way of diffusing a bad atmosphere.

'Yes, thank you, Phil.' Having talked with his mum and rid himself of bad thoughts, Adam was calmer.

'How about you?' Phil turned to Polly with a smile. 'Are you ready for your ice cream?'

'Yes, please, Phil. I'll have a double dollop of strawberry with chocolate sprinkles on top.'

Phil and Adam laughed out loud at that.

'Huh!' Phil tutted. 'And who's been lecturing me to watch my belly, eh?'

'I tell it as I see it,' she retorted with a cheeky little grin.

'There! I always knew it.'

'What?'

'You're a bossy boots!'

Even so, Phil thought her to be a handsome, homely woman, and a fine companion into the bargain.

CHAPTER NINE

'NO, ANNE!' SALLY pleaded. 'You're not ready to go back there yet. Please, stay here with us for a little longer. Just until you feel sure.'

Anne had thought about it more and more of late, and though she shivered at the idea of walking into that house again, she was determined that Edward Carter would not defeat her. 'But, I *am* sure, Sally. Well, at least as sure as I'll ever be, I suppose. Besides, I've put myself on you and Mick long enough. If I'm ever going back, the time is now.'

'But you're not strong enough in yourself.' Sally was worried. 'You still have the nightmares, and I know if you go back to where it all happened, it might be too much for you to handle. Please, Anne. Stay here, with me and Mick, for a few more weeks at least. If you're still determined after that, you can go home, and I'll come and be with you for a week or so, just to see how it goes.'

Sally knew only too well how deeply Carter's vicious attack had damaged her dear friend. It was only when she was checked over at the hospital afterwards that it was discovered two of her fingers were broken, and because of Carter's cruel handling of her, they found that some cartilage in her back had shifted, causing temporary damage to her spine. That meant an operation, and weeks of recovery back to full health.

Edward Carter, though, had not only damaged her physically, he had left her in such a bad state mentally that she was a mere shadow of her former self. It soon became clear that while the outward scars were healed, the same could not be said for her fragile state of mind.

In those first few months after she came to stay with Sally and Mick, Anne constantly teetered on the edge of a breakdown.

In the early days after the attack, she was afraid to go outside on her own. Instead, she would huddle indoors, unwashed, undressed, and unable to cope with returning to work.

At night, she could be heard pacing up and down in her bedroom, and whenever Sally took her out, she would never want to stay out long.

On the few occasions that Sally was successful in taking her into town, Anne would be nervously glancing about, watching people passing, and hiding in doorways if she saw any man who bore even the slightest resemblance to Carter.

All that had now run its course, although even now, she was nervous to be out on her own, which was why

Sally was anxious that she should stay with her and Mick for a while longer.

Presently, in the kitchen, making tea for the three of them, Mick heard the exchange between his wife and Anne. Like Sally, he was greatly concerned that Anne should give herself more time to recover before she returned to the house on Roff Avenue.

Having taken it all in, he now had the beginnings of an idea that might just satisfy everyone.

With this in mind, he quickly made the tea and set it on a tray with a box of biscuits, which he carried into the other room.

'I don't know who made me the servant around here,' he joked light-heartedly. 'It's Sunday! Which, as you know, is supposed to be a day of rest . . . and here's me, waiting on you two hand and foot. Right then! I reckon I've done my chores for today, so now it's up to you lovely ladies. You can now pour a drink for the man of the house, while filling me in on all the gossip.'

He put the tray on the coffee table in the bright, spacious room, and sat himself alongside Anne on the sofa, while Sally sat forward in the big brown leather armchair and set about pouring the tea.

'Mick, tell Anne she's not ready to go back to the house just yet,' she pleaded.

'Mmm. Well, I heard what you were saying just now, the two of you, and for what it's worth, I think you're *both* right.

'Really? In what way?' Sally asked.

'Well, from what I gather, Anne wants to go back to

189

the house, and you want her to stay here. That's right, isn't it?'

'Yes, but Anne is determined to go home. I've been trying to dissuade her, but she won't listen.' Sally appealed to Anne. 'Anne, tell Mick what you told me.'

'I've been here for months now,' Anne explained. 'It's not at all fair on either of you. I've crossed hurdles since I've been here and that's thanks to you two, my best friends. I'm back at work now – another hurdle overcome – and I'm much stronger in myself now. But I need to go home and pick up my life. I really think I can do it. Sally and I have been going over once a week to open and shut curtains, turn taps on and off, and dust around . . . that sort of thing. As you both know, I wasn't at all comfortable with being there at first, but I'm getting used to it now. I'm stronger in myself, and it doesn't frighten me like it did before.'

She appealed to them both. 'I'm sure I'll be OK, and if I'm not, I promise I'll call you.'

Understanding her dilemma, Mick offered his idea of a compromise. 'Look, Anne, what do you think of this idea? Sally is anxious for you to stay here with us for a while longer . . . and so am I. You, however, are anxious to go home, and I fully understand that. But I would not feel right if I let you go back there on your own just yet. So why doesn't Sally come and live with you for a week? I'll pop in straight from work and spend the evening with you both.' He laughed. 'I'll even bring us all fish and chips on my way back from work; save you the trouble of cooking.'

'Brilliant!' Sally was relieved. 'In fact, I suggested

something along those lines.' She appealed to Anne. 'Please, Anne. I would feel a lot better about you going back to the house if you could agree on Mick's plan. Just one week, that's all, and if you feel able to take charge again, we'll back off, although we'll always be here if you need us.'

Mick added, 'Just remember, if you're the slightest bit nervous or worried – about anything at all, however small – then you come back home with us and give yourself a bit more time. The alternative is you and Sally could maybe just go over there at weekends – a small dose at a time, if you get my meaning. That way, you might just reach the point where you feel good about being back home permanently. So, would you prefer that?'

Although still slightly nervous, Anne had to agree with his initial plan. 'I think it might be better to make it the full week as you said, because a couple of days won't be enough. So, if you really don't mind Sally coming to stay with me for that length of time, I would love to give it a try.'

Sally was already thinking ahead. 'I've got clean bedding and towels in the airing cupboard. When we leave work on Friday, we'll go shopping. We'll need to do a big shop: enough for the two of us for a week, and enough to fill the cupboards for Mick.'

'I'm quite capable of getting my own groceries.' Mick could be highly independent.

'I know you are, but while we're there we might as well do all the shopping in one go.'

'OK, Sal. Whatever suits you. So, when are you actually planning to stay at the house?'

Anne had already decided. 'I think we should go over there Saturday. It will be much better to start on a weekend. That way there'll be more people about, and we won't be leaving the house to go to work. It will give us that time to adjust.' She felt as though she was being ungrateful. '. . . If that's all right with you, Sally?'

'Yes, good thinking,' Sally agreed. 'So, this is how it goes. Friday evening after work, we'll go and get the groceries. Then we'll bring Mick's shopping back here, so he'll be all set up. We'll leave our groceries in the boot, except for the milk and such. On Saturday morning, we'll put the bedding and linen in the boot and make our way over to the house.' She clapped her hands. 'Job done!'

'Sounds like you've thought of everything. Thank you, both. I don't know how I can ever repay you,' Anne said.

In a strange and selfish way, she somehow envied Sally's seemingly perfect marriage. From the first meeting with Mick, she had recognised a good and thoughtful man; a man who would never harm a hair on his darling wife's head. Unlike the evil man she had foolishly married as a young girl.

The time came to make one last visit to the house before Sally would move in with Anne.

'We'll draw the curtains as always, and turn on the taps for a while. We'll just spend a couple of hours over there this evening, shall we?' Sally suggested.

'I think so, yes. But why don't we take the bedding and linen tonight?' Anne suggested. 'That way we'll save time on Friday after work. And don't forget the grocery store will be busy at that time on a Friday.'

'Yes, that's very true.' And so it was agreed.

'Do you need me for anything?' Mick asked.

'There's not much you can do, Mick,' Sally reminded him. 'You're terrible at changing beds. And as for housework, if I let you loose it would only have to be done again.'

'Well, thanks for that!' Mick laughed. 'In that case, happen I'll go down the pub, and have a pint or two with the boys.'

'Oh!' Sally sounded disappointed.

'What's wrong?'

'Nothing. It's just that I thought maybe you could put that curtain rail back up, the one that fell down in the back bedroom. Oh, but it's not important, especially as nobody sleeps in there anyway.'

'Mmm!' He had the germ of an idea. 'I'll do the rail, don't worry.'

'No, honestly, Mick.' Sally felt bad now. 'It's all right . . . it's really not important. I don't even know why I mentioned it. I mean, you can fix the rail any time. Go down to the pub. Meet up with your mates.'

'Only if you're sure you don't mind?'

'I am absolutely sure! Honestly, Mick, you haven't had a night out in a while and it'll do you good.' Sally felt mean now even mentioning about the curtain rail, especially as he had genuinely welcomed her friend into their home.

Mick was curious. 'How long do you reckon you'll be gone?'

'Two . . . maybe three hours, I suppose.' She turned to Anne. 'What say you, Anne?'

'Yes. I think that's about right. Check the house. Change the beds and close the curtains. I might just have a quick chat with my neighbour; see if anyone's been hanging about, maybe.'

Sally picked up on her worrying remark. 'Anne, trust me, there won't have been anyone "hanging about". Especially not Carter, because thankfully that madman is well and truly locked up.'

When Anne felt the nervousness creeping up on her, she gave a wide smile. 'That's very true! But I'll go and have a chat with her all the same, if only to thank her for keeping an eye on the house while I've been away. In fact, while we're out getting the groceries, I might pick up a bunch of flowers for her.'

Sally agreed. 'Your neighbour is a real darling. I bet she'd have opened and shut the curtains as well, if you'd asked her. But she's getting on a bit and maybe it would have been too much to ask.'

Mick felt bad about going to the pub. 'I'll tell you what, Sal,' he started, 'I've worked it out. Being as you'll probably be gone the best part of three hours, I can do the curtain rail first and still have time to enjoy a pint or two with the lads. OK?'

Getting out of her chair, Sally went to him and kissed him full on the mouth. 'Course it's OK. I'm sorry if I sounded a bit miffed at first, but I didn't mean it. You go and see your mates. Have a good time, and we'll catch up when I get back.'

Half an hour later, Mick saw them off. 'Drive carefully.' He always worried about Sally in the car. Capable though she was, Sally could be a bit too daredevil at times.

As he waved them away, Mick smiled to himself, thinking how much he loved Sally. He had never had one single moment of regret at having married her. The only regret he had, and would always have, was that Sally was unable to give him a child.

That sorry discovery had floored them both. Yet, even with that, he had never regretted marrying her.

There were still the odd times when he truly ached for a family, especially when he and Sally were out walking, and he saw other men playing footie in the park with their sons, or a father teaching his child how to ride a bike. He missed all that, yet because he adored the ground she walked on, he was always careful never to let Sally know his true feelings.

~

At the same moment that Mick was dwelling on that particular sadness in their lives, Sally too felt a touch of regret at her inability to give Mick the children he craved. She had always planned that the back bedroom should be a nursery, and now, after years with no baby in it, it was looking rundown and neglected. She now felt guilty at having seemed unsupportive when he had mentioned he might go for a pint with his mates instead of putting up the curtain rail.

Anne had noticed how quiet Sally had grown since

195

they left the house. 'Is everything all right, Sal?' she asked.

Sally nodded. 'Sort of . . . yes. Only I should never have let Mick see how I wasn't keen on him going to the pub tonight. It was selfish of me. I should never have made an excuse for him not to go. The back curtains don't really matter anyway. It's been ages since he went out socially, and the first time he suggests it, I put on a sour face.'

'Well, I'm sure Mick didn't even notice.' Anne had seen the tense exchange, but tactfully made light of it.

Now her curiosity got the better of her. 'Tell me if I'm out of line, but can I ask why you don't like him going to the pub?'

'It's not that I don't like him actually going to the pub,' Sally revealed, 'it's just the tarty barmaid . . . she has her eye on him.'

'Oh, I see!' Anne detected the green-eyed monster. 'And you don't like him going there without you, is that it?'

'Sort of. I'm not being paranoid, but even when Mick and I are there together, she's always stealing a glance at him. It's obvious that she fancies him, and when he goes to the bar I hear the two of them laughing together. I think he really enjoys her company. For all I know, he might even fancy her!'

'You don't believe that for a minute, do you? I mean, he might just be being polite and laughing at her jokes, even if they're rubbish. Mick is a lovely man, Sal. You've often said how he makes friends easily.'

'Well, yes, that's right, he does. But what man can resist when a pretty girl keeps making a play for him?'

'A man like Mick, that's who.'

'Maybe.'

'For goodness' sake, Sal, you must know how devoted he is to you. Anyone can see, he's crazy in love with you. You're a fortunate woman, Sal. You have a good man there. I reckon he would rather cut off his arm than cheat on you.'

The atmosphere grew tense and, for a time, neither of them spoke.

Then out of nowhere, Sally made a heartfelt confession. 'I'm frightened, Anne. I'm really frightened that he might leave me.'

Anne was shocked. 'He would never leave you . . . Why would he?'

Sally took a while to answer, and what she confided rocked Anne to her roots. 'I'm always afraid that he will leave me one day . . . if he meets the right woman. And, to be honest, I wouldn't blame him.'

'But why would he leave you? He loves you far too much.'

'I know he loves me, but sometimes things happen that might make a man do what he might otherwise never do.' She searched for the right words to make Anne understand, without giving away too much.

She had always been afraid to say the truth out loud, hoping that if she never actually said it, then it might not be true.

Anne urged her on. 'What kind of "things", Sal?'

Wishing she had not said anything, Sally gave a little

shrug. 'Just "things". Like if someone was told something . . . so cruel, it could break up a relationship. Something that could never be put right.'

'Such as what?' Anne was intrigued, and a little concerned.

Sally went on, almost as though she was talking to herself, 'Sometimes I think I'm just being selfish . . . none of this is his fault. It's been on my mind for a long time that, however much I love Mick, it's very wrong to try to cling onto him.'

Anne was lost. 'What are you saying, Sal? I don't understand. You and Mick have a wonderful marriage. You belong together.'

Sally shook her head. 'All I'm saying is, maybe the best thing would be for Mick to find some other woman who could make his life complete.' She took a moment to think and reflect. 'If that happened, and he would rather be with her than me . . . well . . . I would have to let him go. It would be cruel of me to try and stop him.'

Anne understood that Sally was sorry for trying to deter Mick from going to the pub without her, but she sensed something much deeper in what Sally was saying.

So, because she cared, and because she and Sal now told each other almost everything, she decided to wait for an opportune moment when she might persuade Sally to confide her troubles.

She needed to know why Sally could even entertain the idea that Mick would be better off with another woman. Moreover, why would Sally be prepared to let her beloved man go? The idea of those two breaking up was unthinkable.

With Sally now lapsed into silence, Anne wisely kept her own counsel. She hoped a quiet moment might allow her friend to reflect on the enormity of what she had just said.

That was exactly what Sally did, and she quickly realised that her problem was too hard to bear alone. It would be good just to talk about it, preferably with a dear friend, who would not judge her. But not now, not in the car. So, gathering all her strength, she told Anne, 'I want you to know everything, Anne. I need to tell you. But it's too difficult just now.'

Gently, Anne laid her hand over Sally's. 'It's all right, Sal. Whenever you're ready, you know I'll be here for you.'

'I know.' Sally was deeply grateful to have found such a loyal friend and confidante.

A moment later, Sally drew up at Anne's house.

After climbing out of the car, each took a bundle of linen from the boot, and as they walked up the path, the next-door neighbour gave a cheery wave from her window.

To Anne, it was a warm and comforting gesture, but not enough to quell the nervous flutter in her stomach whenever she returned to this house.

Yet she was determined to rid her mind of her tormentor, and get on with her life. This was her home, and it was where she wanted to be. She must not let him rob her of that.

Yet, even while her determination hardened, she could still hear his threat: *What's yours is mine.*

She dared not even think about it.

Once inside the house, Anne waited in the hallway for Sal to come in from the street.

She felt nervous, as always. She could feel Carter's presence there. In her mind's eye she could see him standing over her . . . wanting to kill her.

Even now, after all this time, there was an atmosphere of evil here. It lingered, making her blood run cold. *Come on, Anne!* she chided herself. *You can deal with it. You have to realise he can't hurt you from where he is.*

Quickly now, before she lost her courage, she made her way to the kitchen where she put her bedding bundle down. While she opened the kitchen curtains, Sally came in to put the kettle on. 'I think we both need a cuppa,' she sighed wearily.

While Sally was preparing the tea, Anne went into the front room and opened the curtains there. It was a well-practised procedure, which they had perfected daily over these many weeks.

But when Anne came back into the kitchen, she found Sally seated at the little kitchen table, her head bent forward on the bundle of bedding, and sobbing her heart out.

On realising that Anne had returned, Sally quickly wiped her eyes and hurried over to the kitchenette.

Rummaging for the cups and saucers, she said, 'The kettle's just boiled. I'm making us a pot of tea,' and she began setting out the cups.

Having set the tray, she carried it across the room and sat herself down.

For the next few minutes, they sipped their tea and

talked about all things unimportant until Anne could bear it no longer.

'Look, Sal, I know I said I would be there for you whenever you're ready, and I will, but I know something is eating away at you. Please, Sal, you can trust in me.'

'Yes, I know that, but there's no use talking about it because nothing can be done. There's no cure. And there's no real future for me and Mick. I'm just a rope around his neck. I know I should end our marriage but I can't. The truth is, I don't know what I'd do without him by my side. But that's just selfish of me. I understand that now.'

Anne had no idea what Sally was talking about, but she did know one thing for sure. 'Talking about it might help . . . more than you realise. I mean, look how you and Mick encouraged me to talk about what happened here. You helped me through it, and before you got me talking I had it all locked up inside and it was tearing me apart. Don't do what I did, Sal. Don't imagine it will all go away on its own, because it never will. So, let me help. Talk to me.'

'But you can't help, Anne. They've tried, but it seems there's nothing they can do.'

'About what? Tell me what's bothering you. Please, Sal, let me help. Remember how in the worst of my troubles, you told me not to shut you out? I'm asking you the same now. Please, don't shut me out.'

For what seemed an age, Sally did not reply. And then, in the softest of whispers, she confided, 'I can't make him complete. I can never give him the one thing he truly wants.' Hanging her head down, she continued,

'I don't know what to do, Anne. All I can think is to let Mick go. To give him a chance to find happiness with someone else. Someone who can give him what I never can.'

Embarrassed and ashamed, she looked away. 'When we first realised something was stopping me from getting pregnant, I underwent so many different treatments. Mick did the same, but it wasn't his fault. It was me. In the end, they said I should reconcile myself to the fact that I can never have children.'

She took a deep breath. 'So now that you know, I'm sure you can imagine how hard it is. Mick is my life, and it really hurts that I will never be able to give him the child he so desperately wants . . . that we *both* want. I know how much he misses out on being a father. I've seen him looking at the parents with children in the park, and it's so cruel.'

As Sally poured her heart out, Anne realised why the business of Mick going to the pub had been such a problem for her.

'It's unnatural for a man not to father a child.' Sally had suddenly shifted the focus of the conversation. 'The barmaid deliberately keeps making a play for him. She makes me afraid, Anne. She's recently divorced and she's got two small children. She even shows Mick photographs of them. It's as though she knows I can't give Mick the children he longs for.'

When, inevitably, the tears began to flow, Anne held Sally close. It was all the comfort she could give.

~

Left alone in the house, Mick closed his eyes and enjoyed the quiet. For a time he had nothing on his mind. Then he had everything on his mind.

He thought about work, and all the things he had to do. He mentally back-tracked on his day at work and the lorries he had loaded up at the warehouse, satisfying himself that he had not missed anything; that the orders had been properly sent out and all the paperwork was done.

He thought about money. Thankfully, he and Sally had good jobs, so financially they were quite comfortable.

He thought about the future stretching far ahead of him, and he hoped it would be with Sally, because without her, there was no future worth having.

Inevitably, his thoughts reluctantly lingered on the cruel fact that Sally could not conceive. Yet even though the idea of never being a father cut him deep, he felt hugely compensated by the fact that he had a wife in a million. And besides, a man can never have everything, or there would be nothing left to yearn for.

He quickly shifted his thoughts to his mates down at the pub. Should he meet up with them? Or should he not?

He thought about all the work waiting to be done. There was a dripping tap in the kitchen, and last night he had heard one of the roof slates rattling in the breeze. That was another thing that needed fixing. Then there was the curtain rail in the back bedroom.

Oh, yes! The curtain rail.

He thought about the way Sally had grimaced when he mentioned going down the pub.

He knew she suspected the barmaid had her eye on him, even though she also knew he would never look at another woman. And why should he, when he already had the best woman in the world by his side?

Sighing, he shook his head, 'Fancy Sal thinking I would ever entertain that barmaid!' Still, even if he wasn't interested, it was still flattering to know a pretty woman had an eye for him.

Getting out of the chair, he thought he'd better fix that curtain rail, before going to the pub.

Going through the hallway to collect the shed key from the kitchen, he paused by the wall mirror to flex his muscles. 'You've still got it, my boy!' He smiled. 'Oh, yes! You've still got it!'

A few minutes later, he went out of the back door and down the garden to his little tool shed. Glancing around at the many shelves, overflowing with bric-a-brac, he groaned. One of these weekends he'd have to spend a few hours staightening all this lot out. Jeez! It was like a junk shop.

He raked the shelves with his eyes. Some of the stuff had been here since they'd moved in.

He searched the bottom shelf for the big black toolbox, but it was nowhere to be found. Then he looked up and spotted it on the top shelf, sitting awkwardly beside an old packing case. He decided he could just reach it without fetching the ladder from the garage.

Finding it more difficult than he'd first thought, he tugged harder at the toolbox. 'Come on, dammit!' Something appeared to be holding it back.

One more huge tug and he had it almost free, but when he finally slid the toolbox out, the packing case tumbled out with it.

Cursing, he collected the case to replace it on the top shelf, but the lid flapped open, revealing a number of items from the time before he was married.

Intrigued, he followed his instinct to have a little rummage in the old case, which in the event, turned out to be greatly nostalgic. There was a multitude of memorabilia from his past, and some precious items he had thought were gone for ever.

There was his old fishing rod; his brown football boots, all cracked and dirty, and stiff as planks after years of being in the damp. There was a pack of cards and a set of darts from the carefree days when he was a young man, with a young man's wayward habits.

It was like his early life was unfolding right before his eyes.

With most of the contents now laid out on top of a wooden box, he dug deeper. He drew out an old football, now sagging and past use.

A moment later, his fingers gripped what felt like a book.

As he drew it out, he did not instantly recognise what it was. At first glance, it looked to be a brown leather ledger. It was only when he blew away the dust that he realised it was an old photograph album.

The photographs were mostly damaged, with bent corners and cracks; also the damp had badly marred the initial one or two.

There was a lovely photograph of his parents, the

original of which was framed and standing proud on the sideboard inside the house.

Alongside that photograph was the last photo of his mother, before she passed on.

When Mick's father was killed in an explosion at work, his mother lost the will to live. After a difficult year, she too was gone. People understood that her grief was too hard for her to bear, especially as the two of them had been inseparable since their schooldays, and were absolutely devoted to each other.

Mick had the smaller print of his mother's photograph in his wallet, but now, when he held the original in his hand, he felt too emotional for words.

Quickly, he began flicking through the album, eager to put it safely away.

As he folded it shut, he saw the corner of what appeared to be a torn photograph, jutting out from between the top of two pages stuck together.

Curious, he eased the photograph out, and was riveted by what he saw.

The photograph was partly damaged at the corners, but he instantly recognised it, and it took him back to the days when he was in his twenties.

The photo was of himself, and a girl. Mick remembered her vividly: small-built, with dainty features and wild, curly hair. She had the softest eyes, and a pretty smile, like sunshine on a cloudy day.

He was shocked. 'Good grief!' He laughed out loud. 'Peggy Farraday . . . the girl I nearly married!'

Mesmerised, he took the photograph over to the door, all the better to see it. Leaning against the doorjamb, he cast his eyes over the girl in the picture. *Southend!* He remembered it like it was yesterday. They'd been going together for only a few days and had decided on a day out in Southend, with a couple of friends.

He relived the day in his mind.

It was raining, but they were having so much fun, they didn't want to go home. So, after the other two had gone, he and his girl found a telephone box and rang their parents to tell them they were staying over with their mates, although they'd already gone back, after promising not to say anything.

All they could afford between them was an overnight room at a tatty old boarding house. And all because Mick had spent the best part of his money on a silver locket she'd seen and loved.

He couldn't help but smile at the memory and the way it had turned out, and now he was laughing out loud. He recalled how the curtains were paper-thin, and the springs in the bed creaked and groaned, but they hadn't cared a jot.

Now, the laughter died away and his mood grew serious. He had dated a number of girls, but Peggy had been his first real love.

With his finger he traced her small, pretty face, now looking up at him from the photograph. Up to that night, she hadn't even let him touch her in that certain way, but once they got into bed, she was amazing . . . In fact, when it got to four in the morning, he hadn't given a damn whether he got any sleep or not.'

For a while he sat remembering how it was.

It was strange, though, how Fate took you one way and then the other. He looked down again on Peggy's smiling face. They might have gone on to be regular sweethearts and ended up getting married, but they kind of drifted apart after that weekend.

He tried to recall the exact date. That weekend in Southend . . . *Must have been, what, going on for fourteen years now.*

He took a moment to gaze at the photograph. It wasn't meant to be . . . but if the rumours were right, she'd got herself a good catch – some bloke with his own business. As for Mick, he'd found the loveliest girl . . . name of Sally. And he considered himself to be a very lucky man.

Thinking of Sally put a smile on his face. If Peggy and her man were as happy as he and Sally, she wouldn't go far wrong, he thought.

Quickly now, he folded his old life back into the packing case.

He had no reason not to keep the photograph, so he packed it away with everything else.

He replaced the case on the top shelf, collected his tools and returned to the house, a smile on his face. *Who'd have thought it, eh? A real jolt from the past . . .*

Then he made a start on the curtain rail, keen to please Sally. Anything to make her happy.

It took him all of twenty minutes to fix the curtain rail. Afterwards, he stood back to view his handiwork, thinking he'd earned a pint and a catch-up with his mates. He gave a cheeky little grin. There was nothing like a chat and a laugh with your old mates to make a man feel worthy.

Even as he climbed the stairs to get himself ready, the romance from the past was already gone from his mind.

CHAPTER TEN

Miss Martin listened intently, while the officer explained, 'We've held on to these personal items for too long. They were passed to us by the new tenants of the Carters' former home. We quite overlooked them and have no legal reason to keep them now.'

Miss Martin was curious. 'But I understood the Carter case was not yet closed. I was of the opinion that because there were no witnesses to the event, and also a certain lack of evidence from the parties involved, it was never actually proved that Edward Carter had caused his wife's death. Indeed, according to the newspaper reports, his wife never once claimed that he was responsible for the injuries that killed her. Surely, if he had caused her death, she would have said so, don't you think?'

'It's not for me to say, but your observations are correct. You would be surprised, however, to know that in matters such as these, nothing is ever black and white.

For my part, all I can do is to apologise for the length of time we've retained these personal possessions.'

'Oh, well, at least they're here now, and Adam will be relieved to have some things of his mother's, I'm sure.'

'Of course, and like I say, I only wish they were returned earlier. It's only now, with Peggy Carter laid to her rest, and Edward Carter sentenced, that we thought to return these files and properties. Having said that, and even though he's proven to be a very dangerous and violent man, we're still not fully satisfied.'

'In what way?'

'I'm afraid all I can say is that we discovered certain documents hidden away amongst old papers that we removed from the house. We suspect there has been another breach of the law, which if proven, could lengthen Carter's sentence quite considerably.'

'What kind of documents?'

The officer gave himself a mental warning. He had a weakness for being drawn in too far. 'I'm sorry, but I am not authorised to discuss that.'

'Well, whatever it is, I'm sure I don't need to know. All I'm concerned about is placing young Adam with a good family.'

Miss Martin was slightly miffed that the officer had cut short the conversation, just when it caught her imagination.

Ready to see him away, she stood up. 'I'm sorry, but if there is nothing else, I'm shortly expecting to receive a family, who might be the right one for the boy.'

'Everything personal to Adam is in that box,' he

assured her, producing an official paper, which she duly signed as temporary guardian.

Miss Martin extended her hand. 'Well, thank you for returning these, officer. I do hope that whatever is in here will bring some kind of closure to Adam.'

'Yes, I imagine it will. These items eventually proved to be of small significance to us, but to Adam, they are part of his mother's belongings.'

'So, there's nothing in here that belonged to his father, is there? Only, I'm not sure he—'

The officer sensed her concerns. 'No. In the light of ongoing enquiries, we have duly retained certain items particular to Edward Carter. Which will in the course of time be returned.'

With that, he shook her hand, bade her goodbye, and left.

On leaving the office, he recognised Adam, seated forlornly on the bench by Miss Martin's office. He greeted the boy, who nodded slightly, but seemed to be miles away in his thoughts.

Once outside, the officer stood a moment, thinking of what that young boy had gone through: no home of his own; his mother lying in the churchyard; and his father jailed for a great number of years. Added to which it had transpired that he had only two distant relatives, neither of which had a yearning to take on a troubled young boy. He hoped that by the time Carter was released, the boy would be a full-grown man. If the police successfully managed to uncover his suspected other illegal activities, this seemed highly likely.

~

A moment or so later, Miss Martin came out of her office and ushered Adam inside. 'We've got a while yet before the family arrive,' she informed him excitedly, 'but in the meantime, I have something for you. Sit down, Adam, please. Sit down opposite me.'

When he was sitting, she informed him, 'The gentleman you probably saw leaving just now was from the police.' Concerned when she saw him press nervously back into his chair, she quickly assured him, 'There is nothing wrong, Adam. He just came to return something that belongs to you.'

Adam was surprised. 'Something that belongs . . . to me?'

'Yes, Adam. This box and everything in it belongs to you, Adam. That's why the officer was here. The police have no further use for this, and so he's brought it here for you.'

'Is it my mother's stuff?'

'Possibly, I don't know. It is not for me to pry into your belongings, Adam. But, he did say there are certain items that might belong to you, and maybe some of your mother's things . . . I have no idea. That's for you to discover.'

Choking back tears, he asked brokenly, 'Can I see it, please, Miss Martin?'

'But of course!' She got out of her seat and gently inched the box forwards until it was within reach. 'Would you like me to leave you alone for a while?'

Adam shook his head.

'So, you want me to stay here, with you?'

'Yes, please.'

'Very well.'

She sat down with a bump. 'Remember, these belong to you, Adam. They're yours to keep.' She added wisely, 'You understand, it may not be good for you to keep it all in the dormitory, but I have a big enough safe here, in this office. I can keep anything precious here, locked away, and of course you may ask to see it any time.'

'Thank you, Miss Martin.' His fingers played on the box lid. 'Can I open it now?'

'But of course! That's why I called you in.'

She asked again just to be sure, 'Are you certain you wouldn't prefer to open the box without me here?'

'No, miss. I'd like you to stay with me . . . please?'

'Of course.'

A moment later, she watched as he tore back the sealing tape and opened the lid.

One by one, he removed the items. There was a diary, beautifully written, seemingly in the delicate, sweeping hand of his mother. Thinking it might be too personal, he put that aside for the moment.

There was his father's old bunch of keys, which he recognised but did not want to touch. Gingerly sweeping them into a corner of the box, he continued to dig down.

He found all manner of things he had never seen before: a small rag doll with one eye; a tray of jewellery, which he tenderly put aside while he continued to empty the box. Then there were a number of items from his own bedroom: a pile of *Beano* comics; his school books; and a tied-up roll of posters.

There were other miscellaneous items, some of which he had occasionally seen and others he had never seen before, such as a pile of documents and letters, neatly rolled and labelled.

Alongside these were his mother's handbag and purse containing little of any significance.

When the box was emptied and all items laid across the desk, Adam began to cry . . . softly at first. Then he was shaking, seared with pain.

He realised how the remains of his old life and that of his mother were now reduced to empty, useless things that only served to hurt him all the more.

Then he felt Miss Martin's chubby arms about him, and he nestled into them. For a while neither of them spoke. Until Adam told her, 'Can you please lock it away?'

'Yes, Adam. I can do that for you. But is there nothing at all that you might like to keep in your own locker?'

He shook his head.

'But you haven't even looked at your mother's jewellery. Maybe you could take one very small thing?'

She understood his pain, but sometimes having some small thing that had been close to the one you love and miss, did actually help. Sadly, she reflected, she knew that more than most, as her fingers now went to the little trinket around her neck.

'I'm sure your mother wouldn't mind. What do you think, Adam?'

It seemed an age before he looked at her with

brimming eyes. It was an even longer age before he told her shakily, 'Yes, please.'

Taking a long, easy sigh, she patted him on the back and smiled. 'I'm glad,' she said, hugging him tight. 'Right! So let's take a look at the tray of jewellery, shall we? And see if anything appeals to you.'

She watched while Adam gently trawled through his mother's precious items. She could see how difficult it was for him, but she also knew it would not be right for her to take charge. This was Adam's moment. It was crucial that he and he alone should complete what must be a very traumatic ordeal for him.

She stayed by his side, occasionally encouraging him, as he lifted one item after another, until finally, he was left with the prettiest silver locket on a chain.

'Mum used to wear this all the time,' he said proudly. 'Father didn't like it. He wanted her to always wear the things he had bought her. Most times she did, because he would get angry if she didn't. But whenever she took me out, she always wore this locket.'

Miss Martin understood. 'It obviously meant a lot to her. Maybe her parents bought it for her, did they?'

Adam tried to remember what his mother had told him. 'No. It wasn't her parents. It was a friend. That's right . . . She said a really good friend bought it for her when they were young. She said it was two days before her birthday. She and some other friends had gone to Southend, and that's when she was given it as a present. She said it was a secret, hers and mine, and that I must never tell Father.

'One time I heard him ask her where she had got

such a cheap thing from, and she told him that she had bought it for herself, because she thought it was pretty.' Adam remembered the conversation he had overheard. 'Father told her she was never to wear it when they went out together, because he did not want people to see her wearing such a cheap and nasty thing, and he certainly did not want his friends to think he could not afford to buy his wife decent jewellery.'

Miss Martin was beginning to grow curious. It was an intriguing story.

'I see. And so, after that whenever she went out with your father, she never wore it, is that the way it was?'

'Yes, I think so.'

'And you think this locket meant a great deal to her, don't you?'

'Oh, it did, yes! She told me it was very special, and she would never get rid of it, whatever Father said.'

'Well, there you go then, Adam. It was obviously a very special present . . . from a very special friend.' She wondered about Peggy Carter and, being a woman, she understood why Adam's mother might cherish that pretty silver locket, though her own romantic past was long gone now.

Adam went on, 'Mum never told me who her friend was, but I think it was a lovely present.'

'And now, it's in your safekeeping. And I think you made a very good choice to keep with you, Adam.'

Adam's tears had subsided and now he smiled up at her. 'Thank you. Miss Martin, would you like to hold the locket?'

'Oh, yes, please. I really would like that, Adam. Thank you.'

When he now raised the silver locket, she held out her hand while he carefully folded it across her chubby fingers.

Turning it this way and that, she took a moment to examine it. Noting the small heart etched into the deep, graceful surface and the raised flowers within, she was impressed by the complexity of craftmanship. 'Your father was very wrong to call this "cheap and nasty". It's incredibly pretty. I can certainly see why your mother might have appreciated it.'

She was convinced that it was a lover's gift and she continued to turn it around, greatly impressed by its simple beauty; so strong, yet so delicate.

She was just about to return it to Adam, when something caught her eye. 'I can't be sure,' she said, 'but I think it opens. Did you know that, Adam?'

'No.' Adam was surprised. 'I've never seen my mum open it.'

Miss Martin showed him. 'Look!' She raised it up to him. 'Can you see that? I might be wrong, and it could be just a natural swelling within the etching, but it does look like a sort of little catch, don't you think, Adam?' She now handed it to him. 'Just there . . . see?' She brought his attention to the rim of the locket and the minutely raised area that was skilfully built into the pattern. 'That's the sign of good workmanship, if I'm any judge at all.'

In fact, the pattern and the catch itself were so cleverly integrated that if she had not turned it over at just the right angle, she would probably have missed seeing the catch.

Excited, Adam tried to move the tiny catch one side and then the other, but it was difficult. 'Do you think there's anything in there?' he asked, wide-eyed.

Miss Martin had seen these lockets before. 'In Victorian times, people would hide a lock of hair in this kind of locket, to remember a loved one, but I'm sure that isn't the case here. And if your mother did put something in there, she obviously didn't want anyone to find it. So, maybe you should let sleeping dogs lie, so to speak.'

Adam had not thought of that. 'What, you think she put something in there to hide it from my father? Is that what you mean?'

'Well, I don't know, and neither do you. But of course the locket is yours now, and it's you who must make the decision to open it or to leave it as your mother left it, well and truly closed.'

Adam was at a loss. 'Maybe there's nothing in it anyway.'

'Yes, that could be very true. As for finding out, I must not persuade you one way or the other. Besides, from the way the catch seems to be stuck hard, it could well be that the locket has never been opened.'

Adam, however, was of a different mind. 'If it has not been opened, then there won't be anything inside, so it won't matter if I look, will it?'

'Well, yes, that's very true.'

'But, if Mum did hide something there, it was so my father could never find it, though I don't think she would mind me looking inside.' Nevertheless, he was concerned. 'But if there is something hidden inside, why did she not show me? She knows I never would have told.'

'Well, of course you wouldn't. Nice people would never tell other people's secrets.'

Adam was in a quandary. 'I don't know what to do now.'

He wanted so much to believe that his mum had been clever enough to outwit his father. That would be just wonderful! But was it too prying to open the locket? What if his mum never wanted him to see what was in there?

'Maybe I should think about it some more,' he suggested.

'Yes, I believe that to be a very good idea. Now then, what shall we do with it while you're thinking?' Miss Martin was relieved at his sensible decision. 'Shall we lock it up now, or do you want to keep it with you?'

'Can I really keep it with me?'

'Of course, but it would not be wise to show it around.'

'I won't do that. I'll keep it safe next to me. I'll wear it under my shirt and when we do PE I'll hide it in my mattress.'

Miss Martin smiled. She had just learned a tiny bit of useful information. 'Would you like me to take care of the other items?'

'Yes, please.'

'Then consider it done.'

At that moment a knock came on the door, followed

by the flustered Mrs Baker, Miss Martin's assistant. 'Mrs Dexter just called.' She explained. 'They apologise profusely. The babysitter let them down, but they've managed to solve the problem, and they hope to be here in about half an hour, if that suits us?'

'Oh, my word, yes, of course. As a matter of fact, it would suit me better. I quite got carried away with other matters and didn't realise the time. Yes, of course. Tell Mr and Mrs Dexter that we're looking forward to receiving them.'

With Mrs Baker gone, Miss Martin smiled down on Adam. 'As you know, it's unusual for me to allow private things of any value to be kept with the child concerned, but I believe you are a sensible boy, that you will be discreet, and inform me if there's a problem.'

'I will be careful. I would never do anything to lose my mother's locket.'

'Nevertheless, if you find yourself growing anxious about keeping the locket safe, you must come and see me. Is that understood, Adam?'

'Yes, miss.'

'Now then, you heard what Mrs Baker said. Half an hour. That should give you time enough to prepare yourself. Off you go then.'

When he hesitated, she asked him gently, 'What is it, Adam? Is there something worrying you?'

'No, miss.'

'Then why haven't you gone already?'

'I just wanted to know, if the dog might be with them?'

'Oh! I see.' Her merry smile was infectious. 'Not this

time, I'm afraid. And nor will the children be with them. The first meeting is just you and the parents. Don't get too worried, Adam. If this family proves not to be right for you, then we shall have to look again. You do understand what I'm saying, don't you, Adam?'

'Yes, miss.'

'Good. Now, run along and be quick. You'll be sent for the minute they arrive.'

'Yes, miss.'

She watched him go out the door. *Dear me,* she thought, *if it isn't one thing, it's another.*

A moment later she was hurrying along the corridor to the library.

As always she muttered to herself. 'Half an hour and they'll be here. All I can say is that it's just as well they did lose their babysitter, considering the amount of time I spent with Adam . . . enjoyable, though. Yes indeed. Quite enjoyable.'

The silver locket reminded her of her own lost youth. *These days I feel so old and lonely,* she thought.

She tutted all the way down the corridor, 'I never did find the right man.'

But Adam was never far from her thoughts. 'They say light will always follow the darkness.' She recalled her own father having uttered those words many years ago. '. . . I hope for the boy's sake, that might be true.'

CHAPTER ELEVEN

Liz Dexter sat at the dressing table, her auburn hair swept up in a ponytail, and her slim figure looking fresh and smart in a long-sleeved blue dress.

Her husband, Jim, stood at the far end of the bedroom, gazing across at this woman he loved. 'You look beautiful, sweetheart.'

'Thank you.' She smiled at him through the mirror. 'Flatterer.' Her face lit up at his warm compliment.

She took a moment to sweep her eyes over him. Of medium height, with the slightest paunch, he had a shock of fair hair, twinkly blue eyes and the features of a handsome puppy dog. 'Change your shirt, Jim.'

'What for?' He examined himself in the long wardrobe mirror. 'A white shirt always goes down well with authority.'

'Maybe. But we're hoping the boy takes to us, and, like you say, a white shirt does smack of authority. Change it –' she gave him a mischievous smile – 'or I might be forced to rip it off your back.'

At that, he rushed across the room, and slid his arms round her waist. 'Ooh! That sounds promising. But I'm afraid it will have to wait because we've got only about twenty minutes to get there.'

She groaned. 'Oh, bugger!' Swinging off the stool, she went to the bed and collected her cardigan and handbag. 'I'd better go and make sure Maureen has everything she needs.'

As she ran out the door, she called back, 'Change the shirt, Jim! Wear the blue one.'

As always, Jim did as he was told. 'I'm a poor, henpecked husband!' he yelled down the stairs, but got no response as Liz went skidding into the sitting room.

Softly whistling, he returned to check himself in the mirror. Finally satisfied that he looked smart and approachable in his dark trousers and blue shirt, he patted his hair down. *That's it! Ready for anything*, he thought.

After a week of nail-biting and worrying, the big day had finally arrived, but it had not been without its problems.

Liz had not slept well, having got herself in a tizzy about whether they were doing the right thing. He hoped he had reassured her.

Downstairs, Liz was talking to Maureen, a sixteen-year-old with a bird's-nest of black hair swept up, and a mouth carefully shaped with the brightest of lipsticks. She was the only daughter of their closest neighbour, and she had babysat many times before. 'I'm off to the flicks tonight,' she told Liz. 'Got a new boyfriend.' She made a swooning noise. 'He's not as good-looking as Danny, but he's all right for now. Anyway, Danny will see me out with my new fella, and he'll get jealous; that'll teach him for giving me the old heave-ho.'

'Well, let's hope the same doesn't happen with this new boy.' Today of all days, Liz did not particularly want to hear about Maureen's turbulent love-life.

'Ah, but it won't happen,' Maureen chirped. 'Hopefully, it'll be me giving him the shove. Y'see, I'm not all that fond of him. I'm only going out with him to get Danny all riled up.'

'Ah! You think that might make him come running back, do you?'

'Oh, yeah!' She giggled. 'He's just sulking. Truth is, he fancies me rotten! Oh, and he's just got a full-time job at the garage. They pay really good money. So, when we go out, I won't have to pay for a thing.'

Liz had to smile. 'Honestly, Maureen. You're incorrigible.'

'What does that mean?'

'Never mind. I'll tell you later. For now, I'm counting on you to take good care of the children. As you can see, Harriet's in her cot. She's been fed for now. I've left the feed times on a list, with the other things you might need. You'll find them all in the basket in the kitchen, with a spare dummy, a pile of nappies and such.'

'OK. Thanks.'

'If there's the slightest problem, go and ask your mum. Now, have I forgotten anything? Do you have any questions?'

'Nope! I've done this job before, and anyway, you told me everything I need to know last night. Don't worry, I've watched the children before and I'm good with them, you know that, Mrs Dexter. I'll feed Buster if you're late back, too, and let him out if he whines to go.'

'Yes, I do know, but this time you've got Alice to look after as well, which is why I'm insisting that you will fetch your mum if need be.'

'I promise.'

'Good. Oh, and do keep an eye on Alice. Let her sleep, though. She needs it after her bad night. I kept her at home today because she's got the sniffles. She was fast asleep just now when I went in. I had a word with her earlier, so I won't disturb her now. I've explained everything to her, so she won't be any trouble.'

'Naw, she never is. Alice and me, we get on just fine. If she comes down and wants to play a game, I've brought some with me – snakes and ladders and all that.'

'That's good thinking, Maureen. There are more games in her room if you need them.'

Jim was getting anxious. 'Come on, Liz.' He burst into the room. 'I've just checked on Alice, and she's still fast asleep. Anyway, Maureen knows the ropes by now. We'd better leave now or we'll be even later.'

He gave Buster an absent-minded pat on the head as he left and Buster retreated under the kitchen table.

~

As they climbed into the car, Liz still had a niggling doubt about their errand today. 'Jim?'

'Yes, love?' Jim was taking extra care as he pulled out onto the road. 'What's up?'

'I can't help feeling just a bit guilty.'

'Why's that?'

'Well, you know, there are so many people out there who can never have babies of their own. We've already got two beautiful children, and now we're about to offer a home to this boy Adam. It does seem a bit greedy, when he might be perfect for any one of those childless people.'

Jim had suspected for some time that Liz was not altogether sure about the fostering. 'Are you saying we should go back, ring Miss Martin and tell her we've changed our minds about having Adam?'

Liz was horrified. 'No! I'm not sayng that. Not at all.'

'Then what *are* you saying?'

Liz was silent for a moment, searching for the right words. 'I'm just asking, do you think we're being selfish fostering this boy? Won't we be depriving another family, who can never have children of their own?'

Jim was not surprised by the question. He had anticipated something like this because of Liz's quiet mood over the past few days.

He took a time before answering. 'So instead of having Adam, you would rather we have another child of our own. Is that what you're thinking?'

'Something like that, yes. And don't tell me you haven't thought of it as well?'

'Yes, I might have given it a passing thought, but

that's all. Because I don't want us to take the risk of you being pregnant again. I know what could happen – what has a seventy per cent chance of happening – and I can't take the risk. I thought you agreed.'

'I thought I did as well. But maybe we should have discussed it further, before raising this poor boy's hopes.'

'No! Haven't we already discussed it until we're blue in the face, and it always comes out the same?'

'What's that supposed to mean?'

'Well, tell me this: would you still want to get pregnant, with such a high chance that our two beautiful children could be left without a mother?'

'It would break my heart to think of leaving them.'

'Yes, and it would break mine too.'

Flicking the indicator, Jim drew the car to the kerb and parked. Then he took hold of Liz's hand to tell her gently, 'Listen to me, sweetheart. I know how hard it is, but I thought we had already faced the situation and come to a joint decision. I love our two girls, and I still have room in my heart for a third child. I honestly don't mind whether it's a boy or a girl, but I don't want a third child if it means losing you.'

He leaned over and kissed her. 'Do you think I don't know just how difficult it is for you? You're a wonderful wife . . . a natural mother. But you seem to have forgotten what the doctor said. He sat us both down and he told us that after the dangerous and traumatic time you had through both births, a third one might well be too much of a risk.'

'I know that. But a doctor can be wrong. It has been known.'

'No, Liz! For heaven's sake, listen to yourself! We almost lost both you and Harriet. Your heart actually stopped! You were in hospital for weeks. Even after you were eventually allowed home, it took you as long again to recover. Have you forgotten all of that?'

Liz had not forgotten the awful nightmare, not for a single minute. 'I just thought that maybe, with a third child, they would monitor me more. That's all,' she said quietly.

'Oh, I see.' Jim made a desperate effort to remain calm, although he was deeply angry at what she was saying. 'So, let me get this straight. You would like us to try for another child. And, regardless of what the doctor said, you think you know better. You think that if they monitor you throughout the pregnancy – if they keep you in for possibly a third or half of the pregnancy – everything will be just fine.'

'But it might be.'

'And the chances are it might not. And what about your two daughters? What if you were kept in hospital in order to "monitor" you? Would you really want them to be without their mother . . . possibly for months? I would take your place with the girls . . . possibly even lose my job. And every minute of every day I would wonder if you were ever coming home to us again.'

Tearful, knowing that he was right, Liz felt ashamed. 'I'm sorry. It's just that—'

'I know it's difficult, sweetheart. But, let's look at this another way. There's a young boy out there who's been through a nightmare. They say he's lost everything: his home, and his family. He has nothing and no one. They've told us what happened to him, and now they're trying to find him a family, some people who might build his belief in humanity again. Some people who might show him that the world is not the ugly, cruel place he has seen so far.' He grew emotional. 'Oh, Liz! We could give this boy so much. And who knows, maybe he'll do the same for us. But we won't do this unless you're happy about it. As for me, I'm ready to show him kindness and love as a substitute father. But before we go on, you have to be sure.'

'You're such a good man.' Liz slid over in her seat and kissed him soundly on the face. 'Jim Dexter, you are the kindest, most sensible man I've ever known. And I love you.'

Jim kissed her back. 'Are you nervous?'

'A bit. But I feel more content about the whole thing now.'

'Good. Now hang on. We're late already!'

Reassured, he pulled back out onto the road and roared away.

~

After seeing them off, Maureen set about her duties.

First, she ran up the stairs to peep in on Alice, who was still curled up in bed, sleeping soundly.

Tenderly, she took hold of the corner of her blanket and drew it up to her chin. 'That's a good girl,' she whispered. 'You sleep, while I see to the baby.'

Running downstairs, she crossed to the cot, where Harriet was happily sucking her thumb. 'It's not your feed time yet.' Maureen collected her from the cot. 'Ooh! You're a fat little lump and no mistake.'

Going over to the sideboard, she switched on the radio, and tuned it to her favourite music, which immediately filled the room. Soon she was jigging and jiving and thoroughly enjoying herself. Even the baby was smiling.

'Like it, do you?' Maureen jiggled Harriet up and down as they went round the room, and the baby laughed out loud. 'You and me, we're a right couple of swingers, aren't we, eh?'

Maureen was never happier than when she was listening to music and dancing the night away. There were all manner of new groups emerging, and she loved the new, exciting sounds that filled the clubs and pubs.

When the song ended, she placed the baby in her cot, dismayed to see that she'd been sick on her bib. 'Too much for you, was it?' She cleaned her up and set about checking her nappy. 'Good! Nice and clean . . . One thing I hate is changing nappies . . . ugh!'

'Maureen?' Alice, woken by the music, had made her way downstairs. 'Where's Mum?'

Small-built, Alice was blessed with big brown eyes and thick, straight brown hair. Normally, she was as sweet-natured as she was pretty, but for some reason she now appeared to be unsettled.

'Mum and Dad have gone out. Mum said you didn't sleep very well last night. Maybe you might be better off going back to bed . . . get some more sleep before Mummy and Daddy come home.'

'I don't want to go back to bed. I want to stay here with you.'

'OK. If that's what you want, that's fine by me.' Maureen could not recall Alice being so irritable.

She brought Alice right into the room. 'I bet you're hungry, aren't you? I'll make you something to eat. I'm sure your mummy's cupboards are full as always, so what do you want?'

'I want my mum.'

'I already told you, she and Daddy have gone out. They'll be back soon, though.'

'Mummy told me about the boy.'

'Oh, did she? Well, there you are then. So, you've no need to worry, have you?'

Maureen had recently overheard her own mother and Liz Dexter discussing the idea of the Dexters' fostering a child. When she later quizzed her mother, she was told never to eavesdrop on other people's conversations, and that she was to forget what she'd overheard. She had effectively put it out of her mind until just now, when Alice mentioned 'the boy'.

Heeding her mother's warning, she changed the subject to take Alice's mind off the idea of 'the boy'. 'I bet you're hungry, aren't you? What if I get you some cereal, or a glass of orange squash and a slice of toast?'

'I don't want anything to eat!' Running across the room, Alice threw herself on the chair beside the baby's cot, where she sat, very quiet and seemingly tearful.

'What's wrong, Alice?' Concerned, Maureen came and kneeled on the carpet beside her.

'Nothing.' Alice turned away.

Maureen persisted. 'There must be something wrong. You've come downstairs in a funny old mood. Why is that? Has something upset you? Or is it just that you're still tired?'

Alice shook her head, but gave no other reply.

Maureen was not so easily put off. 'So, do you want to talk about it?'

'No.'

'I'm a good listener.'

Alice shook her head a second time.

'OK. No more questions then.'

Maureen started on her way to the kitchen. 'I'm really thirsty, though. I'll make us both orange squash. If you don't want it, I expect I'll be thirsty enough to drink the both of them.'

Busying herself in the kitchen, she made two orange squashes and carried them back into the other room. 'Here we are.'

There was no sign of Alice.

Worried, Maureen put the drinks down; and searched around, but Alice was nowhere to be seen. There was just Harriet in the cot, happily kicking her legs and gurgling.

Maureen ran to the window and looked out. She called her name, but there was no sight or sound of Alice.

She ran into the hallway. 'Alice, are you upstairs?'

No answer.

She ran up the stairs two at a time, and found Alice in her bed.

'Why didn't you answer me?' Maureen tried not to sound harsh. 'You had me really worried. Did you not hear me calling?'

'You told me to go back to bed,' Alice answered casually.

'No, Alice! I didn't actually say you had to go back to bed. I just suggested it, because I thought you might still be tired.'

'I am.'

'All right. I'll leave you for a while. Is there anything you want?'

'No, thank you.'

After settling Alice between the bedclothes, Maureen returned to keep an eye on Harriet. She also drank the two orange squashes – waste not, want not – then carried the empty glass and beaker into the kitchen, all the time wondering what was wrong with Alice. Buster was now asleep under the table.

Returning to check on Harriet again, she heard movement from upstairs. Going into the hallway she called out, 'Alice, are you all right?'

'Yes, thank you.'

'You will shout me if you need anything, won't you?'

'Yes.'

'Just try and get some more sleep. I'll let you know as soon as your parents get back. OK?'

'Yes, OK.'

Maureen wandered back to talk to Harriet. 'Hmm! So, Alice knows about the boy, eh?' She tickled the child under the chin. 'You don't know yet, though . . . you're too young to know what's going on, anyway.'

She thought about Alice. 'I'm glad her mum told her they might foster a little boy, because it's not fair when your parents keep secrets and you only find out about them after something happens,' she told Harriet.

She wondered how Alice really felt about having a brother. 'I think it would be nice for you and Alice if they fostered a boy, because brothers look after you. And they don't steal your make-up and clothes like my sister Jan does.' She rolled her eyes. 'She is such a nuisance. I have to hide everything from her!'

Glancing into the cot, she noticed that Harriet was now asleep. 'Oh, I see, don't want to talk to me, eh? You've got your belly full and a nice clean nappy on, so now it's snooze-time, is it?'

Smiling, she went and rummaged in the kitchen drawer, looking for magazines. She found just the one. Bursting with fashion items and kinds of make-up, it was just what she needed.

Curling up in the front room with the magazine stretched out on the arm of the chair, she was soon lost in the many, colourful pages.

Upstairs, Alice sat at the window, silently crying. With her nose pressed against the windowpane she looked up and down the street, watching for the car to bring home her parents. 'Why do you need a boy when you've got me and Harriet?' she whispered.

She went back to lie on the bed. She lay there for what seemed an age, her sorry gaze fixed on the precious rag dolly that her daddy won for her at a fair two years ago.

Taking the doll into her embrace, she cuddled and kissed it. 'We don't need a boy, do we? We just need Mummy and Daddy, and me and Harriet.'

For a while, she hugged the doll tight and softly cried, her tears dampening the doll's raggedy face. She then returned to the bed, where she sat thinking. She was angry, and for the first time in her short life, she felt incredibly lonely.

After a time, loneliness became rejection, and her anger turned to rage. Throwing the doll across the room, she got from the bed and ran across to the window again. 'Don't bring him home. We don't want him here,' she muttered angrily.

A moment later, she collected the rag doll from the carpet and hugged it to her chest. 'We're all right, aren't we, Dolly? Just you and me and Harriet.'

Very gently at first, she painstakingly untied the two bows that tied the doll's plaits. That done, she undid the two thick plaits and, one at a time, she calmly and systematically tore out each hair from the scalp, until there was not a hair left on the doll's head.

That done, she bunched the hair up tight, screwed it round and round until her hands were red-sore, then she dropped the ravished hair into the waste basket.

She hid the waste basket behind her desk and went downstairs. She found Maureen in the front room, intently reading Mummy's magazine. 'I'm hungry now, Maureen,' she said. 'Can I please have something to eat?'

A few minutes later, she was enjoying the beans on

toast that Maureen had made for her, then the two of them sat on the sofa, looking through the magazine together, and choosing the things they would buy if they had the money.

Once or twice, Alice looked towards the hallway door and secretly smiled.

'Maureen?'

'Yes?' Maureen looked up from the pages.

'Can we play match the cards?'

'Yeah, course we can, but no cheating like you did last time, you little monster!'

'I won't cheat . . . honestly,' Alice promised.

But she would if she had to.

~

Adam was nervous.

Having been told to wait in the library, he heard Mrs Baker's excited voice calling out, 'They're here, Miss Martin!' She had seen the car drawing up outside and recognised the driver as Mr Dexter.

'Hurry! Go and greet them, quickly!' Miss Martin tried to suppress her excitement.

While Mrs Baker went one way, Miss Martin went the other, her thick-heeled shoes echoing on the wood-block floor as she hurried to get Adam.

'Quickly, Adam. They're here.'

With great speed, she ushered Adam along the corridor and into her office. 'Don't be nervous,' she told him, fiddling with the neck of his clean white shirt. 'They're just ordinary people, like you and me.'

Adam tried his hardest not to be nervous, but he was excited at the same time. He did as he was told and sat in the straight-backed chair by her desk. 'When they come in, remember to stand up, Adam. Remember to greet them politely.'

Preparing herself for the Dexters, she stood smartly behind her desk; she fussed wth her hair and constantly wiped imaginary fluff from the skirt of her dress.

In truth, she was every bit as nervous as Adam. She so wanted him to be with a good family, and from what she had learned about them, she was satisfied that the Dexters were fine, God-fearing people, with room in their hearts to take in a troubled boy like Adam.

As they walked down the long corridor to Miss Martin's office, Liz and Jim Dexter were somewhat apprehensive.

Although they had discussed the boy with the authorities, and they had met and discussed the matter in great depth with Miss Martin, this introduction to Adam himself was all-important. Everything was resting on it. If Adam was nervous, they were even more so.

As they walked in the door, Adam nervously appraised them. He saw two well-dressed, smiling people. Thinking how much younger they were than he'd expected, he was made easier by the friendly manner in which they greeted him.

Adam took an instant liking to them but, for some inexplicable reason, he was especially drawn to the woman. She had the same soft smile as his darling mother, though there the similarity ended, because where his mother was short and small of bone, this woman was taller and more broad-shouldered. Also, her hair was straight and brown, unlike his mother's wild, curly hair.

Even so, Adam thought she had that same air of graciousness, and when she smiled, it made him feel accepted. He began to relax.

Mr Dexter seemed like a friendly man, who made Adam think he might be a good dad, and friend; something his own father had never been.

Miss Martin introduced them to each other. 'This is Adam,' she announced proudly. 'You've already been made aware of his story and background, and our intention to place him with a good family. This meeting is for you to get to know each other, and for me to answer any questions or concerns that might arise on either side. Before we go any further, I wonder if you might want to be left alone with Adam in order for the three of you to get to know each other better, without myself or Mrs Baker here.'

She looked from one to the other, speaking to the Dexters first. 'Would that help you in any way?'

They thought it would, and Jim Dexter said so.

Liz, however, could see how nervous Adam seemed, constantly fidgeting, and dropping his gaze to the carpet. 'But how does Adam feel about being left alone with us just now?'

From the first moment when she and Jim walked into the room, her gaze was drawn to Adam, this solitary and frightened boy, who needed a family to love him. Right there and then he had touched her heart and banished any doubts she had.

'Well, Adam?' Miss Martin asked. 'Would you like to spend a few minutes getting to know Mr and Mrs Dexter. I'm sure you must have questions that only they can answer.'

Adam took a moment to turn the idea over in his mind. He was nervous and afraid they might not like him. And that would be a shame because he so wanted to be part of a family, and they seemed like kind and decent people.

'Well, Adam? There's nothing to worry about. I won't be far away, and it's only for a few minutes, ten at the most.'

It was the encouraging smile and slight nod of the head from Liz Dexter, that prompted Adam. 'Yes, please, Miss Martin. I would like that.'

'Excellent!'

Both Miss Martin and her treasured assistant departed the office and left them alone. 'Ten minutes,' Miss Martin reminded them. 'Then I'll be back to see how you got on together.'

When the door closed behind her, Jim was the first to speak. 'Adam, for what it's worth – and you don't have to do it if you don't want – but I think it might be best if we don't just ask each other questions. Instead, what if Liz and I tell you all about who we are, what we do, and why we thought you might be the one to come home and live with us, as a son? After that – and only if you want to – you can tell us about yourself. Tell us whatever you feel we need to know. After that, we can ask each other questions. So, Adam, is that all right with you?'

Adam nodded. He liked that idea.

Liz was the first to speak. Without going into details, she told him how she and Jim had always wanted a third child but it was not advisable because her health had suffered greatly when giving birth to her two babies.

She described the baby, Harriet, and her other daughter, Alice, and assured Adam that they would love him as a big brother.

When it was his turn, Jim explained how much they both loved their two children, and that he would be cherished in the same way.

'There's enough room in the house, and enough love in our hearts, to make another child feel as though he belonged. Our preference for a boy is simply because we already have two daughters. Today is the culmination of many meetings that we've already had with the relevant authorities, so we do know a little about you and your background, Adam, and it's only made us want you all the more.'

Soon, it was time for Adam to tell them something about himself. There was much he kept back because he was not ready to discuss some of the really shocking things that had happened.

He told them that his father was a bad man, and that his mother was the kindest and loveliest mother ever, and that he missed her terribly.

He said he thought Mr and Mrs Dexter were kind people and that he would like it very much if they decided to make him part of their family, because he had never had a brother or a sister.

There was one, very important thing that Adam

241

thought could swing his decision either way. 'My only friend is called Phil, and I would be unhappy if I never saw him again.'

Liz was interested. 'Oh, but I'm sure if we take you into the family, and if you want to stay, then your friend Phil can visit . . . if his parents don't mind.'

'Oh, no!' Adam was taken aback at her remark. 'Oh, no! He's not a boy. He's an old man who drives the school bus. He's my very best friend, and Miss Martin lets me go out with him and Polly to the park, and sometimes we go to the churchyard, where I take my mum flowers.'

Jim was a bit taken aback to learn Adam's friend was an elderly man. 'Of course, if you decide that we're the family for you, then we'll need to meet up with your friend.'

Adam's passion about his friendship with Phil, and the taking of flowers to the churchyard had really touched Liz's heart. 'I'm sure we can work something out about your friend,' she said. 'First, though, you need to decide whether or not you would like to be part of our family. And we must do the same.'

Jim tried to reassure him. 'You'll need time to think, Adam. No one is expecting you to decide here and now.'

Almost before Jim had finished speaking, Miss Martin tapped on the door and entered immediately. 'All done, are we?' She had a good feeling about this particular family.

Jim had a question. 'Adam has been telling us about his friendship with Phil. Could you tell us a little about him, please?'

'Of course. Phil has been close to Adam from the first day he was brought here, and even before that. He's a local man. He drives the bus that took Adam to school every day.'

Being careful with her choice of words, she explained, 'Phil was there on the day Adam's father ran off. At the hospital he remained at Adam's side, and he has seen him through all his trials and troubles. He's a stalwart and well-respected member of the local community, and still remains a very important part of Adam's life. In fact, we actually relaxed a certain rule so Phil might accompany Adam whenever he takes flowers to his mother.' She finished with a bright, proud smile to Adam. 'In fact, Phil is more like Adam's granddad than just a friend.'

Both Jim and Liz were impressed.

Liz had no hesitation in telling Adam, 'It's been an absolute pleasure meeting you, Adam. The first thing for us to do is to agree on the next step, I think.' She turned to Miss Martin. 'What happens now?'

'Well, I believe you were informed by the office that the next step is for Adam to have a trial visit to your home, but first, now that you've met Adam, and he's had the opportunity to talk with you both, you and your husband need to discuss it further, between yourselves. This is a very important decision for all three of you. When you're ready for the next step, let me know, and whichever way you decide, I shall act accordingly.'

Liz glanced at her husband and smiled. 'I think Jim and I have already decided.'

Miss Martin was pleased. 'Even so,' she said, 'in something as important as Adam's future and your own peace of mind, you must have space to reflect. I cannot go ahead with arrangements until you've had time to think and discuss it, away from here. Away from Adam.'

She had seen far too many quick decisions, only for them to be overturned later. After what he had already experienced, she had no intention of putting Adam through further trauma.

CHAPTER TWELVE

BEDFORD CENTRE WAS relatively quiet for a Friday, as was the Woolworths store. 'Friday at last!' Sally slunk down into the passenger seat of Anne's car.

Sally and Anne were on their way to work. 'Honestly, Anne, if you'd been just five minutes late picking me up from home, I reckon I'd have gone back to bed.' As though to make her point she gave a long, lazy yawn.

'I know what you mean,' Anne smiled as Sally yawned again. 'I'd much rather be run off my feet than waiting for customers to come to the counter. It just makes the day seem twice as long.'

Sally hunched herself up in the seat, 'Anne?'

'Yes?'

'Are you sleeping better at night?'

'Sort of.'

'And what does that mean?'

Anne shrugged. 'Just that . . . I don't wake up quite as often, that's all.'

'You promised me and Mick that you'd tell us if you were not all right.'

'But I am.'

'It doesn't sound like it to me.'

'Well, if I'm honest I do sometimes wake up at the slightest sound, but I'm getting better. Really I am.'

Sally was not totally convinced. 'If you want me to come and stay with you again, I will. You do know that, don't you?'

She had missed Mick terribly last time, even though he'd come over most evenings to keep them company. Despite this, she would stay with Anne if need be.

Anne graciously refused her offer. 'Thanks all the same, Sal. I do appreciate your concern, but I must learn to fend on my own. Like you said, he can't hurt me from where he is.'

'That's what you need to keep in mind, Anne.' It had been a while now, since Sally had stayed at Anne's house. Only when she thought Anne was confident enough to be on her own did she move back with Mick.

'I really don't know what I'd have done without you, Sal.' Though she would not admit it, Anne still had her bad moments. Sometimes, she was afraid to go into the back garden, even in daylight. And even though she had locked the back gate securely, she still wedged all manner of things against it – wooden garden chairs and even the dustbin – anything to make a noise and alert her if anyone tried to get into the garden.

She was afraid to leave the curtains open once the night closed in. Even now, she did not feel safe upstairs, fearing that if Carter somehow got to her, she would have no way of escaping. She had slept downstairs for a week or so after Sally had first gone home.

Fully dressed, she had slept lightly on the sofa, with a torch beside her, the door secured by the weight of an armchair, and the line from the telephone fed under the door from the hallway, with the phone itself sitting on the pillow beside her.

Nighttime or daylight, and even with the knowledge that he was locked away, Edward Carter still had a hold over her.

She was suddenly startled from her thoughts when Sally said, 'All right, but don't forget, if you change your mind the offer is still there. I've discussed it with Mick, and he's OK with me coming to stay the odd week now and then. Just until you feel one hundred per cent safe.'

'Sally, I'm absolutely fine! Having you for a week was really great.' Anne added light-heartedly, 'Apart from your snoring.'

'I do not snore!'

'You do so! When you get going, it's like all hell let loose.'

Sally was silenced for a minute before confiding meekly, 'Mick said when I snore, it's like a runaway train thundering along the tracks.'

Her throwaway remark soon had the two of them roaring with laughter. 'Poor Mick!' Having experienced Sally's snoring at first hand, Anne had sympathy for him.

'Poor Mick nothing!' Sally groaned. 'Without me knowing it, he sometimes wears the same socks for a whole week! When he takes 'em off, they stand up all on their own.'

They were still giggling as they turned into the car park.

In the cloakroom, they hung up their coats and put on their smart white overalls. 'You and Mick are such wonderful friends to me,' Anne admitted. 'I honestly don't know what I'd have done without you both. You've helped me so much. I know you think I don't listen to your good advice, but I do.'

She hadn't been going to say anything about the positive step she had recently taken, but now she thought it only right that Sally should be made aware of it.

'You might be pleased to know that after the good advice you gave me some time ago, I am now seriously trying to get my life in order. I'm feeling stronger now . . . more like my old self. I'm thinking things through and making decisions that I should have dealt with years back. For all the wrong reasons, I've let things slip for too long, but I'm onto it now, and that's all down to you and Mick.'

Sally was thrilled to hear Anne being so positive. 'That's wonderful, but what kind of decisions are we talking about?'

'Oh, you know, things like I might get the house painted inside, change the furniture and such. It might help me to forget he was ever there.'

She realised she was not quite ready to explain just now. 'I've decided to make an effort to live my life and not be afraid to do things. Important things that have been neglected for too long.'

'Such as what?' Sally was intrigued.

'Like I said, all kinds of things.' Anne realised she would have to be careful what she said, or Sally would never leave her be. 'Just to generally . . . well . . . get my life in order.'

'Oh, Anne, I'm so relieved. It seems to me you have a new fighting spirit.' She reached out and patted her on the shoulder. 'Atta girl!'

Changing the subject, Anne hoped to draw Sally away from asking more questions she was not yet ready to answer.

'Are you going to the works dance tomorrow night?'

'Yes, but you're coming as well, aren't you?'

'I might have other plans.'

'Oh, I see!' Sally playfully taunted her. 'Sounds to me like you're hiding something. So, what are you up to?'

'I'm not up to anything. I just don't feel like going to the dance, that's all.'

'Is that because Tony McDonald asked you to go with him?' She gave a little wink. 'I kid you not, Anne, he's the one bloke that every girl here would love to go with.'

'Except for me.'

'But why? I thought you liked him. You seem to get on well enough. I saw you and Tony chatting the other day and you looked really comfortable with him.'

'I'm not saying I don't like him, Sal, because I do. He's polite and caring, and he doesn't force his attention on you, not like that new maintenance bloke. Bad-mannered oaf. He thinks he's God's gift.'

Sally persisted, 'So, if you like Tony, why won't you go to the dance with him?'

'No reason in particular. I just don't plan on going, that's all.'

As Anne closed the subject, Sally caught her by the arm. 'Anne, I very much doubt if he's the sort of man who would force himself on you, if that's what you're worried about.'

'Huh! I wouldn't even be talking to him if I thought he would ever do such a thing, but he has a kind and thoughtful nature, and like I say, I do like him. I'm not going to the dance, because I have other things to do.'

'Well, I think that's a shame, because he really likes you. He did ask you to go with him, didn't he?'

'Yes, but I'm not ready for dating.' The thought of being close to any man made her shiver.

'Oh, Anne, that's such a shame.'

Sally was used to the shutters coming down where Anne was concerned, but for now she decided to leave the subject alone. 'We're still going out to the café for lunch, though, aren't we?'

'Of course. I'm looking forward to it.'

'Good, because I'm tired of canteen food.'

'Me too. Whatever meal you get, they all taste the same.'

Sally laughed. 'You're absolutely right! But don't let Cook hear you say that or she'll have your head on a plate.'

A few minutes later, the two of them walked through the store and took up their respective places: Sally behind the perfume counter, and Anne fronting the bits and bobs counter, where the selection of threads, needles, wool and bric-a-brac made a lively and colourful display.

As always, there was the initial rush of customers, followed by a slight lull, during which the sales women would have a quick gossip amongst themselves. Today they were all excited about the works dance.

Brazen Pauline from hardware had her eye on a partner for the evening. 'I'm hoping to bag a dance or two with our new assistant manager,' she cooed. 'He's single, probably not short of a bob or two, and he's the best-looking bloke I've seen in a long time.' Clicking her tongue, she gave a knowing smile. 'Oh, yeah! He'll do for me!'

Just then, a colleague nudged her in the back. 'Ssh!' He's on his way. We'd best get back to work.'

As he strolled towards them, it was clear that Tony McDonald was indeed a 'good-looking bloke'. With his wayward mop of dark hair, smiling hazel eyes and a slim body, he walked with a lazy ease that showed authority and a certain sensuality.

He strolled over to Sally. 'How's it going this morning, Sally?'

'Not too bad.' Sally described the initial rush of customers. 'Mostly people popping in on their way to work.'

He thanked her and moved on to Anne. 'Good morning, Anne?'

His manner was different from how it was with Sally. His voice was softer. He stood closer, and when he smiled on her, his kind, dark gaze seemed to look into her soul. 'Everything all right, is it?'

'Yes, thank you, we've already had a flurry of customers.' She felt nervous around him, but not like she was with Edward Carter, because this was a different kind of nervousness. Her stomach danced and she felt hot all over. 'It's always the same,' she answered, 'a bit of a rush first thing, then it goes quiet for a while.'

He shifted nearer to her. 'You look pretty this morning, Anne. As always.'

'Oh?' Not knowing what to say, she shyly averted her eyes, bowed her head and pretended to shift the merchandise about.

Lowering his voice he asked, 'Have you thought any more about coming to the dance with me tomorrow night?'

Anne shook her head.

'If you're worried about driving home late, I could pick you up, and drop you home afterwards. It's not a problem.'

Anne graciously declined. 'Thank you, but I don't know if I'm going. I've got so much to do at home.'

'Can't those things wait even for a day?'

'Not really, no! I have things to prepare for an important meeting next week. And it's kind of complex.'

'Can I help at all?'

'Oh, no!' She began to panic. 'It's private stuff.'

'I'm sorry.' He could see how nervous she was. 'I won't pressure you. If you have important things to do, then I suppose you can't be in two places at once.'

'Thank you, anyway, Mr McDonald. I'm really sorry.' And she was.

His gentle smile enveloped her. 'That's OK. Anyway,

the offer still stands. If you change your mind, it would make me very proud if you could be my partner for the evening.'

Anne nodded appreciatively, and watched him walk away.

She felt a strong urge to call him back, but she resisted.

It was peculiar how he made her feel like a shy little girl, wanting to curl up and hide. In some ways it was a nice feeling.

Tony moved on to Barbara, the smart, middle-aged lady at the help desk.

Out the corner of her eye, Anne was not surprised to see Sally giving a crafty thumbs up as though to congratulate her.

Realising that Sally must think she'd accepted Tony's offer of taking her to the dance, Anne shook her head determinedly, and from the look of disappointment on Sally's face, Anne knew she had got the message.

She thought it comforting, though, how Tony made her feel like she was special. Edward Carter had never been able to do that. For the first time in years, she felt a fluttering of excitement that a fine man like Tony had actually asked her twice to go out with him. It made her feel like a real woman. Maybe, at long last, she really was getting over her fear of men.

Or maybe she was just feeling good because last week she had asked for permission to leave work slightly early, on the pretence that she had a dentist appointment.

The real reason for leaving early, however, was because she had to make a very important decision.

At long last, she had gathered courage enough to take that first step to distance herself from the man who had destroyed her peace of mind for far too long. Sufficient time had passed, and now, thankfully, she was feeling strong enough in herself to deal with issues long overdue.

~

The morning had flown by, with eventually hordes of customers coming in and out of the store, and every assistant run off his or her feet.

It was now midday, and time for the first shift to take their hour-long lunch break.

'Come on, Anne, let's get off before Tony asks us to work through our break.' Sally had already managed to collect their coats.

A minute later they were headed off down the High Street.

'Phew! What a morning.' Sally was glad to get out of there.

They went carefully across the busy road, then through the arcade and on to the café, which they found half empty.

'Good!' Sally made a beeline for the table in the far corner. 'I think you've got something to tell me, and if people start coming in, we won't get overheard back here.'

'Who says I've got something to tell you?'

'Well, let's see. Firstly, you've been acting strangely, such as telling me you're getting your life in order.

Added to which, it's been ages since you wanted to come down here for your lunch.'

'Huh! You know me better than I know myself.'

When Sally continued to hover, she informed her, 'Go on then! I'll have a cheese and salad sandwich . . . and a pot of tea, please.'

'OK, but it's your turn to pay.'

Anne plucked a note from her purse and pressed it into Sally's outstretched palm. 'Go on then.'

She watched as Sally went to the counter, and a warm smile crept over her pretty features. Sally had been by her side through all the troubles. And whichever path her life took from now, Anne knew that she would never be able to thank Sally enough.

Within minutes, Sally was back. 'Oh, dammit!' She took off again. 'I forgot the sugar!'

Meantime, Anne was thinking how best to tell Sally what she'd done. She was wary of saying too much in case nothing came of it. She was also very afraid that it could all go wrong, with her caught in the middle, wishing that she'd left everything as it was.

Sally returned with the sugar bowl. 'Now then, lady!' Seating herself, she poured out her tea and plopped two heaped spoonfuls of sugar into her cup, stirring so vigorously the tea slopped over the brim. 'So, come on, Anne. What are you up to?'

'You're a mucky pup.' Anne laughed. 'Worse than a kid.'

'Never you mind about me, and stop trying to change the subject.' Sally was like a dog with a bone. 'We're here, just the two of us. There are no prying eyes and no one to overhear what you have to say. What's ticking over in that brain of yours? And don't tell me it's nothing, because I know you've got something you're itching to tell me, so come on. Spit it out!'

Anne told her, 'I've been thinking a lot lately, about my life, and everything. You and Mick have given me good advice and so far I've done nothing about it. But, do you remember what Edward Carter said to me, when he trapped me in the house? I told you and Mick about it, and you both said it was imperative that I should seek legal guidance, sooner rather than later.'

'You mean when he made reference to your house, and he said what was yours was his?'

Anne nodded. 'You and Mick were right. I should have done something about it then, and I didn't. But I've been thinking more and more about it lately, and it really worries me. That house was Aunt Ada's home. She and Uncle Bart moved there when they got married, so they enjoyed many good years in that little house. Aunt Ada left it to me, because she wanted me to love it the same way they had.' Her voice dropped to a whisper. 'It really hurts me to think that Carter might get his hands on the house. I don't want that to happen, Sally, and I don't want any link with him any more.'

Sally was delighted to hear Anne talking like this. 'So, have you got a plan?'

'You and Mick were right about a lot of things,' she admitted, 'so I've made an appointment with a solicitor. It's time I stood up and faced the truth. Edward Carter wants to ruin me. He wants to keep me frightened and take everything I have. I know what Aunt Ada would say: she'd say the same as you and Mick. "Fight him!" And that's what I've decided to do.'

Sally was thrilled. 'Good girl! So what did the solicior say?'

'Well, we haven't met yet, but I told him the situation on the telephone, and I gave him as many details as I could. He said he would make a start looking into things, and we arranged a meeting.'

'So, what exactly did you tell him on the phone? What kind of details did he ask for?'

'Well, firstly, he wanted me to bring along a marriage certificate, but I couldn't because I never had one. Edward was such a secretive man. He kept everything squirrelled away. I never knew what he was up to from one minute to the next. I do have the deeds to the house, though. I told the solicitor that I'd get them from the bank, and bring them to the meeting together with anything else that might seem relevant.'

'So, what else did he say?'

'When I asked him about getting a divorce from Edward Carter, he said he would have to make enquiries and such. Beyond that, he said there was much to be done, and that we would discuss the details at the meeting.'

Jubilant but highly nervous, she leaned back in her chair. 'So, what do you think, Sal? Do you think I'm doing the right thing? Or have I opened a Pandora's box? Have I let myself in for more trouble than I can handle?'

'Listen to me, Anne. I won't lie, because even a

normal divorce is never easy. But that man has made your life a misery. He's vicious and cruel, and he doesn't give a tinker's cuss about you. Yes, it might get nasty, and when he's served with divorce papers, he won't be best pleased, but who cares? You and I both know he'll move Heaven and earth to rob you of half the value of your home.'

'He will!' Anne was sure of it, 'I know he will.'

'OK. But everything is in your favour. It will all come out: the beatings he gave you when you were married to him . . . causing the loss of your baby. Then there's the way he tracked you down and held you prisoner, in fear for your life. Don't you worry, the Courts will have a field day with it.'

'I know all that, and I've told myself over and over that if it comes down to it, the Courts will be on my side, but I'm frightened, Sal. You don't know what he's like, not really. You have to live with him before you realise what he's capable of. I've always believed he's a bit wrong in the head. A madman!'

'But he can't hurt you while he's locked up – don't you ever forget that, Anne – and now that you're fighting back, he knows his track record will not serve him well.'

'Yes. Now I'm doing what I should have done years ago. But the thing is, Sal, I'm really frightened it will all blow up in my face.'

Leaning forward, Sally placed her hand on Anne's shoulder. 'It won't. Yes, it's true, divorce is never easy. But you really are doing the right thing, Anne. After you've told the solicitor everything, he'll understand.

I know you're worried, but now that you've found the courage to fight back, you must be strong and see it through. You obviously know that, or you would not have called the solicitor in the first place. And always remember, you're not on your own.'

'I do realise I have to do this, Sal. I'm so weary of being afraid. I just want it over.'

'I know. And I'm proud of you, and if you want me to come to the solicitor with you, I will. I'll tell him everything I know. Calling that solicitor can't have been an easy thing to do, but you did it. Now, like I said, you need to see it through. Mick and I will be right behind you.'

She was greatly relieved that Anne had found the courage to fight Edward Carter. But like Anne, she was nervous of how Carter might react when he discovered that Anne was now taking the initiative and refusing to be the victim.

At the end of the working day, the two of them made their way to the car park. 'Are you sure you won't change your mind and come to the dance with me and Mick?'

'No, but thanks all the same.'

'It seems such a pity, especially as you've made the hard decision to shape the direction of your own life.'

'I know, but I need some quiet time. I intend making a list of every little thing that man has ever done to me. I'm determined that people should know what he is.'

'That's good, but it doesn't mean you can't go to the dance.'

'I know that, Sal, but I really don't feel like going anyway.'

'Is that because Tony asked you?'

'No. Oh, I don't know, Sal. The truth is, I don't think I'm ready for dating.'

'It's not really a date, is it? I mean, it's just the annual staff dance. We'll all be there.'

'I know, but Tony particularly asked me to go with him, and from what I can remember, that's a date. And like I say, I'm not ready for it.'

'OK, but where's the harm in coming along with me and Mick? Just see how it goes. If Tony does ask you to dance, you can always say no.'

Anne could see the reasoning behind Sal's suggestion. 'I suppose it would do me good to get out for an evening,' she agreed. 'Sometimes, the house does seem like a prison. All right then, I don't suppose there's any harm in coming along with you and Mick.'

'Now you're thinking sensibly. So, I'll take that as a yes, shall I?'

'Yes, why not? Besides, I'm sure there'll be time enough over the rest of the weekend to prepare for the meeting.'

'Right!' Sally was delighted. 'So now, the all-important question: have you got a pretty, girlie dress for dancing? And what about shoes? We might have to go shopping. Don't forget the summer sales are still on. Oh, and I'll do your hair, if you like, save you a bit of money going to the hairdresser's—'

She would have gone on, but Anne interrupted her, 'I've agreed to go to the dance, but I am not going shopping for dresses and shoes. There are so many things in my wardrobe that I haven't worn for ages. I'm bound to find something suitable.'

'Oh, no, you don't!' Sally was determined. 'You haven't bought anything really pretty in ages, and everyone will be dressed to the nines. So, the two of us are going shopping. We need a new dress, and shoes, and a hairdo, and I won't take no for an answer.'

And when Sally was in that kind of mood, Anne knew there was no stopping her. In a way, she didn't really want to.

Swept along in Sally's excitement, Anne found herself looking forward to the dance.

More than that, she was also looking forward to a successful meeting with the solicitor, but whichever way it went from now on, she was beginning to feel like she'd been given a new lease of life.

~

Saturday, at the shops, swept by and the moment had arrived.

Right on time, Mick and Sally arrived to collect Anne.

When they drew up outside Anne's house, Mick gave a gasp as she opened the door and stepped out.

Wearing a slinky, black dress and red high-heeled shoes and with a little red bag clutched in her hand, Anne looked like a million dollars.

Apart from one lock of loosely waved hair that hung down to her shoulder, her hair was swept up and gripped in a silver comb. All of this was Sally's doing.

'I know you said she'd knock 'em dead, but she doesn't even look like the Anne that we know,' Mick gasped.

Sally watched proudly as Anne neared the car. 'You have no idea how much persuasion it took to convince her the dress was perfect for her. She's just not used to dressing up.'

Getting out of the car, Sally held the door open for her. 'Oh, Anne, you look lovely.'

'So do you, Sal.' Anne admired Sally's tight-fitting blue dress. Low on the neckline and drawn in at the waist, it swirled out at the skirt. Her pretty blue shoes and bag topped it all off.

When they were settled in the car, Mick drove off. 'I must be the luckiest man ever,' he said. 'I've got the two loveliest ladies right here in my car. When we walk into that room, they'll all be asking, "Where did that ugly devil manage to find those two beauties?"'

Sally kissed him on the cheek. 'You're not an ugly devil. And we're proud to be with you.' She turned to Anne. 'Isn't that right, Anne?'

Anne kissed him as well. 'We're the lucky ones.'

'Mmm,' he laughed, 'you're only saying that because it's true.'

Sally turned round to ask if Anne was all right.

Sally had persuaded her out of her shell, and Anne could not be more grateful. 'I'm glad you made me change my mind about not going to the dance,' she said. 'I'm really looking forward to it now.'

'Good!' Sally was excited. 'Just for tonight, put everything else out of your mind, and enjoy yourself.'

'I will, I promise.'

In this moment, here with Mick and Sal, and wearing a dress she would never have imagined herself in, Anne felt very special, and more excited than she had been for a long time.

When she'd been locking the front door, however, for one fleeting second, Edward Carter crept into her mind. There'd been the slightest, unsettling niggle at the back of her mind that when she came home, he would be there, waiting for her.

But then she'd reminded herself that he was in prison, where he belonged, and that very soon, if all went well, she would be free of him for ever. All these years she had been afraid to stir up the muddy waters, but now that she had started proceedings against him, she felt optimistic. She would not completely rest easy, though, until she'd secured the official papers on which it was written in black and white that she was no longer Mrs Edward Carter.

Twenty minutes later, they arrived at the club. Music blared into the night, indicating that the party was already underway.

'Here we are!' Sally was already twirling as she got out of the car. 'Time to enjoy the evening.'

As Anne followed her two friends into the crowded hall, she reminded herself of what Sally had told her: tonight was her night. It was a night for fun and laughter, with no regrets.

Inside the club, Tony McDonald had been watching for her. When he saw her coming in through the door, he could hardly believe his eyes. She looked so lovely. But then, he thought, she always looked lovely.

Anne saw him striding towards her. For one split second, she almost turned away. But something held her there; maybe his smile, or his genuine delight at seeing her.

Whatever it was, she waited for him. They chatted a while, during which his easy manner made her feel comfortable.

Later, when he swept her onto the dance floor, she went willingly into his arms.

While they danced, he held her tight, and whispered soft endearments in her ear.

Afterwards, they walked out into the terraced garden, where they strolled and talked, getting to know each other. 'I'm so glad you changed your mind,' he said. 'Right up to the minute I saw you walk through the door, I wasn't sure whether I would see you tonight.'

When he reached out to take hold of her hand, she drew away, all her old fears coming back to torment her. 'I'm sorry, Tony . . .'

'What's wrong?' He thought they'd been getting on so well. 'Have I said something to upset you?'

'No. It isn't anything you've done,' she assured him. 'It's just that I'm not looking for a relationship. If I gave you that impression, I really didn't mean to.'

'Look, Anne, I think you already know how much I like you, but I'm not looking for a close relationship either. To tell you the truth, I've only recently come out of a bad situation, and I'm still carrying the scars.' His ready smile was reassuring.

'Oh! I'm sorry if I jumped to conclusions, but the truth is, I need to steer well clear of getting involved with anyone. I don't want to give you any wrong signals . . . if you know what I mean?'

'I hear what you're saying, and I understand.'

'Thank you.' When he smiled down on her, her heart did a little skip. She was both excited and afraid; and ready to flee at the slightest opportunity.

'I'd best go and find Mick and Sal.' Her heart urged her to stay but her head warned her off. 'They'll be wondering where I am.'

Without waiting for an acknowledgement, she hurried away.

She located Sally at the bar, sipping a glass of red wine.

Mick was nearby, talking with the store manager.

Sally turned and saw Anne rushing towards her. 'Where've you been? One minute you were here and then you were gone.'

She noticed Tony McDonald coming in from the terrace. 'Oh, I see.' She gave a naughty wink. 'You've been hobnobbing with the good-looking side of management.'

Anne laughed. 'And you've had one drink too many, by the look of you.'

Sally would not be silenced. 'I want to hear all the juicy gossip.' Taking her drink in one hand, she linked arms with Anne, marching her across the floor to the nearest free table. 'Right, my girl! Spill the beans. I know you've been outside with Tony, so what happened? Did he make a play for you? Was he the perfect gentleman?'

Anne was shocked. 'Ssh! He'll hear you. And yes, for your information, he was a perfect gentleman.'

'Well, that's a pity.' She gave a telltale hiccup. 'I expected him to be a bit more daring that that. One little kiss at least.'

'Well, you expected wrong because there were no kisses, and no canoodling. We just talked.'

'Aw, Anne, I'm sorry.'

'Why? I'm not.' Though in a secretive way, she wondered what it might feel like for Tony to kiss her. But as soon as she thought it, she blocked it from her mind.

'I'll get you a cuppa coffee,' she told Sally. 'Sober you up a bit.'

'Are you saying I'm drunk?'

'No.'

'Right! Then, I'll have another glass of wine. This one's half empty.'

'Oh, no, you don't.' Mick arrived to collect her into his arms. 'You owe your neglected husband a dance.' With a knowng wink to Anne, he swept his wife onto the dance floor.

Anne watched them for a while. She saw how happy they were, and she was genuinely glad for them.

At the same time she wondered why she had chosen a man like Edward Carter. And yet, thinking back, she realised it was he who had chosen her.

Remembering how it was, her mood dropped. Feeling angry with herself, she grabbed up Sally's half-empty wineglass and drank it down in one go.

'Wow! Somebody was thirsty!' Tony McDonald smiled down on her. 'Would it be OK if I sat next to you?'

Taken by surprise, Anne gestured to the furthest chair. 'You're very welcome.'

'Aren't you worried I might pounce on you?' His smile was infectious.

Anne felt foolish. 'Just now, out there . . . what I said, it didn't mean that I don't like you –' the wine was taking an effect – 'because I do. It's just that . . .' She took a deep breath. 'When I was too young and foolish, I trusted a man and I got badly hurt.'

'I understand.' Like Anne, he had not been successful where love and happiness were concerned. 'Sometimes we get swept away with the idea that we'll be happy ever after, but it doesn't always turn out that way. I'm sure it happens to everybody at some time or another.'

'You're right! It's not just me, is it? He was good-looking and charming, and he promised me the world. But he turned out to be a liar and a bully.' She gave a sorry little giggle. 'I wasn't to know what he was really like.'

Sensing a deep confession of sorts, and realising she was not used to the wine, Tony felt like an eavesdropper and decided to bring the conversation to a halt. Getting out of his chair, he rounded the table, slid his hand through hers and bent to whisper in her ear, 'Let's you and me take to the dance floor, shall we?'

'Good idea!' Anne saw a man she might be able to trust; a man who had done nothing wrong. 'Why not? Yes, I'd like that.' And she allowed him to whisk her away again.

Waiting for the music to resume, Mick saw the two of them making their way across the room. 'Looks like Anne has a very keen dancing partner,' he told Sally.

Merry from the wine, Sally waved at Anne, who shyly

put up a hand. 'I'm glad for her,' she told Mick. 'Tony seems to be a decent sort.'

She watched as Tony led Anne into the waltz. She saw how intimately close he held her, and how Anne easily melted into his embrace.

Yet somewhere in the back of her mind, she sincerely hoped that, for the moment at least, Anne would not be drawn in too deep.

PART FOUR

~

Thrown to the Wolves

1957

CHAPTER THIRTEEN

PHIL CLIMBED OFF the bus and started to walk down the road, but he stopped on seeing Adam stitting on a wall at the corner of the street. Adam was so deeply preoccupied with his thoughts, he didn't see Phil heading towards him. He continued to swing his legs, his face looking down and his gaze drawn to the pavement.

Phil was concerned that it was not the first time he'd seen the boy looking so dejected, although whenever he asked Adam if things were all right the same answer was always given with a bright smile: 'Yes, Phil. Don't worry, I'm fine.'

Phil knew he had to be careful. The very last thing he wanted was to stir things up with Miss Martin, and he would never do that, unless he was absolutely certain there was something not right with Adam's situation.

On the other hand, Phil had wondered whether the problem could just be something straightforward, and therefore nothing to worry about. It might be that Adam was still struggling to feel comfortable in his new circumstances.

After all, this new family situation was all very strange to him. It could be that it was taking him longer to settle in than anyone had anticipated.

Phil himself was still fretting because the authorities had flatly turned him down when he offered to take the boy. And whatever he said, they always had a well-rehearsed answer, all tied up in red tape.

Phil had told them, 'You should ask Adam what he wants.' And they assured him it did not work that way.

So, he made up his mind to do the next best thing. He promised both himself and Adam that he would never be far away, and that he would see him as often as the Dexters allowed. It was the only alternative he could offer.

Fortunately, the Dexters had been as good as their word. They had allowed Phil and Adam time enough to be together, to go fishing and walking, and making the regular pilgrimage to the churchyard.

Occasionally, in her own free time, the lovely Polly from the children's home would join them. That was an extra treat for Adam, and especially for Phil, who always looked forward to her company.

To all appearances, Adam was well looked after in the Dexter household. He now had a wardrobe of smart clothes, a fast Raleigh bicycle in the garden shed, and a small amount of pocket money each week. He looked well, and he was growing fast.

Having turned thirteen a short time before he left

the children's home, Adam still had that lean, lolloping gait of a young boy, and that recognisable, ever-untidy crop of brown hair.

Adam had spent two separate visits with the Dexters before approval on both sides was achieved. The next step required formalising the necessary paperwork, along with choosing a school and securing his name on the local doctor's list.

That done, Adam was now a more permanent member of the Dexter family, which included Buster the dog, who had welcomed him with open paws.

With all this running through his mind, Phil slowed his pace. Still unseen by Adam, he took time to study the boy before he should look up and see him approaching.

On his last visit, a week ago, Phil had reason to be concerned. Throughout their wanderings, Adam had very few words to say, and he was distant in his thoughts.

When Phil discreetly questioned Adam, he again assured him that everything was all right. And so, for the moment, he had to be content.

Now, though, he was learning a great deal from Adam's body language, and Phil could see a very unhappy boy. He noticed the way Adam was hanging his head and looking down, as though lost in thought. His shoulders were deeply hunched and there was an air of dejection about him.

He felt troubled. Something wasn't right, and somehow or other, without upsetting anyone, he meant to get to the root of it.

Just then, Adam glanced up, and when he saw Phil,

his face lit up. 'Phil!' Leaping off the wall, he ran up the road, whooping and hollering. 'I've been waiting for you, Phil!'

Adam's excitement was a joy to the old man; so much so that he had tears in his eyes. *They should have let me take him home,* he thought angrily. *Me and Adam, we'd have been just fine. It's true that I might never see sixty again, but I'm not ready for the scrapheap just yet!* His own dear father had lived to be a sprightly ninety years old, and still walked the countryside right up to the day he died.

Adam launched himself at Phil, who was almost knocked off balance. 'Steady on, son!' Catching Adam to his chest, he laughed out loud. 'You nearly knocked the stuffing outta me!'

Adam was so excited, he couldn't stop talking. 'I'm glad you're here,' he confided. 'I've been sitting on the wall for ages. I thought you would never come. I was beginning to get worried.'

'Well, you've no right to be getting worried!'

Taking out his old pocket watch, Phil checked it. 'I'm not late. You should know what time I usually get here on a Saturday morning.'

Adam apologised. 'I know, but it seems like I've been waiting ages, and I was beginning to think you'd never get here. I'm really looking forward to us going across the fields, Phil. I've even got my wellies ready and everything.'

Hoisting his trouser leg up to the ankle, Phil pointed out, 'See there? I've got my new walking boots on, so it seems we're both set for a good old trek.'

When Adam asked why he hadn't got his loyal little

dog with him, Phil explained, 'It's a pity, but since he sliced his paw on that broken bottle down at Badgers Den, the vet said it's best if he doesn't run about. He'll be all right, though. Pat from next door is keeping an eye on him while I'm out.'

He rolled his eyes in frustration. 'She treats him like a baby, and he laps it up, like you would not believe.' Laughing out loud, he confessed, 'I reckon she'd do the same to me, given half a chance!'

Adam innocently remarked how Phil would not want to take up with Pat because, 'You like Polly, don't you?'

Phil was shaken by Adam's observation. 'Well, of course I do. We both do, don't we? Polly is good company.' He added firmly, 'She's also a good friend, to the pair of us.'

He was shocked that Adam had latched onto his fondness for Polly. In future, he would need to be careful, although just now, talking about Polly had brought a warm flush to his old heart.

Side by side, they went down the street together, chatting like the old friends they were, and laughing out loud when Phil described his little dog's antics. 'Rex howled at the window when I set off, but Pat called him back for a juicy bone. It didn't take long for him to choose the bone over me, the little traitor!'

As they approached the Dexters' front gate, Phil had a question. 'Adam, will you be honest with me, son?'

Anticipating the same question that he'd answered last week and the week before, Adam replied with a question of his own. 'Phil! Are you're still worrying about me?'

'Is there any reason why I should worry?'

'No reason at all.' Adam felt uncomfortable. Normally, he would confide in Phil, but on this particular issue, he thought it best if he tried to deal with the situation himself.

A minute later, with Phil going at a steady pace and Adam running ahead, they arrived at the house.

'While you're getting yourself organised, I'll have a quick word with the woman of the house.' He still felt unable to refer to Liz Dexter as Adam's mum.

'But I am "organised",' Adam protested. 'I've been ready for a good hour.'

'Ah! But have you got all your stuff together?'

'What "stuff"?'

'Well, let's see. You'll need a coat in case the weather turns. I've got a full flask, and sandwiches enough for two.' He pointed to the canvas bag he was carrying. 'So we're all right for food and drink, and if we're in need of a treat on the way back there's always an ice-cream cart at the foot of Brent Hill.' He added the most important item to the list: 'Oh, and you'll need your fishing gear.'

'I thought you said we weren't going fishing today?'

'Well, we might, and in any case, it never hurts to be prepared for a change of plan.'

Adam heartily agreed.

As always, Liz Dexter was delighted to see him. 'Phil! Oh, come in. You've time for a cuppa, haven't you? It won't take me a minute. You timed it right, because the kettle's just boiled.'

She led him into the sitting room. 'Make yourself comfortable. I'll be back before you know it.'

Adam ran along the passageway towards the back door. 'I'll just go and sort out the fishing tackle.'

Phil was quietly pleased, because he certainly did not want Adam sitting in while he was talking to Liz. 'We're all right for time,' he called back to Adam. 'There's no rush. Liz is making me a nice cuppa tea.'

As good as her word, Liz was soon back with a tray laden with teapot, cups and saucers, and a plate of shortcake biscuits. 'Help yourself, Phil.' Carefully pouring the tea, she left Phil to add his own milk and sugar. 'So, how's the little dog's paw?' Adam had told her about that the week before.

'Thank you, yes, it's healing well.'

'Oh, I'm glad. It's awful when they're hurt. They look at you with their big, sorry eyes and there's nothing you can do but follow the vet's advice. We had that with Buster last year. He got a thorn in his paw and we didn't even notice it; not until he started limping. By that time, it was infected. The vet confined him to the house and yard. Poor Buster. He was so miserable.' She added casually, 'Jim and Alice took him for a walk. Goodness knows where they've gone, because that was over an hour ago.'

Phil took a long invigorating gulp of his tea before opening the all-important conversation. 'Mrs Dexter, can I ask you something before Adam comes in?'

'Of course you can. But I'd be happier if you'd call me Liz.'

Politely passing over this comment, Phil asked, 'I was just wondering, do you know if Adam is worried about anything?'

'No.' She seemed genuinely surprised. 'Not that I know of. Whatever makes you ask that?'

Phil was careful not to alarm her. 'Oh, it's nothing in particular. It's just that when we were out last week, he was quieter than usual. And just now, when he was sitting on the wall waiting for me, he seemed to be deep in thought.'

Liz was concerned. 'He hasn't said anything to me, and I haven't noticed anything untoward with him.'

Phil was relieved. 'Maybe it's just me. I'm well known for being an old fusspot. That's what comes of keeping a fatherly eye on the youngsters from school.'

Realising he was genuinely worried, Liz made a suggestion. 'It could be that Adam is still finding things a bit overwhelming. Just think of what he's been through, what with the sad loss of his mother and all that terrible business about his father. To be honest I'm not even sure it was right to bring Adam into it, but the authorities claimed they were duty-bound to speak with him.'

Phil harboured the very same sentiments. 'I expect they went by the book. Matters of that sort can be a minefield, if they get it wrong.'

'Yes, I suppose so. But then, as if that wasn't enough to be going on with, he had not long started at a new school and, as far as I know, he hasn't yet made any friends. Then there are all the other intrusions into his young life. Goodness! It's enough to unsettle anyone, let alone a young boy.'

'Yes, of course, you're right.' Phil agreed. 'It's a lot to deal with at his age.'

'It certainly is, though Jim and I think he's coped magnificently. But of course you never can tell how it's affected him inside. But we do talk about these things privately. And we try to keep him busy and make sure he gets plenty of recreation. Jim started teaching him the rudiments of golf, but Adam didn't take to it at all.'

Phil was partly reassured. 'So, do you really think I'm worrying about nothing?'

'Yes. I would say so, Phil. Being fostered into a new family is daunting for anyone. Adam needs time to adjust. But, rest assured, he's doing all right.' She confided, 'Adam and I have an agreement that if he's ever worried about anything at all, he would tell me.'

'That's good.'

Feeling easier, though not altogether convinced, Phil took another long sip of his tea. 'By! I must say, you do know how to make a satisfying cup of tea.'

The sound of the back door being opened heralded the return of Adam, complete with two fishing rods, a basket to sit on, and a small, narrow cart for carrying the load.

Phil was impressed. 'That's a fancy little cart, I must say.'

'Jim made it for him,' Liz declared proudly. 'He even measured the fishing rods so that everything would fit in. It's light and sturdy, so it's easily wheeled over uneven ground.'

Phil got up to take a closer look. 'Well, I never! That'll take the weight and no mistake.'

'I'll pull it,' Adam decided.

Phil was all smiles as he told Liz, 'Let's hope me and Adam catch enough fish to give you a feast at dinnertime.'

A short time later, she waved them off. 'Mind how you go.'

She watched as they went down the street, heading for the bottom lane, which led directly to open countryside. From there it was a ten-minute walk to the canal.

'You might cross paths with Jim and Alice on your way,' she called out as they rounded the corner.

Adam responded with a cheery wave of his hand, but his heart sank at her parting words.

'All right, are you, son?' Phil asked, sensing a sharp change in Adam's mood.

'Yes, Phil. I'm really looking forward to our outing.'

What he was *not* looking forward to, however, was crossing paths with Alice.

~

As it happened, they did not see hide nor hair of Jim and Alice.

Phil was happiest when he and Adam were spending time together. They chatted and laughed, and when they sat down to do a bit of fishing, Adam confided that he really liked Liz and Jim.

'They're so kind and thoughtful,' he said. 'They don't treat me like a baby. They talk to me as if my opinion really matters, and they never force me to do anything I don't want to do . . .' his mood darkened at that point, '. . . not like my father did.'

Phil wisely let him talk on, and eventually, in one unguarded moment, Adam revealed something alarming. 'Alice doesn't like me,' he told Phil. 'She hates me being there.'

'Really?' Phil was taken aback. 'What makes you say that?'

Adam shrugged. 'I just know, that's all.'

'Has Alice actually said she doesn't want you there?'

'Not yet, no.'

'So has she done anything to make you feel she resents you?'

'Not really.'

'So, you could be wrong . . . couldn't you?'

Growing impatient, Adam drew his fishing line out of the water and looked Phil in the eye. 'I'm not wrong, Phil. Alice hates me. She wants me out! And even if she doesn't say it, she tells me in other ways . . . like the time she left a frog in my bed. When I tackled her about it, she laughed in my face. She said it was a joke, but I know it wasn't.'

He glanced about nervously. 'Sometimes she follows me about. It's like she thinks I'm looking to steal something. She makes me feel uncomfortable, Phil. She does it on purpose, because she doesn't want me there.'

For a long, awkward moment after Adam's heated revelation, neither spoke. Adam flicked the line back into the water, and continued fishing as though nothing had happened, while Phil pondered upon the anger in Adam's face when he'd spoken of Alice.

He tried to allay Adam's fears. 'Listen to me, son. It might not be what you think. Girls have a habit of playing tricks. It's just their way. They seem to get a laugh out of it, but I'm sure it doesn't mean she wants you out.'

Adam gave another shrug. 'Well, it feels like it to me.'

'But she's never actually said it to your face, has she?'

'No, but she will. I just know it.'

Phil continued to smooth over the situation. 'It might just be that she's a bit jealous of you.'

'Why would she be jealous of me? What is there to be jealous of? She's far better off than I am. She's got her mother and father. And she's got a little sister. Before I came to live there, Alice had them all to herself.'

'Ah! Well, there you go. I think you've hit the nail on the head.'

'What do you mean?'

'That could be why she's playing tricks on you. Maybe she's jealous. Like you said, before you came along, she had her family all to herself, and now she has to share them with you. Like when Jim gave you a lesson in playing golf, she might have felt a bit left out.'

Phil felt for the boy, but he could also see Alice's side. 'The tricks she played on you, they didn't do you any real harm, did they?'

'Don't suppose.'

'So, maybe you should try and forgive her. Just like you, she's trying to adjust to a new and strange situation. She might be worried that the family haven't got enough love and attention for all of you, and that she might be the one to lose out. It doesn't mean she wants you out of the house. It just means she's desperately trying to hold on to what she's got. It's difficult for her . . . as it must be for you. So can you understand what I'm trying to say, Adam?'

Torn in his thoughts, Adam chose not to answer.

Phil persevered. 'Listen, Adam, try not to worry about it. She's just a little girl, playing silly, childish pranks. It's probably all very innocent.' He lightened the atmosphere with a throaty chuckle. 'You'll find out soon enough that women and girls have a very strange sense of humour compared to us men.'

Adam was curious. 'How d'you mean, Phil?'

'Oh, yes. It's a well-known fact. Women and girls are not at all like men and boys. They get all these silly, immature ideas, and sometimes, no matter how hard we try, us men don't know what to make of 'em.'

He was pleased to see a smile on Adam's face. 'Try and ignore it if you can, son. I reckon she'll soon get fed up of playing tricks.'

He thought it wise for the moment to play down the business of Alice. At least now he had a plausible reason for Adam's sorry little moods.

Though he'd advised Adam otherwise, Phil wondered if the boy might be right. Maybe, Alice really did want him out of the house. If that was so, and it wasn't nipped in the bud quick enough, there might be a real danger that the situation could escalate.

He wondered if he might have a word with Jim and Liz Dexter, but then he instantly thought better of it, because there was still a chance that it really was innocent game play on their daughter's part.

Over the next couple of hours, Phil and Adam enjoyed each other's company. Adam caught three fish, and seemed more like his old self. He made no further mention of Alice and her little tricks, and Phil decided to let sleeping dogs lie. For the moment, he turned his thoughts to giving the boy a memorable outing.

Having secured a good catch of fat, juicy fish, the two of them washed their hands in the water, and wiped them on the towel Phil had thoughtfully put in his old canvas bag.

Then they set about enjoying their sandwiches, before heading back.

'Can we go the long way back?' Adam liked that particular route. 'We can get an ice cream and stop at the ruins.'

Phil had no objection whatsoever. In fact, he was about to suggest it himself.

It wasn't long before they arrived at the ice-cream van.

Parked beside the canal, the van and its colourful owner were a welcome sight to any weary traveller.

'Hello, you two!' Dressed in his blue-and-white-striped overall, the ruddy-faced man was a familiar figure hereabouts. 'Been fishing, I see?' His beady little eyes latched onto the two fishing rods protruding from the cart. 'Hello! What's that contraption, then?'

'It's a purpose-made fishing cart.' Phil liked to wind him up. 'Good grief, have you never seen a fishing cart before?'

'No. Can't say I have. Is it any good?'

'Well, o' course it is. That little cart is carrying two

bags, two nets, a haul of fish and two fishing rods. So you tell me if it's any good.'

'Hmm!' Leaning forward, he peered so hard over the counter, the other two were sure he would fall out. 'I wouldn't mind one o' them for myself. In my spare time I like to do a bit of fishing, but I reckon you could use that little cart for anything and everything.'

'That's my thoughts exactly!' Phil said.

'Oh, yes! I could use that little cart to carry the vegetables home from the allotment. I've got a good strong wheelbarrow, and it's served me very well over the years but it's only got the one wheel and it gets stuck in the ruts when it's wet underfoot. That little cart, with its four wheels, is perfect for the job. So tell me, how much did it cost?'

'Jim Dexter made it,' Adam answered. 'He drew up a plan, then he measured the rods, and he built the cart in his garage.'

The ice-cream man was really impressed. 'Does he sell 'em?'

Now it was Phil's turn. 'He might.'

'Well, if you let me know how much he charges, I might buy one. I know one or two friends up the allotments who would love a little cart like that, too. Does it fold up so's you can hang it in the shed?'

'He can make them any way you want,' Phil said. 'We'll have a word with him and we'll let you know.'

The ice-cream man was so thankful he refused to take payment for two large, chocolate-topped cornets.

'That's what you call drumming up business.' Phil felt proud as he and Adam set off, happily enjoying the biggest ice creams ever, which were all the more tasty because they were free. 'By, I reckon Jim could make himself a small fortune with that little cart.'

On the way home, Adam seemed content enough. When they reached the house, Phil was pleased to see how Adam ran on in front, as though he couldn't wait to tell Jim about the interest his cart had created.

It was as though the worrying conversation about Alice and her pranks had never happened.

Being a belt-and-braces man, however, Phil decided to keep Adam's comments firmly in the back of his mind.

Jim was home. When Adam told him about the ice-cream man and the interest he'd shown in the cart, Jim was most impressed. 'Well, isn't that a turn-up for the book?'

He told Phil how he came to build it. 'Whichever way you look at it, those fishing rods can be a bit awkward to carry,' he said. 'I just thought the cart would make life easier for the two of you, when you're off on your treks.'

Phil thanked him. 'Well, it certainly made an impression,' he said. 'We even got two free cornets.'

'Yes!' Adam spoke up. 'Extra large, they were, with chocolate on top an' all.'

Jim was bemused. 'Maybe I should copyright the design for the future, for when I'm old and worn and I need an income on the side.'

Liz playfully thumped him. 'Don't say that! You'll never be old and worn in my eyes.'

She asked Phil if he'd like to stay to dinner, 'being as you and Adam caught the fish?'

Phil respectfully declined. 'I promised I'd be back by a certain time. Pat, my next-door neighbour, very kindly offered to look after the dog till I get back.'

Liz understood. 'Another time then?'

Phil thanked her. 'Yes, another time. I'd like that.'

'Good! Meantime, you must take the biggest of the catch home to Pat as a thank-you for looking after your little dog . . . Rex, isn't it?'

'That's right. I think I told you . . . I named him after my late father because they've got the same straggly beard.'

Liz chuckled. 'Well, I'm sure Rex would love a bit of fresh fish as well, don't you think?' Without waiting for an answer, she hurried into the kitchen to sort out the biggest fish in the catch.

A short time later, with the fish gutted, cleaned and packed up, Adam accompanied Phil to the bus stop.

'Tomorrow's Sunday,' Adam reminded him. 'I've already got Mum's flowers.'

Phil had not forgotten. 'You're a good boy, Adam. You never forget, do you?'

'No.' Adam's voice shook. 'And I don't forget what Edward Carter did to her.'

Phil understood Adam's bitterness, but nonetheless, he was saddened. 'Justice prevailed and he's being made to pay for his wickedness.' He knew that was not much consolation to Adam.

'I know how hard it must be . . . impossible, even, for you to put him behind you,' Phil told Adam. 'At the same time, I would be distressed if the rest of your life was overshadowed by a man who does not deserve one minute of your thoughts.'

Adam hardened his heart. 'I hate him. He hurt my mother so bad. It's his fault she died.'

'I understand how you feel, Adam. All the same, I'm sure your mother would not want you to spend your life filled with hate and revenge. Nothing good will ever come of it. And besides, if there's any justice at all, Edward Carter will spend the rest of his life behind bars.'

Adam was not convinced. 'I want him to suffer, like he made my mum suffer! I want him to hurt, and be afraid, just like she was.' His voice shook. 'Even if he's in prison, he's still alive, but my mum is in the churchyard.'

When Adam fell silent, Phil feared the boy would never feel any different. But then, why should he? After the shocking ordeal that both he and his mother had gone through at the hands of a maniac, the memories would stay with Adam for ever.

Phil wisely changed the subject. 'I must say your mum would have loved the many bunches of pretty pink flowers you've bought her over time.'

Adam glowed with pride. 'Pink is Mum's favourite colour.'

'I know, son.' Many times he'd watched Adam lovingly arrange the pink flowers in the memorial case, and he did it with such tenderness it always brought a tear to Phil's old eyes.

'Now then, Adam, don't forget to keep the flowers in water overnight. I'll be round here to collect you about midday tomorrow. We'll place your mum's flowers first, then we'll use that little hand spade we hid behind the trees, and we'll tidy round where the rabbits keep digging. After that, we'll go down to the canal and feed the ducklings. I've got half a loaf going stale at home. We'll break it down, throw it in, and before you know it, the ducklings will come out of nowhere and there won't be a single crumb left. So, what do you think? After we've been to the churchyard, would you like to go to the canal?'

'Yes, Phil. I really would.'

'Me too.'

For now, at least, Phil thought the change of conversation had rid Adam's mind of Carter. Though like Adam, Phil firmly believed that such a man should be made to pay the ultimate price for the shocking things he had done.

~

As they made their way up the street, Phil and Adam had no idea they were being watched.

Hidden from view at her bedroom window, Alice followed their progress. When the other two were out of sight, she turned away from the window. Grabbing her doll, she hugged it tight to her chest. 'Don't worry. After he's gone it will be just like it was before.' The idea made her smile.

Collecting the tiny hairbrush from the dressing table, she sang softly as she brushed the doll's long, auburn tresses.

Downstairs, with the dinner almost ready, Liz and Jim were enjoying a few minutes playing with Harriet when they heard Alice singing.

'She sounds happy,' Liz commented.

'That's because she knows we're going out for an hour or so after dinner. She seems to enjoy Maureen coming round.' Jim smiled at the baby. 'See that? It comes to something when your own daughter thinks more of the babysitter than she does her parents!'

Liz laughed. 'Don't be silly!'

'Oh, well, whatever makes her happy.'

He made a monkey-face at the baby. 'Listen to me, Harriet! Don't *you* go shifting your affections to the babysitter, will you? Can you hear your sister singing like a canary because Mummy and Daddy are going out? Most kids would be grumbling, but not our Alice.'

Using two fingers to create long donkey ears above his head, he waggled them at the baby, who stared at him with big eyes.

Liz had to smile. 'Stop it, you big kid! You're frightening her.'

Just then, little Harriet laughed out loud and Jim was forgiven, though there was something else playing on Liz's mind.

'Jim?'

'Yes, sweetheart?' He looked up and paid attention.

'Have you noticed anything different with Adam?'

'In what way?'

'I mean . . . do you think he's happy, here with us?'

'Hmm! That's an odd thing to ask. Yes, I think he's happy enough. I reckon he's fitted into this family really well. But what's brought this on? Has something happened? Has Adam said anything?'

'No! In fact, he never does say how he feels. I was just wondering, that's all.'

'Well, I think he's very happy here with us. Maybe the fact that he doesn't say anything about how he feels, actually means that he's content, and that's all we need to know. So, stop fretting. Adam is an important part of this family now, and as far as I'm concerned, he's our son, in all but name. If he was unhappy for whatever reason, I believe he would confide in one of us.'

'That's what I thought.' Liz was greatly relieved.

'There you are then. You've answered your own question.'

From the landing, Alice was disturbed by the conversation she'd overheard. So, Adam was a son in all but name?

Silently tiptoeing back to her bedroom, she closed the door behind her.

Half an hour later, Liz called, 'Alice! Dinner's nearly ready, sweetheart. Maureen will be here soon.'

A few minutes later, Alice came into the room.

'Goodness! You've been up there a long time, Alice.' Jim was curious. 'So, what have you been up to?'

'Nothing much. Just brushing my dolly's hair.'

Liz gave her a hug. 'You did remember Maureen's coming to look after you later, didn't you?'

'Yes.'

'And you're all right with that, are you?' As if she needed to ask.

'Yes, Mum. I like Maureen.'

'Maureen will probably bring a selection of puzzles and such. So the three of you should have a good time.

I'll have Harriet already fed and changed. She'll be that sleepy, I'm certain she'll be no trouble.'

Alice smiled sweetly. 'If she cries I'll rock her pram and she'll go back to sleep. I've done it before.'

'I'm sure you won't need to do that,' Liz said. 'Maureen is well versed in what to do. Harriet's been crawling all over the place today, so she'll probably sleep well. I wouldn't be at all surprised if she started taking her first steps very soon.'

Jim winked at Alice, admiring the pink ribbon in her hair. 'You look very pretty, Alice.'

'Thank you, Daddy.'

'Would you rather we didn't go out tonight?' She seemed unusually quiet, he thought.

'No! You and Mummy go and enjoy yourselves. Me and Maureen will be fine.'

'And Adam . . . don't forget him.'

'I won't.' She gave a slight nod of the head.

'You know we'll only be gone for a couple of hours, don't you?'

'Yes, and it's all right, Daddy,' Alice assured him brightly. 'You and Mummy don't have to worry about us. Maureen always takes care of us very well.'

'Thank you, sweetheart.' Thinking how Alice was some-times like a little woman in her manner, Liz returned to the kitchen to collect the condiments. Alice had made her smile. Talk about an old head on young shoulders.

On returning to the table, Liz sat herself down. 'Come on, Alice. Tuck in.' Apart from Adam's meal, which was warming in the oven, everything was served.

Alice's meal was already set before her: boiled baby

carrots, buttered mashed potatoes, and a slice of pink, juicy fish, gently cooked in milk, the way Alice liked it.

'We've got Adam and Phil to thank for this lovely fish meal.'

Liz made the casual remark as Adam arrived to seat himself next to Jim. It wasn't long before he was ravenously tucking in.

'Woah! Slow down, son.' Jim was surprised.

'Sorry,' Adam apologised, 'but I'm really hungry.'

'I expect that's all the fresh air,' Liz suggested. 'Still, you don't want to give yourself indigestion, do you?'

Realising he'd been wolfing his food, Adam slowed down. 'Sorry.'

Jim playfully ruffled his hair. 'Aw, that's all right, Adam. I was the same when I was your age. I remember after we'd been out playing footie, me and my brother would run home, cram our food down, and be off out again, before anyone else had finished.'

The meal continued in a civilised if lively manner. There was much laughter at Jim's descriptions of his boyhood pranks, particularly the one about the time when he'd gone home with the bottom of his pants worn clean through, where he and his mates had spent the morning racing each other down the slide.

When the meal was over, Liz noticed that Alice had eaten everything except the fish, which was pushed to the side of her plate.

'What's wrong, sweetheart? You've always liked fish.'

'Well, I don't any more.'

'Really?' Liz glanced at Jim, 'And why's that then?'

Alice shrugged. 'I just don't, that's all.'

Jim sensed an underlying atmosphere. 'That's OK, Alice.' He smiled. 'You're allowed to change your mind.' Though, like Liz, he thought Alice was being unusually picky, for some reason.

By the time Maureen arrived, Jim and Liz were all dressed up and raring to meet up with their friends at the local pub, which was just a ten-minute walk from the house.

Liz wore her new red dress, while Jim looked every inch the sportsman in his dark trousers and black blazer with the darts club badge on the pocket.

'You're dressed a bit severe for a pint and a game of darts, aren't you?' Liz joked.

'No, I am not! I intend for our team to win,' he declared, 'so I thought I'd put on the gear.'

He did a twirl on the spot and was dead pleased when Adam told him proudly, 'You look really good.'

'Thank you, Adam. So, what do you think, Alice? Do you agree with Mummy, or do you agree with Adam?'

'I agree with Mummy.' There was no way she was about to agree with Adam.

'Well, I'm afraid you women are wrong.' Jim placed a kiss on the top of her head. 'To be a winner, you have to look the part, and I think I do. So this time, the men have it!'

After going through the usual check list with Maureen, Jim and Liz started off up the street, with Alice waving them off at the door.

'Have a good time,' she called.

'We will!' Liz called back.

'And don't be late, will you?' Alice reminded them.

'We won't.' Jim replied, and he had an instruction of his own: 'Alice! Go back inside and lock the door.' He waited for Alice to do as she was bid.

He thought it amusing how Alice had seen them off, so concerned and caring. 'When did it swing the other way?' he asked Liz.

'What d'you mean?'

Jim gave a whimsical little smile. 'Alice, just now. She's nine years old, and there she was, standing at the door, telling us to have a good time and not to be late home.'

Liz agreed. 'You're right. It's like we're the kids and Alice is the concerned parent.'

'She's always been like a little woman, though,' Jim said. 'Always so fussy and protective of her family.'

Liz laughed out loud. 'She's always been a little bossy boots!'

'Well, there you are. Now then, will you please stop creating things to worry about. We have a wonderful baby, a bossy young daughter, with an old head on her shoulders, a fine son, who fits into our family like a hand in a glove, and a dog called Buster, who rules the roost.'

Greatly reassured by his wise words, Liz gave him a quick kiss on the mouth. From now on, instead of looking for things to be anxious about, she would remind herself of how fortunate they were.

CHAPTER FOURTEEN

FOR THE BEST part of an hour, Maureen and the children played on the mat with big coloured balls. It was really a game for baby Harriet, who, with screeches of laughter, rolled the balls haphazardly back and forth to the others, while Buster the dog looked on, too lazy to get up and play along.

'Where's Adam?' Maureen asked. 'I haven't seen him since your parents went out.'

Alice simply shrugged her shoulders, as she often did to avoid answering a particular question.

Maureen was concerned. 'Alice, can you keep an eye on Harriet for just a minute,' she asked, 'while I go and see if he's upstairs?'

Scrambling to her feet, she collected Harriet and placed her in the baby pen, but as she went to leave the room Alice called out, 'He's not upstairs.'

'So, where is he then?'

'He's in the shed. He asked Daddy if he could paint

the little cart, and Daddy said yes.' A deep frown betrayed her disapproval.

A few minutes later, Maureen found Adam busy in the garden shed. 'Hi, Adam. I thought I'd come and see if you were OK.'

'Hi, Maureen. Look, what do you think?' He proudly pointed to the cart, all wet and shiny in its brand-new coat of dark stain.

'Great! Looks like you're doing a good job.'

'Did you want me for anything special?' Adam asked.

'No. I just wondered where you were, that's all.'

'Oh, I'm sorry. I should have told you, but I just wanted to come straight in here and get on with it. I'd like to fnish it before they come back. I'm hoping it'll be a nice surprise.'

'I'm sure it will.' Maureen excused herself. 'Now I know you're all right, I'd best go and sort the girls out.'

'Call if you need me for anything.'

'Thanks.' Maureen did not intend taking him up on his offer of help. She had always seen herself as more than capable.

An hour later, with Harriet still happily playing in her pen, Alice was in the kitchen looking out the window at Adam, who she could see through the open shed door was putting the last few strokes to the little cart.

When he stood back to check that he had covered it thoroughly, Alice dodged back, not wanting to be seen.

Suddenly Maureen called out, startling her, 'Alice, are you in the kitchen?'

'Yes.'

'You're not touching the kettle or anything, are you?'

'No!'

'So, what are you doing?'

'Just having a drink of lemonade.'

'Oh, you wouldn't fetch me one, would you, please?'

'OK.'

Carrying the glass of lemonade, Alice found Maureen stretched out on the sofa, her head buried in Adam's *Beano* comic.

Maureen sat up to take the glass of lemonade. 'Thanks, you're a darling.'

Throwing the *Beano* aside, she asked Alice, 'Do you want to play that new Donkey card game?'

'No, it's boring. Mum says I need to tidy my toy box, so I'm going upstairs now.'

'All right then. See you in a while.'

She watched Alice leave. 'Don't go lifting anything heavy,' Maureen advised her. 'If you need any help, just shout down.'

Five minutes after Alice had gone upstairs, Maureen heard the back door open and shut. 'Is that you, Adam?'

'Yeah. I've finished painting the cart. I'm just about to wash my hands.'

'Make sure you don't tread any paint into the house, or I'll get the blame!'

Taking her advice, Adam retraced his steps to the back door on tiptoe and slipped his shoes off on the mat; Maureen was none the wiser.

She did, however, pop into the kitchen to return her empty glass. 'Alice is cleaning out her toy box,' she informed Adam. 'Apparently, her mum's told her it was well overdue, so you'd best do what I'm doing, and leave her to it.'

Adam gave a wry little smile. 'I'm sure she wouldn't thank me if I interfered anyway.'

From upstairs, Alice heard the two of them talking together, and it wasn't long after that when she heard Adam coming up the stairs.

Quickly, she ran to softly close her bedroom door, while not actually clicking the lock.

Adam called out as he walked past her bedroom, 'Hi, Alice.'

'Hi.'

Going softly to peer through the chink in the door, she watched him go into his room, which was directly opposite.

She watched as he went to the wardrobe and chose a pair of clean trousers and a jumper.

When he turned round and seemed to look straight at her, she ran quickly to the back of her room, where she sat on the toy box, wondering if he'd seen her peeking.

She bided her time, and when she again heard Adam clattering about in his room, she edged towards the door. Stooping down to peer through the narrow chink, she followed Adam's every move. She saw him tidy up the clothes he'd taken off, then he was behind the wardrobe door, hauling up his trousers, and now he was slipping on a clean shirt and rolling up the sleeves.

That done, he came nearer to sit on the edge of the bed, head down, and seemingly faraway in his thoughts.

After what seemed an age, he stood up and, going across the room, he seemed to be reaching down into an area near the wardrobe.

Highly curious, and irritated that she could not see clearly what he was doing, Alice cautiously inched open the chink and watched him return to sit on the bed.

She was excited to notice that he was holding a small, decorated box.

Unaware that Alice was spying on him, Adam held his mother's box for a while. Just to hold it in his hands was an emotional experience for him.

He was in no hurry to open it. Instead, he ran his fingers over the ornate brass panel on the lid. He thought of his mother and the wonderful, happy times they had enjoyed together; the laughter they'd shared. The small adventures they had enjoyed were unforgettable.

And now, for the umpteenth time, he lived the memories again. In his mind, he could almost touch her. He could see her lovely smile and hear her laughter.

He now recalled the many times he had seen her holding this very box.

For the longest moment, he simply sat there forlorn, his eyes closed while he brought his mother's face into his mind and heart. And as always, the pain was unbearable.

With aching curiosity and a deal of resentment, Alice watched his every move. Why had she never seen that box, especially when twice before when he was out, she had gone through his things? So, where did he hide it? What was in it, and who did it belong to?

When Adam held the box close to his heart, it took but a moment for her to realise that it must be his mother's. For one fleeting moment she felt pity for him, but that rare moment of weakness was forgotten as she eagerly watched him open the box and take out what looked to be a long neck chain, which he wound into his hand.

Attached to the chain was a locket, not as flat and small as the one her own mother had, but, oh, it was so pretty. Just now as it emerged from the box, the light caught its brilliance, and the locket seemed to come alive.

Alice was mesmerised.

She saw how Adam caressed the locket in his hands, and she felt his joy. She saw how he pressed it to his face and when she heard him softly crying, she looked away.

In that moment, for whatever reason, Adam instinctively walked across the room and quietly closed his door.

Alice was not best pleased, though in her mind's eye she saw the bright, shimmering locket still, and knew she would not rest until she had it in her hands.

In his bedroom, unaware that Alice had been snooping on him, Adam quickly replaced the locket and hid the box underneath the deep, wooden skirt of the wardrobe, where he believed it to be safe from prying eyes.

Suddenly, he could hear the telephone ringing downstairs, and then Maureen's voice calling up: 'Can somebody please get the phone? I'm changing Harriet's stinky bottom!'

Adam was there in no time. Grabbing up the receiver, he asked, 'Hello, who is this?' Then: 'Oh, right. Yes, we're all fine. Maureen's changing Harriet's nappy, and you'll be pleased to know that Alice is upstairs tidying her toy box.' There was a moment when he just listened, and then: 'Yes, I will. Yes . . . see you later.'

Replacing the receiver, he went into Maureen, who had already guessed from the short exchange: 'That was either Liz or Jim, so is everything all right?'

'They'll be about an hour later than expected. Some friends they haven't seen for a while have just turned up.'

'That's OK.' Maureen was ready for every eventuality. 'I hadn't planned on going out anyway.'

With the baby struggling in her arms, she gently pushed the lazy dog aside with the tip of her toe. 'Shove up, Buster! Harriet wants to play ball.'

She placed the baby into the playpen and watched as she quickly crawled away to get the big, blue ball from the far side. 'I reckon Harriet's gonna be a foot-baller when she grows up.' Maureen reached down and gave the ball a gentle pat; she laughed out loud when Harriet screamed with delight as she scuttled across the playpen after the ball.

Adam, meanwhile, had gone to make sure he'd locked the garden shed.

Up in Adam's bedroom, Alice was on her hands and knees, frantically searching for the box. She had just about given up when she spotted the corner of the eiderdown oddly tucked up at the bottom of the bed. Quickly now, she ran her hand beneath the bed but found nothing. Then, she reached under the skirting of the wardrobe and there it was: a square object with raised features on the lid. Yes! It had to be the box.

Delighted, she withdrew it and, quickly locating the silver locket, she plucked it out, closed the lid and slid the box back again. Hurriedly, she went to the door and peeped out. Satisfied that it was safe, she went straight back to her own bedroom.

As Adam ran up the stairs, she was already sliding the locket underneath her mattress.

She almost leaped out of her skin when there came a tap on her door. 'Alice. You've got a bit more time to tidy your toy box.' As the door was slightly open, Adam poked his head in. 'Do you need any help?'

'No, thanks. Oh! Was that my mum on the phone just now?'

'Yes. She said to tell you and Maureen that they should be back within the hour.'

'That's good, because I haven't really started on my toy box yet.' This was her moment, just before her parents were due home.

Smiling sweetly, she invited him in. 'Come and see. Honestly, Mummy makes such a fuss. I think it's tidy enough already.'

Adam would rather have got on with his own tasks, but thinking to humour her, he came across the room.

When he was almost beside her, Alice calmly opened the lid, deliberately watching Adam for his reaction.

Adam was horrified by what he saw. Lying neatly on top of a mountain of toys, six mutilated dolls lay in a row, each with her hair pulled out by the roots. Their raggedy arms were hanging off, as though they'd been viciously swung round, and their pot faces were busted to a pulp.

Unable to speak for a while, Adam was visibly shaken, then he was gabbling, 'Alice, what's happened to them? Who did that?'

'*You* did that, Adam!' Alice was calm. 'You came into my room when you thought I was asleep and you broke all my dolls. I saw you, but I was frightened in case you hurt me too.'

Adam was shocked, but from her manner and the way she was smiling, he knew the truth. 'You little monster! You did this yourself, didn't you?' He was so shaken he could hardly think straight: 'Alice! Why did you do this? And why are you blaming me? I would never do such a terrible thing!'

She came back at him, calm and smiling. 'But you *did* do it! You thought I was asleep but I wasn't. I saw you do this, Adam. And when Mummy and Daddy get home, I'll tell them what you did, and they'll send you back to that children's home, where you belong! You don't belong here with decent people.'

'Oh, now I see!' Adam grabbed her by the wrist. 'I should have known. All your snide little glances; the way you always butt in whenever I get some attention from your parents; and I know why you wouldn't eat the fish even though it's your favourite. It was because me and Phil caught it. And now this . . . busting up your best dolls, so you can blame it on me, and get me sent away. Well, it won't work! Because you can tell Maureen what a bad thing you've done!' He grabbed hold of her wrist. 'Come on . . . tell her right now!'

When he tugged her forward she started to yell and scream at the top of her voice, 'Help! Maureen, get him off me!'

Alerted by Alice's frantic cries, Maureen ran up the stairs; she was horrified to see that Adam had Alice by both wrists and was trying to force her downstairs. Greatly distressed, Alice was sobbing as she tried to fight him off.

'Stop it!' Grabbing Adam by the arm, Maureen managed to pull him off Alice. 'What the devil do you think you're doing?'

Breaking free, Alice clung to her. 'I know what he did!' she yelled. 'That's why he wants to hurt me . . . because I saw him do it. He broke all my dolls. He did it, Maureen. I saw him.'

'Sssh.' Maureen calmed her, before asking Adam, 'Did you do what she said? I want the truth, Adam.'

Although Adam vehemently denied it, Maureen chose to believe Alice. 'I can only go by what I see now.' She pointed to Adam. 'You were deliberately hurting her, and she's got the bruises to prove it. What's wrong with you, Adam? Why would you do that?'

Adam could see that he had little defence and, not for the first time, he felt alone and vulnerable. 'What's the point?' He glanced at Alice, who was nestling up to Maureen; a look in her eyes that told him she would lie through her teeth until everyone saw her as the victim.

It was then that he realised no one, not even

Maureen, would believe him against Alice, because she was a part of this family, while he would always be an outsider.

'I'm waiting, Adam.' Maureen was insistent. 'I want to know why you hurt her like that?'

'I was not hurting her. I was trying to get her to come and tell you the truth, and she began screaming and fighting me.'

Maureen tenderly stroked Alice's face. 'That's not true. I saw you with my own eyes. You were deliberately hurting her. The poor kid was terrified. So don't you try and lie your way out of it, because I know what I saw.'

'Well, you saw wrong. I didn't mean to hurt her, but she was like a crazy thing, kicking and screaming. I promise you, I never touched her dolls. I just wanted her to tell the truth about what she'd done, and how she deliberately put the blame on me.'

He gave a wry little smile. 'I can see you've already made up your mind that I'm a liar, when the truth is, it's *her* that's lying. But if you can't believe me, then nobody else will.'

He was not surprised to see Alice smile at him from Maureen's protective embrace.

Deep down, he'd always known Alice hated him. He had even confided in Phil, but being the caring man he was, Phil had tried to dismiss Adam's fears.

'You don't know her,' Adam told Maureen. 'She's worked this all out. She's never liked me being here. She told me that I should go back to the children's home, where I belong. She said I don't belong with decent people. And now, that's what you think as well.

So she's won and I'm the bad one, and if you can believe the tale she's told you, they will all believe it.'

Maureen could feel Alice trembling in her arms. She could not believe how Adam was desperately trying to justify what he'd done. 'Adam, I don't know what to say, except that I'm shocked at what you did. I really am sorry that it's turned out like this . . . for Alice's sake mainly. But she could be right. Maybe you did leave the children's home too soon.'

She looked at him, and what she saw was a boy not much younger than she was herself; a boy who had seemed the perfect son for Liz and Jim; a boy who had been much loved by those good people. And, seeing the look on his face now, she saw a goodness there, and for one split second she was actually made to wonder if Alice was lying.

But then she recalled the evidence of her own eyes, and she quickly dismissed that fleeting instinct. The truth was, Adam had hurt Alice. That was what she had witnessed, and Alice had been terrified. She was the one who got hurt. She was the one in distress. She was the one who carried the bruises.

Moreover, from what she had learned through various sources, Maureen reminded herself that Adam had come from a violent background, while Alice's family were decent, God-fearing people, whose only mistake was making a wrong judgement.

'The truth is, Adam, you hurt a terrified nine-year-old child. She was screaming for you to let her go, and you wouldn't. I have to believe what she's told me, and what I saw with my own eyes.'

She looked at him, at his soulful expression, and the way he kept glancing at Alice as though warning her. It only confirmed her belief that he was a bully and a liar.

Maureen held on tight to the girl. 'I'm sorry, Adam, but from the little I know, I believe you must take after your father.'

'*I'm nothing like him!*' Her cutting words ignited a fury in him. 'Don't you ever say that!' He took a step forward, his anger focused on Alice. 'She's the warped one, not me! She never wanted me here. That's why she's done this . . . to make me look bad. To get rid of me!'

When Alice clung harder to her, Maureen slowly backed away from Adam. 'I'm calling the pub to speak to Liz and Jim,' she said coldly. 'You can explain yourself to them!'

'Maureen, I'm not lying,' Adam pleaded with her. 'Please . . . you have to believe me. If one of us is lying, it's her! I never went near the dolls! And I did not deliberately hurt her. She was fighting me because she didn't want me to bring her down to tell you the truth.'

Maureen was already halfway down the stairs, with Alice clutching onto her. 'Stay away, Adam!' she warned him. 'After what I've seen, I don't blame Alice for wanting you away from here!'

When they were out of sight, Adam stood at the top of the stairs for what seemed to him a long time, though in fact it was only a matter of minutes.

Realising that he might be sent away, he was frantic. Liz and Jim were bound to believe Alice over him, and why shouldn't they? Alice was their flesh and blood, after all. Maybe Maureen was right; maybe he did take after his father. Maybe he really was a monster in the making.

He could hear Maureen on the phone. 'No, she's OK now. I've got her down here with me and Harriet. No, he's still upstairs. I don't know . . . but I'll keep an eye on things until you get here.'

On hearing that conversation, Adam could see no alternative.

He went into his room and collected his hessian bag from inside the wardrobe. He filled it with the basics, together with a complete change of clothes and a spare pair of boots.

Next, he took out all his savings, which he had in a jar under the bed. After transferring all the money to one of his clean socks, he stuffed the sock into the deepest crevice of his travel bag.

The money was not a vast amount – well-earned from his paper round, and other odd jobs – but it had filled the jar, and now it would help him get by until he decided what to do.

For now though, he must be quick. He needed to be out of here before Liz and Jim got back.

Quickly, he checked in his mind that he had enough for his immediate needs.

I'll need to get a job, he decided as he hurried about his business. He'd lie about his age. No one would guess he was not yet fourteen. Everyone always said he was tall for his age.

He now collected the most important item of all: his

mother's box, which he withdrew from under the ward-robe and carefully placed in the bottom of the bag. He had an idea for keeping it safe. Taking a pen and paper from the chest of drawers, he pushed them into his pocket.

Shortly after that, he crept softly down the stairs, and out of the house at the back. He had no idea where he might end up, or if the authorities would catch up with him and put him in care again. He desperately hoped not. He had no intention of going back to the children's home. He longed for the day when he would be out of their jurisdiction; when he would be free to do as he pleased. But that was many long months away yet.

~

Following Maureen's frantic phone call, Liz and Jim left the pub to hurry home.

Jim broke the silence. 'I still can't believe it!'

'It's not like Adam,' Liz agreed, quickening her footsteps.

'Liz, think back. Did Maureen actually say that Adam had hurt Alice . . . that she was bruised and upset?'

'Well, yes, as far as I could understand her.'

'But why would he want to hurt her? What's happened? He's never done anything like that before. Jeez! When I get my hands on him, I'll make him answer for this.'

Seeing how he was getting worked up, Liz tried to calm him. 'I can't help but feel Maureen might have got the wrong end of the stick,' she said, breathlessly, hurrying along beside him.

'No. She's a sensible girl. All the same, I'm damned if I can understand it, because Adam's never shown any sign of violence before. What's going on, Liz? Is it maybe something we've done wrong?'

'We've done nothing wrong, Jim. We've given him a good home and we've looked after him like our own. I don't know what's happened exactly, but I do know one thing for certain: if he has lashed out at Alice, he can go back where he came from; and the sooner the better.'

Yet, even though she was concerned, Liz was convincing herself that Adam would not deliberately hurt Alice.

Jim quickened his space until he was almost running. 'I'm sorry, Liz, but it's beginning to look like we've made a big mistake.' He couldn't get home quick enough. 'Come on, Liz. Hurry up!'

Hobbling along in high heels, Liz urged him on. 'You go ahead, Jim. I'll be right behind.'

Just then, as they passed the bottom of the street, Liz caught sight of Adam out the corner of her eye. 'Jim, it's Adam . . . over there, look!'

Jim caught sight of him. 'It looks like he's making a run for it. So there's your answer! Why would he run off like that if he hadn't done anything wrong? You get home and check on Alice. I'm going after the bugger!'

By this time, unaware that they'd seen him, Adam was away like the wind. As he neared the canal, he realised he was being pursued.

On recognising Jim, he was tempted to stop and explain that Alice had set him up, that he had not deliberately hurt her. But then Jim began shouting, 'Come back, you devil! Face up to what you've done!'

Jim was relentless. As fast as Adam ran, Jim was right behind. 'If you're innocent, come back now. Or maybe you're just a coward, like your father!'

The idea that he was being seen in the same light as his father only fired Adam to keep going, to get away from here, and never come back.

Breathless and stumbling, Jim kept after him, over the fields and onwards, towards the canal. Intermittently calling Adam, he had to stop a couple of times to draw breath, but though the terrain slowed him down, he soon renewed his pace, determined to make Adam face up to what he'd done.

When Adam scampered over the stone wall alongside the water, Jim did the same, though being less fit and lithe than the boy, he paid the price.

As he swung himself over the wall, he caught his foot in a deep crevice between the boulders. Propelled forward out of control, he tumbled headlong down the rough, slippery bank until there was nowhere to go but into the murky waters below. He tried desperately to keep himself from going under, but the harder he struggled, the quicker the waters seemed to cover his head and draw him down.

Being some distance ahead, Adam had no idea that Jim was in trouble, though he wondered why he'd given up the chase.

Jim had been yelling for him every few minutes but

now there was only an eerie silence. Adam was puzzled, but somewhat relieved.

Stopping to catch his breath, he smiled to himself. Jim wasn't as fit as he thought. But something felt wrong. It wasn't like Jim to give up.

In the short time he'd been with the family, Adam had grown close to Jim. He knew his ways and, knowing them, he now grew uneasy. Jim's family were everything to him. If Jim thought he'd hurt Alice, he would never give up. So, Adam thought, Jim had either found a different route and he was planning to waylay him at the other end or, for whatever reason, he had decided to let Adam go. But that idea didn't feel right to Adam.

Now convinced that Jim was in trouble, he stuffed his travel bag between the knotted roots of an ancient tree, then he ran as fast as his legs would take him. He carefully retraced every step and kept his eyes peeled at every turn.

When he got to the canal, he saw that the boulders had been disturbed, and the earth was stripped in a jagged line from the boulders to the water. He suspected Jim might have slipped.

'Jim, where are you? It's Adam. Answer me!' he shouted.

On hearing a weakened cry from somewhere beneath the canal bridge, he swiftly ripped off his jacket and shoes, and eased himself into the water. Straightaway, he caught sight of Jim. Visibly shivering, and badly bleeding from the head, he was desperately clinging to an overhanging branch, which was too thin to hold his weight so he might climb out, but it was sturdy enough to help him keep his head above water.

'Hold on . . . don't let go, I'm here.' Adam swam to him. 'I'll get you out, but you'll have to trust me. All right?'

Jim nodded. He was never more relieved than when he saw Adam approaching.

'Don't worry, we'll get you out, Jim,' Adam continued to reassure him, though he soon realised it would not be easy. It was obvious that if he were to go for help, Jim would not have the strength to hold on. 'There's no time to go for help, but you'll be all right . . . I promise. I'll get you out.'

Going under the water, Adam discovered an even more desperate situation than he'd feared. Both of Jim's legs were badly tangled in a mass of thick, binding weeds. Also, judging by the gaping wound and the peculiar angle of a jutting bone, his left knee appeared to have been broken in the fall.

Coming up for air, Adam was concerned to see Jim drifting in and out of consciousness. 'Stay awake, Jim. You have to stay awake!' he yelled. As gently as he could he explained that the weeds were tangled round both his legs, and that his knee appeared to be broken.

He saw the despair in Jim's eyes. 'I will get you out,' he promised again, 'but you have to help me. It's going to hurt, but I need to free your legs. You must try to stay awake!'

Growing weaker, Jim was concerned for Adam. 'Leave me,' he said. 'Go for help!'

Grabbing the collar of his jacket, Adam yelled back, 'There's no time! I won't leave you here to die, like a drowned rat!'

Cold and weary, Jim could hardly keep his eyes open.

'Keep awake, Jim. Hang on. You can do it, I know you can.' Smacking Jim's face, Adam hardened his voice: 'Jim! Don't make me ashamed of you!'

When Jim smiled at his last remark, Adam felt a huge surge of relief. 'You have to trust me, Jim. I need to release you from the bindweed, and then we'll work together and get you out of here. OK?'

Jim gave a curt little nod, then he laid his head on the crook of his shoulder, and watched as Adam slid back under the water.

Adam quickly set about loosening the bindweed that was tightly coiled about Jim's legs. It was a long and laborious task, but eventually the legs were free. With the removal of the bindweed, the broken knee was now hanging open.

From above the water line, he could hear Jim screaming in pain as the dead weight of the lower leg seemed to be tearing the knee apart.

Adam came up for air, before going back down.

Breaking off some lengths of the drifting weeds, he loosely plaited a makeshift bandage. Tying one end above the knee, he wound the bandage down the leg, to secure the other end around Jim's ankle. That done, he drew the two ends together as far as was possible without actually bending the leg until the gap in the knee was made smaller, thereby taking away the drag of the lower leg.

Jim's agonised cries told Adam it was a painful procedure for him to bear, but he urged Adam on.

On surfacing, he could see the pain etched in Jim's

face. 'I'm sorry,' he said, but there was no time for explanation.

Hauling Jim out of the water was the most difficult part of all.

Hoping that someone might be walking the fields, Adam cried out for help, but no one came so the task of heaving Jim onto the bank was left to him alone.

Little by little, Adam managed to get him onto the upper bank, where the two of them lay side by side, totally exhausted, with Jim slipping in and out of consciousness.

Jim's knee was a real concern. When he'd got his breath back Adam knew exactly what he had to do next.

'I'm going for help.' Adam threw his jacket over Jim's wounded knee. 'I'll make you safe so you don't fall down the bank . . . I'll be as quick as I can.' With Jim lying prostrate, eyes closed, and his breathing unsteady, Adam was beginning to fear the worst.

'No . . .' Jim raised his hand. 'Please . . . help me . . . up!'

Adam refused, but Jim was in such a state that Adam feared if he didn't somehow take him from there, Jim would try to follow and end up in the water again. With Jim so determined, and no time to argue, Adam reluctantly decided to help him up.

～

The farmer's wife was at the kitchen window, when she saw two figures struggling up the field.

Alerting her husband, who went outside to check the strangers, she continued watching from the window.

She then followed her husband out, and the two of them watched in amazement as the boy continued towards them, part supporting, part carrying a man. They both looked to be in trouble.

Realizing the emergency of the situation, they began running towards the boy.

Adam saw them coming. 'We're all right,' he said to Jim, who made no reply. By now, he was too far out of it.

Bent double with the weight of Jim, Adam was hardly able to stagger on, but seeing the couple hurrying towards them gave him renewed strength as he pushed himself forward. He'd promised Jim he would get help, and he had kept his promise.

When the farmer took some of the weight onto himself, Adam was close to collapse, but between the two of them, they managed to get Jim to the house, where they laid him on the big oak table in the kitchen.

In the front parlour, the farmer called the ambulance while his wife tended to Jim, who was slightly delirious and making little sense.

Adam bent to tell him, 'You'll be all right now, Jim. The ambulance is on its way.'

Adam had given Jim's name and address to the farmer, urging that he should call Liz, and the farmer went quickly away to make his calls.

A short time later, after Adam was rested and Jim was made more comfortable, Adam whispered in Jim's ear, 'I need you to know, I did not hurt Alice.'

Not yet fully conscious, Jim seemed not to have heard.

Deeply unsettled, Adam sat on the bench outside the farmhouse door for a while. His every bone ached, and his heart was heavy. What to do now?

He thought about going to see his dear friend, Phil. Then he wondered if he should see Liz. But Alice had put a bar between him and the family, and knowing he would not be welcome, he quickly dismissed that idea.

So, while the attention of the farmer and his wife was on Jim, Adam decided it was time to leave.

He did not say goodbye, nor did he linger for them to ask questions. He simply walked away, and kept going until he found a good spot from which he could think.

His plan was to collect his bag and make his own way in the world.

He did not plan on going back to the children's home. Nor did he feel comfortable returning to the family who had taken him in. The family he had come to love.

He thought of Alice, and he was sorry it had turned out the way it had. But thinking back to Phil's earlier explanation, he understood how she felt about his being here.

Now, though, it was time to leave all that behind, and move on.

More importantly, it was time to leave the boy behind, and become the man.

Again, he thought of Phil, and decided to contact him at the first opportunity.

Now, though, for what seemed an age, he sat down on the grassy bank some distance away from the house, just watching and waiting.

When finally the ambulance arrived, he stood up to see the ambulancemen bring Jim out on a stretcher.

Satisfied, he gave the whisper of a smile, and reluctantly turned away.

~

In the ambulance, Jim constantly asked for Adam, but no one knew where he was. No one had seen him leave.

All they knew was that the boy had saved the man's life, and now he was gone.

The ambulanceman questioned the farmer's wife as to the boy's condition. She told how the boy was completely exhausted and in considerable pain when they took him in, but that he was given a hot drink and some clothes that had hung in the wardrobe since her husband was a young man. The boy had changed into them, and seemed much easier in himself. He was not injured as such, but he was very concerned about his companion. 'When we told him the ambulance was on its way, he was greatly relieved,' she said.

When the farmer had called Liz and explained the situation, she was shocked, but as the ambulance was already on its way she decided to head straight to the hospital.

When the ambulance doors were closed, ready for departure, the farmer and his wife could still hear Jim calling, 'Adam . . . where is he? Where's the boy?'

By then, though, Adam was long gone.

~

It took a deal of searching before Adam located the tree under which he'd left his travel bag. He was devastated when he discovered that the bag was gone.

With his bare hands, he dug deeper into the roots of the tree, but it was definitely not there, and he was in pieces.

For a long time, he sat on the ground, rocking back and forth, thinking of Jim, hoping he would be all right. He thought of Alice and the way of things.

When he crossed his arms over his knees and the tears began to fall, it was not because of the small amount of money he'd lost. It was not for Alice, nor the lost bag, and it was not even for Jim, whom he believed was safe now.

His bitter tears were for the loss of his mother's precious locket.

It was the only part of her he had left. And after all he'd been through this was the hardest loss to bear.

Emotionally and physically exhausted, he curled up beneath the tree. It was not long before he drifted into a deep, troubled sleep.

CHAPTER FIFTEEN

I T WAS LATE when Liz got home from the hospital. Maureen had managed to get the children to sleep at long last, but was so tired herself, that she'd fallen asleep on the sofa.

On hearing the key in the front door lock she leaped up, desperate to know that Jim was all right.

Liz looked haggard. 'His knee was badly damaged,' she revealed, '. . . his leg was in a shocking mess.'

'But will he be all right?' Maureen was very fond of the family; it pained her to see their suffering.

'They operated, and the doctor said it went well, but that there was a long way to go yet,' Liz explained. 'Jim had lost so much blood, they had to give him a transfusion. He's sedated now and they seem pleased with his progress. I wanted to stay, but the doctor said he would be out of it for quite a time, and it wouldn't hurt for me to come home and get some sleep. They promised to call me if I'm needed.'

Maureen thought Liz was right to come home. 'I'm sure they would have let you stay if they were unduly concerned about him,' she said. 'And anyway, if you don't mind me saying, you do look like you need a good night's sleep.'

Liz didn't argue with that, though she was more concerned about the children. 'Have they slept?' She recalled how upset Alice was at the awful business of Adam running away, and her daddy having to go into hospital. 'I've been troubled about Alice,' Liz quietly admitted. 'I hope she didn't get herself in a state again after I left. Did she?'

'Well, Harriet went to sleep straight after her milk, and she hasn't woken since. But it took Alice ages to get to sleep, and even then she kept waking up and coming down . . . getting herself upset all over again. In the end, I lay in bed with her until she went to sleep. She kept saying it was all her fault that her daddy nearly died and Adam ran off.'

Liz was surprised. 'How can it be her fault? Unless it was that business with Adam hurting her.'

'That's exactly what I thought,' Maureen said. 'But I told her that even though he got her daddy to safety, it still did not excuse what Adam did to her. I said it was not her fault, and she should never think that.'

'You're absolutely right,' Liz agreed. 'I will never be able to thank Adam enough for getting Jim to safety, but then again, if it hadn't been for Jim chasing after him because of what he did to Alice, Jim would never have got hurt in the first place.'

When Liz sank into the nearest chair, Maureen went

off to the kitchen to make them each a cup of cocoa. 'It'll help you sleep,' she told Liz.

Upstairs, Alice had got out of bed and was sitting at the top of the stairs. She'd been waiting for her mother to come home. She needed to see her. To know her daddy was all right.

Just now, she'd overheard the conversation between Maureen and her mummy, and she felt afraid. She returned to her bedroom. There was something important that she needed to do.

Liz and Maureen were sipping their drinks when Alice came into the room. 'Is Daddy all right?' she asked her mother tearfully. 'He won't die, will he?'

Liz ran across the room and led Alice back to the chair, where she told her sincerely, 'No, sweetheart, Daddy's not going to die. He's had an operation, and he has to stay in hospital for a while, but the doctor told me that he should be all right. It might take a long time, but he'll be fine.'

When Alice burst into tears, she kissed her on the forehead. 'Listen to me, Alice,' she said, stroking her face. 'None of this is your fault. If anything, I'm sorry to say, it's Adam's fault, because if he hadn't hurt you, Daddy would never have been chasing him.'

'Maureen said Adam saved Daddy and got help for him. Did he do that, Mummy?'

'Yes, sweetheart, he did. Daddy told me that he was in a bad way. He was trapped in the water and badly hurt, but Adam managed to get him to safety, and we should all be very grateful for that. But I will not forgive Adam for what he did to you, because that was a cowardly thing.'

'But it's all my fault, Mummy!'

'No, sweetheart. None of this is your fault. Adam did a bad thing when he hurt you. When he ran away, Daddy went after him to bring him back, to explain what he had done, and why. But Daddy was hurt. It was not your fault, and you must never think that.'

Liz was surprised when, without a word, Alice got off her knee and went away upstairs.

'Shall I go after her?' Maureen asked.

'No. Let her go for now. I'll go up in a couple of minutes and see if she's asleep. I think she just needed reassuring, that's all.'

A few minutes later, just as Liz was about to go upstairs, Alice returned. She didn't say anything. Instead, she stood before her mother, her hand outstretched and tears running down her face.

'Alice? What's wrong?' Looking down at the girl's outstretched hand, she was surprised to see a locket and chain, so pretty, and shimmering in the light from the table lamp. 'Alice, where did you get that?' Liz had never seen it before. 'Whose is it?'

'It belongs to Adam.'

Liz was confused. 'If it belongs to Adam, what are *you* doing with it?'

'I stole it.'

'You did what?' Liz was shocked. 'Why would you do such a thing? Was it because he hurt you? Is that why you stole it – to hurt him back? Because if you did, it was wrong to steal, and you know that! Adam was very wrong to hurt you, but you had no right to take his belongings.'

'Adam didn't hurt me, Mummy . . . not on purpose.'

'How can you say that? You had the bruises. You told Maureen that Adam had done it, that he had deliberately hurt you.' But from the look on her daughter's face, Liz knew she was now telling the truth. 'I think you'd better explain yourself, young lady.'

Growing nervous, Alice went on: 'It was me who broke the dollies. I did it to blame Adam, so you and Daddy would send him back to where he came from. I showed Adam the dollies and I told him that I would tell everyone it was him who did it. He got upset and tried to get me downstairs to tell Maureen the truth.'

Liz was shocked, but she sat silent as Alice finished. 'When I didn't want to go downstairs, he got hold of me and I started fighting him. That's how I got bruised. He didn't do it on purpose. I did it, because I wanted him to go back to the children's home.'

Liz was truly shaken by what Alice told her. 'How did you get Adam's locket?'

'I stole it from his bedroom. I saw him looking at it and he was crying, because, I think, it was his mummy's locket. He hid it, and when he went downstairs, I went into his bedroom, and found it.'

When Alice now broke into tears, Liz made no move to hold her. Instead, she told her firmly, 'Give me the locket.'

When Alice passed it over, Liz folded it into her plam. 'What you did to Adam was very wrong. Do you understand that?'

'Yes . . . and I'm sorry, Mummy. Truly, I am. I want to make it better. I want to see Adam. I want to say thank you for helping my daddy, and I want to tell him I'm sorry.'

Reaching out, Liz drew her close, her voice firm yet quiet as she told her daughter, 'You did a very bad thing, Alice. You destroyed your beautiful dollies and turned us against Adam, when he'd done nothing wrong. And then, to steal something that obviously meant a lot to him was cruel. If you were so unhappy about Adam being here, you should have told me or Daddy. You must never, *ever* do such bad things again.'

'I won't.' By now Alice was in floods of tears.

Liz made no effort to comfort her. Instead, she said, 'We need to find Adam, and you must return his mother's locket to him. Then you apologise . . . for everything. And hope he can forgive you.'

'I'm really sorry, Mummy.'

Liz could never have imagined her daughter doing such wicked things. She had always believed that if Alice was unhappy she would confide in her and Jim. But at least she had found the courage to own up, and though it was not enough, it was something. 'Well, I suppose there is one saving grace. At least you've now told the truth about what you did. And I can see that you really are sorry. So, maybe now, we can put the record straight.'

She held Alice at arm's length. 'We know now that Adam was not the villain you made him out to be. In fact, as far as I'm aware, he's done nothing wrong since we took him in. I truly hope you've learned a very valuable lesson here, Alice. Have you?'

'Yes, Mummy.'

'Well, that's something. But I'm shocked and disappointed that you found it difficult to confide in me or your father. In future, if you find yourself worried, about anything at all, you must talk with me or Daddy.'

She gently pushed her away. 'Now, I want you to go back to bed, and think about what you did. I want you to think about how Adam must be feeling, and what you might say to him when we find him.'

'If he's run away, how will we find him, Mummy?'

Liz had been thinking about that. 'I'm hoping Phil might know where he's gone. Now you get back to bed, and remember what I said.'

'Good night, Mummy. Good night, Maureen.' Feeling very sad, Alice gave them each a kiss.

With Alice back in her room, there was no more talk of what she had done. Instead, feeling shocked at Alice's deception, Maureen went home, and Liz slept, fully clothed, on the sofa.

It had been a worrying day, during which she had learned a great deal about human nature.

~

It was dawn when Liz opened her eyes.

Aching in every bone, she struggled to sit up and for a moment she sat stretching her arms and thinking about Jim. Then she began to panic. She had to phone the hospital and check on his progress.

She hurried across the room and into the hallway, where she dialled the hospital.

It seemed to take an age before anyone answered.

'Oh, hello, I'm Liz Dexter. My husband, Jim, was operated on yesterday. Can you please tell me how he is?'

Tapping her fingers on the top of the small table,
she waited, and she waited; and just as she thought no
one was coming to put her mind at rest, a warm, caring
voice lifted her spirits.

'Hello, can I help you?'

'Oh, yes, please. I'm calling about my husband, Jim.'
She paused while the other person confirmed Liz's
identity. 'Please, how is he this morning?'

She listened again and her fears were soothed. 'Oh,
thank you so much. So, he had a good night?' She gave
a sigh of relief. 'That's wonderful, thank you. Could
you please tell him I'll be there very shortly? Thank
you.'

She decided not to tell Jim what Alice had done.
There would be time enough for that when he was
stronger.

With an easier mind, she replaced the receiver and
made her way upstairs on tiptoe. Satisfied that the
children were still fast asleep, she went down to the
kitchen and made herself a cup of tea, which she carried
into the other room. Placing the cup and saucer on
the arm of the sofa, she opened the curtains.

Already the street was coming alive. John Miller,
opposite, was off on his bike to carry out his postman
duties, and down the street she could hear a car revving
up. Liz gave a hint of a smile. Through thick and thin,
good or bad, life still went on. Thank goodness.

Returning to the sofa, she collected her cup and
saucer, and as she sat down, something glittering on

the carpet caught her eye. On closer inspection she saw that it was Adam's locket.

Realising she must have dropped it in the night, she feared it might be broken. She carefully examined it. On first sight it seemed intact, but when she turned it around, she was concerned to notice a slight twist on the side, where it seemed to have a split along the rim.

Curious, she took it to the window and examined it closer. 'That's strange . . .' She moved her finger along the side rim, and, yes, she could feel the slightest bump. A closer look revealed the tiniest catch, woven into the pattern in such a way that it was hard to see at first glance.

Liz was curious. She guessed it was probably hiding a lock of hair, maybe Adam's from when he was a baby.

She knew lockets were often used for that purpose. She examined the filigree patterns and the intricate raised heart on the front. The design was very special and unlike anything she had seen before.

She turned it over in her hand, thinking it had to be a lover's gift. The way the morning light danced off the front, reflecting its glory, was simply breathtaking.

Liz was curious. From what she knew about Edward Carter, she could never imagine him buying such a lovely thing.

When taking Adam for fostering, she and Jim were officially made aware of Adam's background. They knew Edward Carter was now imprisoned.

Curious, she turned the locket over again to see if

there was an inscription anywhere, but she could see none. The only marks on both chain and locket were official hallmarks.

She ran her fingers over the tiny catch. Feeling guilty, she put the locket down. A moment later, intrigued, she picked it up again.

Twice, she tried to shift the catch and each time it held fast.

Frustrated, she laid the locket on the arm of the chair while she finished her tea, before taking the cup and saucer into the kitchen.

On returning to the front room, she stood a moment just gazing at the locket until her curiosity got the better of her. When she now made a determined effort to open it, the catch suddenly popped up, and the locket sprang open. To her surprise, a small square of folded paper fluttered to the carpet.

Liz bent to pick it up and carefully unfolded it. The writing was tiny, but readable:

My darling Adam,
   This locket was a gift from Michael Slater, a man whom I loved as a girl. You are the only one who knows where I keep the locket, so if you now have this note, I am probably no longer alive. You need to know that Michael Slater is your true father. He gave me this locket before I met Edward Carter, who always thought you were his son.

Please forgive me, Adam. Be strong. I love you so very much.
Mum X

Liz was mortified that she'd pried into the locket, for the message was both revealing, and extremely private. It was not meant for a stranger's eyes.

With the locket clutched in one hand and the note in the other, she sat heavily on the sofa and wondered about the ramifications of what it meant for Adam.

Edward and Adam Carter believed they were father and son, when in fact his true father was a man called Michael Slater. She worked it out in her mind: Adam's mother said she loved this Michael Slater *before* she met Edward Carter . . . so she must have been pregnant with Adam, when she married Carter. And he never even knew.

She wondered about Adam's father, Michael Slater. Why had she and Adam's true father gone their separate ways? Maybe Michael Slater was already married. Or maybe she told him she was pregnant, and for whatever reason, he didn't want to know.

It was a mystery, and one that was not altogether uncommon. Sometimes, these things happened, and the girl might have no other choice but to trick a man into marriage, because she needed the child to be legitimate.

Liz paced up and down for a time, wondering how she might deal with this information. *Talk to Phil! Yes, that was it!*

Her first priority for now, though, was her own family,

not least the love of her life, who she may so easily have lost for ever if it had not been for Adam. A boy not quite fourteen years of age, with no home, no family, and nowhere to go, and he was out there, possibly alone, and afraid.

Unless Phil could help to locate him, that innocent boy, through no fault of his own, was headed for a bleak future.

CHAPTER SIXTEEN

THE SUN HAD risen, but Adam was still sleeping.

Having run ahead of its owner, the dog quickly found Adam, fast asleep and bundled up against the chilly night. Excited, it pounced on him, licking his face with its leathery tongue.

'Hey!' Taken unawares, Adam scrambled up, greatly relieved when he saw it was just a friendly, scruffy little dog. 'Hello, you.' He ruffled its coat and waggled its ears, and not for the first time, he wished he had a dog of his own.

'Come 'ere, boy!' The dog's owner was a ruddy-faced man with a walking stick. 'Sorry about that,' he told Adam. 'He were just being friendly.'

Adam assured him it was all right, and the man went on his way with the dog, occasionally glancing back. Wiping the dog's slaver from his face, Adam gave him a little farewell wave.

After the man and dog were out of sight, he leaned

back against the tree and glanced about. The skies above were morning grey, while the sun was trying its utmost to break through. The ground beneath his feet was hard and rocky. There was not a soul about; not even a bird singing. All around was eerily silent, save for the gentlest whipping of the tree branches when the breeze began to play.

In that moment, it seemed to Adam that he was the only person left in the world. It was an exciting, though somewhat disturbing, feeling.

'Come on, Adam. Move yourself!' he said aloud. Drawing his coat about him, he knew he had better get well away from these parts.

He thought of Jim, and he truly regretted what had happened, though he was greatly relieved to know that Jim was now in safe hands.

He took stock of his own situation. *I'd best get word to Phil*, he thought. *But I'm not going back, not ever.*

He was the one who had made the decision to leave, so why did he feel abandoned? *What do I do now? Which way do I go? How do I live?* So many questions passed through his mind, and so many fears, too.

He stood up straight, shoulders taut and head high. He dismissed each question with an answer. *First, you find work. Then you find lodgings. You say nothing about your age, or where you come from.* The sad truth, for now at least, was that he had no idea where he might be headed.

After living with Jim's family, he now felt incredibly lonely, but he also felt stronger, more able to face the obstacles life might put in his way. *Don't lose sight of who you are,* he told himself. *What you do from now on is up to you and no one else. It's time to make your own way in the world.*

Before he set off, he spared a moment for his mother. 'Someone took your locket, Mum,' he whispered sadly. 'They took everything.'

When the inevitable tears fell, he sat on the ground; folding his arms over his head, he sobbed as though he would never stop.

When the tears were spent he felt a rush of anger. 'I hope Edward Carter gets what he deserves,' he said aloud, his voice grating like the hatred within him. 'I hope he suffers for what he did to my mother!'

He shook the bad thoughts clear and stood up. Where to go?

He glanced back in the direction of the farmhouse where he'd left Jim. He wanted to thank the farmer and his wife for what they did, but in the end he could not bring himself to go back. It was enough for him to know that Jim was now being taken care of.

Turning his head, he looked in the direction of the place where he had found a family, and a measure of peace for a time, and he thought of Liz, and Alice.

For a moment, he was sorely tempted to go back, but the moment passed and he decided to take the same route as the man with his dog.

The minute he started walking he felt as though he had the body of an old man; every bone creaked and groaned. This was the price he must pay for having got Jim to safety, and for choosing the cramped and rocky place where he'd laid his head to sleep.

He kept his pace steady, and the further he walked, the easier it seemed to get. When he got to the neck of the canal, which was far from the spot where Jim got caught up in the bindweed, he walked along the towpath until he found a private little curve in the bend. Here was where the water narrowed, and the risk of anyone seeing him was remote.

Stripping naked, he rolled his belongings into a tight ball and with great care he hid them under a pile of leaves and branches. Then he dived lazily into the water, shivering as he floated free for a time.

The experience was heavenly. The weight was gone from his joints and the water was immensely soothing. And now that the sun was coming alive, he could feel the warmth caress his bare, wet skin. He closed his eyes and let the water take him where it would.

After a time, he spun over and swam back to the place where he'd hidden his clothes. He clambered out and, finding his clothes, he quickly put them on, before anyone might come this way.

Feeling cleaner and fresher, and much easier in his bones, he walked on, following the path taken by the man and his dog.

The dog had reminded him of Phil's little dog, Rex. He missed Phil. He wondered how long it might be before he would see him again.

First, though, he had things to do, and places to go. But wherever he went he would let Phil know. He owed him that much at least.

As his journey progressed, he wondered about that boy who had been taken to the children's home. He made himself forget, for that boy was not him. Never again would he be that boy.

Time had moved on, and life had taken his childhood.

He had lost not only his darling mother, but, with her, the only real and true love he had ever known. Nothing on earth would ever replace that.

It was time to face up to the harsh truth. From now on, he must take responsibility for himself. It would not be easy, he realised, but he would learn, because life itself, with all its trials, joys and impossible journeys, was the best teacher of all. Like it or not, he was already on the longest journey.

At this moment, in this place, he had no idea where the journey might take him.

It was a daunting thought.

PART FIVE

~

The Girl

1959

CHAPTER SEVENTEEN

PHIL HAD MADE this journey many times when Adam was living at the children's home, but this time he was angry, and deeply worried.

Miss Martin had grown to know Phil very well since Adam had gone missing, some months back. 'Hello, Phil. Come inside,' she greeted him. She led him down the hall to her office, talking as she went. 'I'm afraid there is still nothing to report.'

After ordering tea and biscuits from the kitchen, she told Phil, with much regret, 'Although the police have not been able to find him, they do assure me that they're still on the case.'

Phil had heard it all before. 'That's not good enough.'

Dipping into his pocket, he slid the letter across the desk. 'That one arrived this very morning. It's the fifth letter I've had in these past months, and they're all stamped from different parts of the country. And still they haven't been able to trace Adam. Why is that? *Tell me . . . have* they given up on him?'

Miss Martin was adamant. 'Dear me, no, Phil! The boy is not yet fifteen. It's their bounden duty to find him, and they will. They have traced the letters as far as they can, but still no sight of Adam. We just have to be patient.'

'So what do we do?'

'There is very little to be done, except to let the police get on with it,' she answered sadly. 'I know it's frustrating, but sooner or later they will find him. You mark my words.'

'I'm worried about him.' Phil had suffered many sleepless nights since Adam had been gone. 'In the letters he tells me he's well, and that I'm not to worry, but how can I not worry? He says nothing about how he lives, or where he gets his money from. Or what kind of work he might be taking on. And what kind of people would take him on, anyway? He's just a boy. I can't even write back to him because he never gives me a return address.'

Growing emotional, he could hardly keep his voice steady. 'To tell the truth, I'm at my wits' end.' Dropping his sorry gaze to the floor, he gave a long, drawn-out sigh. 'Oh, dear lady, why doesn't he come home?'

Miss Martin gave a sympathetic little smile. 'I'm sorry, Phil, I can't answer that question. But for now, we must be content that he's keeping in touch. At least we know he must be safe. Isn't that so?'

Phil nodded his head, but he was too choked up to speak.

Just then the assistant arrived with tea and biscuits.

Miss Martin thanked her, and the woman quickly departed.

Phil grew unusually quiet, his mind heavy with troubling thoughts.

Liz had only recently entrusted him with the information concerning the stolen locket and the ensuing discovery of its contents, which Phil so wanted to share the amazing news with Miss Martin. But he realised how strongly Liz and Jim felt about not releasing the information to anyone else.

They had rightly argued that it was Adam's private business and no one else's for the time being. They pointed out, quite rightly, that Michael Slater was a complete stranger, and that Adam might not even want to know him. Also, it was painfully clear that this man had not stood by Adam's mother when she needed him, or he would have been with her and Adam from the start. So, the question remained, what kind of man would desert a woman who was carrying his child?

With that in mind, Liz and Jim were adamant that it was for Adam to decide whether he wanted this man in his life, or not.

Phil himself was undecided as to the best way forward; although his every instinct urged him to discuss the issue with Miss Martin. After all, she seemed a wise and kindly woman, who Adam liked and respected. Moreover, she had many contacts, and she had a canny way of getting to the bottom of things.

Phil's deep thoughts were interrupted by Miss Martin's kindly voice. 'Are you all right?' She smiled at him across the desk. 'You seem to be miles away in your thoughts.'

'I'm sorry,' he answered lamely, 'it's just that I'm so worried about Adam.'

'I understand that, but I can't help feeling that you have something else on your mind.'

Phil confessed, 'You're right. I do find myself in a sort of dilemma, and I'm not sure which way to go.'

'Is it something I can help you with?'

'I'm sure you could, but I believe I'm not at liberty to confide in you.'

'Really?' She was both curious and concerned. 'And why might that be?'

Phil was hesitant. 'I wonder . . . if I was to share something with you . . . something very private and a little difficult, d'you think you could be discreet?'

She smiled. 'People do say that I'm the soul of discretion. Yes, you can rely on me, I promise. I can see that you're deeply troubled about something or other, and in my experience a niggling problem is always better out than in. So, if you want to share the burden, I can just listen. Or, if you want, I can maybe give advice.' She gave a little knowing smile. 'Or I can do absolutely nothing . . . if that's what you want.'

Miss Martin was nobody's fool. She had come to know and like Phil, and she could see he was deeply troubled. 'If you're concerned about me gossiping, have no fear. Whatever confidence you share with me, will never go beyond these four walls.'

Phil believed her, but still he agonised with his conscience. He desperately needed to confide in this dear soul; to tell her of the exciting discovery regarding the locket and the note within it.

Suddenly he was confiding the knowledge he had learned from Liz and Jim. And when he was finished, he shook his head despondently. 'I should never have told.' He felt guilty, and yet curiously relieved.

Growing hopeful, he dared to ask, 'So, will you help us then?'

'Yes, but firstly, I think you must speak with Liz and Jim. I will help, of course I will, and they must remain determined in their efforts to find Adam. However, if he does return, you should persuade them not to tell Adam of their new-found knowledge regarding his father; at least, not until we can substantiate it. Conversely, once Michael Slater *is* located, then of course Adam should be made aware that he may have a father whom he knew nothing about.'

Phil was in full agreement as she outlined her terms. 'There are too many unknown issues here that must be dealt with before Adam is brought into the equation,' she went on. 'Firstly, it might take months, even years, to track him down. Secondly, suppose it turns out that this man is not Adam's blood father? Thirdly, even if he is, it does not follow that he would want to take on a boy he doesn't even know, and possibly doesn't even care about.'

'I agree with everything you say.' Phil was delighted by her response. 'It's just that Liz and Jim are eager to give Adam the news that the unsavoury character he believed to be his father was never his real father at all. The thing is, nothing is certain yet.'

'So, do you think you might persuade them to keep this discovery to themselves, at least until I've had a chance to verify some of the possibilities?'

Phil was thrilled. 'I can't thank you enough, because I know if anyone can locate this man, and get to the truth, it's you.'

'You know I can't promise anything, except to do my utmost, for you, and Adam. I do have numerous contacts in far-flung places, and if you promise to speak with Liz and Jim, I can get on to it straightaway. So, do you think you can persuade them not to tell Adam . . . at least for now?'

Phil did not hesitate. 'I know they'll understand when I tell them that you've decided to help us. With you searching for the man we all hope is Adam's real father, that leaves us able to throw all our efforts into finding Adam.'

They shook hands, and while Phil left with a smile on his face, Miss Martin was already sifting through her contacts list.

~

On a fine, dry day, Miss Martin turned her little black car into the street, some time after Phil's visit to see her.

Parking the car halfway down, she shifted it out of gear and turned off the engine. She then gathered her small briefcase into her arms, and got out of the car. After a glance up and down, she mentally registered the number sequence on the doors. 'Ah . . . this way,

I think.' She proceeded to walk along the pavement, checking the door numbers.

The house with the two flowerpots outside was numbered to correspond with the number in her notepad.

She made her way up the path and knocked on the door. By nature, she was a stalwart and confident figure, but this particular errand today felt more like a part of her own life than a matter of professional interest. Realising how important the outcome of this meeting was to Adam, she felt decidedly nervous.

When there was no answer to her modest tapping on the door, she took a deep breath and gave a resounding knock on the door panel.

Inside the house, Sally was running the upright Hoover over the carpet, and had not heard the first knock. 'Oh, who the devil's that?' It had been one of those mornings. She had already changed the bed, done a pile of washing and baked a cake for the woman next door – it was her daughter's tenth birthday tomorrow and she was hopeless at baking.

'All right! I'm coming.' Switching off the Hoover, Sally rushed to the door and flung it open. She was surprised to see a very matronly looking woman standing on her doorstep. 'Can I help you?'

Miss Martin was relieved to see this very ordinary though pretty woman answering the door. 'Thank you, yes. I hope you don't mind this intrusion, but I'm looking for a Michael Slater. He does live here, doesn't he?' After flicking through her notepad, she showed it to Sally. 'This is the right address, isn't it?'

'Well, yes . . . that's our address.' Slightly frazzled by piles of housework and a late Friday night that left her tired, Sally was somewhat impatient. 'Sorry, but . . . might I ask what you want with my husband?' Thinking her visitor both polite and official, she was a little concerned.

'I'm sorry, please forgive me, but it's a rather delicate matter and I do need to speak with Michael Slater . . . if he's at home?' She felt awkward. She had hoped he would be alone, but now that she was faced with his wife, she was uncertain as to whether it might be wise to come back another time. The news she was bringing, would no doubt be a shock to Michael, but possibly even more of a shock to his wife, who in the event must surely be made aware of her purpose for this visit.

Miss Martin, however, felt her responsibility was to speak with Michael. It was then for him to speak with his wife.

Suddenly he was there. 'Yes, I'm at home.' Having come in from the shed, he was still in his work overalls and with oil stains on his smiley face. He opened the door wider. 'So who wants me?' He smiled at Sally, but Sally was not amused.

Miss Martin was staggered to realise how much Adam resembled Michael: the same bright eyes and smiley face. The same thick, wild hair. She was deeply shaken but excited, yet managed to compose herself. After all, a smiley face, and a mop of wild hair was not enough to go on.

'This lady asked for you, Mick,' Sally said lightly. 'She

needs to discuss a delicate matter, but doesn't seem at all keen on talking to me.'

She opened the door wider. 'Please . . . do come in.' After ushering Miss Martin inside, she then ordered her husband, 'You go and get cleaned up, while I put the kettle on.'

Gesturing to the lounge door, she asked Miss Martin, 'Please . . . go and sit down, while I make us a pot of tea . . . or would you prefer a cold drink?' She was curious as to why this woman might want to speak with Michael.

Upstairs, Mick was wondering the very same. 'What the devil does she want with me?' he muttered as he washed and changed. 'I don't believe I've ever clapped eyes on her before.'

Miss Martin thanked Sally for her kind offer of tea, which, after her journey, would go down very nicely. 'Tea would be lovely,' she said, and watched as Sally went away. She hoped her visit here today would not wreck this marriage.

It seemed no time at all before Sally was back with the tray. 'So . . . what's this "delicate matter" you mentioned?' She set the tray down and poured out three teas. 'Sugar . . . er . . . I don't know your name?'

'It's Miss Martin . . . and please, forgive my manners.' She smiled up at Sally. 'Oh . . . yes, two sugars, thank you.'

She felt awkward. 'I'm sorry, but . . . would it be possible for me to see Michael alone?'

'Mick and I have no secrets. I'm sure he would want me here.'

'Yes! Of course I want you here.' At that moment, Michael returned to find the visitor seated in the armchair. Sally was seated a distance away, on the sofa. 'Right! So, what's this all about?' He addressed the visitor, but glanced at Sally. When she looked away, it made him curiously uneasy.

Miss Martin was also uneasy. She felt awkward with Sally in the room. 'It's difficult,' she said, as Mick sat down in the chair opposite. 'I'll be honest with you both. I was hoping I might talk with Michael, first, and then the two of you could discuss the matter after I've gone.'

'Nonsense!' Mick was adamant. 'Sally and I always deal with everything together. So, who are you, and what's the purpose of your visit here?'

Miss Martin first verified that he was the right person. She checked his name, recent addresses, and ran through the information she'd collated. When he asked light-heartedly if she'd come to tell him he'd been left a deal of money by an aged unknown relative, she chuckled. 'No, nothing like that, I'm afraid.'

She informed him of her name and her work, and both Sally and Mick were taken aback. Why would someone in charge of a children's home be coming to see Mick? Sally was unsettled by the information.

Mick, too, was irritated. 'Why in God's name would you be wanting to speak with me?' he asked impatiently. 'Where do I fit into all that?'

Miss Martin drew out a sheaf of details. 'Firstly, let me tell you that there is no certainty in anything I have to say, or show you. Like I say, it's a difficult situation.'

She glanced at Sally, who was now on the edge of her seat and thinking the worst.

Miss Martin went on: 'We're here simply to determine whether or not this has anything to do with you, or means nothing at all to you. In the latter case I beg your forgiveness, and I'll be on my way.'

Sally was growing increasingly nervous. 'What have you to say?'

And so, she told them about Adam, and how her enquiries had brought her here, to their home.

She informed them of what she knew of his mother, while carefully withholding her name.

'His mother was a lovely lady, but she married a monster, and that monster hurt her so badly that she died. The husband was arrested and is now safely locked away. With his father secure in prison and his mother buried, young Adam became an orphan and was subsequently brought to my children's home. He is now with foster parents.'

Sally was intrigued. She felt for the boy, Adam, but wanted to know, 'What has all this to do with us?'

'Please, I'm getting to that.' Miss Martin went on: 'Adam has his mother's gentle nature, and though he appeared to be content with his new foster parents, the daughter resented him being there and there was a disagreement. Adam ran away, and despite everyone's efforts to find him, he has not been seen since. And of course we are all deeply concerned for his safety.'

She took out Adam's birth certificate and held it out to Michael. 'Does this tell you anything at all?'

He took the certificate and as he ran his eyes over the page, he took in a great gasp of breath.

'What is it?' Sally leaned over to see. 'What's wrong, Mick?' She saw the blood drain from his face, and her heart turned over. 'MICK! TELL ME! Please?'

He handed her the certificate and while she perused the details, he paced the floor, saying not a word, but looking as though his world had fallen apart. 'I knew her,' he said quietly. 'The boy's mother . . . I knew her.'

Sally flung the certificate onto the couch. 'What are you trying to tell me, Mick? What has this boy to do with you?'

Suddenly he had her by the shoulders. 'Please! Listen to me, sweetheart . . . it was a long time ago. It was before I met you. It was a fling, that's all. A young man's fling, and it meant nothing to me. It was one night, and I never saw her again.'

'So . . . what are you saying to me?' She had an idea, but dared not say it out loud.

When Mick looked at her, he realised that one way or another, their lives were about to change, and he prayed he would not lose this woman, who he loved with all his heart. With tears in his eyes, he explained, 'The boy's birth-date . . . he could be mine. I can't know for certain, but it all tallies.' The tears flowed shamelessly. 'Oh, sweetheart! I'm saying . . . that boy could be my son!'

When Sally turned away and ran to the bedroom, he sat for a while on the chair, his head in his hands and his mind in pieces.

'You need to see something else.' Miss Martin gave

him the tiny note Adam's mother had written, and as he read it, she told him, 'I don't think there is any doubt, do you?'

When he sank down into the chair, she knew it was time for her to leave. 'I'm leaving my contact numbers here,' she told him. 'Whether you get in touch is now up to you.' Lowering her voice, she told him, 'I can see now . . . you did not abandon her. You just didn't know . . . did you?'

When he looked up, he seemed a man devastated.

'Go to your wife,' she murmured. 'Anyone can see that you and she are devoted to each other. You have a lovely relationship . . . strong enough to come through this, I'm sure. But right now she needs you, more than ever.'

She told him, 'Whichever way you decide, I would be grateful if you let me know . . . for Adam's sake.'

Through his tears he asked, 'The boy . . . you said he was missing. Will he be safe, do you think?'

She nodded. 'He has many friends, people who love him dearly. And we won't rest until we find him.'

He gave a little smile. 'I'd best go and talk with Sally.'

'Yes, I think you should.'

She left copies of all the information she had collated. Then she let herself out.

~

Late the same evening, Jim and Liz sat talking together.

'Jim, are we wrong in not trying to contact this Michael Slater?'

Jim poured out two glasses of wine, and passed one to Liz. 'No. It has to be Adam's decision. That aside, I've been thinking.' He took a sip of wine and placed the glass on the side table. 'The last letter Phil got was from Dorset. Oh, I know it's a long shot, but what if I went down there and drove about for a while? You never know, I might just catch sight of him.'

'Look, I'm just as desperate to have him home as you are, but Dorset covers many miles,' Liz reasoned with him. 'How could you even hope to get a sight of him? He could be anywhere. In fact, by the time you got into Dorset, he could well have moved out of the area.'

'Yes, you're right.' Jim let out a long sigh. 'I just worry about him . . . what he's doing . . . who he's with, and why won't he come home?'

Liz quietly reminded him, 'He went away thinking Alice doesn't want him here. That's maybe why.'

Jim had no answer to that.

'Jim?' Liz knew how concerned he was.

Jim looked up. 'Yes, sweetheart?'

'If you could get time off work, and you really want to go and look for Adam, I'd be right behind you. You do know that, don't you?'

Jim came to sit on the arm of her chair. 'I do know that.' He slid an arm round her shoulders. 'I also know how lucky I am to have a wife like you.'

They talked for a while and when they were weary of talk and weary of worrying, they went off to their bed.

Another day was ended.

Another day when Adam continued to weigh heavy on their minds.

CHAPTER EIGHTEEN

I T WAS SATURDAY, and the work was almost over. In the relatively short time he had been here, Adam had become accustomed to the noise, colour and excitement of a day working on a fairground. His particular training had been on the waltzer. One of the main attractions, the waltzer consisted of a wide ring of large metal chairs, which spun madly round on their own axles as the machine rotated at great speed. The riders would scream and laugh, as they were thrown every which way, out of control. Adam's job was to collect the money and keep an eye out for anyone who might want to exit early.

His working day was long and hard, but he enjoyed the independence and freedom of having a reasonable wage at the end of the week, and a place to stay, however humble it might be.

Now, as the last ride finished, he noticed the boss heading towards him. Jack Langdon was a man of some considerable size, a kindly but firm man who was well liked by the workers. He ruled his large, nomadic family with a mixture of sternness and humour; the one exception being his second wife, who had an acid tongue, and a delight in seeing men fight amongst themselves.

Apart from Adam, and another, older, man, all the fairground workers were of the Langdon family. Following long and often dubious traditions, the family were close knit and fiercely independent. Occasionally flirting on the wrong side of the law, they answered to no one, and on the first sign of interference into their cherished way of life, they would swiftly move on.

When Adam came looking for work, they did not ask his age or situation. Instead, the boss-man gave him the once-over and, satisfied that this boy looked well capable of doing the job, he was given a month's trial period.

In return, Adam worked hard and long. He kept himself to himself, and made no ripples. At the end of the month, he was taken on for another month and then longer, until now he was just a stride away from his fifteenth birthday.

In the evening, after everyone and everything was accounted for, Jack supervised the securing of the stalls and rides for the night.

One of Adam's late duties before settling into his tiny caravan was to feed and groom the two riding horses belonging to the boss-man. Jack Langdon was an accomplished rider, and the horses were his pride and joy. Everywhere Jack went, the horses went with him, being drawn behind the convoy, in a smart, motor-driven horsebox.

Today, while Adam made his way to the stables, Jack embarked on his regular check: making sure nothing had been missed and that every ride and stall was safely locked down for the night.

From the main caravan window, the girl watched as Adam made the trek towards the portable, makeshift stables. Built from large wooden panels and securely bolted to the ground, the stables were sturdy and warm, with two doors that swung to and kept the horses safe. Inside, the earthy ground was dressed with a thick layer of straw for the horses to lie on.

When moving on, the stables would be taken up and packed onto the wagon, ready for the next stop.

While she watched Adam, her grandmother watched Amy. She had always thought the girl was far too pretty. Small of face, with her sleek black hair and sea-green eyes, she was a magnet for any man, even at sixteen years old.

'Amy! What are you doing looking out the window?' The shrill voice of Maggie Langdon startled the girl. 'I hope you're not fawning over that boy . . . because if you are you'd better forget it. I've told your grandfather he should send the bugger on his way, and the sooner the better. So if you're planning to throw yourself at that boy, you'd best think again, 'cause we don't want no little bastards running about here!'

Amy shrank away from the window. 'That's a dreadful thing to say!'

Like many members of the family, Amy had no liking for her grandfather's wife. 'I wasn't looking at Adam,' she lied. 'I wasn't looking at anything in particular.'

Amy had learned long ago that however hard she tried to please this bad-tempered woman, nothing she did would ever be enough.

The older woman would not let it go. A small creature with birdlike features, she poked the girl in the chest. 'Little liar! I've seen the way you fawn over him. You're turning into a slut, just like your mother. You've got the look of her, and the same appetite for men. If you ask me, you're getting to be a handful. No wonder she ran off and left you. I must have been crazy to let your grandfather take you on; especially when we've already raised our own children.'

When Amy tried to defend herself, Maggie shouted over her, 'Don't lie to me! I saw you gawping at that boy the first day your grandfather gave him work. I warned him not to take him on, but what did he do, eh? He went against me, that's what – like he always does. And now it's only a matter of time before that boy proves me right. He's a lazy article and a waste of space.'

Amy was used to her grandmother's spiteful tirades, and normally she would just walk away. This time, though, she was not only hurt by her grandmother's cruel remarks regarding her and her mother, but she felt the need to speak up for Adam. 'You're wrong, Grandma! Adam is not useless. He works hard. He doesn't steal, and he doesn't fight, not like the others. Grandfather says he's doing really well.'

'Huh! He does, does he? Well, more fool him! It wouldn't surprise me if that little devil hasn't already dipped his hand into the money-bag. Your grandfather's too soft. Too trusting. If this was my business, I'd run it the way it should be run. Unfortunately, it was handed down to your grandfather long before I met him, so he thinks he knows best. If he'd listened to me he would never have taken that boy on . . . same as I never would have taken you on, if that silly old fool hadn't kicked up the divil of a fuss.'

'I never asked you to take me on.' Amy was always hurt by that particular comment. 'It wasn't my choice to stay here with you.'

'Maybe it wasn't, but I had no choice either. I certainly didn't want a bawling kid round my backside . . . not again. But your grandfather has no backbone. He insisted you stay with us, and no matter what I said I could not change his mind. Anyway, you're coming up seventeen. It's almost time for you to take off in the big wide world and make your own living. Oh, but why should you, eh? When you've got it so cushy here.'

Tutting and ranting, she stomped to the bedroom, where she could be heard slamming and banging about.

Within minutes, she was back. 'That boy . . . what did you say about him fighting?'

Amy thought back. 'I said he would never fight, not like the others.'

For the longest moment, the old woman remained silent; and then she was chuckling. 'There you are then. So, he's a coward into the bargain.'

'I never said that, and he's not a coward. Anyway, I'm glad he doesn't fight. He's a decent boy, not like the ones Granddad had to get rid of.'

'Oh, decent is he? Well, if I know anything, it's that the

boy will show his true colours soon enough.' With that she went away and shut herself in the bedroom.

Amy took the opportunity to sneak out.

Once she was free of the caravan, she took to her heels and ran to the stables, where she looked through the door to see Adam gently stroking the long neck of one of the horses. She could hear Adam softly talking to him.

'You're a real beauty,' he was saying. 'It's no wonder Mr Langdon wants you everywhere with him.'

He dropped his voice to a whisper. 'Whenever that wicked old woman has a go at him, at least he's got the two of you to come and be with.' Nuzzling up to the horse, he continued to whisper, and as though understanding, the horse rested his head on Adam's shoulder.

This was always Adam's favourite time of day, when his ordinary day's work was done and he came out here. Trusting and friendly, the horses settled his fears and warmed his heart, and he was glad that Langdon had trusted him with such a special task, because settling the horse for the night also settled him.

Their gentle natures reached him deep inside, where no one else could, except for his darling mother, and, like her, these magnificent horses seemed to know when he was sad and lonely and needed reassurance.

Taking the brush, he ran it over the horse's mane. 'You and your pal are lucky to have each other. I have a special friend too. His name's Phil. I haven't seen him in a while, though, but I send him a note whenever I can to let him know I'm all right, and to say that he's not to worry.'

Thinking of Phil made him think of Alice and the family, and as always the sadness crept over him. 'I ran away,' he whispered, 'so now I have to pretend I'm older than I really am. I can't wait until I'm sixteen, when I'll be free to go and see Phil and the others.'

That particular birthday could not come soon enough for him, because he so wanted to see his dear friend. Phil had been with him through all his trials, and Adam sorely missed him.

Listening from outside, Amy was surprised to hear that he'd run away, and that he was not yet sixteen, and now she was unsure whether or not she should make her presence known. Wanting to be with him, she pushed everything she'd heard to the back of her mind, and stepped back a few paces, calling his name as though she had just arrived.

'Adam . . . it's me . . . Amy.' She shuffled her feet as though she was coming along the path, and when she got to the door, she stood outside looking in. 'Grandmother's off on one of her rampages, so I thought it best to get out of her way.'

'Hello, Amy.' Adam was pleased to see her. 'I'm just finishing off here,' he said. 'Come in, if you want.' He hoped she would, because he really liked her.

Amy went inside. 'You really love these horses, don't you, Adam?' Reaching out, she stroked the neck of the stallion. 'They seem to trust you, and you're so natural and easy with them. Did you ever have a horse, Adam?' she asked.

'No.' Visions of his father dampened his spirit. 'My father would never have approved.'

'Oh, that's a shame.' Noting the bitterness when he spoke of his father, she wisely changed the subject. 'So, did you never have a pet?'

'I once had a cat, but my friend Phil has a dog, and we used to take it on long walks through the woods.' He cautioned himself not to talk about anything connected to his background. 'But that was a while ago now.' He made an effort to close that particular subject.

Amy sensed his concern and changed tack. 'Do you like it here, Adam?'

Adam's face lit up. 'Oh, yes, I really do. I'm earning money and I'm kept busy, and, oh, I do love to be with the horses.'

Amy smiled. 'Did you know that, apart from me, you're the only person grandfather allows to be in here, with his precious horses?'

'Really?' Adam felt a surge of pride. 'He never said.'

'Ah, well, I'm telling you now. These horses are his pride and joy. He bred them, raised them, broke and backed them, and they've both won him championships.'

Adam was in awe. 'Wow! No wonder he doesn't want anyone else near them. But why does he trust me to feed and bed them? I mean . . . I know nothing about horses.'

Amy smiled. 'You don't have to know anything about horses,' she explained, 'because the horses will know whether or not you're safe to be with. I was ten years old when Grandfather first took me to see these horses, and I remember when I stroked this stallion I was really nervous. But he stood tall and let me stroke him, and he even nuzzled me. I was not afraid after that. Granddad told me that a horse has a sense about you. On first meeting, he'll either back off and refuse to come to you, or he'll let you touch him. If he responds like that, it means he feels safe with you, and that you would never harm him.'

Adam was amazed. 'But that's exactly what happened to me. On my second day here, your grandfather brought me to see the horses. He told me to approach the mare and raise the back of my hand near her face. I had to wait until the mare came up to sniff my hand, and then I was to very gently stroke her nose and move away, to see if she would come to me. And she did. It was amazing.'

Amy smiled. 'Grandfather told me that the back of the hand does not represent a threat. If you had gone straight up to the mare with your hand flat out, and she didn't like your scent, she might have bitten your fingers off. Granddad was introducing you to her, like he did with me. The horses obviously liked you. That's why he lets you feed and bed them down.'

'Well I'm so glad he did, because I really like being with them.'

From a short distance away, Grandmother Langdon spied on them. She could not hear their conversation, but she heard them laughing together. She inched closer. Enraged by the sight of Amy leaning in to the horse, with her hair touching Adam's face, she made her way back to the caravan, where she sat by the window, impatiently waiting for Amy to come home. *I should go and get her,* she thought, *but then she would only defy me even more.*

It was half an hour before Amy came back; her face warm with pleasure at having spent time with Adam.

'What have you been up to?' Grandmother Langdon assumed the worst.

'What do you mean?' Amy was angry. 'I haven't been up to anything. For your information, I've been in the stables with Adam and the horses. We just talked, and I helped him so he could finish early.'

The older woman gave no reply. But she was determined to finish this relationship. Maybe Amy was telling the truth and nothing happened this time, but there would surely be another time, when things would not be so innocent. She had never wanted that boy on site. She neither liked, nor trusted him.

When it came down to it, that boy would have Amy, take his pleasure and then he would move on, leaving her with child. They were all the same; only ever after one thing, and then they were gone in the night. She knew about these things.

She also knew she had to do something about it, before these events came to pass.

Retiring to her bedroom, she could not get the idea out of her head. She began pacing back and forth, her mind alive with plans. *If he stays here, before you know it, he'll have her in the sack and there'll be a young 'un to care for,* she thought. *And who would end up being expected to look after the little bastard? Me, that's who! Well, they're wrong. I've done my baby-raising, and there'll be no more of it!*

Soon, her plan was hatched in her mind and she could not wait to put it into action.

~

The following afternoon a horse-trader, Bob, called in on Jack Langdon, telling him there was a young thoroughbred up for sale in the village some fifteen miles away. 'I heard you were on the lookout for a high-class filly, being as your one isn't as young as she used to be. As you know, the best filly thoroughbreds are not only hard to come by, but they fetch such prices as might put anyone off. But being as you can swing a bargain, I reckon you might fetch the price down to suit.'

Jack was excited. 'What made you think of me?'

'That's easy, Jack. You helped me out once, so I thought it was time to return the favour. The filly is out of a top thoroughbred, so you don't want to hang about if you're interested.'

Jack could hardly hide his excitement. 'I've already had three foals from the mare I have now, and sold them on at a tidy profit. And you're right, I've been looking for a filly to bring up alongside her; get it ready for breeding, so to speak. So, what d'you reckon, Bob? Should I go tonight?'

'Well, that's up to you, but if it were me, I would not leave it till tomorrow, that's for sure.'

Before he left, Bob gave Jack the name and address of the breeder, and left him to think about it.

As the visitor left, he looked up to see Grandmother

Langdon at the caravan window. They exchanged a knowing smile. These two were long-time buddies.

~

Adam had just finished his day's work, when Jack approached him. 'I've to go out for an hour or two this evening,' he told Adam. 'The other blokes are already off, and Pete's been called away unexpectedly – there's a spot of trouble with family, or something of the sort. It means I'm one security man short, though. So d'you think you're man enough to fill the breach?'

Adam was thrilled. 'Yes, Mr Langdon. I already know Pete's routine. I walked round with him the other night, and I can do it, no bother.'

'Good! So, after you've seen to the horses, go and check with Seamus. He'll put you right. Just make sure everything is as it should be. If there's the slightest sniff of trouble, you must call Seamus. He won't be far away, but you probably won't need him. I'm counting on you, young Adam. Don't let me down.'

'I won't let you down. Thank you, Mr Langdon.' Adam was pleased to be trusted alongside Seamus.

~

A short time later, after Adam had seen to the horses, he went to his caravan and hurriedly cleaned himself up. He then made himself a sandwich, but he was so excited he couldn't eat it. He put the sandwich aside, collected his torch and went off to find Seamus.

Seamus had already been briefed by the boss-man and he showed Adam the ropes. 'Every half-hour, you check all the locks. You look for anything suspicious, like a flap of tarpaulin turned back, or a light on somewhere, or some little thing that doesn't seem right. You check everything, however insignificant it might seem, but if you do find anything untoward, don't take any chances, just call me and I'll be there in a jiffy. Have you got that?'

'Yes, I've got that.' Every word was emblazoned on Adam's mind.

Some hour and a half later, he and Seamus had done the rounds three times, and the only misdemeanour they could find was that one of the workers had left a bucket across the walkway. In the gloom, Seamus accidentally knocked it over, startling both himself and Adam. Other than that, everything appeared to be normal.

'I'd best go and tell the women not to worry.' Seamus thought the clatter of the bucket might have made them nervous. 'I'll not be a minute,' he told Adam. 'You just hang on here.' He left him by the caterpillar ride.

Adam did as he was instructed. Keeping his eyes and ears open, he waited for Seamus to come back. Everything was quiet. There seemed nothing untoward.

He almost jumped out of his skin when Seamus came up behind him. 'It's all right. Young Amy is safely locked in the caravan, listening to her music. Apparently, the grandmother's in her bedroom having a nap.

Seamus was relaxed. 'Look, Adam, I'll go round and check the rides. You have another walk round the stalls. We'll meet up at the candyfloss stall. Oh, and we should swap torches. Yours looks a bit low on battery, I reckon. I'd much rather it died on me than you.'

Adam thanked him. 'It's all right, Seamus.' He gave the torch a shake. 'I'm used to this one. It's never let me down yet.'

Seamus took him at his word, and each went his way.

Halfway round the site, Seamus thought he heard a noise. Standing still and quiet as a mouse, he listened a while. 'Damned cats!'

Taking out his cigarette packet, he plucked one out and pressed it to his lips, then he struck a match and lit the cigarette. Relaxing, he sat on the steps of the carousel and took a few puffs, blowing the smoke out in perfect circles.

Leaning back, he thought of his girlfriend at home and enjoyed the cigarette all the more. *Adam's a good boy*, he thought, his mind now back on his responsibilities. *Not many young boys actually listen to what you say . . . at least not some o' these chaps we often hire through the summer. Think they know it all . . . lazy little sods!*

On the other side of the fairground, Adam was investigating the very same noise that Seamus thought he had heard.

When a cat ran out from under the tarpaulin, Adam breathed a sigh of relief. But the relief was ended when suddenly he was spun round and before he could shout for Seamus, his mouth was taped and a sack was thrown over his head. Propelled forward, he had no idea what was happening, or who the men were that held him in such a lock-hold he thought his arms would break.

Terrified, he felt himself being dragged over rough ground, and then he was lifted and thrown into what he imagined must be a vehicle of sorts. He could hear an engine running, but he couldn't see or even cry out.

Behind him, Seamus heard the vehicle take off at speed. He ran as fast as his legs would carry him, only to see the back end of a vehicle, partly hidden by flying dirt, and thick smoke rising from the exhaust. Just a fleeting glance, then all he could see were the lights as the vehicle sped away along the top lane. 'Adam!' He screamed his name as he ran back to the stalls. 'Adam, answer me, dammit!'

When it became obvious that Adam was nowhere to be found, he ran towards the Langdons' caravan, only to be greeted by a frantic Amy.

Having heard the speeding vehicle and then Adam's name being called out, she was already running down the caravan steps. 'What is it?' she screamed at Seamus. 'What's happened? Where's Adam?'

Seamus wasn't altogether certain exactly what had happened. 'I sent Adam to check the stalls while I checked the rides. I heard a sound and ran round to the stalls, and there was this vehicle racing off – a van, I think, but I can't be sure.'

Amy was fearful. 'Where's Adam?'

Seamus threw out his hands in despair. 'I can't find him. I've searched high and low and I can't locate him. I checked the horses, but he's not there either.'

'So, where is he, Seamus?' Amy was beside herself. 'Where could he have gone? And who did the vehicle belong to?' She had a really bad feeling. 'I'm frightened, Seamus. What if he's lying hurt somewhere? We've got to search. We've got to find him.'

'I've searched every nook and cranny, and he's nowhere on site,' Seamus told her again. He took hold of her by the shoulders. 'Listen, Amy, it's no good us looking again. You'd best call your grandmother.'

'No!' Amy was adamant. 'Leave her be. She doesn't care about Adam.'

Inside her bedroom, Grandmother Langdon listened to the conversation for a while, and then she turned over, a devious little smile on her crinkled old face.

Outside, Amy ran past Seamus. 'I'll find him,' she said. 'He must be here somewhere.'

Going after her, Seamus held her back. Looking down on her tearful face, he told her what he suspected. 'I don't know who was driving that vehicle, but whoever it was, I think they took him.'

'No! Why would you say that?' Then Amy remembered what Adam had told her. 'He said his father was a controlling man. He ran away. He said he couldn't go back. Oh, Seamus, maybe Adam's father took him?'

'But why snatch him like that? Why not come here himself, in daylight? Why did he not speak to your grandfather, like any other man would do? Amy, fetch Grandmother Langdon. Maybe she can get hold of Jack. Maybe he'll know what to do.'

Fearful for Adam's safety, Amy relented, and ran into

the caravan bedroom where she shook the older woman. 'Grandmother! Get up, quick!'

Opening one eye, the older woman cursed. 'What d'you want?'

Impatient, Amy shook her again. 'We need Granddad. Adam's gone missing.'

'What? You mean he's run off? I knew he would. I said all along he was trouble, but nobody would listen.'

'No! He hasn't run off. There was a van. Seamus thinks someone's taken Adam. We need Granddad. Where is he, Grandmother? Can we call him?'

'No, we can't, and even if we could, he wouldn't thank you for it. He's doing an important deal just now. You know he won't like to be interrupted.'

'He'll want to know about Adam and the van. Please, Grandmother, give me the number and I'll call him.'

'I can't! I don't have a number. And if I did, I would not give it to you. I knew all along that boy was trouble. Good riddance to him. I won't be shedding any tears at his going. Now get out and leave me be!'

When the door suddenly opened to admit Jack Langdon, Maggie was shocked. Drawing the covers over her, she demanded, 'What's brought you home so early? You said you'd be gone for most of the evening doing a deal or something . . . buying a filly thoroughbred, so I was led to believe.'

'Really? And who told you . . . about the filly?'

'Well, I don't know. *You* must have done.'

'No, I didn't. There wasn't time.'

'Well then, I suppose Bob must have told me . . . We had a few words before he came to find you.'

Jack was suspicious. 'We'll continue this conversation when I get back.'

'Where are you going?'

His face set with anger as he stared down on her. 'You get back to sleep. You and me . . . we'll talk later.'

Hurrying outside, he shouted for Seamus. 'Fetch the Land Rover. Be quick! And think hard . . . which way did they go?'

When Amy came running down the steps, he told her, 'Go back. Lock all the doors and windows and keep an eye on your grandmother.'

'I'm coming with you two. I'm coming to find Adam.'

'Do as you're told, Amy!'

Amy's answer was to fling the caravan door shut and run across to climb into the back seat of the Land Rover. 'I'm coming with you, Granddad.'

'Well, if I'm right, there'll be no time for arguing. So keep quiet, sit still, and hold onto your hat!'

When he put his foot down hard on the accelerator, the capable Land Rover responded at speed. As they fled along the lanes, Amy clung on with both hands. She had no idea where they were going. She had a feeling that her grandfather knew something, and from the way he spoke to Grandmother Langdon, maybe she knew more than she was saying. It was a bad situation with undercurrents she did not understand, and Adam was right in the middle of it.

She could hear the two men talking in the front. 'They wouldn't have gone along the main route,' Grandfather Langdon was saying. 'Not from the way you described how the lights were bouncing up and down as they sped off. I reckon they went along the top lane?'

'That's right. I could see the lights clearly bobbing up and down, which means they were on a rough surface. Besides, if they'd been along the bottom lane, the spinney would have blacked out the lights, but I could clearly see the lights travelling on.'

'Right! So, that's the way we'll go – along the top lane – and let's hope to God we're right.'

～

After a rough and frightening journey, Adam was yanked out of the van. Blindfolded, and completely unaware of why this was happening, he could feel himself being dragged along rough terrain. He heard the voices of his attackers, but he was not able to recognise them.

Suddenly his abductors came to a halt and he was dropped to the ground. All was quiet and for a moment he thought they'd gone, but then came the vicious kicking, and a harsh warning. 'Somebody doesn't like you! So don't come back. You won't get a second chance.'

Time and again, Adam felt the impact of their boots against his battered body. Then he was rolling away, faster and faster before the darkness swept over his mind, and took away the pain.

～

Jack Langdon senior had grown up in the countryside. What he didn't know about tracking was not worth knowing. Amy's grandfather was his only grandson, and it had given the old man the greatest pleasure to teach him everything he knew.

It was this knowledge that Jack drew on now.

While he walked in front, following every dip and scar in the road, Seamus crawled on behind in the Land Rover. Amy watched her grandfather and she knew if anyone could find Adam, it would be he.

The abductors' van had left behind a trail of clues: the peculiar swerves, and the deep tyre tracks were still fresh and telling a story.

Amy had wanted to walk with him, but Jack told her to stay inside, and so she hung her head out the window and watched her grandfather's every move. When suddenly he stopped to call out, 'Here! They pulled in here!' both she and Seamus jumped out and ran to see.

The evidence of a vehicle having swerved towards the edge of the steep bank was clear. The ground was stirred up by the heavy-booted footprints from at least two people, and between the footprints the track of flattened dirt suggested that something heavy had been dragged along the ground.

Jack drew their attention to where the flattened ground carried on right to the recently broken edge. 'Here!' Jack knew straightaway, and his fears were very real. 'Go back and lock yourself in the Land Rover,' he instructed Amy. 'If anyone comes near you, press the horn, and we'll be right there.'

When she opened her mouth to argue, he told her firmly, 'Amy! Do as I say. We don't know what we might find down there.' He had an idea, and it was not pleasant. If Adam had been thrown down there, Jack knew his chances of survival were very slim indeed.

For a painfully long time, Amy sat in the car, frantic and increasingly impatient. She wanted to go after them, but the lane was dark, and she was nervous. Granddad had looked really worried.

All she could think of was Adam. 'Please, let him be all right,' she whispered, over and over again. There was no comfort, no reassurance, and now Seamus and her grandfather had been gone for so long, she began to worry about them too.

She was curled up, eyes closed, when a gentle tap came on the window. It was Seamus, and he looked fraught.

Quickly, Amy unlocked the door, and Seamus jumped in and started the engine.

'Seamus! Did you find Adam? Is he all right? Where's Grandfather?' The questions came thick and fast.

'Yes, we found him.' Putting the engine into gear, Seamus sent it hurtling forward, keeping a sharp eye on the road ahead. 'He's bad, Amy. I'm sorry, but Adam's real bad. He's alive, though, thank God. Your grandfather's watching over him.'

'Did Adam tell you who took him?' Amy could not hold back the tears.

Reluctant to tell her that Adam was in no fit state to speak, Seamus avoided the question. 'We've to find a telephone quickly. There's one in the next village. Hold

on, Amy!' he warned her again, as he sent the Land
Rover surging forward. 'Hold on tight!'

Amy remained silent. There were no more questions.
Just a desperate prayer, that they had found Adam in
time, and that he would recover.

PART SIX

~

Home is Where the Heart is

1960

CHAPTER NINETEEN

'I'M NERVOUS ABOUT meeting up with Jim and Liz.'
Sally linked her arm through Mick's. 'And I've got
my fingers crossed that Adam will let you explain.'

Mick reassured her: 'Stop worrying, sweetheart. Miss
Martin told him everything, and for now, I'm just
delighted that at least, he's agreed to see us.'

Sally relaxed. 'You're right. If he didn't want to know
us, he would have said no straight off.'

Mick was also nervous, though he was determined
not to let his nerves get the better of him. This first
meeting with Adam was too important. 'I can never
thank Miss Martin enough,' he said now. 'If it hadn't
been for her, and the others, I would never have known
about Adam.'

He glanced at Sally. 'As for you –' he squeezed her
hand – 'you're amazing. That day when Miss Martin
came to see me, you could have packed your bags there
and then. Instead, you took the time to listen to what

I had to say, and once you understood, you supported me all the way.' Leaning down, he kissed her on the cheek. 'I loved you from the first day I saw you. Truth is, my life would be empty without you.'

Sally smiled up at him. 'I'm sorry I couldn't give you children.' Her smile brightened. 'But you now have a son . . . *we* have a son, and I so hope he'll accept us, because from what we've been told, he's had a bad time of it.'

'Yes, he has, but if we're given the chance to make it up to him, we'll turn all that around, won't we?'

'Yes, God willing.' She gave a private little smile, 'Oh, Mick . . . just imagine . . . a son, to love and care for. We'll help him forget the bad times, and look forward with him to a better future. Oh, Mick! With us, he'll have so much love.'

Mick was filled with emotion by Sally's enthusiasm. 'You do realise that if he accepts us—'

'Yes . . . what?'

He gave a happy smile. 'There might come a day when we'll be granddad and grandma. What do you think to that?'

Her smile said it all. 'Babies . . . oh, how wonderful!' She clung to him. 'First, though, we need to be thankful for Adam. Like you say, if he accepts us, all the lovely things will follow. And I for one won't mind having grey hair, with a bouncing grandchild in my arms.'

Falling silent, they walked on, growing more excited, more nervous. This was a major day in both their lives. Miss Martin would be waiting for them at a café near to the hospital, where Adam was recovering, along with

Adam's foster parents, Liz and Jim. Also, they would finally meet Phil. According to Miss Martin, it was that dear man who had kept Adam under his wing, and never once faltered in his loyalty to the boy.

Deep in thought, Mick remained anxious. Meeting up with all these fine people was a daunting prospect. Suppose they took against him and Sally? Suppose they were able to persuade Adam against accepting them?

When he voiced his concerns to Sally, she told him in no uncertain manner, 'Stop worrying. Adam will see how genuine you are, and I just know he will love you.' Looking up at him with adoring eyes, she squeezed his arm. 'I mean . . . who wouldn't?'

Meeting up with the others in a café near the hospital, Mick saw them all as having Adam's welfare at heart. He confessed his anxieties.

'I'm just a stranger to him. I'm concerned that he might not give me a chance to explain. He could even reject me out of hand.'

Phil assured him, 'In spite of his bad experiences, Adam is a good and balanced young man, without an ounce of spite in him.'

'He might think I abandoned his mother, but I didn't know she was with child. She never told me.'

Phil put his mind at rest: 'Miss Martin and I have already spoken to him, and though he was deeply shocked, I think he's had time enough to mull it over in his mind. I'm sure he'll listen when you put your case. Like us, he'll see you both as good people, and to tell you the truth, although all of us sitting round this table have done our best for Adam, we are not his parents, and that's what the boy needs, more than anything.'

He smiled at Mick. 'Don't be nervous, either of you. I'm sure Adam will like you both straight off. Trust me.'

~

Adam had been in hospital for two long months.

His broken bones were mending, and the deepest scars he carried from that terrifying ordeal were the memories of it. There was a faint scar along his cheekbone, but apart from that his face had escaped unscathed.

Today, the nurse would take him for final X-rays and a check-up. If everything was headed in the right direction, he would go home this afternoon. Phil was due to arrive before too long. And if all went as planned, maybe Liz and Jim would be with him.

'Excited, are you?' the nurse asked.

Adam told her he was grateful for the care he'd had there, but that he would be pleased to leave now. 'I can't wait to see Phil and the others,' he said.

'Well, I'm sure they'll all be excited to get you home again. You're a very lucky boy to have such good friends.'

Adam smiled. 'I know that.'

'And that little Amy is lovely. I know I shouldn't ask, but I'm naturally nosy. Is it serious between you and her?'

Adam blushed. 'I don't know yet.' For him, it was.

The check-ups all showed that Adam was well on the mend. The doctor was delighted with his progress.

'I'd feel comfortable if you use the wheelchair for at

least another two weeks or so, and then you can progress onto crutches. Within a month or so after that, you should be strong and able enough to climb Mount Everest.'

Adam was slightly disappointed that he needed the wheelchair for a while yet, but at least he was mending, and that was the most important thing.

As the nurse wheeled him back, she suggested, 'You should get a couple of hours' sleep before your folks start arriving. It will stand you in good stead for the travelling.'

In the ward, she tucked him up in bed and left him drinking a glass of orange juice. 'Miss Martin brought your clothes in yesterday. They're hanging in the wardrobe to loosen the creases. Oh, and I'll have the medication waiting for you by the time you're ready to leave. Meantime, you get some rest.'

After finishing his orange juice, that's exactly what Adam did.

First, though, he checked the clock: half-past one . . . another hour and they would be there. He was disappointed that Liz had not offered to take him back, but he accepted it because he thought maybe Alice was uncomfortable with the idea of him living there again.

Still, he comforted himself with the knowledge that it would not be too long before his sixteenth birthday, when he could choose where he might live.

He thought of Amy, and his heart melted. Wherever in the world he went from now on, he would not want to be far away from her.

~

Seated in the nearby café with Phil, and Liz and Jim, Sally and Mick grew increasingly nervous. 'I'm worried that Adam might be upset when we tell him the truth,' Mick said. 'Maybe he won't even like us.'

He was highly nervous of speaking with the son he had not even known he had. He spoke to Liz on that point. 'It's thanks to Miss Martin's valiant efforts to track me down that I found out I had a son. But that was months ago. I should have talked to him about it long before now. He won't forgive me, will he?'

'There is nothing to forgive,' Liz promised him. 'You couldn't tell him when he was lying at death's door, and you certainly couldn't tell him while he was recovering. But you came here every day to see him, while he was unconscious and such dedication tells its own story. Adam will see that, and of course he won't be upset. One thing I would say, though: when you do tell him the truth, do it gently. Think of how the truth came as a shock to you. And as you're well aware, he's already been through a lot these past months.'

Phil endorsed that. 'Adam is a surprisingly mature boy for his age. He has a depth of understanding. I know, when you tell him, he'll be shocked at first, yes, but I can assure you, Adam will be greatly relieved to know that the monster who raised him was not his blood father.'

Sally had a different concern. 'What if he doesn't want to come home with us? We can't force him, and neither would we. So, what do we do?'

'I think we should leave it to Adam,' Mick decided. 'One thing we are sure of, he won't have to go back to the children's home, not now he's got me and Sally. And don't forget, I'm his father – named and verified by his own mother – and I think that means I can say whether or not Adam can stay with friends if he wants to.'

Sally agreed. 'But we would love him to be part of our family. To call us Mum and Dad would mean so very much to us.'

She smiled shyly. 'I'll admit, it was a shock when I first found out that Mick had fathered a child. When Miss Martin traced us and showed us the locket and the note Adam's mother had written, I was truly shaken. I didn't know what it might mean to us. But now, after being by Adam's bedside for hours on end when he didn't even know we were there, I've grown to love him as a person in his own right, and as a son. And I really would love him to come home with us.'

Phil ended the conversation, with wise words: 'Trust me to let the boy know the truth, and we'll go from there.'

~

Adam was surprised to see Phil on his own. 'I thought you were bringing Liz and Jim with you?' he asked. 'Or did they not want to see me?' He was disappointed.

'I came alone because I have something to show you.' He took the locket from his pocket, and pressed it into Adam's hand. 'This belongs to you.'

Adam was amazed and confused. 'Oh! It's my mother's locket! But it was in my bag. Someone stole it . . . However did you find it, Phil?' Holding the locket in his hand again brought tears to Adam's eyes. 'Oh, Phil, I don't know how you found it, but I'll never be able to thank you enough. Where was it? Did the thief try to sell it, or what? I don't understand.'

'The locket was not in your bag when you left Liz and Jim's house,' Phil carefully explained. 'Alice took it from the box. She hid it and told Liz about it later. Now then, I have something here that will change you life for ever, Adam. Something very precious. Liz found it when she took the locket from Alice.'

Intrigued and somewhat afraid, Adam held out his hand. 'What is it, Phil?'

Phil laid the folded note into Adam's palm. 'This was inside the locket. It's a beautiful thing,' he said, 'and it's in your mother's hand.'

With great trepidation, Adam unfolded the tiny piece paper and read what his mother had written for him.

When he had read every word, Adam looked up at Phil, his eyes filled with tears. 'I never knew,' he said, 'I never knew.' He put his face in his hands and he closed his eyes. His mother was strong in his mind. He was sad for her, for the way she had lived with Edward Carter all those years, not because she loved him, but to give her child a father.

He looked up at Phil. 'She made a terrible sacrifice, Phil . . . for me. She lived with that man for all those years, and she probably never even loved him.' The tears ran down his face. 'She did that, for me, Phil. For me!'

Phil warned him against feeling guilty. 'Your mother

was a very strong woman, Adam. She had a choice and she took it. It was what she wanted. And as long as she had you, she was a happy, contented woman. You must never, ever forget that.'

Adam nodded. 'And this man . . . my father. Does he know about me now?'

'Yes. He's a good man, Adam. I can see why your mother fell in love with him. But he never knew she was pregnant with you. She never told him. He's married now but, ironically, Mick and his wife, Sally, can never have children. Miss Martin told them about the letter, and they have been at your side from when you were first brought in to when you began to open your eyes. That's when they decided not to come any more, until you knew the truth. And you could make up your mind as to whether or not you want him in your life . . . him and Sally.'

Adam shook his head. 'I don't know, Phil. I'm confused at the minute. I need to think about it. Are they here now?' he asked suddenly.

Phil nodded. 'They're waiting, but they will go away and come back again to see you . . . if that's what you want?'

Adam was about to answer when both he and Phil became aware of someone bearing down on them.

Mick had decided he needed to know what his son thought of him.

Phil stood up. 'Adam . . . this is Mick, your father.'

For the longest moment neither of them spoke. Instead, they looked at each other and the moment was heavy with emotion. Then Adam opened his arms and

Mick went to him. 'I'm sorry, Son,' he whispered. 'If I'd only known, I would never have let your mother go. She was so very special. But I have a wonderful wife now, and in many small ways she's very much like your mother. She's kind and loving, and she so wants you to be with us . . . if it's what you want too.'

Adam thought of the horses at the fairground, and how they could sense whether they would be safe with a particular person. Just now, he felt the same way with Mick.

In that precious moment he could see his mother's smile; he could hear her voice. And now, having read her heartfelt letter, he knew she would be content if he were to accept this man who was his father.

In answer to Mick's request, Adam smiled and nodded, and his future was sealed.

~

Later, Phil made him aware of Carter's downfall.

He told Adam of a recent report, detailing how Carter had tried to install himself as the big man inside prison. Unfortunately for him, he had set himself against hard and dangerous men, who meant to teach him a lesson.

Edward Carter earned his comeuppance.

After a fierce and bloody skirmish between the prisoners, the officers found Carter, crouched in a corner, badly injured and mentally unstable.

After treatment in hospital, he was transferred to a mental institution, where he was destined to spend the rest of his days.

Phil said it was an eye for an eye; despite all the pain, fear and suffering he had heaped on others, his innocent victims had grown stronger, while Edward Carter was now a broken man.

CHAPTER TWENTY

THROUGHOUT HIS RECOVERY, Amy was never far from Adam's side.

Amy's grandfather, also, was a constant visitor and had neglected his work duties to be there for Adam. Throughout Adam's painful recovery, Seamus had yet again proven himself to be a loyal friend.

When Adam was strong and able enough, he was determined to return to the fairground, of which he had wonderful memories, alongside his darling Amy.

Also, it gave him a measure of pride and satisfaction to repay their loyalty and love.

One evening, after a busy day, Adam made his way across the yard to check that the horses were all put away safely.

Having checked around the buildings and grounds, he then went over to the young colt's stable. The colt had only recently been separated from his mother, and like other young horses weaned from their mothers for the first time, he was somewhat fretful and jittery.

Inside the stable, Amy pacified the colt. 'Ssh . . . you're a big boy now, and you can't cling to your mummy for ever. You have to learn to be on your own at night-times, but don't worry, you'll see her tomorrow in the fields.'

She nuzzled its face. 'I think I know how you feel, though,' she confessed. 'I can never imagine being too far from Adam. When I'm not near him, I feel empty inside, and so very sad. And then –' her eyes lit up and a warm passion coloured her voice – 'when I'm with him, my heart sings and jumps for joy, and I feel kind of . . . complete somehow. Sometimes, when he smiles at me, it's like I can't breathe. I love him so very much, but I'm afraid to tell him, in case it might frighten him away. Oh, I think he does like me a lot, but I don't know if he loves me in the same way that I love him.'

'Then you must be blind,' Adam's voice gentled across the stable.

'Oh, Adam!' Flustered to see him there, she was lost for words, and then she was in his arms as his tender words brought tears to her eyes.

'Oh, my darling Amy . . . how could you not know, I've loved you from the first time I saw you?'

Taking a small, red box from his pocket, he told her, 'I've been carrying this about for over a week, not daring to give it to you, in case you might turn away.'

When he handed her the pretty red box, she gingerly opened it. Inside was a tiny ring, with a bright, blue stone set in a heart-shaped centre.

With tears streaming down her face and her heart about to burst, Amy was lost for words.

'Well?' Adam whispered teasingly. 'Will you marry me . . . or have I got it wrong?'

Amy gave her answer by flinging her arms round his neck. She held onto him as though she would never let go.

'I love you,' she whispered softly in his ear. 'I've always loved you.'

After slipping the ring on her finger, Adam held her for what seemed an age. Then they were laughing, and running hand in hand, so excited. And impatient to tell everyone the good news.

Find out more about
Josephine COX
and her bestselling books

Dear Reader,

The first thing I do when I'm about to start a novel is to profile the main characters, and, from that moment, it is they who write the story. Along the way, I might laugh or feel sadness with all the characters – I share their every emotion. Sometimes my characters catch me by surprise when they commit an act of cruelty that I might never have originally anticipated. But I remain true to my instincts. The characters are alive, the plot is shaped by what they do – just as in life, we as readers are swept along in their world. In our own lives, we have no say in who we are, and just like the characters, we have no idea how our lives will shape us – and often we are at the mercy of life itself, helpless to change our journey.

In this book, the character that shapes the story is Edward Carter, more monster than man. Through devious actions and callous intent he drives the other characters into situations that will either make or destroy them. But along the way, there are some wonderful characters who cross Edward's path, characters who are as good as he is evil. So, as in life, this story touches upon fear and hatred, but there is also laughter and joy, and a sense of fulfillment.

I am thrilled to live in my characters' world for a time, and I hope you are too – enjoy the journey!

Lots of love and take care,

Jo x

JO ANSWERS QUESTIONS FROM HER READERS

If you could live in another time, which era would you choose?

It would have to be Dickensian London – I'm absolutely fascinated by the world of Charles Dickens.

Are you superstitious?

No, I'm not superstitious, but I always carry a sports whistle in my bag when I travel. I like to think that if the plane went down in water, I could attract attention, which gives me a bit of security.

Have you always told stories? Can you tell us a bit about your earliest memories?

Yes, I've told stories for as long as I can remember! I remember one teacher at school in particular who encouraged me, Miss Jackson.

When I was young, my family was very poor – we often went without, and our clothes used to come from the rag and bone shop. I used to collect up newspapers and take them to the paper factory to save up enough money for something 'off the rack', which was the height of luxury to me then!

One of my earliest memories is of my granddad. He always wore a flat cap and a really long overcoat. He had long whiskers, and a terrier that followed him everywhere. I remember that the shoes I had from the rag and bone shop were hurting my feet, and one day we walked past a shop displaying a pair of red shoes with ankle straps – I pressed my nose up to the window and said to Granddad, "Look at those!" They were so beautiful, and I couldn't ever imagine owning a pair of shoes like that. But my granddad went back to the shop and bought them for me. They were the only pair they had, and they fitted me perfectly – it was meant to be! I've always loved shoes from that moment – so much so that my husband, Ken, built me some cupboards all along the bedroom wall to keep them in, but I still manage to have some in boxes on the floor!

What would you do if you won the lottery?

I would share it with my friends and family – by paying off their mortgages and other bills, for instance. I always try to help anyone who is in trouble if they come to me, and helping the people I love most in this way would be a great joy to me. I think I would also treat myself to a really fast sports car! If I won enough money to do it, I would also really enjoy helping to grant the wishes of children who are very ill, or in difficult family circumstances. I would love to do that, and to see the look on their faces when they got their wish!

How do you come up with new ideas for your books?

New characters just present themselves to me; I see them everywhere, quite often when I'm halfway through writing another book. They stay with me and simmer along until I'm ready to give them their story.

I have writing pads all over the house – I covered eight pages of A4 last night writing a story I've called *The Kissing Tree* – it meant that I only slept for about three hours, but it was worth it!

What have been the proudest moments of your life and career?

The proudest moment of my life, without doubt, was giving birth to my sons. I think the greatest achievements in my career are the beautiful letters I receive from my wonderful readers, and receiving the Outstanding Achievement Award from the RNA in 2011.

Which famous person, and which of your own characters, would you most like to meet?

Without doubt, I'd like to meet Kirk Douglas! I've got every edition of *Spartacus* ever made (and quite often with an extra copy for back up), except for the original unedited film. My brother even bought me a huge framed picture of Kirk Douglas in his loincloth in

Woolworth's years ago. I had it enlarged, and it still hangs in my office. Recently, my wonderful agent Luigi surprised me with a copy of *The Broken Man*, signed by Kirk Douglas himself – needless to say, I was absolutely thrilled! Kirk wrote that he's looking forward to reading my next, 50th book…

Of my own characters, I'd most like to meet the bus driver in *The Broken Man* – he's a wonderful friend to Adam. He is a really warm and lovable person, and he certainly lingered with me after I'd finished the book.

Which character from your books is most like you?

I think probably Emma Grady, from *The Emma Grady Trilogy* (*Outcast*, *Alley Urchin* and *Vagabonds*). I really put myself in her shoes – her uncle, who was supposed to be her guardian, frames her for murder, and she is transported to Australia. She is lined up with all the other convicts and picked out to work for some awful men. I could really feel everything she felt, and I just wanted to cuddle her and tell her that it was going to be all right. I won't give the rest of the story away, but I will say that I made sure she came back to England and gave her uncle his comeuppance!

What's your favourite book?

My favourite book of all time is Charles Dickens' *Oliver Twist*. I heard that story at school when I was about seven years old and was mesmerized. The characters are amazing – you never forget them. It definitely inspired me to become a writer.

What is your writing routine?

I don't have a routine as such. I don't have eight hours sleep, eight hours work and eight hours play – it just doesn't work like that for me. If I wasn't sleeping well I would go into the office and work for four or five hours – I love being with my characters. The story and characters just take over so I have pen and paper in every room of my house in case I need to hurriedly jot something down.

What do you do in your spare time?

That's a very difficult question because I don't have a lot of spare time. I like to go dancing, swimming or walking – basic things make me happy. When I've finished a chapter, I often sing and dance around the kitchen with the radio on. I'm a creative soul.

Are any of your stories based on real life events?

My stories are a mixture of real life and make believe. Sometimes I feature a street that I grew up in or a character that struck me as a child. But often a character just pops into my mind without me even realising.

How do you feel when you finish a book?

I live with my characters while I'm writing a story so when you come to the last page, you do feel sad. There is an element of excitement that the story is written but you miss the characters, as they become so real. A lot of readers say they re-read my novels if there are characters that they particularly relate to.

I have to clear my mind and have a break once I've finished a book so that the new characters can materialise. I'm soon living with them and I have a new set of people in my life.

How do you choose the settings for your books?

I pick up the setting on location – how a street looks, the houses...

I also set a lot of my books in and around Blackburn because it's where I grew up. I think it's natural for most writers to go back to their roots. It was my stamping ground when I was a kid – we used to play in the streets, swing round the lamppost and dream of the future. When you're a child your emotions are very raw and you live life full on – it was a fantastic time and so I feature most of my childhood, filled with memorable characters that I transfer into my stories.

Josephine
COX

Have you read all her
No. 1 *Sunday Times* bestsellers yet?

THE JOURNEY

Three strangers are thrown together by chance.
It's an encounter that is destined to change all of
their lives for ever.

When Ben Morris comes to the aid of Lucy Baker and her
daughter Mary, he is intrigued by the story behind their
frequent visits to the local graveyard. Later, invited into their
home, an old Edwardian place suffused with secrets of the
past, Ben hears Lucy's remarkable tale – one she must tell
before it's too late.

The story of Barney Davidson, his family and the part
Lucy played in his extraordinary life, is one of a deep, abiding
love and an incredible sacrifice, spellbinding in its tragedy
and passion. And it still exerts a powerful
influence in the present day…

The first in a two-book story, *The Journey* is Josephine Cox
at her mesmerising best. Spanning decades, generations
and continents, it will stay with you for ever.

⊕ ebook • audio

JOURNEY'S END

Like a ghost from the past, she walked along the platform towards them …

It has been over twenty years since Vicky Maitland set foot on English soil. Twenty years since she left Liverpool with her three children, bound for a new life in America, leaving her beloved husband Barney behind.

But this long journey home is the hardest of all. She is here in search of the truth, afraid of what she may find. Why did Barney turn against his family so suddenly, so cruelly? Only her old friend Lucy Baker knows what happened. And Lucy promised Barney she would never tell his secret. Is it time she broke her silence and explained the events of so long ago?

As the past weighs heavily on Lucy's heart, other ghosts are stirring, intent on revenge. Will they finally catch up with Vicky and Lucy?

⊕ ebook • audio

THE LONER

Home is where the heart is – but it's also where the pain lies…

Young Davie Adams is all alone. Devastated, he flees his hometown of Blackburn to escape the memories of the worst night of his life. With little more than the shirt on his back he sets off on a lonely, friendless road, determined to find his father.

Two people are stricken by his departure – Judy, his childhood friend who is desperate to reveal a secret she has kept close to her heart for so long, and Joseph, his grandfather, who is racked with guilt about that fateful night.

Exhausted and afraid, Davie finds friendship and a place to stay but when fate deals him another disastrous blow, he must decide whether to keep running or return to face his demons …

Josephine COX

The Loner

THE NEW BESTSELLER

ebook · audio

BORN BAD

Harry always knew he would go back one day…

Eighteen years ago he made a decision that drove him from the place he knew and loved. In those early years he carved out a life for himself, and somehow, he had found a semblance of peace.

Every waking moment during those long aching years he was haunted by what happened when he was a boy. He had never forgotten that warm, carefree girl with the laughing eyes.

For Judy Saunders, the pain of her past had left her deeply scarred. Cut off from her family and stuck in a stormy marriage to a man she didn't love, the distant memories of her first love were her only source of comfort.

Now for the first time in all those years, Harry is heading back, and he needs to know the outcome of what happened all those years ago.

And, most importantly, he needs to find forgiveness.

THREE LETTERS

Eight-year-old Casey's mother Ruth is
a cruel woman, with a weakness for
other women's husbands.

Casey's father is gentle and hard-working and, though
Tom Denton has long suspected his wife of having
sordid affairs, he has chosen to turn a blind eye to keep
the peace. But then, out of the blue, Tom's world is
cruelly shattered when he receives two bits of devastating
news. Because of this, Tom realizes that from now on
their lives must change, forever.

Tom is made to fight for his son, determined to
keep him safe. But when fate takes a hand, life can
be unbearably cruel, and Casey is made
to remember his father's prophetic words …

'It's done. The dice is thrown, and nobody wins.'

But, unbeknown to Casey, there are three letters penned
by his father, that may just change his destiny forever.

Josephine Cox's
Chatterbox

News from Jo's life … straight into yours

Sign up to receive Chatterbox in your inbox!

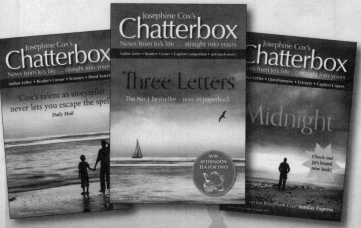

If you would like to receive regular updates about Josephine Cox, you can register to receive Chatterbox, Jo's free newsletter packed with exciting competitions plus news and views from other fans.

For details, visit: www.josephinecox.com

Keep up to date with Jo!

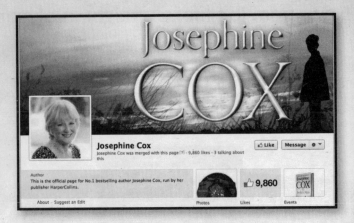

 /JoCoxBooks

Join Jo on Facebook for the latest news, photos and competitions. It's a great place to talk to other readers and keep up-to-date with Jo. Plus, there'll be even mor exclusive content in celebration of Jo's fiftieth book.

And why not log on to Jo's website

www.josephinecox.com

and sign-up to receive Chatterbox, her popular newslett